Play Ice

Brittany Carson

ISBN: 978-1-7636279-2-5

Dedication

For the *private* lovers, you don't have to prove anyone a damn thing.

Content Warnings

Hello reader, this book is predominantly a sweet story with mild miscommunication between two childhood best friends. I will preface that there are brief mentions of fatphobia and mental illness. Please take care of yourself and act in your best interest.

love, Britt

Contents

Playlist

Too Little Too Late – Jojo
Science – Niall Horan
Almost Is Never Enough – Ariana Grande ft. Nathan Sykes
Last Christmas – Ariana Grande
Back To December (Taylor's Version) – Taylor Swift
The One That Got Away – Katy Perry
We Don't Talk Anymore – Charlie Puth ft. Selena Gomez
Sorry – Justin Bieber
Loser – Charlie Puth
Over Again – One Direction
Ghost – Justin Bieber
November Rain – Guns N' Roses
Paper Rings – Taylor Swift
Smells Like Me – Charlie Puth
Since You Been Gone – Kelly Clarkson
Baby – Justin Bieber
Crying In The Club – Camilla Cabello
Promiscuous – Nelly Furtado ft. Timbaland
Cold As Ice – Ava Max
It Takes Two – Katy Perry
It's Nice To Have A Friend – Taylor Swift

Long Live (Taylor's Version) – Taylor Swift
Teenage Dirtbag – Wheatus
Teenage Dream – Katy Perry
I Like You – Post Malone ft. Doja Cat
Today Was A Fairytale (Taylor's Version) – Taylor Swift
Just A Girl – No Doubt
Welcome To The Jungle – Guns N' Roses
Hot N Cold – Katy Perry
The Reason – Hoobastank
Boyfriend – Justin Bieber
Never Really Over – Katy Perry
You Are In Love (Taylor's Version) – Taylor Swift
Marry Me – Jason Derulo
Fairytale – Justin Bieber
Purpose – Justin Bieber
Nothing Like Us – Justin Bieber
This Is Why We Can't Have Nice Things – Taylor Swift
No Air – Jordin Sparks ft. Chris Brown
Afterglow – Taylor Swift
If I Could Fly – One Direction
Cinnamon Girl – Lana Del Rey
Good Graces – Sabrina Carpenter

ONE

Too Little Too Late

January

Ten Years Ago...

Well, this is just fucking shit.

I think to myself over and over. *This is so fucking shit.*

Steadying my erratic breathing, my lungs take in the abrasive, cool air. But my heart is still breaking. My furrowed brows can't possibly express my reluctance any more than they already do, and my nose flares with frustration.

This is so fucking shit. I can't leave Noelle.

Noelle Winter Darlington is everything to me. She's been with me every minute of every day since my family and I moved to Colorado. Noelle makes this isolated ski lodge live up to its marketed slogan as a "Snow Paradise".

To leave Noelle behind will be the exact opposite of paradise, even though Phoenix is peppered with palm trees, which most people associate with paradise.

Sure, joining the Phoenix Badgers will come with a lot of benefits, especially financially, and it'll make me incredibly famous.

But it's not Darlington Snow Paradise.

My idea of paradise? Cold weather, an adorable redhead I've secretly pined over since I was 11 years old, and this quaint little ski lodge all to ourselves.

Darlington Snow Paradise is far more picturesque than any rink I skated on back in Ottawa. Each time my stick connected with the puck, I'd watch to see if it made it into the net. My gaze would always drift to the snow-capped mountains hovering over the placid resort like Titans. But my eyes distractedly strayed to my biggest cheerleader, applauding loudly to catch my attention—*though it never wandered far from her, anyway.*

Noelle Winter Darlington.

The absolute best thing to happen to me. The best thing to happen to this place, really. She makes this meek, rickety ski lodge glitter brightly, even as the dying Christmas lights that skirt the gutters flicker weakly.

Noelle works her butt off to be hospitable to the very few guests the lodge receives during the year. Often forgotten amid the blur of the flashy huge ski resorts sponsored by Warren Buffett or some other gross billionaire.

Maybe that's the first thing I'll do with my hotshot pro hockey player money.

My favorite thing about this place is that it's quiet most of the time. I get Noelle all to myself. We have time to venture into the crevices of the lodge we've explored one hundred times before. But I never tire of it. Being with Noelle is never boring. She can make something mundane feel like a trip to Disneyland, each activity more exhilarating than the next. Whether we're heading into town to visit Cocomo, a tropical-themed cafe known for its fancy, eccentric hot chocolates.

No one pulls off a hot chocolate mustache better than Noelle Darlington.

Or chasing down snow bunnies in the small forest that circles the lodge, hearing her infectious laugh every time I would miss and face plant into the snow.

Or doing what we're doing right now.

Well, me at least. Sitting atop her lodge's roof, waiting to have her all to myself one last time. No, this can't be the last time.

This is so fucking shit.

I never even got to tell her how I feel. Is now the right time? There have been moments where I've nearly slipped up and honestly, my blood always runs cold at almost ruining our beautiful once-in-a-lifetime friendship.

Most of the time, I am pretty stoic and hide my romantic feelings behind a surly pout. Keeping my infatuation unassuming. Being a grump pays off sometimes, but I'm fuming at the path my parents have carved in ice for me.

I guess that's why I am always a little angry at the world. My parents took my childhood away from me, plucking me from Ottawa and isolating me here on this lodge.

But my anger dissipates when I'm with Noelle. Her imagination brightens the bleakness of my lost childhood.

When I'm with Noelle, I feel the whimsy of a child again. Her company is free from expectation and discipline. It's all play with her.

I can't leave all of that behind. I can't leave her behind.

But she can't come with me either, not with her vicious dizzy spells. Thankfully, she's sheltered in the snow here in Aspen, but Phoenix is famously hot with its desert sun. I know heat is a major trigger for her spells, not to mention fast-paced environments.

Thank God, I have months of training before I'm thrown into the most hectic playing schedule I've ever seen, games every second day, performance evaluations, and training sessions. I'm getting dizzy at the thought of it. I don't know how I'm going to bear it without my personal cheerleader glued to my side.

Shit. Shit. Shit. Just fucking shit.

"Janny, Janny, he's the manny. He will beat you, 'cause he canny!" A flurry of fiery red locks burst onto the scene, slipping through the upstairs window.

My mouth almost twitches into a smile. I train myself into stoic stone. Now is certainly not the time to be all heart eyes for Noelle. No matter how cute she looks with her reddened nose. I train my eyes on the monstrous mountains instead.

I plan on being just like them, rigid and unmoving.

I nonchalantly offer my palm to guide her down to the roof shingles. The electricity that sparks in my veins is unsettling to my nervous system.

Diminishing my feelings for this shitty circumstance is going to be harder than I thought.

She runs her fingertips across my palm first before clasping at it for support. She is always so delicate with *everything*, and it kills me inside a little every time she is so gentle with me.

Absolute fucking torture.

"Thank you, Janny." Noelle flashes her appreciative smile.

I can still remember when we first met. Her endearingly jagged teeth were on full display, along with an eagerness to befriend me.

A first impression I will never forget.

I just hope my leaving doesn't leave a lasting impression on her. I hope she can forgive me for leaving months at a time.

"I'm so sorry I'm late. Dad needed help with the database system again." Noelle unscrews the top of her Thermos, placing two tin mugs onto the rug before pouring thick, steamy chocolate into them. It may as well be fondue. It's going to be quite the 'stache Noelle will be sporting.

"Did he forget your super secure password again?" I deadpan to the mug as she hands it to me, careful to avoid her galvanizing touch. Maybe I'm just imagining it because I'm so in love with Noelle, but it seems like she deliberately touches me.

"Iwishjustinbieberwasmyboyfriend1 is a great password." Noelle turned her Rudolph nose to the clouds stubbornly. This girl had to have the most striking profile. If only the password was Iwishjanuarysnowwasmyboyfriend1.

"No one is cracking that one." I roll my eyes, mostly to avoid her gaze when it meets mine.

Noelle turns to me with a suspicious hum, flashing her beautiful eyes my way. The palest of blues that remind me of an iced-over lake with tiny sapphire-like fractures, as though the murky water beneath is trying to break through the surface.

"Possibly because you're about the only girl in the world that is still willing to defend J-Justin Bieber. You have the worst taste in b-boyfriends," I stumble over the jab pathetically. She really drives home my fluster by snorting adorably.

"That was pathetic, Janny."

"I'm better at insulting in my native tongue, *sac de merde.*"

"Hey! I know what that means. You taught me that," Noelle whines, giving me a hard nudge. "I am not a bag of shit."

I can't help but snicker as her proper British accent peaks shrilly. She's correct. I taught her some French to mutter under her breath when dealing with not-so-pleasant guests.

"Oh god, that made me dizzy."

All the urges to laugh hysterically flees my body at Noelle's declaration. I come to a stand, ready to swiftly scoop her up, carry her through the window, down the narrow stairs—carefully avoiding the balustrades—and lay her gently on her bed.

"Relax, Janny, I'm not having a spell," she giggles. I plant myself back on the picnic blanket, my quick-thinking plan wiped from my mind. My eyes scan her shivering figure. I wrestle my parka off.

"January, what are you doing?"

"You look cold, Nono." I lace the black parka over her shoulders, cocooning over her white snowsuit. Her angelic beauty remains uneclipsed.

"I promise, I'm fine." She nuzzles her head into the crook of my neck. My stomach feels like a goal net being slammed with puck drills. "We should have our little meetups at lower altitudes."

"I suggested that Nono and you always argue with me."

"Because it's so fun to see you riled up," she clicks cheekily, snuggling further. "You're so scared of emotions, Janny."

She pinches my cold cheeks, thankfully inhibiting a smile from cracking through. Her warm fingertips feel like bliss on my skin.

I'm particularly scared of one emotion in particular, love, and especially how much I have for Noelle.

Now my heart is receiving puck drills just thinking about it.

"Such a great way to pass the time here, huh?"

Being in love? Absolutely. Couldn't think of a better way to kill time. A part of me hopes time is immortal, so I can stay in love forever.

"You're so quick to temper." She pokes her finger into my cheek repetitively.

Oh, she was referring to her taunting as an effective way to occupy the day. I'll take it. It's what we do. We jab, we taunt, we insult. Doing anything to get under each other's skin, since I'm too cowardly to get on her skin. The teasing is how I sneakily get my feelings across to her, but I think her provoking may just be strictly friendly.

Surrendering to the voice in my head telling me to hold her close, I wrap my arm around her waist. I press my fingers into the plush of her snowsuit, wishing I could get my hands on her already heating flesh. I feel her thread her arm around me, her fingertips wrapping near my rib cage.

I tilt my head onto hers, admiring the landscape of soaring mountains.

This is my paradise.

"Finally, a change of scenery, lucky you," she lilts calmly, her tone steady and her words drawn. Which means she's probably feeling a little feverish. Another impression I will never forget was when Noelle fainted after a very excitable match of MarioKart. One second she was trash-talking me as I sulked like a sore loser, and the next thing she dropped like a sack of potatoes.

"Noelle?" I retract from the lovely embrace.

"I'm fine, January, I'm just...going to miss you," she croaks. I tilt her chin, making her eyes meet mine. Her sweet lips part invitingly as I inspect her flushed, freckled face. "Is everything okay?" She asks.

Her voice is like sugar personified, with the same addictive quality. It wraps around my ears pleasantly.

"I'm going to miss you too," I say, resisting the urge to kiss her sugary lips. Ignoring her concern, I immerse myself in her candied airy vocals. The truth is something I'd rather avoid now and enjoy Noelle instead. "I'm going to miss you," I repeat in a whisper, my lips brushing her crown as she bows her head. I catch myself before I plant a love-blind kiss there.

"But not this view, right?" She looks up once again, a precious blush coating her cheeks, burning them an even deeper shade of pink as her lips spread into a conniving smile. "Total snoozeville. Yawn." Noelle feigns the motion. I'm hypnotized by her tongue and how I want it wrapped around mine, like right now.

Her delicate voice pokes at my curiosities. I want nothing more than to press Noelle Darlington into the picnic blanket. Make out with her so fiercely that we tumble off the roof and have the snow become our mattress instead.

"Change is good," she declares with a thick swallow. I watch the gulp travel down her throat. I wouldn't mind chasing after it with a trail of kisses down her neck. "January?"

"Huh?" I catch myself staring obsessively at the pulse thrumming on her neck.

"I'll ask again, is everything okay?" Noelle's sweet voice, laced with concern, asks again, her pale blue eyes piercing me with worry. How I just want to kiss them all away.

There's no escaping this one. No, everything is not okay. I need Noelle. She made me realize there's more to life than ice hockey. There is laughter, there is turmoil, there is friendship, there is love. Sweet unconditional love, even at our absolute worst, we make space for understanding one another. No one has ever connected with me on this kind of level before. All that we've built is going to be challenged, because I'm moving away.

Sooooo fucking shit.

Her mouth shapes into an O, shaking me from my trance as realization dawns on her face. Mine is probably displaying all the underlying love I have for my best friend, love that should stay hidden. Or should it?

"Noelle, I'm scared," I pinch out dryly.

Christ, this is not a great way to start a confession of love.

"January, you have nothing to worry about. You're really good, great even!" Noelle gushes, the wind catching her exclamation with an echo. "See, even the mountains know it."

Jesus, I want to kiss her so badly.

Her lips tint darker with the abrasive chill in the air. I can visibly see how fast my panted breaths become at the sight.

"I believe in you, Janny, if that helps," she timidly encourages.

Ugh, it does help—a little too much. But please, Noelle, tell me I'm in over my head, that everything I need is right here with you.

"You're going to be recognized for how talented you are in the rink, and then you're going to be famous and probably get free fancy stuff! Janny, free fancy stuff!" Those beautiful ice-colored eyes sparkle enthusiastically. I don't have the heart to ruin her good mood with my complicated feelings. "And when you're famous, you'll probably meet some really cool people."

"You're the coolest person I know, Noelle."

"I'm the only person you know, Janny," she snorts gorgeously.

I guess that's true. None of my friends back in Ottawa are people I keep in touch with. I've been far too busy secretly pining for my best friend here in Aspen.

"Not for long though. Just don't forget me when you hang in the same circles as Justin Bieber. Please try to get me an autograph. I will love you forever."

I love you too.

My blood runs cold at my blunder.

"Christ, did I say that out loud?"

"Huh?"

"Oh nothing, also I don't think Justin Bieber and I will ever run in the same circles." *Nice save, January, now bury those feelings before you do something idiotic.*

"A girl can dream. I'm still bummed you're not even remotely related," Noelle sighs, and although I know she's putting on her disappointment, my brain is itching for me to comfort her.

"And I'm still disappointed that you're not related to Prince Harry."

"Not all British redheads are related. That is highly offensive." She turns her adorable red nose to the marshmallow clouds again.

"Neither are Canadians," I snipe back.

"I could pass for royalty, though. I am your Princess after all." She beams her glowy smile my way and I'm melting. Even being surrounded by snow, I can't help but warm around her.

My bare arms don't even get the chance to texture with goosebumps with the inferno Noelle causes inside of me.

"You'll always be my Princess, Noelle."

She turns away before I have time to see her adorable blush. I stare at the blank canvas of snow while the memory unfolds. We used to create Noelle's fantastical visions of faraway lands, dangerous creatures, and magic, always featuring a prince and princess fighting together.

It is an honor being Princess Noelle's Prince. How does anybody expect me to give that up? Even though we haven't played pretend for such a long time, the dynamic of me being her Prince always stuck.

"No doubt when you meet Justin Bieber, he's going to introduce you to one of his super gorgeous model backup dancers, then I guess you can call her Princess."

"But you're my Princess, Noelle." My heart is breaking that she gives up the nickname so willingly.

"January, don't you want a famous girlfriend instead?"

"Instead?" My eyelids snap open wide. We're doing this, we're actually bringing it up. I've always felt the nicknames had a sentimental shift somewhere amid our adolescence, the pet name becoming less innocent in my mind. It sounds like it may be mutual.

"Huh? No, I meant- I'm not saying I'm your girlfriend or anything," Noelle flusters pathetically, and it's setting off a chemical reaction inside of me. I can see her panic in her hard-coming breaths.

"You're not?" My throat is going dry. I have to wonder if these spells are contagious.

"No, I know I'm not," she says evenly. Her composure escapes her quickly, though. "I know you don't want me as your girlfriend, otherwise I'd be your girlfriend. It's that simple."

Is it fucking really?

Is she insinuating that all I have to do is ask her to be my girlfriend because she's also really into me?

"Wait, Noelle, wait. Is there something you're not telling me?"

"No, Janny, that came out really wrong. I know I'm not your girlfriend. I'm your friend who is a girl. All I'm saying is, you should probably reserve the nickname Princess for the girl you love." She averts her gaze. I swear disappointment settles in those beautiful eyes of hers.

Shit, here goes nothing.

"What if...what if I already call her that?" My heart feels like it might explode.

"Huh?" Noelle's breathing has stopped as the clouds escaping her lips disappear. Now, I'm narrowing in on her lips. *All or nothing, January, finish what you've started.*

I cup Noelle's face in my hands, hoping they aren't too cold against her reddened cheeks. My palms warm as her cheeks grow darker. "January."

The way she says my name is satisfying, like the feeling of how cotton candy dissolves on my tongue. I bet her kisses feel just the same.

"January." The cotton candy cloud is back, and it's hitting hard on my lips as I inch closer to hers.

"Noelle."

Her whole body releases all its tension at that moment. Her lips part as her breathing becomes healthy. I can feel her steadying pulse on the pad of my thumb.

I give her time to comprehend what is happening, knowing high stress can trigger one of her mysterious hot spells.

She licks her lips and tilts her head to the side and I take that as a sign to kiss her, my seven-year-long daydream finally coming true.

Cinnamon fills my senses, a memory of her rolling perfume on her pulse points.

How she would hold a normal conversation whilst she performed the wicked seduction. I was always so entranced when she rubbed it along her neck. Who knew putting on perfume could be so arousing?

"Cinnamon." I moan into her lips, my tongue catching hers briefly.

"Vetiver."

She's right. My cologne has notes of vetiver and from the sounds of it, the scent has the same torturous effects on her.

I want to seek where she's translucently stained her skin with the perfume, so I can paint the swatches with crimson and violet.

I press my nose into the crook of her neck and inhale unabashedly.

"January," Noelle hisses. I feel the shiver that runs through her whole body. It makes me want to explore what other reactions I can get out of her. I test by splaying my hand on her back, between her shoulder blades before following the slope to her lower spine. "Let's go inside!" She yelps suddenly.

"Sorry, I'll stop." I remove my hand.

"No...don't stop. I just want to continue inside." Noelle's blue eyes bead apologetically.

"You want to continue?"

"Can we?" Her eyes look more pleading, and I've always had trouble saying no to Noelle.

"We can." I steady myself on my feet as Noelle gets up and practically throws herself at me. Fame and fortune could never compete with this moment. "Alright, let's head inside. Ladies first."

Noelle pecks my cheek before dipping her tall stature in the window frame.

She hurries down the stairs of her lodge. I follow to keep up. My eyes can't help but catch on her ass as she excitedly crawls onto her bed as I reach the last landing. I have to close them just to compose myself once again.

It's all such a rush right now. I get to kiss my best friend a little more in her bed, which smells like a cinnamon wonderland.

"Okay, I kept all the condoms from our Sex Ed classes."

"What?" I open my eyes to see an array of rippled square packets laid out on Noelle's snowflake-printed duvet.

"I just need to find one that hasn't expired. Mrs. Donovan always stressed that the condom can't be expired."

Mrs. Donovan, our childhood tutor at the ski lodge, endured elaborate pranks every year.

Safe to say she won't be missing teaching us. We weren't terrible students all the time. There were some classes we didn't prank her in. Take Sex Education, for example. Noelle and I were far too busy being flustered by rolling condoms on bananas to even execute a flawless prank. The embarrassment would grow tenfold when she would hand out condoms at the end of the class.

Well, I guess Noelle kept all hers.

"I found a couple. I guess I could just bin the rest." Noelle sashays a fistful of condoms to her desk bin. "Unless we blow them up like balloons."

"Noelle." I need clarity on what she is exactly expecting from me right now.

"Actually, on second thought, I suddenly feel winded. I need to lie down." Noelle drops the bunch into the bin, the bag sinking under the added weight. It was quite the condom collection she had.

"Um, Noelle."

Even when she's dizzy, she sprawls on her bedspread seductively. I'm thinking it's intentional.

"I won't be long, I just need to cool down," she wrestles her arms out of her adorable white snowsuit. "Can you give me a hand?"

She nods her head toward her limb-tangling predicament. I perch on the edge of her bed, pulling at the cuff as she untangles her arm from her sleeve.

"Thanks, Janny." Before I know it, she's pressing her cushiony lips to mine once again, and I'm only realizing how much I've missed Noelle's hot breath mixed with mine. How did I survive the whole five-minute intermission?

I crawl atop of her, feeling where our bodies lock into place like a puzzle piece. She wriggles underneath me, her snowsuit now inched down to her hipbones.

"Noelle, are you expecting us to..."

She pauses, her blush crawls across her entire face and down her neck. I don't allow my eyes to dart lower until I have some clarity on the situation.

"I thought you loved me too, don't you?"

"You love me?" Oh my god, this is the best day of my life.

"I asked first." Her British accent comes out with a posh hiss.

"Yes, Noelle Winter Darlington, I love you. I have loved you since forever." It feels so good to get that off my chest.

"January Cameron Snow, I love you too."

I reignite the fervent kiss, finessing the snowsuit further down her legs.

The rest of the events that took place were a blur of passion. Noelle and I collapse, our breathing ragged and labored. I turn to her, wearing my biggest smile to date. I didn't even know my lips could stretch this far. Only it's short-lived as pained whimpers leave Noelle, her lids squeezed excruciatingly tight.

"Noelle, are you okay?" I press the back of my hand to her forehead.

"Snow."

"I'm here."

"No, January, I need snow. Get some snow please."

I act with such urgency I nearly crash into the glass porch door. Thankfully, the thing is never secure, so I can hastily whip it open and tumble outside. With my bare hands, I round a ball of snow the size of a cantaloupe and hurry back beside Noelle.

I'm unsure if those are tears or sweat running down her temples.

She takes the clump from me; the form collapsing into her decolletage, and her eyes ease from their tight squint. She breaks off a solid chunk of snow and glides the icicle on her forehead.

"Thanks, Janny." Her eyes finally flutter open and lay on me amorously.

"Noelle, I'm so sorry."

"What for? That was fun," she weakly giggles, "and interesting. But it was fun once we figured it out."

"It was? Look at the state it left you in." I press my palm to her cheek. It's dangerously hot.

"It's not like I was going to die a virgin. "I'm burning up and not feeling great, but I had a good time," Noelle says, her winning smile reminding me of our first encounter.

"I'm glad you had fun, Princess. I had fun too."

"Just give me a few more minutes to simmer down and then we can cuddle."

My God, this has all happened so fast. To think that Noelle felt the same way about me all along.

"How long have you loved me?" I watch as she sheets the ice over her red, splotchy torso.

"I've always loved you, Janny. You're like family to me. But when did I fall in love with you?"

I'm hanging on her every word, and from the mischievous look on her pretty flushed face, she knows she's got me wrapped around her finger.

"That's a good question, Nono."

She presses her frosty palm to my cheek. It counteracts the piercing heat my cheeks are supplying.

"You should answer it then, Janny," she taunts.

I can't remember a time when I wasn't in love with Noelle Winter Darlington.

"I'll try not to be insulted by your hesitation," she snorts, trialing her dizziness by shifting on to her elbows. I have the potent temptation to dive for her lips as they inch closer to mine.

Think, January, think. When was the time you truly fell in love with Noelle?

The day my life changed for the better was the day Noelle, sporting a snowsuit, greeted me enthusiastically. A flash of that friendly jagged smile and I was a goner. Throughout the day, as I learned more about her personality and interests, I became convinced she was the coolest girl on the planet.

I still think that Noelle is the coolest, kindest, bubbliest girl I've ever met. I'm lucky enough to say I love her, and even luckier to have her reciprocate that love.

"I've always loved you, Nono, and I've always been in love with you."

"Even when I had braces?" She raises a suspicious red brow, pursing her kissable lips.

"You rocked that steel like no other, Noelle." I taunt back and the giggle that leaves her lips is infectiously sweet.

"I did, didn't I?" She flashes the product of enduring three years of metallic torture. "Bet you didn't want to kiss me then."

But I'm not fooled by her cotton candy marshmallow demeanor. She's really the most devious girl I've met. Being a mastermind goes both ways. It's simply all a saccharine facade so she can charm you with her cunningness.

She's always been the brain and the beauty behind all the pranks on Mrs. Donovan and I guess I was her brawny henchmen. She'll always be my villainous princess, tinkering with her techy gadgets.

"Seems like you don't want to kiss me now." Her plush lips sink into a pout. I want to nip at the sunken cushion.

"I just want to make sure you're feeling okay, Nono." I swipe away a soaked tendril of scarlet from her forehead. It's still searing hot from our interesting fun.

"I'm okay enough to jab," she pokes a finger at my hip, "so I'm clearly in good enough shape for kissing."

"Well then, let's get smooching." I balloon her snowflake-printed sheets over us, the linen floating down dreamily, caressing our skin before hugging our figures. The piles of snow fall underneath her as I pull her towards me. I can only imagine the icy temperature is bliss on her bare back. I shimmy my palm beneath her, trying to disperse it before laying her on the mattress of snow.

"Oh, January." She swoons.

Fuck, that's my name.

She's a fucking angel, and that's my name upon her lips, spoken with such heavenly softness.

"Noelle." I sound far more pathetic than I would like. She cools my embarrassment by igniting the kiss once again.

Why can't *this* be my prophecy, kissing Noelle until our lips hurt?

And they may bruise now. I hiss as Noelle acts on my impulse to pinch her lip between my teeth.

"Nono." I practically whine. Am I okay? Why am I falling apart on top of this woman?

I quite like having my lips imprisoned between Noelle's teeth. I want to be detained in her room forever. My cinnamon-scented jail cell, with the sweetest and most devious jailer.

I will gladly be Noelle Winter Darlington's bitch.

She's got me whimpering like a clingy pup, anyway.

"Oh, Janny, I'm so excited."

To kiss again? Me too, Noelle, me too.

To do all of it again, when we can, that is. I'm quite content with just tame kissing at the moment.

"I'm going to see the world!"

"Huh?" I pull back, but she doesn't stray from the daydreamy spiel she's about to undertake. Did I really do that good of a job for my first time? She's comparing it to a trip around the world.

"Well, not the world, but Phoenix is a good start. I'll be there cheering on the sidelines at a real hockey game! I'll try not to let my competitiveness steal your thunder."

Her competitive spirit is evident, especially during our post-school gaming sessions.

Every time she zipped past me in Mario Kart, she'd remind me to *eat yellow snow*. She was usually way ahead, though, so it didn't happen often.

I might not have great luck with gaming, hitting more banana peels than rainbow mystery boxes, but I don't need luck in the virtual realm. I got lucky here in real life. Or as Noelle calls it, IRL.

"But I won't shy away from being a supportive girlfriend unless Justin Bieber is in the room. In that case, I'll pretend I don't know you, but could you keep an eye out for Selena Gomez for me?" She bats her thick lashes. I would gladly do the favor under her hypnosis.

"What are you talking about, Nono?" I chuckle. She's clearly gone loopy from her spell. She tells me sometimes she sees stars, maybe unattainable daydreams are also a side effect.

"When I come with you to Phoenix, duh."

"Noelle, you're not coming with me."

There's no way her body could handle it.

"What?"

"What makes you think you would be?"

"Are we not...?"

"Together?"

"Oh god." She looks the most sickly she's ever looked. I act quickly, tossing the blanket from us again, and hurry for more snow. Only when I turn, I see Noelle on the other side of the door wrapped up in her sheet. She looks like a Greek goddess. Aphrodite herself was a redhead, I'm sure of it, and Noelle is probably a descendant of hers.

I tug at the handle, but it doesn't budge. Something is wrong. This door is never locked. "Noelle, I think your doors iced shut somehow."

"In the three seconds it took you to go outside."

I don't know how I missed it before, but her red face wasn't the result of a spell but a product of her being pissed the fuck off.

"The only thing iced shut here is my heart."

"What?" I try the door again. I'm supposed to be locked in, not locked out. "Noelle, open this door."

"Fuck off, January, don't ever speak to me again."

"What are you talking about?"

She threatens to whip her blinds down.

"Wait, Noelle, wait. Talk to me. What's going on?"

"I thought we'd finally gotten over ourselves, January, and finally admitted our undeniable feelings for each other. But no, I didn't account that you were already in a very loyal, committed relationship with your hot shot pro hockey player ego. Have fun having babies with yourself, jerk!"

I flinch as a spray of white hurdles towards my face, instead hitting the glass with a hard thwack. The snow slumps to the ground, revealing an enraged Noelle. Her chest rises and falls quickly, her breath coming hot and fast, obscuring my vision of her as it fogs the glass.

"Noelle, breathe. You're going to trigger yourself into another spell." I drop the clump of snow I was holding and rattle at the door with all the strength I can muster.

"I am breathing, you motherfucker!"

"Noelle, please let me explain," I ensure she's listening, her breathing now loud and wheezy, but hopefully my words can soothe her worries. "You can't come with me to Phoenix, firstly you'll be too vulnerable with your spells."

"I'm vulnerable right now because I thought I could let my guard down around you. I thought you felt the same."

I know for a fact that the tears streaming down her face aren't doing any wonders in cooling her down.

"I feel the same, Noelle. I love you. But you can't come with me, you're not built for the big city, those kinds of places are stressful and loud. It's peaceful here at the lodge. You should stay here."

"You're not the person I thought I grew up with," she sneers calmly.

That will certainly bruise my ego for life. No amount of compacted snow could relieve the wound.

"You're a horrible person, January Cameron Snow."

"Please, Noelle, I'm just trying to protect you."

Can't Noelle see I love her so much that I can't take her with me? That would go against every innate instinct. Her well-being is my responsibility. I don't even know if I'm completely ready to take on this lifestyle myself. I can only imagine what sort of havoc it would wreak on someone in poor health. She's not getting it. I don't know how to tell her I'm trying to save her. I feel like I'm hurtling towards the earth with no parachute. In minutes, I've gone from cloud nine to the pits of hell.

"The only thing I need protection from is you."

She punctuates her statement with a dramatic rumble of her shutter blinds.

My heart stings listening to her thunderous wails.

Fuck, I should've kept my mouth shut.

Even though Noelle likes me back, even loves me back...probably not anymore. I should've just let us stay as friends. Now she thinks that the whole friendship was a lie, she's wrong about that. Noelle was right about one thing, though.

I am a horrible person.

Two

The Prince Is Depressed

January

Present Day

I'm finally the fuck alone.

Which means I can begin my daily morning routine. Gym—done. My chef has just finished preparing my açai bowl—done. My housekeeper has also finished tidying my room—done.

And most importantly, my publicist, Samantha, is off my ass—

"CAMERON!"

Or not. She calls me by my public name, Cameron, insisting that my birth name is not marketable enough. *Cameron Snow, The Prince of Ice.*

"For fuck's sake, go away, I'm..."

Quick January, think of something off-putting.

"I have a girl in here," I wobble unconvincingly, looking down at my phone. It's a half-truth, I'm with a girl virtually, or I will be once I get the chance to type her handle into my search bar.

"Nice try, you don't bring girls over," Samantha snarks, her voice coming from outside my door. "Like ever, and you probably should, because then you wouldn't be such a big grump."

"Fine! I'm masturbating," I grumble, only providing evidence for her observation of me being a big grump.

I'm half tempted to flop my cock out just to scare my publicist away, but considering she has bigger balls than me, I doubt it would actually work.

She's 4'11 and truthfully, I'm more scared of her than I am of wild bears.

"I'm convinced you don't even do that," she snorts as she welcomes herself into my bedroom, "because there's no way you'd be this wound up."

"Samantha," I press through my teeth.

"Cameron, you fucking genius!" Samantha flops out her extra limb, her mobile phone. Her acrylic nails clack frantically on the small device. "I should get you a brand deal with TickleMeKink. They have a new line of male self-care toys, and my husband and I—"

"Samantha, I'm trying to eat breakfast," I gruff, gesturing to my unappetizing fruit vomit.

"You said you appreciate how unfiltered I am." Samantha arches a suspicious brow at me, and my stomach sloshes nervously.

"I do, but there's a time and a place for that kind of thing," I mumble, stirring the rainbow mixture into an unpleasant gray. "And person. I feel you shouldn't be discussing sex toys with your client. What would Vinnie say?"

"He'd say, bro, you have to try the vibrating cock ring!" She exclaims.

"Sounds painful." And I already have my means of torture, which I would like to indulge in if only my boundary-lacking publicist would fuck off already.

"I think Noelle just did a brand deal with them. This could be your means of reconnecting." Samantha's eyes lift from her phone, anticipating my reaction.

I train my face into an expression of stoicism.

"Pleasure isn't a part of my brand, Sam." I brush straight past the mention of *her* because this will certainly not be the way I reconnect with Noelle after ten long years.

I am glad Noelle found a bit of success after I broke her heart. She's now influencing on social media and endorsing women's empowerment. And I guess that includes doing brand deals with adult toy companies.

My cock awakens in my sweats at the thought of her using such devices.

Thankfully, Samantha is too immersed in her phone to take notice of my growing predicament.

"But pain is, they've got a whole drop-down menu sorted for that," Samantha gasps, her eyes light up like the Aspen city Christmas tree, as her fingers undertake a scrolling frenzy. "Ooh la la, nipple zappers."

"Samantha, get the fuck out of my room!" I roar, standing from my cloud-like mattress, using my intimidating 6'3 height to back my tiny invasive publicist out of my room.

Samantha's face twists into an expression of offense. But really, I should be the one offended. She tosses her mane of blonde over her shoulder, sticking her nose in the air with a disgruntled hum.

"Right, got it. You need to do your morning routine in peace." Her eyes roll so far back that only the whites are visible, yet I still feel judged by her. "I'll pretend I never stumbled across your burner account. Bad move for using your personal email, mister, big mistake, huge." She gesticulates theatrically upon her exit.

Embarrassment floods through me as I remember the day Samantha discovered my burner account. What began as a suspected hacking—someone using my email to create an Instagram account—almost led to the deletion of @NovemberRain. Samantha's no-nonsense attitude made me admit to how I stalk my "pretty redhead Angelface best friend," as she calls her.

"Thank you, Julia Roberts. Can I please be alone now?" I grimace, my grip tightening around my spoon. I only know that's a quote from Pretty Woman because Noelle was an obsessive movie fanatic and often adorably quoted films. It is far from endearing when Samantha does it. She is so lucky I am not holding a butter knife right now.

The urge to stab my breakfast savagely leaves my body, thankfully, along with the wish that I had a more solid breakfast to stab.

But now I can undergo my morning routine.

I pay no attention to the daily generated suggestive feed of models, models, models, and skip straight to the search bar. I finally type in the username of my muse.

@DarlingNoelle.

Along with eating breakfast and working out, checking up on Noelle is a daily practice of mine.

I'm completely aware of how pathetic it is, but I need the reassurance that she is happy, while admittedly, I'm still miserable.

I make my way across my snow-colored tiles to the glass balcony door, so pristinely streak-free I almost crash into the invisible glass, I'm so engrossed in Noelle's feed.

This fucking stupid mansion is always meticulously clean.

I slide the door handle once I have located it with my air-grasping hand. The sound is hauntingly similar to a certain porch door that is never locked. I shake the memory before my mind fully settles on it.

I abandon my AC-chilled bedroom, decorated in soft faux furs that remind me of a certain snowsuit, taking in the view of the canyons that landscape my view. The stunning copper hues of the canyon are available for me to admire. But the color only reminds me of a certain redhead I haven't been able to forget for ten years.

The balcony is big enough that it houses a large sofa, where I plop myself down carelessly. Some coconut flakes that survived my aggressive stirring fly from my açai bowl and snow onto my chest.

And now I have the vision of Noelle's naked body covered in snow in my head.

January, pull it together.

A notification pinging from my phone brings me back to earth.

@DarlingNoelle is live

She's live. Like every morning, she makes breakfast with her followers, and I eat it up with each scrumptious moan after every spoonful she takes.

It's where I got this very açai bowl recipe, which I'm sure she got from one of her healthy eating influencer friends. It tastes like ass, and I have to wonder if Noelle actually likes it herself. But I could never ask, even disguised under an undetectable name, @NovemberRain. My secret account peppered with pictures of the beloved rock band Guns 'n' Roses. It's pretty convincing since I am a fan of their music. They act as a substitute to get me geared up for a game...since my Angelface cheerleader hates my guts.

"I'll just wait for a few more to join," Noelle sweetly announces as she continues to chop away at some strawberries.

There's no mistaking that she is in the ski lodge's kitchen. My memory betrays me by revisiting that time Noelle and I snuck into the kitchen to pinch the Christmas cookies for the annual banquet.

"Everyone must be sleeping in on this fine Friday morning," she giggles, her laugh coming in clipped snorts that often earn disturbed looks from guests, but it's my favorite sound in the world.

"Oh, Nono, I miss you," I whimper pathetically.

"Okay, I'm going to start now. Welcome everybody." She chops up an array of colorful fruits. All I can do is stare at the strawberry juice that has glossed her lips.

Those pretty fucking lips.

That's one memory I can't seem to grasp back.

How do your lips taste? I can't remember.

She moans as she slips a slice of mango into her mouth, dragging the skin through her perfect teeth, hollowing her cheeks, and punctuating with a pop.

"Jesus fucking Christ!" I moan aloud.

"These mangoes are great, considering they're not in season." Noelle pops her hip happily at that news. My length twitches with an enthusiastic rhythm as her curvy derriere is emphasized.

Her fingers sprinkle granola flakes around the edging of the aesthetically laid fruits. "Finished!"

My cock is just about to do as she says, pressing uncomfortably against my sweatpants as it becomes firmer.

"Questions?" she asks her thousands of adoring fans who have volunteered to be influenced by her charm this morning.

My keyboard is the next thing to spring up. My wandering hand hovers over the letters. I fear she might recognize me from the way I type.

Even though our cabins neighbored each other from across the hall, we still texted our little hearts out when we first got phones.

I taught her French; she taught me text lingo.

Is this my chance? Do I ask her if she actually likes this ass-ai bowl?

"Oh, here's a question," she gingerly points out, the light in her eyes dulling.

My disgusted gaze lifts from the rainbow slosh in my bowl back to Noelle. I feel the displeasure melt from my face.

"Are you dating Cameron Snow?" She sighs. "This again. I've heard rumors he has a burner account and watches my live streams every morning. Hi, Janny."

Noelle always likes to stir the pot a bit, and I want to join in on the fun.

"Hi Nono," I breathe out the nickname, and it rolls off my tongue like second nature.

Thankfully, I don't type it out whilst under my alias.

She clears her throat awkwardly as the jarring comment in all caps jumps onto the screen.

> *@CameronNoelle4Ever: YOU AND CAMERON WOULD LOOK SO HOT TOGETHER! I CAN'T BELIEVE YOU GREW UP TOGETHER AT DARLINGTON SKI RESORT!!!!!!*

Fans of Noelle really ought to know the correct name of the establishment she lives in.

> *@NovemberRain: Darlington Snow Paradise**

I correct.

> *@NovemberRain: And yeah, they would look hot together.*

That's a wrap on my social interactions for the day.

But I want to talk to you, Nono.

I piano my fingers on the back of my phone, carefully typing out something.

"You didn't answer the question."

My heart drops when she reads what I wrote, her eyes flicking seethingly to the camera.

Fuck, she's onto me.

"I'm not dating Cameron Snow, we've never even met before." She distracts herself by sloshing around her own rainbow mush aggressively.

The chat goes feral with accusations.

> *@wh0re4CamSnow: SHE'S LYING GUYS!!!!!! SHE LOVES HIM!!!!!*

@CamSnowLovesNWD: Haven't you met? You grew up together. Wikipedia literally has photos of you two together.

It's concerning how Noelle's *Darlings* got those private photos, but it's consistent with her brand of teaching women to leverage technology to their advantage. I would say I was surprised to find out she made a tutorial on how to track someone's location, but honestly, that sounds like something the cunning Noelle Darlington I know would do. Of course, she inconspicuously used her investigative methods to hunt down a donut shop Justin Bieber had visited in the Swiss Alps.

The chat going bonkers for Noelle and I's couple suitability pulls me from my malicious thoughts of when I acted on my darkest impulses.

@NoManButCam: NOELLE AND CAMERON FOR LIIIIIIIFFFFEEEE!!

So, I do my best to course-correct the conversation back to the topic of this Instagram live. Making @WhatIsCandyEating's Tropicana Açai Bowl.

The question Noelle should ask Candy is, *what is she thinking? Because that looks disgusting.*

"Do you even like this crap?" I say as I type out.

The live ends suddenly. I'm met with my own desperate reflection as my screen flashes black.

Seconds later, she posted a story excusing her very sudden departure because of connection issues.

There are certainly connection issues, the main one being you obviously don't want to reconnect with me.

"CAMERON!" Samantha screeches from down the stairs.

"NO!" I bite back. I sound like a whiny brat, but my publicist's intrusive behavior is driving me crazy.

"Cameron! Bud! It's pretty urgent!" She's closing in on me. I hurry back inside to lock my bedroom door, so I can tend to my other unwelcome guest.

Seriously, she was making breakfast. You're going to get hard at her making breakfast.

"Samantha, I just want to be left alone," I groan, cupping my balls as they ache painfully, muttering curses in French under my breath. What could be of urgency? Unless someone I love died or the house is on fire, leave me the fuck alone.

But maybe drop off the vibrating cock ring first.

I make it just in the nick of time, the *click-click* sound of my door locking hits my ears orgasmically.

"Cameron, you should come downstairs," Samantha reasons with a maternal softness. Just the sound of her voice is causing my erection to disappear. Just goes to show the lack of attraction I have to the entire female race except for my best friend...the same best friend who clearly wants nothing to do with me.

"Why should I?" I remove my palm slowly from my bulge; the shape defined in my sweatpants.

"Christ, I'm not your mother," Samantha huffs, "but the woman in your living room is."

My mom?

All concerns for my cock disappear. I'm sure this is just a scheme on Samantha's part to lure me out of my room and into an interview I'm reluctant to partake in. When will she learn? I will not stop giving these interviewers the same amount of grief they give me, asking me the most utterly invasive questions?

How's my game? I know exactly what they are insinuating, and I know exactly what image they are trying to paint me, an arrogant prickly playboy. When really, I'm just arrogant and prickly. I'd like to see them run an article about me and my left hand. *I am so pathetic.*

"Cameron, don't make me count to three."

Now that's far more pathetic.

"Mom's here?" I call out hesitantly.

"Your dad too. They have some news that you might find...interesting."

Oh god, don't say interesting, Samantha. That word will forever be associated with the night that went from bad to worse.

"Why are they here? Please send them away." I don't know why I am using my manners when everybody is being incredibly rude and invasive. And more to the point, my parents are most definitely not in my living room. But I bet some Sports Illustrated columnist is. Confident they can tame their desired answers out of me, make me admit to the imaginary playboy image they've crafted for me, or dish on my dwindling sponsorships. At least that story won't be false. My sponsorships have been hot garbage lately. So much so, Samantha is considering having me sponsor vibrating cock rings. And I bet that is exactly what is waiting downstairs for me.

The connection between Noelle and the brand makes it only slightly tempting. But I know Noelle is not in my living room, and she won't be in my life ever again.

"Cameron, they're your parents. You shouldn't take them for granted. I lost my father—" Samantha starts with her reasoning once again.

"I don't care, Samantha, tell them verbatim to fuck off," I roar, my bedroom door trembles.

My reaction is completely unwarranted, but I made a promise to myself all those years ago, Noelle Darlington will not be wrong about me ever again. If she sees me as a horrible person, I will live up to her perception of me.

"Cameron," Samantha scolds. Even though she's only seven years my senior, she treats me like a child. I guess I'll always be the eighteen-year-old she and Vinnie scouted all those years ago.

Mom and Dad's plan actually paid off; it all started with them recognizing my innate ability to balance on a set of blades. Next thing I know, I'm being enrolled in junior ice hockey. Witnessing my parents argue with coaches, claiming the lessons are far too leisurely for their intended trajectory for my life. They completely cut off my contact with my friends from the league. Then, they went to extremes by taking me from Ottawa and moving us to a secluded ski lodge so I could stay focused. Finally, free of distractions.

Not!

My parents didn't account for the most incredible girl living at the lodge.

Noelle Winter Darlington.

My parent's plan prevailed, and that distraction is now eliminated from my life. Possibly for forever.

"Cameron, your parents," Samantha presses through her teeth.

"I said tell them 'fuck off'."

And tell them how much I hate this stupid fucking path they've stoned for me.

I hear her footsteps trekking away, her heels announcing every departing step.

A moment of peace, finally. I peel myself from the door, only to transfer myself to my pillow-top mattress, sinking into its pliable softness. It reminds me of Noelle's hugs in her cumbersome snowsuit, how we seemed to mold into one. And there I go again, thinking about Noelle.

Whatever, it's not a crime to indulge in a nearly two-decade-long musing. I flutter my eyes closed, and the darkness behind my lids plays out images of Noelle happy and content with her life. Only I've edited myself into each milestone.

Her standing on the podium accepting her degree in IT. Her robe is the same forest green color as the Phoenix Badgers team colors, but she pulls it off better than any of us meatheads. Even more than me, after being coined *the prettiest man* in the sport on multiple occasions in many Sports Illustrated articles.

Now if I had to write an article about the 10 prettiest STEMinists on this ball of water hurtling through space, Noelle Winter Darlington would take up all 10 spots.

A thundering against my bedroom door jolts me from my heavenly daydream. My hand flies from my crotch, hurtling my body from the sunken plush.

"GO AWAY!"

Seriously, take a hint. I don't want to do any fucking interviews or scare another sponsor away. My parents are not here. Nice fucking try.

The thundering continues. I toss myself from my bed and whip my bedroom door open.

"WHAT!" My framed medals jitter nervously at my outburst. I watch, anticipating the accolades to collapse to the ground.

"January."

I turn my gaze back and I'm met with my spitting image.

Nicholas Snow, Former Pro Ice Hockey Champion, and my father.

And who is he with? None other than Camille Snow. The world may know and adore her as Olympics' sweetheart on skates, or Camille Roux back in the 80s, but I know her as Mom.

And obviously, they need a reminder of my name.

"I told you guys, my name is Cameron. You have to call me Cameron. It's an image thing."

"Your name is January," Mom huffs, clicking her tongue at my casual dress. She's dressed to the nines, as expected. The day I don't find my mother decked out in rhinestones will be the day something is terribly wrong.

Why do I get the sense that something is already terribly wrong?

"Not to the masses, it's not. You wanted me to be a hotshot pro hockey player." I can hear Noelle's voice taunting me. "This comes with the territory. My image must stay shiny." I daringly pluck a loose rhinestone from the lapel on my mother's suit jacket. Her heavy, kohl-rimmed eyes bore into me with horror.

"You really are out of control, child," she huffs, muttering insults in French under her breath.

"Camille, sweetheart," Dad tries to soothe my mother's temper with the tender pet name. How the world could see my mother as such is beyond me. "We agree. Your image should remain pristine. That's why we're here."

My mother nods her head curtly in agreement with my father.

"Huh?" I snap my eyes to him, all sense of stoicism fleeing my body. I need answers. What could they possibly have in store for me now? They've taken me away from my birthplace, away from my friends, and away from the love of my life. What else can they take from me? Haven't I suffered enough?

"We feel you've become lost in the fame. We think it would be best for you to go back to your roots," my mother says, finally calm, smoothing her palms down her blazer.

"Huh?" I repeat, my eyes flick back to her. They're not taking anything away from me...well, my career, I guess. "Back to my roots?"

"You should visit the lodge again," Dad suggests.

"Why would I do that?" I hiss. Mom can call me whatever she wants in French, but suggesting I go back to the lodge is the most insulting thing anyone can say to me.

"Because you miss her, January, I'm certain she misses you too." Mom unearths my painful truth.

There's the insulting part. I've been tempted to return to the lodge, but it's clear that Noelle doesn't want me there. Disrespecting her twice in my life was out of the question. I still haven't forgiven myself for the first time.

My parents really ought to obsess over Noelle as much as I do; then they'd know as much as I do about her. Beyond her lack of missing me, she pursued her IT degree despite my concerns about her health in a fast-paced city. But she stuck it to all of us and actually graduated, and I couldn't have been more proud of her.

Noelle is right about me being a horrible person, but I was wrong about Noelle and her capabilities.

Now she's vocal online about how your shortcomings only hinder you if you let them. Even if she's subtly criticizing me with that reference to shortcomings, since I could be considered someone who doubted her.

I couldn't be more pleased with being proved wrong by Noelle. What I didn't find pleasing was that she met someone by the name of Sean.

Who is the only normie @NovemberRain follows?

But @SeanWhittaker89 leaves much to be desired, his account has zero posts, no bio, and worst of all, no profile picture. I sure as hell bet Sports Illustrated has not coined him the prettiest man. But what does it matter when he's got Noelle's hand in marriage?

He gets to be coined *husband* by Noelle.

That thought makes my heart hitch in my chest. I wanted to marry Noelle. It seems entirely unfair that some random guy who probably hasn't even seen Noelle on her worst days gets to do that instead.

Who is this motherfucker?

It drives me crazy that there is absolutely no information about him. He doesn't have a digital footprint.

Inspired by Noelle, I even hired a hacker to track this creep down and find out how he came to be in Noelle's life. And how the fuck he put a rock on her finger.

But from the looks of things Noelle is back at the ski lodge, and here's to hoping she left that motherfucker in Chicago.

Oh god, what if that sac de merde Sean is at the lodge?

She hasn't mentioned him since her location pinned in her profile changed back to Darlington Snow Paradise.

But it's clear to see Noelle is a private lover, she has never broadcasted Sean's face on her social media. Which makes me worried he could be with her right now, possibly fucking her on the same sheets we took each other's virginity on.

I haven't been laid since I broke Noelle's heart. I have absolutely no sexual drive, besides when I'm looking at Noelle. I drool over that jacuzzi picture nightly, though.

"Oh, he is so gone for her," Samantha cackles. "I'm chartering your jet for Colorado tonight."

I thrust from my salacious thoughts. Great, I'm being puppeteered once again, and Noelle is pulling the strings on my cock.

Bad time, Noelle.

"The lodge? Why would I find my roots at the lodge?"

Fuck, I might find a root. Or how Noelle would put it sweetly, a shag.

"Because it's where you grew up." Samantha's motherly tone has made a comeback.

"I grew up in Ottawa." Clearly, no one can fight facts. I feel a small smirk twitching on my lips.

I win.

Only when I finally see the concerned expressions on everyone else's faces. I drop my crossed arms, my eyes averting with embarrassment.

"I can't go back to the lodge if she's there." My rare vulnerability must make everybody uncomfortable as they all shuffle on the spot skittishly. "I promise you; she wants nothing to do with me. I don't blame her."

"We heard otherwise, kid," my father shares with a hopeful smile, but his demeanor still exercises caution.

THREE

Long Time, No See

Noelle

It's a quiet day at Darlington Snow Paradise, but that's not really new for this place. It's so quiet it's eerie. I can hear every deafening click of my keyboard. The delay between typing the letter and it appearing on the computer seems to grow longer with each passing day.

Maybe having no guests is a blessing. It would take me three hours just to look up their booking details.

I sure am bored though, now that I've smoothed out all the bugs of the software I created for Dad, one he admittedly still doesn't know how to use. Despite the interface being so user-friendly, a toddler could use it effectively.

But I don't mind my dear father delegating all the administrative tasks to me. He was even nice enough to coin me the title of Database Administrator to add to my very lackluster resume. Not that I'll be seeking other employment anytime soon.

This repetitive job will most likely be mine for the rest of my life.

It's a family business, after all. My estranged uncle suddenly bestowed my father as the owner when I was four years old. One cold wintery day, my family and I left London in a hurry. I fainted on the plane and woke up in a place called Aspen, Colorado. A strange phenomenon has overtaken my body since that day. Doctors could not pinpoint my decline in health. All I know is that it has caused my parents to become chronic worriers.

It took all my energy—the small pool of it I have to begin with—to allow me to pursue my degree in Information Technology at the University of Illinois.

Not only did I survive, but graduated with top honors. Admittedly, I had to return to the lodge because my studies did a number on my health over the years.

How was I to know that a diet of two-minute noodles wasn't sustainable? And would not only worsen my mysterious condition but also lead to a severe case of iron deficiency.

But at least my iron deficiency led me to get a diagnosis for my mysterious spells.

POTS.

My initial reaction to the doctor was, "Never heard of it."

Which led her to break down the acronym Postural Orthostatic Tachycardia Syndrome.

That cleared up a lot of things, Doc.

POTS explained to me in basic layman's terms is a blood circulation disorder that mostly relates to my heart rate acceleration. Symptoms mostly occur when I go from sitting to standing too quickly. Suddenly it's nighty night for me.

However, episodes can occur at random times, such as when I get overly excited, angry, or...aroused, causing my heartbeat to spike suddenly.

Fortunately, and unfortunately for me, my parents are chronic worriers and they have done everything in their means to accommodate my diagnosis. Starting with the comfiest desk chair to accommodate my ass whilst I sit calmly all day, and click clack away.

This job would be far more painful if I wasn't a huge fan of computers, considering it's all I'm acquainted with for hours on end.

The slow pace of the job allows me to work on my video game, The Battle of Blizzard. A fantasy quest game in an alpine setting, that I have been working on since I was a teen.

Only this piece of outdated shit computer does everything in its means to make my shift agonizing with how slow it is. I suspect they overspent the budget on my desk chair.

It is like sitting on a cloud, the ergonomic shaping inhibits me from slouching, which can also trigger spells unnecessarily. I can't even win when I'm just sitting.

Well, if I'm going to black out at least the last view I get a glimpse of is the picturesque views of the lodge. Mountainous slopes that rise as high as the heavens, or so I imagine, I've only ever been to where the fog blankets thickly. Even then, that wasn't possible without January piggybacking me some of the way.

Speaking of triggers.

My eyes roll as he invades my thoughts suddenly. I carefully compose my breathing again, so my heart can conclude its drum solo.

Even ten years later, January Cameron Snow has my keyboard-clicking fingers curling into fists.

He once had a different effect on my heart, by all means, still making it race rapidly, but only because the sight of him took my breath away.

And now the thought of him makes me want to punch this slow-ass monitor.

I didn't even hit the Z key, for fuck's sake.

I'm getting far too riled up. My vision is spotting. I close my eyes, relishing in the cushiness of my chair. My heartbeat in my throat, but it appears to be slowly sliding back to where it belongs in my chest as it decreases in speed.

A shuffle approaching the reception desk sends my heart into a frenzy. I activate my customer service voice, which will undoubtedly leave me breathless once I've finished being exhaustively polite.

I love being hospitable, but my body doesn't seem to agree.

I do my best to not squeeze out the greeting in agonizing pain.

"Hi, Welcome to Darlington Snow Parad—" I stop myself, my heart continues to thrum loudly in my ears. I feel my face completely blanch as I register those haunting green eyes that seem to still glow evilly like they did in their childhood. He's changed, but not completely beyond recognition. His dark hair is still shaggy and unkempt, he still dresses like the lead singer of that whiny rock band, his wardrobe color scheme only comprising black, black and black.

I recognize the shirt. I could've sworn I have that shirt. He gifted it to me himself, as some sort of token for helping him hunt down *this* shirt he had an unhealthy attachment too. Now I have an unhealthy attachment to it, sleeping in it almost every night. This had to be a different shirt, because I wore my one just last night. Although his shoulders fill out this shirt more, they've grown broader and manlier in his ten year long absence. I can't tear my eyes away from the stretched Guns N' Roses logo on his chest.

"Janny."

I slip out meekly, my voice regressing to its teenage airiness; a soft whispering I had to adapt to regulate my heart, something I found quite annoying as I had to repeat myself often to elderly guests. I forced the placement deeper into my adulthood as many misconstrued it for my bedroom voice.

The nickname I gave January in our youth now tastes like poison on my tongue.

"Cameron." I try instead, but that is simply his public persona and someone I do not know. "Snow." I tilt my head with a welcoming smile, assuming he is simply *only* visiting and not returning.

For whatever reason, I don't care, but I will do the courtesy of treating him as a guest.

My initial rage bypasses as I take in the company he keeps, January's parents. I have absolutely no issues with them, and I am more than happy to be personal and not just professionally cordial with these two.

"Nicholas, Camille, it's so good to see *you* again." I'm hoping to get the underlying subtext through to Snow, that it is *so not good* to see him.

"Nono. Noelle. Winter. Darlington," January mocks back.

My stomach twists, I had forgotten how polarizing January's voice was to mine. Still so buttery to my ears, and how seemingly overnight it became that way after years of tortuous voice cracks during Karaoke Nights at Cocomo. "Darlington. I was told you would not be here," he smugly drawls, his bassy voice causing an earthquake in my soul.

"At my home? That's a bold assumption."

"Still the little snark, I see," he says through a nose scrunch, an action he would do to cover up his obvious endearment for me. His large hand slaps over the bell.

"Hm." I swipe the bell from the desk.

"Oh, my bad, I was hoping to get some *good* service around here."

I know exactly what he's trying to do, knowing very well that I don't respond well to negative feedback on my service. Usually, he's siding with me and reminding me of the notion that the customer isn't *always* right.

Camille sneered, "Noelle's always so hospitable, nothing's changed," pushing past January to get my attention. I will gladly be blinded by a million rhinestones if it means I don't have to look at January Snow's stupid face. "*Belle-fille*, you've gotten a lot prettier. My goodness, leave some beauty for the rest of us." I see January nodding in agreement with Camille's statement. I realize then we've been having a staring contest.

Wait, was January just nodding?

"Thank you, Camille," I swallow nervously. "If anyone should leave some beauty for the rest of us, it's you." I can tell my flattery doesn't sit well with January as his lip twitches up in a snarl. I'm fully aware of how he resents his parents, and me siding with them will certainly get under his skin. All because he's bitter about them pushing him into a career of ice hockey, even though he detests the path they've chosen for him.

I recall that one night where he dropped his surly demeanor and confessed that he'd rather stay here at Darlington Snow Paradise, all because it meant he could be here with me. January was rarely sentimental, which had my teenage heart palpitating and me falling deeper in love with the idiot.

"Oh, you charming thing," Camille gushes, turning to her son. "You're a buffoon."

Good, it worked. I know how to get January riled up, too. He should think twice before messing with Noelle Winter Darlington.

"I get it, Mom. She's the daughter you always wanted. She's hopeless on ice skates, though."

Oh, he wants to play dirty. I can get downright filthy just for you, Janny.

I feel my cheeks warm at my vengeful thoughts.

"She's the *daughter-in-law* I always wanted, such a sweetheart."

Camille is qualified to have that opinion; she was, after all, labeled Canada's Sweetheart On Skates in her prime.

"Well, I can't have the best of both worlds, Mom. It was Noelle or ice hockey." January grumbles. His attitude is reminiscent of how he was as a teen. I guess that much hasn't changed.

"You've made your choice very clear." I mutter under my breath. January's eyes narrow on me.

"Mom, Noelle's heart is anything but sweet."

"Coming for my health is low, January," I snarl, typing furiously, despite the frozen program. I sniff as I bite back feigned tears.

January's eyes roll at my ploy. "I was referring to you being an evil tech genius."

"That's more complimentary than you think."

"Say thank you then," January's snarl almost shapes in a smile. Does his face even remember how to smile?

As far as I know, I'm the only one who has seen and made him smile.

"I was never good at accepting compliments." I turn back to the monitor with another dramatic sniff.

"You just accepted my mom's—forget it," January huffs, swatting my antics away, turning back to his parents. "I told you we aren't welcome here."

"Don't be silly, child, this is our home." Camille gestures to the grand lobby with a dancerly flourish of her wrist.

I really love this place. My home.

"Not my home," January ruins my daydreamy appreciation with his man-child grumbling.

"I assume you're just visiting then," I press through my teeth as I bare them. January's judgemental scan of the lodge transfers to me.

"Hopefully, a very, very short visit," January's nose scrunches once again, and those haunting green eyes obviously drop to my lips. "You, however, live here again?"

Awe parts my lips, but I quickly close them. My breathing checks in and out of my body like a hotel guest.

"Yes," I manage through a dry swallow.

"Was there nothing worth sticking around for in Los Angeles? Houston? New York?"

"Chicago," I cut in bluntly. "And I would've stayed with my fiancée—"

"Fiancée?" January looks insulted, his eyes frantically searching my hands. I give my left ring finger a wriggle, relieving him with its lack of sparkle. He resigns from his overreaction, stepping back into his publicized character of The Prince of Ice.

"Yes, Sean and I were briefly engaged, and we really talked it over but, I hate to say it, January, you were right about me. I couldn't stand the city." My fingers fall from the keyboard and limply into my lap, my shoulders curling in with defeat. It amazes me how this keeps happening to me. I will never be suitable for anybody with POTS. I'm simply too much of a burden, too high risk. No one will love me enough to even just tolerate it. I guess I should accept the fact I will probably die alone.

POTS. It may as well be the acronym LRS.

Life Ruining Syndrome.

I nearly had everything, everything I wanted with January, I nearly had it with Sean.

"I broke it off with Sean, and now I'm back here. Where it's quiet and boring and..." Maybe I don't love it here, I simply loved what January made of this place. "Anyway, I would've married the love of my life if I weren't metropolis intolerant."

"Is the love of your life ski lodge intolerant?" January scoffs.

"His work requires him to stay in Chicago." I purse my lips.

"How did you two even meet?" January narrows his eyes suspiciously on me. That question alone reminds me of an indiscreet DM I received to my cyber private investigation side business account I ran whilst at university. The message was from a handle by the name of @NovemberRain requesting background information on Sean Whitaker. My fiancée! I didn't bother looking into it, fluffed some basic information, apologizing that I couldn't assist any further, and went on continuing to love the fuck out of my fiancée.

But not without running cyber diagnostics on @NovemberRain, and sure enough, it was hooked up to the router with the billing information tied to none other than January Cameron Snow. And of course, I withheld the advice of getting a VPN for his router. The idiot deserves to have his credit card information stolen.

"Are you interviewing me? Because from what I heard, you aren't a fan of interviews."

"You keep up with my movements, too?" He leans smugly over the reception. My heart doesn't betray me by getting giddy at the proximity, my stomach might though as I feel bile building in the sack.

Again, I can read him like JavaScript. He's trying to bring back the dynamic we had in our adolescence. Pokes and teases, with undeniable undertones of flirting. I was never subtle with my flirting. The idea of flirting with January now makes me sick, but I smell an opportunity to weaponise it.

"The algorithm hates my guts, no matter how much I tell it I'm not interested in seeing *The Prince of Ice loses his cool at an interviewer...again* on my timeline, it continues to push it like drugs. It's a pusher, January, it pushes people...and my buttons," I quote endearingly. A laugh slips from the corner of his lips, followed by a nose scrunch.

"Just laugh, January, it will not break your soul, might even heal it," I poke further, trying to ignore the fuzzy feeling it gives me being ridiculous with him...again.

"I'll laugh when you are actually funny." January retracts from his advancing stance against the timber reception. His features are all sharp angular lines of disgust, only his eyes are always a giveaway.

"You used to find my movie quoting—"

"Annoying."

"Don't inter—"

"I was talking, not interrupting—"

"Yes, while I was talking, therefore interrupting." I come to a stand, and it's a bad call. My simmering blood runs cold quickly, I collapse back down hard in the chair. All the galaxies are having a soiree in the lobby. Why must they spin the room too?

It's deafeningly silent as I come to, my vision clearing up.

January's concerned gaze is the first thing I see.

"You also interrupted me, by the way," he digs after confirming I'm okay.

"Whatever," I huff, cradling my head in my palms. "I'll go make some hot cocoa. Make yourselves at home." I flick a pleasant smile to Nicholas and Camille, both of them wearing a queasy expression, obviously feeling unwell at their son and I's vomit-inducing conversation.

Along with feeling sick at January's presence, I must have contracted some sort of infection that affects my neurological state. As I enter the small tearoom, a memory plays out like a movie and I can recite the quotes easily.

A tiny January and I hid under this wonky table, waiting for one of the daytime staff to take an unassuming perch in the chair that heads the table, just for us to slip the coaster from under the table's leg, making whoever's lunch splatter to the floor.

January is right, I am no sweetheart. I was quite the terror as a child.

But I learned my lesson one day when Norman, one of the seasonal ski instructors, launched his huge snow boot into my teeth.

Come to think of it, that whole interaction with January just now felt like a kick in the teeth.

I remember prying my trembling hands from my face. Nestled amongst a pool of blood was a chip off my tooth, ending the day with an impromptu trip to the emergency dental hospital five hours away. Where I received horrendous news that I would be getting braces.

At least January had the heart not to poke fun at me for it. He even made me feel better by saying they suited me...which may have been a dig now that I think of it.

January Cameron Snow was no angel either.

Four

Lodge, Sweet, Lodge

January

Noelle's presence is unmistakable, her cinnamon scent filling the lobby. She's wearing her most hospitable smile, the kind that radiates warmth and beauty. I've always thought so, even when her teeth sat in awkward jagged spurts before metallic wires corrected them.

"Shall we move this awkwardness into the reading room?" she presses through her teeth, the waft of hot cocoa following her out along with her signature scent that violates me over and over again.

Cinnamon. Cinna-fucking-mon.

"We shall." I click with a nose scrunch, mostly to mask my adoration. Fucking hell, she is prettier than I remembered, even though I have the privilege of getting glimpses at her on my burner Instagram account. Photos don't do her justice. Filters gloss over her beauty, filters she doesn't need and only mute the constellation of her freckles.

How I would kill to kiss every single freckle on your body, Noelle.

"Ahem, you coming?" her British accent tickles my ears. I feel the hairs on the back of my neck stand at the almost playful tone in her voice...although it's mostly irritation. "Too many pucks to the head, I see."

My eyes dart from freckle to freckle on her nose. *Kiss, kiss, kiss, kiss, kiss, kiss, kiss.*

"Yeah, I'm coming." Those words felt dirty leaving my lips, maybe because it was one of the many last phrases I had spoken to her before it all went to shit. Noelle turns sharply on her heels but not quick enough to hide the blush that amplifies those freckles.

As I move from the lobby to the reading room, I am transported through a portal of memories. The room is completely unchanged, still housing an array of sofas and wingback chairs. These are the seats Noelle and I would share simultaneously. Her legs swung across my lap as she snuggled into my shoulder. I devoted myself to holding her book and turning the pages. But I didn't mind being Noelle's bookish servant. Noelle rewarded me with head scratches. What wouldn't I do to have her fingertips caress my scalp again? I look to Noelle hoping maybe those intimate memories have also formed in her mind and she may even be keen to rekindle our touchy-feely ways.

She moves toward the mahogany coffee table. My eyes drop low as she places the tray down on the table, the chocolatey steam dancing around her angel face. My eyes journey further down her body again like a snowy slope.

She clears her throat, pressing her rouged lips into a thin line.

She is a vision.

Noelle turns away when I challenge her disapproving glare, her eyes scanning for a wingback chair to throne her cute ass, only to find them occupied by my parents. That leaves the cozy two-seater for the both of us, and if Noelle is going to be petty, so will I.

Her thought process reflects in her beautiful icy eyes, her shoulders slouching in defeat.

I swing my long limbs onto the second cushion she's approaching. She stunts herself. I expect her to wrestle me off the couch. That's what she would have done all those years ago, but from the look on her face, she looks utterly repulsed at the thought of touching me.

So much so, that she resigns to the sofa arm, perching on the edge as my enormous feet take up most of the arm too.

"Noelle," I sigh, tucking my legs off the couch. She continues to sit statuesque on the edge of the arm. "Noelle." My goodness, she is far more stubborn than I remember.

Fine. She doesn't want to acknowledge me. Things have changed drastically between us. But being back in the reading room, recognizing everything is exactly as it was, makes me yearn for our dynamic to be the same.

The tall mahogany bookcases lined with Blu-Ray DVDs of the most quotable movies, as well as fantastical books Noelle would disappear into every night before bed.

The tender crackling of the fireplace creates a glowy border around her angelic silhouette, but also brings out the mischievous glint that sits in those precious icy blues.

She wants to be playful too, but she's definitely got her reservations about me. I don't blame her. I was an absolute jerk that day. We shared possibly the most vulnerable act two people can share, only for me to flub my words and tell her I was leaving her.

It's not like I wanted to leave her. It was the moment I was dreading all along.

Divine fucking timing that we just happen to confess our clandestine love for one another that very day.

And now we couldn't be further from lovers, we may as well be strangers with how frosty she's being with me, even with her figure spotlighted with a fiery glow.

She tussles her hair to shield herself from my admiring stare. I clear my throat and reach for the platter stacked with a familiar sweet.

"Is this my Snickerdoodle recipe?" Mom pipes up as her bejeweled fingers pinch at a cookie.

"It sure is. It's my little welcome snack for guests," Noelle trills enthusiastically. She really is the most kind and open-hearted woman I've ever known, or ever knew...She won't give me a chance to remind myself of the person she used to be.

"It's good to know that my recipe is in excellent hands, your Toad In A Hole recipe is also practiced in our household. January invites us over after a win and I cook a big batch of it on his request."

Noelle fights an amused glance. I know she wants to shoot my way. I try to will it my way by focusing intently on her. I soften my brows and untense my jaw.

I slip my trainers off and replace my feet on the arm, launching my toe into the base of her spine. She yelps as she springs to her feet, shoots me a glare, and then quickly resumes a plain and pleasant expression.

Unfortunately for her, I know just how to ruffle Noelle Darlington's feathers.

"Let the girl sit down, boy, don't be so selfish." Mom inhibits me from reconnecting with Noelle. If she knew I was trying to reconnect with her beloved wanna-be daughter-in-law, she'd be far more grateful.

"I have a reputation to uphold. I would hate for Noelle to be wrong about me since I'm always right about her," I snicker, wiggling my toes at Noelle's face, her pretty features contorting with disgust.

"Stop torturing the girl," Mom dusts my limbs off the couch, "demon child, I swear. Sit, angel."

"I'm okay to stand actually," she says stiffly.

I straighten out my parka, and I'm reminded how many times I've offered this very parka to Noelle while she would chatter away. Moments where she would stubbornly decline, only to show the tenderest of gratitude after I laced it around her shoulders anyway.

Noelle is trembling right now, uncomfortably shuffling on the spot.

Her gaze flinches to her parents as they enter the room. She couldn't have fled to them any faster if she tried, exerting all the remaining energy she had to get as far away from me as possible.

"Mum, Dad, look who it is." Noelle turns presenting my parents with an affable smile, before turning to me, stripping her expression of any nicety.

"Nick, Camille, January, it's so good to see you all. My god, it's been years since the three of you have visited," David, Noelle's father, the man I wish my own was like. He cares so deeply about his daughter's wellbeing, but supports her to no end. He's the man I should strive to be.

"David, Johanna," I greet gingerly, springing from my seat. Noelle disperses from the Darlington collective. My palm runs along her waist as I pull the three of us into a tight hug.

A pained whimper leaves Noelle, and that's my cue to release.

"It's so good to see you all again," I press through my teeth.

"Er...so good to see you too, buddy," David responds hesitantly, smoothing out his flannel shirt while Johanna fluffs her hair. Noelle, looking sickly green against her normally snow-white skin, is clearly trying not to vomit. "Noelle, darling, you okay?" David asks.

"Yes, yes, everyone sit," Noelle snips, rigidly gesturing for everyone to take a seat once more.

Johanna and David occupy one cushion of the two-seater, leaving the remaining one to me, and Noelle with my knee.

I give my kneecap a welcoming pat and an audible heave leaves her mouth.

Christ, really making your feelings known, huh?

I resign from my taunting and wriggle over, making room for her.

"Sit down, Noelle, for crying out loud."

"I can stand," she says, looking anywhere but at me. I wonder if she is also taking in the room and remembering all the shenanigans we got up to in this room alone.

"The color of your skin and the fact your eyeballs are rolling back every five seconds says otherwise."

She scoffs fiercely, narrowing that icy glare at me. It makes my fingers tingle to touch her again. I want to tug on this invisible string we still have connected. She must feel it too, as her weight sways toward me. Only it's more like she's about to faint.

I'm up and out of my chair before David can exclaim his worries about his daughter's health. My hands fit perfectly around her waist as I guide her to the couch from behind. I welcome her weight as she leans back into me; I slowly slip us both into the seat. Her head lolls back on my shoulder as her comprehension comes back to her.

"What happened?" She blinks her eyes; I groan as she plants her palm into my crotch. Her body weight goes flying forward, only inches from sending the cookies soaring across and into the fireplace. I act quickly to tug her back into my lap once again.

"Maybe just listen to me next time, Nono," I whisper into her ear.

"Get your hands off me right now!" She thrashes about on top of me. The little guest has checked into the ski lodge in my pants and if Noelle isn't careful, she's going to cause a blizzard.

"You still get those dizzy spells?" I refocus my thoughts.

"Yep, and they are called episodes, not spells," Noelle curtly confirms, resigning her weight into my chest. "I got a diagnosis."

"Diagnosis? You're sick." I watch as the skin on her neck turns red, and her diaphragm tenses under my palms. "Noelle?"

She sharpens her spine at my sympathetic drawl.

"Yes," she answers simply.

"Wait, you're sick. Why didn't one of you tell me sooner?" I hike Noelle out of the way, so I can perch my chin on her shoulder and glare at my parents. Feeling utterly betrayed, knowing they come here at least annually without me. They only watch me with amusement. Noelle being on my lap and willingly staying, something she'd never do, makes me think. "Are you dying?"

That's it! That's the whole urgency of this trip. I don't need to find my roots; I just need to reconnect with the love of my life before she's gone forever. So much time I've wasted not loving her, all out of complete pettiness.

"No, I'm not dying." I can picture those icy blue eyes rolling with the amount of sarcasm that drips from that airy drawl.

"Psh, whatever, what's the diagnosis?" I sit back nonchalantly, trying to focus on my cock, not growing harder. It's not the first time Noelle has sat on my lap, so I don't know why it has to get all firm on me.

Noelle twists to face me, and the hard gaze she gives me puts the steel of the rod in my pants to shame. "POTS."

"Never heard of it," I wince out. She grimaces as she shuffles from my lap into the tiny space between me and her mom. I quickly tug my parka over my lap with as much discretion as I can muster by coughing loudly and drawing all eyes to me. So none.

"It's a relatively new discovery." Noelle flicks her eyes away from my crotch. The fireplace compliments her flustered cheeks beautifully.

"Is it serious?"

My erection is fucking terminal, Christ, down boy.

"I don't know, but it has to do with my heart." Noelle's voice is meek as she speaks.

"Your heart?" I couldn't sound more pathetically desperate if I tried.

"Yes, January, my heart. Nothing you should be concerned with." She swipes her fiery locks over her shoulder, exposing her pulse that I want to kiss. I feel my tongue run over my bottom lip.

Only to remember that the pulse comes from a defective heart.

"A heart disease sounds serious."

"It's not a heart disease, it's a disorder. Like I said, you shouldn't worry about it so you can wipe that expression off your face," she sneers, narrowing her eyes on me as she closes in for dramatic effect. I'm this close to kissing her. If she doesn't pull back in three seconds, she's got a one-way ticket to Smoochville.

"So typical of you not to listen to me," she scoffs, crossing her arms and long legs. Her adjustment thrusts my weight towards the crevice that we are now slowly sinking into.

"I am listening," I squeak. My voice hasn't pitched that high since Noelle and I sang karaoke at Cocomo, and my throat hasn't been this tight since I fumbled my feelings for Noelle all those years ago. The same thoughts are plaguing my mind from that very day.

I want to kiss you, only this time again and again and again and again.

"You're thinking about kissing me." Her icy blue eyes roll, and her lips trill as she slips out a *psh* sound.

"I was not."

I totally fucking was. Noelle has always had a good read on me, if only I had the same capabilities with her.

"You so were."

"Was not," I queasily tease, leaning in and puckering my lips. Her cheeks tint a faint rogue, and if my observations don't deceive me, she's enjoying me flirting with her.

This is odd. It feels like the old dynamic Noelle and I had, our taunting and poking, only there is a new layer to it. *Flirting*. I am dying to explore it more with her.

"I'm not playing your immature game, January."

"Just admit you were thinking about kissing me, too." A slimy smirk tugs at my lips, and I hope Noelle reads it as endearing.

"I haven't given you any thought in years," she sulks, sitting back hard with a harrumph, wearing the most adorable pout. It feels like we're sixteen again and she's sulking because I beat her at *The Battle of Blizzard*, a game that she invented from her own incredible brain. Of course, she blamed my win on a glitch. It was in the beta stage, after all.

I feel my own eyes roll at the memory. The faintest of gasps leaves Noelle's lips. She's got her eyes locked on mine; I daringly wrap my arm around her.

"Only enough thought to follow my anger-induced scandals." I slip a fiery lock of her hair around my finger, and I have never craved intimacy with a woman more than I do Noelle.

"I don't *follow* you or your scandals." She dry heaves, pinching my limp finger between her nimble ones and discarding my advancing arm from her shoulder.

I guess she's not so keen on exploring this very enticing new dynamic. Fine. It takes two to play multiplayer.

"I also don't *follow* you," I spit, mimicking her tantrum from before. I guess being with each other has made us regress right back to where we left off as teens. Whiny, bratty teens. God forbid we act like the 28-year-old adults we are.

"Right." An all-knowing smirk forms on her lips, and it takes everything in me to not turn sickly green. There's no way she knows @NovemberRain is me. I do such a good job at covering my tracks, considering how many hackers she breeds amongst her *Darlings.*

My vision sharpens and I catch her beautiful, mischievous smirk once more. My body involuntarily jerks toward her lips.

She slips from the cozy crevice between me and her mom. I almost end up kissing Johanna's boob.

"I need to lie down. Dad, can you take me to my room, please," Noelle wheezes airily. I snap to my senses. She cradles her head, her brows pinched together in pain.

"I'll take her." I'm quick to stand as I detect her slight swaying.

"Isn't it obvious I'm trying to escape you?" she hisses, gnashing her teeth at me. The color runs from her face, and now it's at the point that our egos need to be put aside.

"Noelle, you don't have to get so worked up. We're only jabbing. It's what we do." I run my palm across her back and just like many times before she surrenders her weight, which means she still trusts me.

"There is no *we* anymore, January, only *I*," she pinches out agonizingly. Her eyes roll back. Things could get ugly if she doesn't rest soon.

"Well, *I* will ensure you make it safely to your room." I'm not sure if my approach is leaning more towards being ego-driven, but I know my concern is genuine.

"I'm locking the door on you; you will not be coming inside."

"I fear that the metaphorical door of this friendship is locked, bolted, and sealed."

"You are correct." She threads her arm through mine, sneering to make her reluctance known that it is simply for the benefit of her health.

"Well then, perhaps our friendship has expired." I sigh, gently guiding her from the reading room as our parents watch opportunistically. *Weird*. Are they not seeing what I'm seeing? All hope for Noelle and I to rekindle our friendship is gone, so I do not know what that optimistic twinkle is in their eyes.

"Typical of you to give up on us so quickly." There she goes, jabbing away as if she's not at risk of collapsing. Now would be the time, I suppose as we cross the threshold and into the snow, knowing that just laying in the snow is an effective way to calm her heart.

"On the contrary, Princess, I propose a new dynamic instead." Here I go, testing the limits of this new camaraderie whilst the abrasive chill tests at my flesh. No matter how many layers I'm wearing, the Arizona heat has made me sensitive to the Colorado chill. This is just a reminder that things have changed, including my biology.

"New dynamic?" She turns to me with the most adorable confused expression, also the rosiest of cheeks.

Change isn't always a bad thing.

"Well, Noelle, I know things will never be what they were because we lost a certain level of trust, but I honestly feel like we were never friends—"

"Are you proposing enemies, because I may very well be on board already," she huffs, a cold cloud slipping from her lips.

"Nono, it's obvious that we liked each other the whole time, so now that we know of the feelings, we should just be unabashed and flirt."

Noelle charges her shoulder into the door of a smaller lodge that leads through to a narrow corridor. What awaits us on the other side of this door, I know for a fact will be incredibly confronting for me. Her room, the scene of the crime, and mirroring her room, is my old room.

"To what end, January, you think you can just march into the ski lodge and propose a situationship?"

"Is that what that is?"

"Flirting with no label. Are you kidding me? Yes, that's a situationship."

"Then let's date!" Fuck, I've got Samantha-sized balls today, which is ironic considering how the cold is making my penis contract. I know my knee jerk reaction stems from my desperation to have Noelle be a part of my life again.

"Here is fine." She snatches her arm from my forearm, aggressively pulling at the doorknob of her bedroom door.

I am not letting Noelle get away this time. I must rescue my Princess.

Five

Change Of Season

January

We'd often play pretend as Princess and Prince, but right now Noelle is the epitome of the fire-breathing dragons we would fend off.

"I said safely *inside* your room." I calculate the few inches that stand between her door and us, still decorated just as I remembered, an amalgamation of her personality on a door; stickers of video game characters, Christmas tinsel and staples that remain from where Polaroids of her and me once were. I watched her tear those down firsthand, calling me many colorful things in French and English.

"And I said you're not welcome inside." She places a flaccid palm on my chest, her eyes rolling back once again.

"I believe the wording you used was coming inside," the smarmy expression falls from my face, as that may test the waters a little too hard. It's now become a murky mess. "Safely. I meant coming inside, making sure you make it inside safely."

"Then you can observe from the doorframe." Noelle pushes through the door. She's clearly forgotten about her work obligations this morning, as a package stuffed to the brim with pleasurable items lay aesthetically on her bed.

"If that isn't an invitation, I don't know what is." I snort.

Noelle's skin somehow turns even more sickly.

"It's for a sponsorship. I had to make a video for Instagram. I don't use these."

"You don't have to justify your pleasure to me." I lean against the doorframe; fully aware I'm wearing the most idiotically charming smile on my face. I just need Noelle to stop averting her eyes so I can take her breath away.

"You're right, I don't because along with my heart, it doesn't concern you," she says, still not looking at me. She hastily scoops the sex toys into the box, finessing the hot pink tissue paper to hide the toys from sight.

Whilst she busies herself with hiding the sponsored gift, I do the pleasure of welcoming myself into her room. It's mostly unchanged, much like the door. Leafy garlands still adorn the beamed ceilings, and she has kept her bed pressed against the window, for easy access to the window seat where we played MarioKart on our Nintendo DS consoles.

Colorful race courses she was confident she could best. Only by some miracle I would win...by a landslide. Leading to her wrestling me onto her bed. That's when things were innocent between us, I miss that more than I crave the undeniable sexual tension between us.

"Get out! What are you doing?" Her attempt at pushing against my large stature is pathetic and entirely useless. With two fingers to her forehead, she easily tips onto her bed.

"I see you're keeping up with all the gadgets and gizmos."

"I already told you I don't use toys," she huffs, seeing I'm referring to the only modification to the room; a desk cluttered with technological bits and bobs that probably only make sense to Noelle.

The damn thing looks like a pocket-size nightclub.

She harrumphs, pushing me aside, and wriggles her mouse around. "That's my gaming setup."

"Looks like an evil professor's liar."

"Well, I have to stay current with all the gadgets and gizmos. I'm sort of a big deal in the gaming world."

I am aware that Noelle has made quite the name for herself on streaming platforms. I'm also aware of all the incredibly misogynistic comments left by thirsty teens that get left on her streams. Just because she's a woman who enjoys gaming. Correction, excels at gaming, until she goes up against me, of course.

"Oh, you stay quite up to date with all the gadgets and gizmos." I wiggle my brows, my eyes flicking to her bedside drawers, where she had stuffed the PR package bursting with vibrators and dildos. "Remind me what *that* has to do with gaming."

"Well, I'm more of just a feminist lifestyle influencer. I'm known for my coding stuff mostly, spreading the message that girls can work in Information Technology too." The way her pride glitters puts all those hoity-toity ski resorts with their fancy schmancy expensive Christmas lights to shame. Her cheeks blushing over modestly like that jolly motorized Santa at that one resort.

"You were always so smart, Noelle." I can't help but compliment her. Even if our relationship is a big fat question mark right now, the truth can't be denied. Her icy-coloured gaze locks on me, her eyes sparkling with validation. It's a hall of mirrors as the acknowledgment has me lighting up, too.

"Yeah, um, well, anyway," she stumbles, catching the computer mouse as it slips from the desk. "Now I sort of partner with any brands with feminist ideals. Nothing screams girl power like destigmatizing female pleasure."

"Oh, we're still talking about the vibrators?" I poke daringly.

"No, we're dropping it now." She clears her throat awkwardly, turning back to the monitor and wiping away her screensaver, a slideshow of images with her friends...none of me, though.

"But I like where this conversation is going," I croak. I plant my palm on her desk, misjudging how low it is. I catch myself before I smash my head through Noelle's secret intelligence-grade monitor.

Her nostrils flare. The sparkling princess is gone and the fire-breathing dragon has returned.

"You don't get to talk to me like that. I'm not one of your little *puck bunnies,* as they like to call them."

Ugh, surely, she doesn't believe the rumors. The one where the media not only depicts me as an asshole but a playboy too, when only the former is true.

"So, you *do* follow me." I wiggle my brows, which brings on an instant headache since my eyebrows have only been accustomed to frowning for the past ten years.

"Get out!" She barks. Despite her angelic face, I'm quite scared of the little demon. Not that she's little, but she sits perfectly at 5'10. I could easily lean in and place a peck between her pinched brows.

I restrain myself, though, picking up on symptoms of an incoming episode.

"For the record, Nono, I'm an asshole, but I'm not a sleaze," I say calmly, hoping she will match me in energy.

"Well, the news my followers distribute to me says otherwise."

"Right, your followers. What do they call themselves, Noelle's *Darlings*?"

"So you do follow me," she lilts in her usual airy trill. She's obviously flirting with me.

I'm getting whiplash as she shifts from dragon to princess in a flash. *My fire-breathing ice princess.*

"Maybe I have a secret account, and I am the president of the Noelle's Darlings." I'm playing with fire now, basically masking the truth in a little playful taunt.

"And what a fierce leader you make." Her weak trembling fingers caress my face with the weight of a feather.

"I lead them ferociously, yes," I pathetically spatter out. But I don't let my embarrassment consume me. It only provides evidence that I don't have any game and, therefore, can not catch *puck bunnies* for intimate burrowing.

"Okay, we're done with this conversation," she concludes, guiding me out of the room.

Wait, I don't want this to end yet. We're flirting again! Noelle, stop!

"I kind of missed you." I seem to be on a streak with my patheticness.

"I kind of didn't. Bye!" The last thing I see is that beautiful angel face of hers and that signature mischievous glint in her eyes.

Okay, fine, I wanted to kiss you. Now let me back in, this is me begging!

All the blood had rushed from my head to my cock.

"I kind of missed you. How could I be so stupid? What was I even doing? I don't talk to Noelle like that. She's my best friend."

Well, she was.

I'm flying close to the sun, testing this new dynamic of ours out, but truthfully, I just want to be friends again. I want what we had.

Looking back, I regret abstaining from sex for so long, but I couldn't bring myself to be with someone else after hurting Noelle. A good lay would probably do wonders for my temper or whatever this animalistic urge inside me is.

But only if it's Noelle.

"Well, that's not happening anytime soon. Woman hates my guts," I huff under my breath. I train my facial features into their natural frown as I enter the reading room once more.

All I truly need is a little privacy of my own. If I can't have Noelle right now, I have to get rid of these naughty thoughts I'm having of her.

"She's sleeping now," I announce to the room. Both sets of parents look at me as if I caught them doing cocaine on the mahogany coffee table. Many a card game had turned into a wrestling match on that coffee table.

"Poor girl, it must be hard living with such a disease," Mom coos, patting her rhinestone fingernails to her heart, wearing a pitiful pout.

"It's not a disease, Mom, it's a disorder," I correct bluntly. "Any chance I can get a room?"

"Sure, kid, we still have your room just the way you left, in case you ever felt called to visit," David notifies me.

Shit! That means every inch will remind me of Noelle. My Polaroids are probably intact on those walls.

"I now realize I should've taken that opportunity when I could." So much regret, so much time wasted, over such stupid petty shit.

"It was Noelle who said to leave it the way it was. I think she hoped you might visit." David's voice is tender as he delivers the most heartbreaking news. Now, I can picture Noelle sitting behind the reception, anticipating my visit, perking up every time someone would sweep into the lodge's lobby. Only to be disappointed, it wasn't me.

Time wore her down, her patience ran thin.

And now she's disappointed that it is me.

"It pains me that Noelle was wrong about me. I should've visited." The old me would have but the new me, *Cameron Snow*, post breaking-Noelle's-heart January is not the January she knew like the back of her hand.

My feet can't decide whether to run to or from my old room as I approach it. Of course, it's the one situated across from Noelle's in the staff lodge. All I want to do is go into her room, hold her, and tell her how sorry I am for breaking her heart. Something I have been trying to do for the last 10 years.

"Nono," I slip from my lips as I take in the door once again.

Instead, I do what I do best, make a mess of a situation and run in the other direction. This time finding safety in my old room.

The guilt that washes over me is like an avalanche. My breathing thins at the sight of my untouched room. The bed sheets are still tangled, just like they were that morning. Where I rolled out of bed reluctantly, because I knew I would leave Noelle, with no indication of when I would see her next. It could've been months.

And it ended up being 10 years.

"I should've visited. Why didn't I visit?" I don't even bother crossing the threshold of my room. The ghosts of our adolescence play out before me.

One specific memory vividly plays out in the corner of my old room, that homed a leather bean bag chair and CD player. The vision of Noelle's long limbs sitting cross-legged on the mystery carpet we found in the ski shed and relocated to my room. Her face twisted in a feigned pleasant expression as a Guns N' Roses CD plays out. She said Axl Rose *sounds like he's trying to let out a fart.*

I got the hint and immediately succumbed to swapping the CD out for Justin Bieber. She was up on her feet in an instant, and so was I to rescue from her sudden faint spell.

Playfully reciting the lyrics to *Boyfriend*, meaning every single word sincerely.

I wanted to kiss her at that moment. Her body pulled close to mine, her hot breath hitting my lips in a hard pant. Her grateful gaze locked on me. She looked remarkable. There were a lot of moments when I wanted to kiss her, but I couldn't risk ruining our friendship. It was the most important thing to me.

It still is the most important thing to me.

I shut my door as if pulling a theater curtain on that nostalgic memory, deciding to not go in. I glance back at Noelle's door, it's radio silent in there.

I ignore the urge to barge in and press the back of my palm to what is no doubt her steaming forehead.

I scrap my trainers on the large welcome mat of the lobby, somehow getting myself here in a subconscious daydream.

"That was a quick nap?" Johanna pokes as we cross paths on my way back into the reading room. She's armed with the platter of cookies. Only a few remain. I pinch one from the plate.

It's just a cookie, January. The scent does not remind you of Noelle.

If anything, it reminds me of heartbreak now.

"I got a second wind, I guess. I'm not tired anymore."

"Okay, kiddo." Johanna swallows thickly, averting her eyes guiltily.

What the fuck was that about?

The same sketchy air from before is still present in the reading room.

"Okay, I'm calling it out. Why is everybody acting fucking weird?" I chomp into my cookie; my parents sigh in synchronicity.

"Should we tell him?" My mom turns to my dad with an air of dramatization that wouldn't look out of place in a soap opera.

"Tell me what?"

Six

Paper Rings

Noelle

I slip a sigh of relief as the door snaps shut behind me. I process what just took place. And all I seem to have is a buttfuck load of questions. Why is January here? Why, after ten long years, is he back at the ski lodge? Why did Camille call this place home on his behalf? If Darlington Snow Paradise is *home* to January, why was it so easy for him to leave? And how was it even easier to stay away all these years? A decade. A whole fucking decade.

I don't know what to feel at the moment, so I just let the sensations pass through me. My head feels like a carousel with a broken gear, spinning around impossibly fast. The imaginary hokey pokey music sped up to a headache-inducing pitch. January's snarky remarks echo in my head, his deep, bassy voice still sends a shiver down my spine. It's only then I notice my whole body is shaking. Until it stops suddenly, like I've gone into a state of shock. Only it's not the shock I'm feeling. I know exactly what is happening to me.

I'm having an episode.

My flesh crawls hot in a flash, and it's only seconds after my vision blurs. I push my back off my door in hopes of blindly finding my bed. I can only just make out the shape. My hip bone stings with pain as a metallic *prang* rings out.

Well, I found my bedpost, my bed can't be too much further.

Relief washes over me as my back sinks into my mattress. I can now let this tortuous episode wreak havoc on my cardiovascular system. At least I'm comfortable. I close my eyes, trying to not hyper-fixate on the fire streaming under my flesh.

I would usually just crawl outside and belly-flop from my porch into the cushiony snow below.

Great, now my mattress is on fire, I think.

Thinking about January is making this episode worse. All I have to do is think of absolutely anything else and I'll relieve my pain.

For someone who hasn't seen me in ten years, he sure is comfortable around me. And the sad thing is, it's kind of nice.

What I told him was a straight-out lie. I missed January this whole time. I don't mean to downplay my accolades and achievements, but January's friendship was the ultimate prize. And if I were to put my stubbornness aside for one second and ask him, what's his most prized possession in life? He'd probably say to hell with all the shiny medals and big stupid trophies. *Our friendship was gold.*

You only have a friend like January once in a lifetime, a friendship that turns into true love.

Only for it all to go down the toilet, because fame shits on true love every time.

Fame. How I gained a tiny shred of it is beyond me. Well, I sort of know the answer to this. It's that girls and women see a piece of myself in them. Intelligent, strong, independent women who don't allow those who let them down keep them down. Take that and veil on a mysterious cardiovascular disorder and I'm the feminist poster child of perseverance.

I genuinely love the message I'm spreading and the comments about how inspiring I am. They encourage me to keep going. But it's tough. My *Darlings* only see the glossed-up version of me, filtered beyond recognition. They don't see the ugly side of me, the episodes, the failures of having to return home, breaking off an engagement. Because sometimes perseverance can lead to burnout, and you have no choice but to give up. Your body is screaming at you to give up, give up, give up.

My followers never see that. They don't see all of me, the real me. January sees me. Or rather, saw me. Now, I'm just a piece of ass to him. He has some nerve.

New dynamic, psh, go to hell.

I want the old one back.

I reach blindly for my phone as it pings and vibrates constantly. The click notifies me that the device has recognized my face and allowed me access to my phone.

I finally see my hearts, and wow, 113 more Darlings! I'm grateful but also very, very tired.

I click on notifications to find the adoration isn't for one of my posts, but rather a post I'm tagged in.

@TheCameronSnow.

"That motherfucker!"

Janelle is the first of my influencer friends to bombard my inbox with messages, but I'm far too busy scrolling through these ridiculous comments for January and me.

@CamIsMyMan: CaMeRon SNoW are you cheating on me with some girl named Noelle how dare you????

@FriskyDiva: She's not even pretty. What do you see in her?

Just when I thought those comments were bad, the comments actually in favor of us being an item are far worse than the ones against this monstrosity.

@NoelleCamEdits: Oh my god! Guys, it's happening! I knew they were fucking!

@CamSnowThirstArchives: Noelle girl pls you gotta tell us how big.

I drop my phone with that one. It springs from my mattress with magical inertia, planting with a smack to the ground. I hesitantly cradle my phone in my hand, inspecting for fractures.

Janelle is so eager to pry answers from me, she doesn't realize she's doing it from her business account.

@TickleMeKink: NOELLE YOU'RE GETTING HOCKEY DICK AND YOU DIDN'T TELL ME!!! YOU'RE A HOCKEY DICK JOCKEY!!!

@TickleMeKink: Tell me everything!!!! Does he make it snow *wink wink*

@DarlingNoelle: Nelly! Make like snow and chill the fuck out! I do not know what January is trying to pull on me right now! I wasn't aware that the photo was taken, and I certainly wasn't aware it was going to be posted.

@TickleMeKink: wow Noelle, go check out the Darlington Snow Paradise Instagram account. The follower count is going up like crazy!!!

I investigate @DarlingtonSnowParadise, but instead find the comments section for the unapproved post has been turned off, leaving me face-to-face with the post itself.

Don't even get me started on the photo. How did I gloss over the photo? It's truly heinous.

It is so obviously taken from Camille's phone only moments ago, when we all congregated in the reading room and I was forced to sit on January's lap.

Well done, Camille, you captured a moment of tenderness.

Well, I won't be supplying any more of those. You think the Prince of Ice is bad? Move over, January, and make room for the Ice Princess!

I can only just make out January's roaring through my custardy pulse in my eardrums. It's like my gaming avatar is on its last health. The screen is flashing with a warning, the heartbeat audio playing thickly in my ears.

"There's no fucking way she would do that. She shouldn't fucking have to!"

Oh, he better not be talking to my parents that way. I march into the reading room once more, finding January pacing back and forth with his phone pressed to his ear.

"Noelle, darling, you're awake." Camille rises from the couch with open arms but retracts her offer to embrace when she catches my piercing, icy stare.

"Great, you've got me yelling, Samantha, and now I woke her up," January huffs. "No, I will not put you on speakerphone. Fine. Fuck! Happy?" January throws his phone carelessly onto the mahogany table, and I wince.

It's very obvious at that moment, we are not in the same tax bracket.

"Noelle? You there?" A voice comes from the phone and it wants to talk to me. Why?

"Um, yes, who am I speaking to?"

"Oh, Angelface, you don't remember me? Samantha, Cameron's publicist."

Cameron. Maybe that's the secret to becoming the most loved and most hated hockey-playing millionaire in the world. I will swiftly change my name to Winter. I like it. It pairs well with my frosty new demeanor.

"I can't say that name rings a bell."

"We met very briefly. I was with my now husband, Vinnie. He's the one who scouted Cameron's talent."

"Oh, I remember you."

"Oh, course you do, sweetie. I make impressions. It's why I'm the best in the biz."

I hate to knock a powerful woman down a peg or two, but I am feeling extremely violated by what the Snow family has done to me. Posting that photo, which I know his impression-making publicist was merely another puppeteer mastering the strings.

"I was talking about Cameron. I don't know a Cameron."

"Oh, that's right, you know him by—"

"January, my actual name." January cuts in. He is exhausted from this play-pretend narrative.

"Wow, kids, see this engagement!" Samantha completely disregards January.

I hold my phone up to my face. My screensaver of my friends, Janelle, Candy, and I are swiped away. I'm face to face with a flood of likes, comments, and follows. It looks like @TheCameronSnow has a lot more influence than me. I don't even get this kind of engagement on a good day.

"Who fucking cares!" January has turned back to yelling, I see. "The plan is stupid and unethical."

"What plan?" my controlled volume pierces through, catching January's attention with a vicious snap of his head my way.

"Well, Samantha, take the floor. Tell Noelle your stupid plan," January huffs, slumping onto the couch. He arranges the faux fur cushions to create space. His eyes soften slightly from their irritation when he looks at me. "You should sit down for this. I have a feeling you'll take the news just as well as I did."

I slowly lower myself to the couch, ensuring I am on the furthest end possible.

"You ready, Angelface?"

"I guess." How does anyone prepare for vague ominous news?

"You and Cameron are going to get married!" Samantha announces, followed by applauding.

Christ, January was right. I did need to sit down. Even lay down, and am I about to pass out?

"Samantha, I told you to ease into the news when you tell her," January scolds, "she gets these—"

"Spells, yes, Cameron, I know. I'm just so excited for you two."

Silence fills the room as I process what I've just been told. I'm marrying January Cameron Snow. Under what circumstances would I be crazy enough to willingly marry January?

"Noelle," January's voice is everything I need to hear right now. It's gentle and concerned. I'm thrust from my spacey thoughts. My face melts from its confused contortion. "Are you okay?"

I meet January's haunting green eyes. The jade green and cerulean blue blend to make the most hypnotic muted mint color, its equal parts disturbing and comforting to stare into them.

"I'm...okay," I say calmly, to my surprise. "Really, I'm okay."

January takes the cue and sits back, but his concerned eyes remain trained on me. "Can someone slowly explain to me why I'm marrying January?"

"Well, Darling." My dad speaks. I didn't pick him to orchestrate an arranged marriage, color me shocked. "The truth is the Snow's, your mother and I-"

"Sorry to cut you off, David, but the Snow's excludes me." January bluntly interjects.

"Right, Camille, Nicholas, your mother, and I were discussing the prospects of Darlington Snow Paradise. I know you have plans to inherit this place when we retire and it breaks my heart that business isn't doing well."

This is not news to me. I manage the bookkeeping on the odd occasion, and from the lack of people I'm greeting, even in the busier seasons, I am fully aware we are not generating revenue.

"I'm doing my best to spread the word with the influence I have, Dad. I don't know why it's not working."

I work tirelessly to make aesthetically pleasing videos of the lodge, highlighting its peaceful quality with its secludedness, and how romantic the scenery is. It would be perfect for a honeymoon or a couple's getaway. I can vouch that it would be a great place for people in love to escape to...because I fell in love with January living here.

"We appreciate how hard you work on social media, getting the lodge's name out there."

"I even have Janelle and Candy post, and share the lodge when they visit. I'm trying to engage not only the honeymoon crowd but singles, too."

It's just the place for introverted college students to spend their winter break. Although most of them end up at ski resorts that host huge rowdy parties where the booking fee includes booze. How am I supposed to compete?

"Actually, I really like your honeymoon angle, Angelface," Samantha pipes up from the phone on the table. "I think your followers need evidence to back it up. It's all about the proof in the pudding."

"So, I'm going to pretend to marry January and we'll stage a honeymoon publicity stunt?" I can plaster a fake smile on my face. I often had to do so at university as an attempt to mask my agonizing fatigue.

"Pretend? Aren't you two head over heels in love with each other?"

"No, Sam," January sneers.

"Hey, don't get cranky at me. I'm just relaying what you've said in the past." Samantha is biting back her giggles. January grumbles quietly in French under his breath. I disregard his disgruntled state, really considering the stunt and how it might save the lodge.

"Why January? If you want to stage a honeymoon, why don't I do it with the man I love?"

I'm sure Sean requires a getaway with how hard he works, so why not make it a romantic reunion with his ex-fiance? Then I wouldn't have to tap into my acting chops. The staging will look authentic because I genuinely love Sean, and those who are lucky enough to marry the love of their lives will come flocking to the lodge.

"Again, is that not Cameron— sorry, I mean January?" Samantha pipes up once again.

"I believe she's talking about Sean, her ex-fiance." Mum clarifies to Samantha.

"Oh," Samantha drags out as realization dawns on her. "The one I had to write up an NDA for. Weird that you call him by his middle name."

I don't understand what she's referring to. Maybe she's finally realizing how weird it is to be calling January by his middle name.

"It has to be Cameron. Have you seen the following on this kid's account!" Samantha reasons enthusiastically.

"I'm marrying January because he's famous. Is that not degrading for him?" I don't know why I suddenly give a shit whether January is exploited.

"No, because, The Prince of Ice here needs a new angle on his public image. He does not make my job easy," Samantha tuts.

"And getting married just wipes away how much of an asshole he is?"

Samantha chuckles, January slipping a harrumph.

"Oh, I like you, Angelface. It's undeniable he's far more tolerable when he's with the person who makes him happiest, and that is you, Angelface."

"So, I'm responsible for keeping him happy. No pressure," I scoff. "He's never been the chipper type. He barely cracks a smile for me." Just to prove my point, January purses his lips into a flat line.

"Won't it be all worth it? If I were you, I would take another look at your social media. I should've acted on this years ago," Samantha cheers, more solo applauding sounds through the phone.

I look at my phone, which has been buzzing non-stop at my side.

"Wow," I slip out before putting my phone on Do Not Disturb, the influx of notifications draining my battery with every second.

"...tomorrow."

I catch the tail end of Samantha's sentence.

"So, Noelle just doesn't get a say in this," January snipes, his brows deepening in their furrow as he becomes more enraged.

"Well, legally, we can't force her to marry you. But it sounds like she can see the benefits of it all." I can hear Samantha's snarky smile through the phone.

"And she only has today to decide?" January's hands ball into fists at his sides.

"Yep," Samantha pops.

"You're absolutely vile, Samantha."

"I'm in," I barely whisper.

My knee-jerk reaction paints everybody with an expression of surprise. I can swear Samantha is also wearing the expression.

"Nono, No." January's features are turning stony once again. "No," he firmly reiterates.

"Great! I'll be visiting tomorrow and we'll settle the contract," Samantha cheers. The line goes dead amid January's protest.

"Samantha, stop. Noelle is not marrying—she hung up."

"I'm marrying you, January. I have to do this."

I can't lose this place. It's the only place that truly accommodates me.

SEVEN

Shhhhhh...

January

Noelle hasn't looked at me once this morning. Her eyes are glazed over, and she's clearly lost in thought.

Now there's a door I wish was unlocked; I would love easy access to what the hell is going through her head. Besides, not a lot of sense. Why can't she be open with me? Just like her stupid porch door, which I'm sure she still leaves unlocked after ten long years.

She's absolutely crazy going ahead with an idea like this. I know why I'm doing it, it's because eighteen-year-old January didn't think I'd have to read the fine print of my contract. So technically my publicist forcing me to marry someone isn't unethical. Clause 22.8a made sure of that.

Thankfully, it's Noelle—*even though it very well shouldn't be*—she's forcing me to marry.

Now here we are twiddling our thumbs nervously waiting for this Sean fucker to arrive and sign an NDA. Everyone's eyes avert from me as I flick a steely gaze of disappointment. Lucky for them, my eyes hurry back to Noelle.

I'm tracking her every move, like I'm a predator scanning for any signs of weakness in its prey, only I don't plan to pounce and devour her for dinner. Her hands wring together so tightly that her knuckles turn white. I just want to hold her tight and apologize for this stupid fucking catastrophe.

It's deafeningly quiet besides the tender crackle of the fireplace. Noelle and I would usually indulge in a quaint scene like this when the snowfall was heavy. She'd be curled into my side with a good book, me trying to keep my heart steady as I would watch those pretty ice-colored orbs run along the words. I could only imagine what sort of otherworldly visions were materializing in her head. She admitted to swapping the protagonist out with herself. It was the closest she ever got to living out adventures. I often wondered if she ever substituted the hero in her books for me.

I couldn't be further from a hero in her eyes nowadays.

"Noelle?" I do the honor of breaking the silence. Clearly, Noelle doesn't want the quiet ambience broken.

I gauge from her spaced-out expression that she's not actively ignoring me. So, I keep my temper at bay and try again calmly. "Nono?"

She turns to me with a cute, confused hum. I have to remind myself of my concern and not become a blubbering mess at her adorableness.

"Are you okay?"

"M'fine," she muffles.

She's so not fine. *Christ, Noelle, you don't have to be a warrior all the fucking time. Just let the feeling wash over you, please. I hate that you're concealing your undeniable rage under these circumstances.*

"What are you thinking, Noelle?"

Let me in, Noelle, I need to know how you see me after I've ruined your life...again.

"Just thinking what Sean is going to think when he sees I've hit rock bottom."

My lips purse at her hurtful connotation. I don't disagree; it is a pretty low-life circumstance she has succumbed to. Many consider arranged marriages to be a last resort option. But add the fact she has to marry me, the person she despises most in life, and well, *rock bottom* is a perfect description of where she's at in life.

"Yes, I agree, Noelle. Marrying me is the equivalent of hitting rock bottom," I tut bitterly. How could what was once my biggest dream, marrying Noelle Winter Darlington, turn into possibly my biggest nightmare for the both of us? Truthfully, there's still a glimmer of that dream that burns inside me. I've been clandestinely in love with her the ten years we've been apart. Of course, I still long to be bound to her in marriage. But not like this. I hoped for a more rejoiceful union. Not this forced, contractual arrangment.

"Exactly," she shudders. I can't even get mad at her honesty, not with how much it breaks her. My eyes drop to her balled fists. "Oh god, I'm ashamed," she presses through her teeth, her cheeks flustering with a petal pink stain.

Fuck, I'm doing it again. I'm hurting Noelle again. I fucking hate how I keep doing this.

What I suggest may make up for it though, as it will hurt me just as badly. As painful as it is to admit, Noelle loved this Sean guy, and I would hate for him to have a negative perception of her. Since that negative image is of my making, I'll do whatever I can to make Noelle happy once again.

"Hey, Nono." My hand envelopes her fist. "We're not technically married yet. Why don't you see if Sean can stay a couple of nights? Just to assure him you are as incredible as you were all those years ago."

Noelle turns her tear-constellated eyes to me, beading with surprise and contemplation at my suggestion, before she finally nods in agreement.

"And I want to have sex with him," she sniffs. I slowly retract my compassionate hand holding, sighing at that disappointing announcement. I was hoping for just a friendly chat over some hot coco, I never planned on her having sex with the guy. "Wait!" Noelle's objection jerks me into alertness. Maybe she has come to her senses. Noelle dulls as realization washes over her. "Can we see other people whilst this stunt is happening?"

Noelle turns to me again, her eyes pleading for permission. She wants to see other people? It hurts that she even wants to, insinuating I'm not enough. Even though my affections for her are real, I guess hers have melted away with the decade we've spent apart.

"No, Angelface, it's all in the contract you signed," Samantha explains.

At least Noelle is the same breed of stupid as me.

"Lesson learned. Always read the fine print." Noelle inhales tensely. Someone comes barreling through the door, Noelle springs from her seat as an average-height man with blond hair approaches the table. His eyes narrow in on the contracts laid on the table. I'm feeling physically sick as Noelle throws herself at him, eager for his embrace and attention. Meanwhile, here I am ready to burst at the seams with how much I love my best friend. But none of that matters because she'd rather have *other people*. And at this very moment, it's Sean.

He halts back from Noelle's incoming embrace, swatting her away as if she were a mosquito carrying an infestation. My affections grow into an ugly monster as I want to squash this rodent beneath my snow boot.

That fucker has the nerve to reject one of Noelle's hugs. He should be so lucky to receive one in the first place.

Holding Noelle is the equivalent of the gentle sunrise peeking from above the snow-capped mountains, her radiance melting away the thick cast of snow that buries my heart. I'm renewed with life and warmth once again.

Somewhere in that thought, I must have stood up and wrapped my arms around Noelle's shoulders from behind. From her lack of resistance, she clearly has taken no notice. Her face pinched in an expression of devastation as her eyes remain locked on her aggravated ex.

"Pen. Give me a fucking pen, for fuck's sake," Sean huffs urgently. He hasn't even acknowledged Noelle's distraught state. I can feel her breathing labor under my hold, her heart working overtime, no doubt punctured by Sean's neglect.

It's okay, Noelle, I'm here to shower you with love. I nuzzle my nose into the crook of her neck, where her pulse hits my lips with concerning rapidness.

"Sean?" Noelle calls out to the man, trying to garner his attention. Which is clearly taking priority over swatting me away. I'm not complaining, I adore holding Noelle so protectively. "Sean, Pookie?"

And maybe soon enough she'll realize this shit bag isn't worth her time and may just fall into my embrace.

"We never met, got it?" Sean turns sharply to Noelle. She startles backward, only now acknowledging my hold around her. She throws my arms away. My palm moves possessively to her waist. She resigns from our tiff with a reluctant huff.

"Sean, what are you talking about?"

"I swear to god if this gets out to my wife and kids, I'm so fucking screwed." Sean rubs at his temples.

"You remarried." Noelle's voice is tepid at the news. Remarried is also a strong word she decided on. They were barely engaged.

"No, I didn't remarry. You're so fucking stupid. I've been married this whole time, Noelle. You were my fucking mistress."

I feel an immense weight as Noelle surrenders into me. I'm worried she's fainted. Only when she speaks, I am reassured she hasn't.

"Mistress?" I feel the fire alight in her core as my palm runs along her stomach. Her entire flesh is warming with each passing second, like she's a boiling kettle. I anticipate her ears to blow steam cartoonishly. "You proposed to me!" she roars, thrashing against my hold. As much as it would delight me to see Noelle beat this man to a bloody pulp, I can't risk her burning herself out before she's really put through her paces.

This is a huge mistake.

I'm tempted to reach for our contracts that lay vulnerably on the table and tear them to shreds, freeing Noelle from this shitshow. Before things become too detrimental to her health. There's no way she'll be able to keep up with the refined public image Samantha demands, along with my fast-paced lifestyle comprising press conferences and training sessions. No, it'll ruin her. I can't let that happen. We'll go our separate ways, and Noelle can go on living her life slowly and peacefully at the lodge. And I'll return to my miserable, lonely darkness.

"I wasn't going to marry you; I knew we'd break off the engagement, eventually. With your whole *Upon-A-Star* chronically ill child vibe." Sean's eyes scan Noelle with a sneer. My eyes trail the very path Sean's did and Noelle looks her healthiest. Since moving back to the lodge from Chicago, Noelle has lost that sickly fatigued twinge to her complexion. Her cheeks are rosy and plump again, no longer gaunt from what I assume was an imbalanced diet typical of a university student. Her eyes, although currently beaconed with rage, are full of life and passion.

Noelle looks incredible these days! If she weren't amid defending herself against this scumbag, I'd kiss her. I'd cup her beautiful face in my calloused hands and kiss her like I did all those years ago.

"You look worse for wear now, no longer that pretty bubbly redhead I met at work."

Fuck this guy!

Sean pulls a face at Noelle that does not sit well with me. But then again, Sean's entire face doesn't sit well with me.

I should rearrange it with my fist!

"Oh, that's it." I reach a loveless hand and bunch the collar of his shirt. "I suggest you sign the contract and scram before I beat your face until it looks worse for wear, broomstick."

The nerve of this guy to comment on Noelle's appearance, when he literally looks like a broom, turned into a human that escaped some high school janitors' closet.

My clench softens slightly as I feel Noelle turn around to nuzzle into my chest. My fist unfurls completely when quiet pretty sulks leave her lips. I disregard the loser and wrap my arms tightly around Noelle. Her sorrow sings out unabashedly with horrendous wails.

"Oh, Nono," I whisper into her hair, pecking her crown before returning the nestling. I train my eyes back on Sean. "Leave now," I grit through my teeth.

Sean cautiously backs away and out the door.

"Is he gone?" Noelle muffles into my parka.

"He's gone."

My chest puffs out heroically. I want to be Noelle's hero every day. That was exhilarating. No doubt Noelle is hearing the epic thrashing of my heart.

She lifts her icy blue eyes to me, stalactites of red occupy the whites of her eyes. Her crimson nose is polished red from her tears.

"If only I'd taken on your PI request." She squeaks shamefully, burrowing her head.

"PI request? What are you talking about?"

I have a feeling Noelle is about to completely humiliate me. I would rather have Samantha walk in on me masturbating than know whatever humiliating information Noelle is about to expose.

"I know I would've found out about me being the other woman if I'd just done a little digging. Oh god, January, I was the other fucking woman. I'm only good for temporary use. Even you left me."

Her perception of her self-worth has been shattered. This looks like a job for Prince Janny to save.

"I was young and dumb, so dumb for doing that Noelle." I cradle her head to my chest, embracing her tightly before tipping her chin to meet my gaze again. "I still have so much regret from that day. Believe me, you are not just good for temporary use. I wish I could have you by my side forever."

"Wow, I have never seen Cameron so...romantic?" Samantha's harsh vocal fry has my eyes rolling to the back of my head.

"Thanks, Sam," I sneer over Noelle's shoulder. I return to Noelle's gaze, only to find her wearing a judgmental stare. Well, there goes that rescue mission. "Please, tell me what are you are talking about?" I sigh in defeat.

"I know you're @NovemberRain."

FUCK.

No amount of media training—or just plain training my face into silly stoicism from all that practice in my adolescence—will be enough to hide my utter embarrassment right now.

"I'm so embarrassed." I scrub my hand over my face, hoping the warmth that prickles under my skin manifests as a blush.

"Makes two of us. Fucking mistress, I'm so mad at myself. At him," Noelle huffs at the lobby's doors.

"At me?" I regret it as soon as I ask it. How could I be so self-interested?

"You're definitely up there with the people I hate right now. If I had just completed your case on Sean Whittaker, I would've never been fake engaged to him. I guess that makes me qualified to fake marry you."

Noelle Winter Darlington, an expert at seeing the positive in everything. But for once, there is no silver lining. This is a shitty circumstance we find ourselves in.

Well, except perhaps seeing Noelle in person again. To hold her again. To feel her skin become unbearably warm against mine. To relish in her warmth that penetrates my thick parka.

"You're aware his name is Gregory, right?" Samantha pipes up again. I am only moments away from tearing out her voice box. Noelle pries from me to acknowledge her.

"No...who's Sean then?"

"His adultery alter ego, I suppose. It's his middle name. Says right here on the contract." Samantha leans over and points out the address information.

Noelle and I should orchestrate the ultimate prank on him. A special delivery of Cocomo's aromatic hot chocolate, only it'll be a steaming hot shit in the bag.

"All of this information must have been pretty accessible; I was just so blinded by love." Noelle sighs. "If you'll excuse me, I feel an episode coming on and must lie down."

"I'll walk you back to your lodge," I insist.

"No thank you, January."

I watch as she shivers upon entering the chilled air, her shoulders relaxing with relief as the cold washes over her body.

My poor Nono.

Eight

Exposure

Noelle

I am completely drained by the time I reach my lodge, collapsing face-first into my mattress. I would slip into a spell coma if it weren't for my phone ringing non-stop.

Who could be calling?

I flip the device that had fallen an arm's reach away from me. Janelle. Possibly the person I need most right now. I calibrate my thumb over the green accept button. At least I think I did. It's hard to see through my blurred vision.

"Hi Nelly," I groan, propping my phone up against my pillow, pressing my cheek into the mattress, noticing that it was a Facetime request.

"Wow, why is my little hockey dick jockey so glum?" Janelle, to no surprise, looks absolutely gorgeous, blonde hair always styled in a bouncy blow wave, and make-up done in a way that enhances her already pretty features. Meanwhile, in my rectangle, I look like a pale goblin.

I sigh, mustering the energy to explain the news I just found out about Sean...or Gregory, I suppose.

"Nelly, I just found out I was the other woman."

"Cameron! That mother fucker is so dead! I'm heading to the airport right now-"

"Not January...Sean. Can you believe he has a family and everything?" My throat becomes tight again, as I'm left arrested by the fact.

"Sean? I can't believe it, actually. It was rather unbelievable that he could score a babe like you. Let alone the chance to reproduce. I mean, the man's hair looks like a toothbrush," Janelle dry heaves.

"Janelle, it doesn't matter. I was a mistress for a man I genuinely loved."

"How did you find this out? Did you finally run those diagnostics, my little hacker hottie?" Janelle teases, trying to keep the mood light, but my mood may be a permanent, surly blizzard.

"I'm not really supposed to discuss this arrangement, but you're my best friend, so surely that's an exemption...you may have to sign an NDA."

"I'd do anything for you, Noelle. Starting with commiserating, now tell me how you found out the crustiest man in Chicago is a cheating pig," she scoffs, giving her copious mountain of blonde a sassy toss over her shoulder, showcasing her perfect tits that I would die for.

"Well, I am under a publicity stunt contract...I'll be marrying January—"

"You're getting married! To Cameron Snow, now that is one tall glass of water, the upgrade of the century," Janelle cuts in with a gasp.

"6'3 to be exact."

"Ugh, Noelle, you lucky girl." Janelle's eyes roll back. "How big?"

"Janelle, please," I scold, a small smile crawling onto my lips.

"Okay, yes, you're right. My one-track mind and I. Tell me more about this classified information I am privy to." She bats her thick lashes at me, perking up like an obedient schoolgirl.

"Well, Sean...actually his real name is Gregory."

"Ew."

"Yeah, he had to come to the lodge to sign an NDA, and that's when the shit hit the fan." I try to force the memory out of my head. I don't want to keep reliving the hurt.

"And where was Cameron in all of this?"

I let those minor details slip into the reenactment in my mind, I shiver as the recollection of January's warm embraces comes back to me. My body craves it now, flashing completely cold at the abandonment of his kindling warmth.

"He was comforting me..." I reluctantly share.

"Sounds like you've got yourself a rebound, and then report back to me how big. Please and thank you."

"I'm still mad at him, though." I slip out despite the contradicting sensations that take over my body, still relishing in the memory of January's compassionate touch.

"For what? He sounds like a catch. You thawed the Prince of Ice, Crumpets."

"I'm still mad at what he did to me all those years ago, Nelly. It left me traumatized. You share a magical night with someone just for them to leave you, years of thinking you were someone's equal, someone's rock, someone's everything. Discarded with a single declaration that he is leaving to chase his dreams while I stay and let my health rot me away."

"Okay, The Tortured Poet's Department called. They want their depression back. Do you know what this means, Noelle?"

"I'm not getting laid." I sigh. "I was really looking forward to getting railed tonight, Janelle."

"Oh, it keeps getting better. You must exact revenge. It's the best cure for heartbreak. I would know, Darlington, I'm the queen of comebacks and coming."

I chuckle at that. If only I had a guarantee of getting railed. I might be as peppy as her.

"I am far too exhausted to exact revenge, Nelly." I snort, the action leaving me more winded.

"That's the beauty of it. It's being handed to you on a silver platter," Janelle snickers. "Does the sucker have hope of rekindling the spark?"

"January? He's uncharacteristically hopeful," I scoff, reminded of his proposal of a situationship.

He gets on my nerves.

My heart rate spikes at just the thought of him.

"Oh, how the stars align. You get revenge by doing what he did to you."

"Sleep with him and then cut all contact. I sort of can't do that whilst I'm under this contract."

"Hm, you're right, we can figure this out..." even Janelle's scheming face is utterly beautiful. "I've got it!" She exclaims. "You fuck him and friendzone him. Guys hate to be declared as just friends after hot, raw fucking sex." She comes to a stand, thrusting her hips enthusiastically into the air as she moans and grunts.

"I don't know about raw. I don't even have condoms." Just when I was regaining hope, the plan was foiled. I'm positive all those condoms I had collected from Mrs. Donovan's sex ed classes—hoping January and I would get over ourselves and finally put them to use—have expired.

"Ahem, check your PR box, babe. You don't have to thank me, you are very welcome. Also, you can use those toys. It sounds like you could use a pick-me-up. On that note, I will leave you to your self-love session. Kiss, kiss, love you."

Before I have time to say my send-off, she hangs up. I finally come to a sit, my episode has mostly subsided.

Maybe I should do some self-loving.

At least I can use these unabashedly now that Sean is erased from my life and my wank bank indefinitely. I don't have to be so careful about accidentally moaning January's name. I can be rightfully mad at someone and still touch myself at the thought of them. That is a very sane thing to do, and I don't owe anyone a justification. Not that anyone is questioning me. I've done a great job of being inconspicuous about my physical attraction to January.

I wrestle the PR box from the side table drawer I crammed it into. The box flies from my drawer and splatters a decadent selection of TickleMeKink pleasure toys. A hot pink holographic box winks at me. I turn the product over. Condoms. An entire box of them.

My heart whirls with giddy just looking at the toys.

Fuck it!

I fight my jeans off as they sit tightly around my sweltering core.

I'm careful not to overly arouse myself, especially since coming off a terrible episode. My fingers stroke my inner thigh sensuously, keeping my touch featherlight as my heart is quick to excite. I inhale deeply, hoping the oxygen will steady the throbbing in my throat.

My eyes roll backward, fluttering to a close, my skin textures with arousal. I blindly reach for the vibrator, thumbing at the on button, greeting me with a tantalizing purr. I run the pleasure device over the cotton of my panties.

I'm instantly wet.

Janelle makes a powerful product for a powerful woman. I know the vibrator will not underperform. I wipe my mind of the lingering question of whether I will achieve an orgasm.

Instead, I indulge my thoughts in my muse. My fingers curl into my duvet as I imagine them threading through January's soft raven locks. I swear I can feel his hot, alluring breath between my thighs. I slip the bullet-shaped toy under the elastic band, January's tongue working in tandem with the vibrator humming on my clit.

"Oh, January," I moan airily. The ache inside me is a yearning for warmth. My hand palms at my tit. "Touch me, Janny." My pleasure suffocates in my throat.

January's handsome form configures on the back of my eyelids. I can completely feel January's sensual presence.

"Nono, are you awake?"

I gasp, my eyes snapping open. I didn't even hear the porch door screech open, so entranced by this gorgeous man in my musings...and now he's here in the flesh. His physique is far more decadent than my imagination could conjure up.

I bale my duvet to conceal my soaking pussy. My stiff nipples are pressing sensitively against my bra. I lock eyes once again with a very real and very flustered January.

"I'll just be going." His bassy voice melts my core.

I want him. All of him. Now.

"January, wait." I huff wetly from my searing throat. I drape my sheet seductively as I lift myself from my bed. Dizziness strikes me, but I push it aside to lure him into my charm. "Janny," I lilt flirtatiously.

He turns to the side, his gaze trained on the ground.

"Don't hurry away too soon. Why don't you join me?" I lick my lips, anticipating his answer. I'm already having visions of our mouths knotting together in a kiss.

"Join you?" January strains. I watch the thick gulp run down his neck with a bob of his Adam's apple.

"Someone's got to finish what I've started. I'm afraid you've seen too much; I can't let you go." I flutter my lashes and I swear I see his knees give a little.

"Finish what you've started?" He chuckles nervously. It's freaking adorable.

"Don't act all coy now." I give his bicep a flaccid slap, shooting him a taunting wink.

"I just came to see if you were okay. I'm really sorry about what Sean did to you," January says genuinely. His authentic concern throws me off my jabbing game. I want to surrender to his care.

"I'm handling it...okayish." I shrug, readjusting the sheet around my body, only for the blanket to fall seductively from my shoulder. January's eyes snap to the tantalizing sight of my freckled skin, licking his lips.

"Okayish?" January is doing everything to keep his composure, but I love seeing him crumble at the sight of my shoulder. What is this, the 1800s? "Anything I can do to make you feel better?"

Bingo! Now we're talking!

"Oh January, it would be an absolute pleasure if you joined me in bed."

"I...I could do that," he stammers, his cheeks rouging as he moistens his mouth. His questionable tongue motions remind me of a dehydrated husky.

But, what a sight! Seeing January Cameron Snow thirsty for me.

"Well, then." I welcome him into my world by cocooning him in the sheet.

I grunt as I'm sent dizzy when I'm swept off my feet. My world stops spinning, finally gaining clarity on my delicious predicament. Bridal style. He's carrying me bridal style.

"Committing to the bit, huh?" I poke. My game is back, baby, I'm doing a metaphorical sassy hair toss in my head right now.

January shoots me a smile that has me clenching my wet thighs together. January isn't a smiler, so when he does, it's game over for my panties. Especially when I'm the one to cause that smile.

He lays me down with such ease, displaying his strength with a casual air that has my heart palpitating in a frenzy. January was already strong at eighteen. I'm feeling some type of way since his fitness has grown tenfold in ten years. Weakness overwhelms me. I quickly scan my body, detecting any signs of another episode coming on. The only signs I'm picking up are that I'm extremely fucking horny and I need this man to handle me more than *okayish*.

My breath dissipates as January hooks his fingers under the band of my panties. I fixate on the sensation of the cotton and January's knuckles journeying down my legs.

"Janny." Now I'm acting pathetic.

"Nono," he says tenderly.

My eyes snap open. I don't recall even closing them, but I find January's palms planted beside my shoulders. His raven hair frames his electric jade and cerulean eyes. I feel my lips part as I take in the raspberry color of his lips.

"Noelle." He says my name like it gives him salvation from his sins. I certainly feel my healing from all the wasteful pettiness I've had since he broke my heart.

Maybe he really wants this. From the looks he's giving me, there are no blurred lines. He wants *me*. I feel like he's always wanted me.

"You want me," I purr, not as a question but as a statement, because I'm certain.

"I need you, Noelle."

I need you too, January. I need you now more than ever.

My god, this has turned quite sentimental. Allow me to take the reins and make things saucy again.

"You need me to what?" I lilt with a flirtatious smile. My hand slips between us, my palm catching all the contours of his toned physique beneath his parka.

"I need you to stay with me this time." He links my wandering hand with an alarming fluidity, pressing my knuckles to his lips.

I moan at the warmth of the kiss, splaying my fingertips featherlight along his stubble.

"You left me, remember?" I try not to let my pettiness resurface again.

"Noelle, I know. I can not tell you how sorry I am."

"So don't." I press a finger to his lips. There's something about how his breath hits the racing pulse on my wrist that really turns me on. "Show me how sorry you are by playing with me."

"Can I touch you?" January whispers.

"I already said you could," I mimic his volume, giggling airily.

He sighs dreamily.

"You're just as slow as I remembered."

"Hey, not all of us can be cute coding geniuses, okay?" January's flirtatious expression drops instantly, draining of its color. "I am so embarrassed that you found out about my burner Instagram account. But then again, it was pretty obvious, huh?"

"You definitely put little thought into it. I'm sensing a pattern." I rap my knuckles on his skull, indicating its hollowness.

"Nono." The whispering is back.

"Janny."

He's staring at me so intently, I didn't realize I was so captivating. Then it becomes abundantly clear he is anticipating my reaction as he slips his fingers between my folds.

"Can I have a little help from your friend?" He smirks, his eyes flickering to the bullet peeking out from my pillow. "I'm hoping to finger you, if that's okay? I'll get you wetter first."

I'm already wet enough but aching to see how January is going to get me geared up.

"Yes?" He searches for consent.

"Yes, Janny." I may as well be butter hitting a hot pan with how my body sizzles and melts blissfully. My bud feels entirely too large for his fingers, but he's doing an excellent job at touching all the sensitive areas. I flinch whenever he manipulates my clitoral hood to his advantage and for my pleasure. "January, fuck."

"I've missed you saying my name."

"Especially like that, I bet." My pulse launches into my throat when his fingers run lower. "Mm, fuck." My legs quiver under his touch.

"I've missed my actual name being said altogether. I used to hate being named after a month. That was only until I heard your pretty voice say it breathlessly. It makes me so fucking horny."

My clit is met with an exhilarating sensation, a frenzied hum paired with the powerful vibration.

"January," I moan, my hand wraps around his wrist.

"Yes, like that, Noelle."

"My name too. I like how you say my name too. A little Frenchy." I huff out. I can barely hear myself over my thundering heartbeat.

I watch January lacquer his lips with his tongue, ogling my chest.

"Can this come off?" He gestures to my sweater.

"Yes." I thrash my head back on the pillow, shuddering as I feel January's warm palm sliding up my torso and toying with the lace of my bra. "January, yes."

"You think you can take over for just a second, Princess?"

I hum deliciously. I'm absolutely mesmerized by how January is looking at me. Sultry, yet compassionate. It's driving me crazy.

I grip the bullet once more with my trembling hand. A vicious inhale of breath escapes me as January's knuckles brush past my ribs whilst removing my sweater. I didn't even realize I had punctured my pussy with the device, fucking myself gently.

"January, fuck, January." My words muffle momentarily as the wool swipes my cheeks. It feels like my skin is hyper-sensitive to every touch.

"So beautiful, Noelle."

A weird noise between a cry and moan slips from my mouth, the pleasure I'm giving myself, and that January is actually here is becoming extremely overwhelming. I just want to surrender to the magic of it.

"Nono," he said, his voice dripping with mischief, "I'm going to take over again."

"Please," I say, more air than word. I release my hands from the device, which still tingles from the vibrator. "January, kiss me."

"I've been waiting for you to say that."

I can feel my insides wrapping tightly around the bullet as January's lips spark a fire in my mouth and an inferno in my core. He edges the bullet out meticulously slow, all without faltering our make out. He rims my entrance before the vibration returns to my clit, and I instantly miss the intoxicating penetration. But

January is quick to replace it as he slips two fingers inside of me, punctuating the moisture that only thickens with his addition.

"That's my Nono, getting nice and wet." His praise drowns in his saliva.

"All for you, Janny," I whisper, cradling my head forward, my eyes rolling back at the sight of the protruding veins on his forearm. He makes my cum look delicious when it's served on a platter like that.

"Taste me," I request. Half a heartbeat later, January is licking his arm clean like a feral feline. His jade-colored eyes lock with mine as he moans with pleasure.

"Oh fuck, I really want to fuck you," he huffs wetly. Planting his palms beside my shoulders once more, his eyes glow with amorous hunger.

"You should." I encourage with a flutter of my lashes.

Reality dawns in his orbs, he retracts as a disappointing thought festers in his brain.

"I don't have condoms, Nono. And I'm positive the ones from Mrs. Donovan's class have expired."

"Aren't you lucky my friend Janelle has us covered?" I roll onto my stomach as I reach for the package from my side table. I can feel January's heated stare on my ass. And I could honestly go for some doggy. But between my heartbreak, my spell, and the incredible experience January has provided thus far, I am far too fatigued to prop myself on all fours.

"You actually want to do this?" Every muscle in my body tightens. My core melts as his buttery bass drawl hits my ears.

"Yes, Janny, you're really driving home this consent thing. It's really fucking hot." I gnaw at my bottom lip, craning my head back as far as I can. I'm adamant about staying in this position. My entire muscular system is waving its white flag.

"I'm just putting feelers out. Just yesterday you wanted nothing to do with me." January's concerned expression makes me roll my shoulder to get a better sight of it. The exertion of energy was worth seeing that adorable pout.

"Well, I've had some time to reconsider your proposal." My weary fingers run along his five o'clock shadow. That phrase slips out a little too genuinely for my liking, considering my original intent of inviting January to bed was to exact revenge.

"The marriage one or the..."

"Situationship." I clarify with a teasing flick of his chin, extinguishing his enchanting gaze from my sight to not fall under his compassionate spell.

"Noelle, that's not what I want." His tone is the same as milkless coffee, bitter.

"Well, there's obviously some sexual tension between us, so that's a good start. Don't you think?" My seduction is anything but milkless. It's milky like my thighs.

"I thought we established, I don't think." He dominates me with a smile. Now my thighs are really milky.

"Then don't think, just do. Here you go." I present a holographic *Cock Cozie*.

Janelle is quite the innovator.

January rolls the geode-printed condom on his cock. It's been years since I've seen the thing and I can happily say it's big. But I won't report that to anybody, no matter how much they beg.

"You ready?"

"Ugh, so fucking ready." I wiggle my tush to press against his thigh.

I moan as I feel January enter me. I've spent the last decade imagining this scenario in many positions. It's one thing to fantasize about having sex with January Snow and a complete dream come true when actually having sex with January Snow. Even after all these years, it feels like we're still drumming to the same rhythm, fast and erratic, with each fleshy slap of his hips against my ass. I'm in fucking paradise.

"Janny! Yes!" With the very minimal energy I have in me, I'm *charging* my pelvis backward into his. My weak form causes the motion to ricochet, throwing the rhythm into a syncopation. And it's fucking heaven. "Janny, I'm going to, oh yes!"

"Noelle, look at me," he huffs. He slows his pace, bringing the tempo back to a steady rhythm.

I tend to his request, pinching my shoulder blades together and tilting my head back. He looks pathetic and I wouldn't have it any other way. His cerulean jade eyes hold a sense of worship, and they're looking at me.

"So beautiful, Noelle, you are so beautiful."

He's so good to me...despite that one time. But I almost don't want to exact revenge anymore. I just want to surrender to this orgasmic sex.

He pecks at the constellated freckles on my shoulder. I watch in awe. His lips latch onto a soft and sensitive part of my neck, his lips sucking in tandem with my heartbeat. The sensation has me pulsing in other places on my body.

I don't know what to do.

He suddenly breaks me from my dilemma by pressing his lips to mine.

"I'm so fucking close, Noelle," he whimpers, looking at me cross-eyed. The epitome of simp is pressed to my forehead. "Are you fucking close too?"

"With a little kissing, definitely." I lick my lips immediately, knowing January will act with fierce attentiveness.

"Noelle, I—" January doesn't finish his sentence, but he may just finish inside me, "Close, so fucking close."

He speeds and I'm right there with him on the edge.

"January," I whine.

"Noelle," he whines. "I can't get enough of your incredible pussy."

I'm almost certain January is seeing a fireworks show behind his eyelids, his neck tilted back as if he were spectating one.

"You're so excited to be inside me right now." I giggle, he winces, and it's game over...for me. Thankfully, I'm not alone when I fall apart attached to January's waist. He's having one hell of an orgasm too, as he cocoons me in his muscles. I purr primitively, welcoming the intimacy.

It feels like January's cock is a mile long as he slowly slips out of me. The chilling abandonment replaces the intoxicating heat, making me shiver. His limbs tangle with mine as he crawls, collapsing onto my other gel-cooling pillow.

January slips a dreamy sigh, tucking a loose piece of hair behind my ear.

Curses. That piece of hair was a shield from his enchanting gaze.

"Noelle, that was incredible."

"It was..." I drawl hesitantly.

Follow through with the revenge, Noelle, don't be a coward...even though I'm exacting my revenge by mimicking his betrayal.

"Nono?" he calls, his face dawning an expression of anxiety.

"Fun..." I gulp. "We really are just friends, after all. I suppose that settles the age-old question."

"Friends?" He strains in his deep bass.

"Yeah, that one!"

"Noelle, you came twice," he reasons with a huff.

"Bad time to bring up I was thinking of Justin Bieber." His features pinch into their signature surliness, clearly unamused by my mischief. "Swaggy." So, I will continue to drive it home.

"Noelle." His lips barely move as he scolds me, but they still garner my full attention in their firm stillness. I have the uncontrollable urge to kiss them into softness.

"I should probably start packing for Phoenix." I escape from January's embrace, stalking my naked, tingling ass to my dresser. I can feel January's gaze on me, conflicted, unsure whether to be annoyed or aroused. Welcome to my world, Snow.

I received notification this morning that January's private jet is scheduled to pick us both up and fly us directly to his glorious penthouse in the Arizona mountains.

My childhood best friend sure has a knack for showy things. Which only whips back into a memory of how he never lambasted me for my appreciation for the finer things.

I'm not materialistic, I just don't get to experience life to the fullest with my unpredictable health. Hence the heavy importance of physical gifts.

"Arizona is known for its heat waves. Maybe I should pack some ice." I pick out a strand of diamonds from an eclectic jewelry box—both were gifts from January, given on different occasions.

"You're ridiculous, Nono." He rolls his eyes, fighting back a smile I'm bringing on. I ignore the flutter of my heart that comes with knowing how to thaw January Snow's heart.

"I don't care if it's gaudy, your penthouse is equally gaudy. I'm only trying to fit in." It feels like a declaration of us only being friends has reverted me to my flirtatious jabbing, which revives January's smile. "Akin to Elsa's snow palace." I flutter my lashes. "World's most quotable movie."

"I'll ensure it's a part of the inflight entertainment." January winks, which sends my heart into a giddish whirl.

"I think I'll take this instead." I distract myself by showcasing the bullet with a baton flourish of my wrist. Only to find January's face void of amusement.

"You don't have to do this, Nono."

"But I do." I toss the vibrator aside. "Now out, I must curate a faux wife wardrobe." I whip my duvet from January. His hands fly to his ballsack with a wince.

"Noelle, this is actually ridiculous." He quickly tucks himself back into his pants. It's rather difficult to take him seriously when he's touching his penis.

"Out, mister." I stamp my foot, crossing my arm and tilting my chin heavenwards.

"Noelle, I'm not playing right now." He is now scooting off my bed like a dog with fleas, and I really can't take him seriously when he does that.

"Me neither. I'm a horrid over-packer. I require intense focus," I lilt with a tranquil air.

"Overpacker?" January's confused expression hovers over me. I hum to confirm. "How are you overpacking? You don't go places."

"Okay, fuck off." I plant my hands on his chest, whipping my bedroom door open and shoving his pathetic ass out.

Slamming the door in January's face never gets old.

Nine

Mile High Club

January

Noelle is driving in on this whole silence treatment thing. She hasn't uttered a word to me since we left things on a sour note after we had incredible sex. I'm still convinced I dreamed the whole thing. It felt like I was running purely on instinct when I agreed to her seductive offer to join her in bed. But from the crimson bruises on her neck, I have all the evidence I need to know that I had sex with Noelle Winter Darlington.

My icy flesh pressed to her searing hot skin, the polarizing temperatures made the experience comforting as I cooled her down and she heated me up. Just to see those cheeks tinted with a rose color in real-time is incomparable to anything. No renowned symphony is a match for Noelle's airy moans. Nothing has ever hit the ears with such delicateness. Her body wriggled beneath my tender petting, her fingertips caressing my skin so feathery. I could've combusted on the spot. My vision was bursting with color at the sight of my angel.

It was magical; it was *intimate.* Something I have longingly wanted with Noelle for years.

There was a moment there where I felt her open up to me. Not only was she taking my cock welcomingly and wantingly, but there was also something emotional happening. It was real and raw, vulnerability at its peak. Dogmatically, it was love-making in its truest form.

Only for us to conclude and have her turn to me and declare we are just friends. I know she felt what I felt. No doubt this is just ego-stroking. Which I suppose I can allow. She certainly received some rough news prior. Being the other woman. That is certainly not what Noelle is in my eyes. She's all I've ever wanted. She is the only woman I've ever wanted, and for a moment yesterday, she was mine. I have always been hers, whether she is completely aware of it. I have devoted my heart, body, and soul to Noelle.

The way her body was surrendering to my pleasure, it felt like she was devoting herself to me.

But, no. Just friends. I'm not even sure I can say that after my stupid blunder. Certain things are off-limits to jab about. Noelle's health is at the top of the metaphorical list in bright red marker.

"I'm such a jerk."

"Agreed." Noelle's eyes don't lift from the tablet she's been toying with for the past 30 minutes we've been on my private jet. Slipping out sporadically impressed hums as she explores the techy interface.

"At least you're talking to me." Beggars can't be choosers. But if I'm honest, I'm this close to getting on my knees and pleading my case for why we should at least be friends again, even after my insensitive remark.

She purses her lips, showing our stream of communication has ended.

"Well, that was fun while it lasted." I sigh.

"You two are so adorable," Samantha squeaks, collapsing into the snowy leather upholstered chair next to Noelle. "I need that, Angelface."

Noelle holds the tablet possessively to her chest, before handing it over to Samantha with a pout.

Samantha's perfectly manicured fingertips clack away, triggering a computer screen to replace the varnished wood on the table where I've been attempting to play footsies with Noelle underneath.

"So fucking cool!" Noelle leans forward, practically pressing her nose to the screen in wonder.

"I can't explain the plan if you're fogging up the screen, Angelface." Samantha tugs back at Noelle's jumper hood. My fingers curl in on themselves as an urge to protect Noelle overcomes me.

"You better fix your face, kid, before it gets stuck like that." Samantha lilts with her maternal air, like usual. I slump back with a harrumph, which only provides proof to view me as a tantrum-throwing toddler.

"Explain this ridiculous plan." I flourish my wrist, slumping further into the custom leather of my chair, the picture of nonchalance.

"Now that you're done having your tantrum."

"Thanks, Sam."

"You're welcome. Let's begin with phase one, which is currently in process. Validating the dating. You can laugh, don't be shy."

Noelle hesitantly giggles, cupping her hand on her cheek. I realize she's mouthing something to me.

"She's scary."

"Terrifying." I mouth back. I can't fight the smile that tugs at the corner of my lips. Noelle giggles authentically.

"Huh? That wasn't supposed to be funny. Ok, you two, pay attention. You can flirt later."

"Oh, we weren't flirting. I can't stand January."

Gee, thanks for clearing that up, Nono.

"Right," Samantha drawls in a tone that shows *she's not buying it.*

Which is odd because Noelle is dead serious about hating my guts right now.

"So, like I was saying. That's why the post at Darlington Snow Resort was essential."

"Paradise." Noelle and I cut in together, our eyes meeting one another's.

"It's Darlington Snow Paradise." Noelle clarifies, averting her gaze as her cheeks blush.

"Oh right, it doesn't matter—"

"But it does. I'm only doing this to course correct the lodge's image, capitalizing on January's and I—although mostly January's—fame. It must take priority, right, Janny?"

Incredible, just absolutely incredible how she sticks up for herself.

"She's right, Sam. That's the only reason I'm doing this, too."

"I thought it was because of your contract, sounds more like a jail sentence to me. That *Hot Shot Pro Hockey Life* is not all it's cracked up to be."

"It absolutely isn't."

"Fine, Darlington Snow Resort—"

"Paradise." We correct again in unison.

"Yes, yes, paradise. I heard you the first time." Samantha dismisses us both with a wave of her hand.

"I mean, clearly you didn't." Noelle snickers, shooting a wink my way. Her eyes sparkle mischievously and I know exactly what she is thinking.

"I wouldn't prank her if I were you, Nono. Samantha may be pocket-sized, but she has the power to transform into a dragon."

"Well, we're pros at fighting dragons, Prince Janny." Noelle shoots me a flirtatious smile. We're flirting. There is simply no other way to describe it. And I am only now realizing it is identical to the smile she'd often flash me in our adolescence. I was just so in my head about preserving our friendship and restraining my flirtations from coming out. I was completely blind to her very obvious advances.

"That we are." I mirror her expression. Only hers falters a little to beaming idolization. Time falls still. We are both so wrapped up in each other that my aching ears from the intense pressure in the cabin no longer bother me. That sweet smile of Noelle's is a cure for everything.

"Snap! Snap!" Samantha's camera sounds off, making her onomatopoeia redundant.

"Did you just take a photo of me?" Noelle looks at her, dazed and confused.

"And me? Separately."

"Sure did. These are going to be your phone screen savers."

"But I like this one of my friends." Noelle turns her phone to me, and I recognize the girls from her Instagram page. The promiscuous blonde with her own sex toy company and the dark curly-haired, tan woman always sporting Adidas and Nike.

"Noelle doesn't have to change her screensaver." I notify Samantha, giving Noelle a curt affirming nod.

"It's a part of phase one." Samantha interjects, I hold a threatening glare on her. "Whatever."

"Another dragon slain, go Janny!" Noelle exclaims, bouncing excitedly in her seat.

"She is your little cheerleader, after all. Perhaps she can encourage you to change your screensaver."

"Can I see the picture first? I want to approve of it." Noelle crosses her legs, straightening her posture to professionally assess the fresh pic on Samantha's phone. Her profile is angelic as she reaches up to retrieve the device.

"I have a few pictures of Noelle already that I really love," I say as my eyes hold on the crimson hickey on her neck.

"Oh, now this I have to see. Do you have them in a separate folder labeled Nono red heart?" Noelle taunts. Little does she know how accurate she is.

"You're a better hacker than I thought. Have you tapped my phone? Here." I can feel Samantha analytically watching every minute interaction with Noelle. She perks a brow up when our pinkies brush as I pass Noelle my phone.

Noelle's ice-blue eyes widen, flicking quickly at me. "These are all the photos of you and me from when we were teenagers. Oh wait a minute, these are from my Instagram. I see you've hearted this jacuzzi picture specifically, I guess that's the one then." She hands my phone back with a smirk. "I'll send you the outtakes and you can choose from those, a saucy little shot of my cute ass that didn't make the feed has your name all over it. Janelle begged me to post it."

"Janelle Cox? CEO of TickleMeKink." Samantha's brow quirks up opportunistically.

"The goddess herself."

"Yes, about that, her and the pretty Portuguese girl. What's her name again, the one that makes cooking videos?" Samantha snaps her fingers as she tries to recall.

"Candy."

"Yes, Janelle and Candy are going to need to sign NDAs, presuming you've already told them everything."

"It may have made its way into the group chat." Noelle gnaws at her lip, her eyes sparkling naughtily. I have to keep the natural primitive instinct that climbs my throat at bay. My lips tingle with want as she releases her bottom lip from her teeth.

"I figured, that's why I did the pleasure of contacting their PR companies and flying them out to Phoenix as soon as possible. They should make it by the boys' practice for the charity match."

"Oh, they'll love watching those meatheads chase around a gliding disc." Noelle snorts prettily. "Candy is totally a sports kind of girl."

"Great, that's all sorted. This brings me swiftly to phase two, integrating your circles," Samantha chimes theatrically. "Cameron, since you don't have any friends-"

"Ha! No friends." Noelle yelps a laugh.

"I took the liberty of selecting Seymour and Aaron as your buddies," Samantha finishes.

"Speaking of meatheads," I groan, rolling my eyes heavenwards. Samantha couldn't have chosen more difficult teammates if she tried. Inflated egos galore. Suppose they'll fit right in with me and my asshole ego. "One literally knocks players' teeth out, and the other is a player who knocks chicks up."

"Aaron Nightingale?" Noelle's posture straightens again. My eyes can't help but slope down the arch of her back.

"That's the one," Samantha confirms with most of her attention on her phone.

"Oh, he's hot. Can you pass on my number when this is all over?"

"Noelle," I press through my teeth.

"Stop being such a baby, January," she hisses.

"Excellent, now phase three, public appearances. I have booked you a table at Luigi's at 7 pm."

"But that's shortly after we land." Even in my experience of masking my shock, I can not believe the level of running around Samantha is already expecting from us. I'm rather accustomed to the fast-paced nature of my job, but I know Noelle is prone to burnout quickly.

"Surprise! The limo will await you two on the tarmac."

"I'm in my tracksuit." Noelle looks down at her oversized sweats. She looks utterly adorable when she's bundled up like this. But that really shouldn't be her biggest concern right now.

"I have hair, makeup, and wardrobe ready for you in the car," Samantha informs.

"In the car?"

"Yes, this industry is very fast-paced."

And you're doing a wonderful job at ensuring it stays that way, Samantha. Seriously, is no one stressed about the woman prone to dizzy spell attacks?

"That's my biggest worry for her." I voice my concern.

"I'll be fine. It's only temporary." Noelle resigns herself.

"Temporary, right?" Samantha snorts. Noelle is far too caught up in her incredibly calculative mind to notice Samantha's comment. I'm barely present, far too wrapped up in my concern for Noelle. "So the marriage."

Noelle perks up. "Yes, the marriage, go on."

"Once I have flawlessly executed all the phases, as I always do, phase four should proceed with no issues."

"Phase four: marry January." Noelle nods curtly to herself.

"Eager beaver you are, Angelface. Not quite, firstly the charity match will take place and the following week is a huge gala, where a grandiose auction will take place."

My stomach drops when an image zips onto the coffee table's screen.

"A snowflake pure silver ring, encrusted with 14-carat diamonds, is the prize of the night."

I'm well acquainted with the jewelry. In fact, it's already in my possession. I paid a hefty six million just to have that specific ring. I had to have it. Why? Because it reminded me of Noelle.

This isn't the first time I've made a purchase with Noelle in mind. We work with the *Upon-A-Star* Foundation every year and I often shop their catalog ahead of time. I have an entire collection of flashy items in the back of my wardrobe that I would have gifted to Noelle if we had stayed in contact.

"14 carats, my oh my, all the *puck bunnies* of yours will go hungry if I hoard all the carrots."

"Very funny, Nono."

"I already rang ahead and secured the ring. The auction will simply be a spectacle for the press."

The tension in my shoulders eases as Samantha leaves out the embarrassing detail that I have been hanging onto. The idea of Noelle and I reconnecting so badly that I still actively buy her gifts.

"Oh wow, that's quite the jewel. I'll be wearing that rock on my finger." Noelle's fingertips reach for the screen, retracting her advances when she catches my gaze. A grimace grows on her lips. *She thinks it's bait.* I give a nod of permission. She rolls her shoulder before placing her feather touch to the screen.

"Yes indeed, Angelface."

"It's so pretty. What will happen to it after the wedding?" Noelle's finger delicately traces the star-like pattern in the center of the snowflake.

"You can keep it. I know you'll actually appreciate it," I reassure. It was always hers to begin with.

"Thanks, Janny. I really appreciate it." Noelle smiles softly at me, her cheeks rosy with gratitude.

"I knew you would." I return her a gentle smile.

"And lastly phase five, return to Darlington Winter Galore, and make a whole show of your love, ring on your finger, ring in the likes, ring goes the phone with all the bookings, the resort is saved, and becomes a romantic honeymoon destination." Samantha rambles in an enthused enchantment.

"And how do we keep the hype of the lodge being a romantic destination when we get divorced? Which I assume will be at the soonest legal requirement." Noelle inquires.

"That would be a month, but I'm afraid you'll have to stay together longer than that," Samantha distantly informs, distracted by her phone again.

"Okay, like two months?"

"Forever, Angelface."

"What?!" Noelle jumps from her seat, only to crash back down.

Ten

The Appearance

Noelle

After being told that dreadful news that I will be married to January forever, I feel I have every right to screw up my face like a shriveled-up raisin. Despite the persistent makeup artist telling me to relax my features, I stubbornly maintain the pinch. Even though it's causing me a headache.

Resulting in her tossing her brush and throwing her hands in a declaration of *I give up*.

"She's beautiful as she is," January comments. I flick him a charcoal bordered glare, hoping the smoky eyeshadow emphasizes my absolute abhorrence to all of this.

Oh, don't you say another word. Prince of Ice? More like Prince of Deception.

"I promise I didn't know, Nono."

"Save it." I scrunch my nose, feeling brush fibers tickle my cheeks. *This is one persistent make-up artist.*

"Agreed. You two need to pull it together. We're almost at Luigi's." The dragon is about to be outranked. I can feel my nostrils flare wide as my hot breath hits my upper lip. The make-up artist backs up warily, as my exhalations become heavier and louder.

I cast one more look at January. His face is a mask of complete boredom. Which from memory actually means he's observing for any signs that my health may be wavering. Like whenever we would be on our feet for hours preparing the massive annual Christmas banquet for the guest. What looked like a teenager trying to amuse himself by rolling cookie dough into inappropriately suggestive shapes was all just a cover up as he subtly monitored me. Analyzing for any washes of fatigue, any dip in energy, or flashes of temperature.

Little did he know his risky creations were the main reason for my flustered nature. Once, he fashioned the cookie dough into a life-sized replica of a dong. I didn't have the courage to ask him if his penis was his artistic reference.

I shake from the memory and spare one final soft glance to January, his jaw tensing into a reluctant pout. Which could only mean he's feeling an immense amount of affection for me right now.

Too bad we'll only be making miserable memories from now on.

"We're here," Samantha announces. "Cameron, fix your face, and be a gentleman and open Angelface's door for her. This moment is imperative to the image, so don't roll your eyes at me."

A twinkle of remorse flares in January's cerulean eyes before he ducks his large stature out of the limousine. I watch through the tinted window as he smooths his palms down his blazer.

The red in my vision finally clears and I can now take in the gorgeous forest green color of my dress. I thought this material was known for its breathability, but it's actually trapping my sweat by clinging to me like a satiny second skin.

As enraged as I am right now, I have to acknowledge that we both clean up nicely. January looks unfairly handsome in his pristinely tailored suit. I've never seen him in a suit, not even for the small self-held prom we had at the lodge. With January looking so dapper, I find my blood-boiling rage faltering and perhaps even my opinion on the marriage swaying.

"Noelle."

I'm startled as Samantha calls me by my name. I've become so accustomed to answering to *Angelface*, in her hard valley girl vocal fry. As I turn to her, I feel a bead of sweat trickle down my forehead, unsure if it's the heat or my nerves.

"I understand you're a little upset, but think of the results. You and Cameron being legitimately married and staying together forever..." I try to hold my concentration so I can hear Samantha's point, but those collections of words strung together still terrify me. "...will validate the resort's appeal, and I'm sure you want nothing more than the resort's life expectancy to be as long and fruitful as your marriage. Who knows, you might even fall in love again. I know that's what he's betting on."

Fall in love again? I don't see that happening, but I can't deny my physical attraction to him. Any woman would feel the way I do if they saw The Prince of Ice looking so...princely. Besides, I've always been hot for January in that regard, so technically my view will remain unchanged from before this arrangement. Except, maybe that small voice inside begging me to acknowledge the longing for our friendship again.

"I don't think I could love him again...I miss our friendship, though."

"Who better to marry than your best friend?"

That would be Janelle, which gives me the idea to leave January at the altar and run off with my bestie. She's already in the land of shotgun weddings. I may as well use it to my advantage.

"My husband and I are just like you and Cameron. Friends have their differences, but at the end of the day, they are the ones you can count on most. Vinnie will always be that for me."

"I don't know about January being the one I *count on most*."

The man has a history of leaving me stranded. I guess my mind isn't protecting me from the more unpleasant memories, as it takes shape in my head. I try to bypass it and rewind back to the blissful vision of Christmas Banquet preparations.

"Cameron is really trying for you, Angelface. I'd have a good think about whether the pettiness is worth it in the long run. This stunt is quite valuable."

The turducken of complex-inducing advice handed to me on a silver platter. There is so much I could benefit from this arrangement. My future becomes more stabilized, for one. But to use this opportunity to rekindle January and I's friendship. That I'm undecided on.

"Stay focused, Angelface. Your Prince is here." Samantha's acrylic nails click me into alertness.

I turn to see January's god-like figure strobing hypnotically. I take a second to realize it's not him that's alight but the paparazzi that's spotlighting his handsomeness.

I plant my heel onto the pavement, and the crowd's muttering turns into a frenzied roar. The cameras flash so constantly, there is not a moment I'm not blinded.

I push myself up from my seat. The intense Phoenix heat is far more lethal than any camera flash.

My head spins instantly. I blindly reach for January, feeling his palm run along my stomach, and his broad torso presses to my back. My shoulder blades pinch together tensely.

After being apart for ten long years, having January hold me like he used to doesn't feel out of place. And I appreciate him for ensuring I don't face plant into the curb. I've lost enough teeth in my lifetime, thank you. And I really don't want a moment like that to be inevitably caught by one of these gossip columnists.

January's guiding touch will forever be ingrained in my memory.

His palm leaves my stomach momentarily to pull at a gold-plated door handle.

"I'll get that, sir." A faint foreign accent fades into my senses.

"I've got it." January's voice booms in my ear, creating a tsunami in my belly. The door closes behind us with a controlled seal, and the chaos outside reduces to a quiet muffle.

I beam up at January with as much grateful adoration as I can muster in my starry eyes.

Words are far too taxing after that ordeal, but thankfully January knows me well enough that words aren't necessary.

"You look like shit, Noelle." January comments loud enough for the front of house staff to hear.

My appreciation dissipates with the speed of light. I scoff, hastily turning away and stumbling to a velour ottoman close by.

"Reservations?" A maître de pesters January with a disapproving snarl. But I am far too busy tending to my sudden dizzy spell to indulge in his deserved lambasting.

"Snow."

"Oh, Mr. Snow, my apologies. Right this way."

Screw January and his intimidating influence. He's not a god, people, you don't need to tremble in his presence.

I can't decide whether the memory that occupies my reeling head is pleasant or self-inflicted torture. The soft cushion I'm sitting on reminds me of the seat of snow I would perch on, as I would watch January skillfully glide across the ice and strike puck after puck into the net. I really saw him as a god in those days. So blindly enamored by his sweat-soaked swoopy locks and his subtle smug smirk, he would shoot me after every impressive score.

January's game did not translate off the field, even still to this day. Who tells their date they look like shit?

"A seat in the far back, and air conditioning on blast before my girlfriend passes out."

I sober up from my symptoms at the title January has coined me. *Girlfriend.* We're doing this, just getting straight to the point. I am January Snow's girlfriend, something I dreamed up for years. Teenage Noelle would be screaming into her pillow, overjoyed, if she knew.

"Of course, Mr. Snow."

"Trying to make up for that rude comment," I say, far woozier than I would've liked. January hums disapprovingly through tight lips.

"I'd like to get you sitting down before you faint."

"I'm not jabbing, I'm genuinely..." I trail off as January leads me to the darkest part of the restaurant. It's practically pitch black. What is happening to me?

My knees give in a little. January has already scooped me up and is now laying me against a velour couch.

"AC. Now!" January practically barks.

"Yes, sir." I hear the waiter flee in a panic.

The spots in my vision clear and I'm met with one of two of January's expressions. It's certainly not the surly stoicism, rather the soft concern.

"Can you order some champagne?" I slip giddily, hoping to unlock his rare third expression.

And sure enough, he smiles. His smiles make me feel like a complete lightweight.

"I can do that."

"And request to leave the bucket of ice," I whine as I come to a sit, only inches from January's lips.

"Sure thing, Nono."

January backs away from his hover over me. He slicks his locks that had fallen loose back into place. I examined his fine dress, the one he was given in the limousine. A pristine white shirt that hugs his sinewy frame artfully, and creaseless black slacks to match his glossed back hair. So lacquered I could pick at my teeth for leftover dinner on the reflective surface.

"I knew this would be too much for you," January huffs. "You don't have to do any of this, Noelle." *Valuable.* That Valley girl vocal fry will haunt me for the rest of my marital life.

"Who are you to decide what I can and can't do? Haven't you learned from all your years of stalking me I am far more capable than you think?" My words are fighting ones, but my body is surrendering with contradiction.

My shoulders curl, my neck rolls weakly, unable to support my head as a tornado cements itself inside. I feel my nape flashing hot.

I moan when a satisfying coolness presses against my neck. My palm splays over January's, sinking into the familiarness of his touch. I lock eyes with his grounding mint cool ones.

"Thank you," I thread my fingers delicately through his knuckles, enjoying their rough manly texture, "you're still dead to me though."

"Noelle, I suggest we do our best to get along. The situation is already working against us. Although I think you're crazy for doing this, but I stand with you and your decision."

"I'm doing this for my family, January." I swat January's palm away. Now I notice he has ice bundled in a cotton napkin, realizing that's what was pressed to my neck. I can't help but be impressed by how quickly he put together the aid to fight off my symptoms of an incoming episode.

"Yes, you've made it abundantly clear that I am not included in your motive. I'm just a pawn in all of this. Play your game, Noelle, but at the very least, for your health, play nice."

"Then stop being an asshole with your backhanded comments," I snipe. Play nice. The nerve of this guy. My anger is completely justified. I've been thrust into such a confrontational situation. I've lost everything by being here. But I also have so much to gain. That doesn't retract from how miffed I am, though.

"I mean this when I say this, I'm sorry, I haven't practiced niceties in a while, I'm a little out of practice." January slops the half-melted ice back into the bucket, burrowing a frosty bottle of champagne.

My absolute favorite. I can still remember how giddy I was when January and I finished an entire bottle for my 18th birthday. Though it's technically illegal here in the States, I felt it was important to celebrate adulthood with my best friend. I wasn't sure if he would have the chance to mark any more milestone birthdays in the future. Besides, both of our parents were fully aware of the alcohol consumption, finishing a bottle of their own as they enjoyed the open fire.

And even with our parents present, I hoped with the liquid courage that night would be the night where we really let go and just fell into each other completely. But no, Mr. Out Of Practice decided at the very last possible moment to talk about his feelings.

My birthday was the perfect opportunity to strip me of my completeness. I was giddy from the bubbly and totally all over January. Playing footsies with him, burrowing into his parka. I couldn't be more willing if I tried. Even my parents were giving me side eyes at my obvious promiscuous advances. Every time I would swoop in for a kiss, January would quickly shield himself with his champagne flute, clinking it with mine as a diversion.

As much as the rejection hurt, I miss moments like that with January. Moments of us just being idiots together, no expectations, no curfew. Just great company and excellent choice of alcohol.

It was all so...nice. Which only polarizes how unpleasant all of this is.

"Looks like playing nice will be difficult for the both of us," I said cheekily.

January resigns back to his side of the booth. The abandonment is hauntingly familiar.

I'm thrust back into the memory full of pain that took place months later, after my birthday, on December 27th, 10 years ago. Where it felt like both my emotions and my body were out to end me. The pain that January caused.

I couldn't go through that again. So that decides it, I will not be seeking a friendship with January.

I'm also suddenly reminded of Janelle's ploy to seek revenge and how I can inflict the same pain on January.

Maybe I will play my game, January, only this game will be single-player.

I'm out for revenge and there will be blood.

ELEVEN

Clean Up Your Act

January

I'm still scrubbing away the red stain on my shirt, put there by a catapulting meatball Noelle swears she flung by accident. Her maniacal snickers and devious expression suggested otherwise. But I took the attack lying down. She was completely herself at that moment. Her naughty self.

"There goes another sponsor. Not to mention, I gathered reports that you were quite snippy with the wait staff." Samantha hounds me from behind her phone screen. If you asked me what color my publicist's eyes were, I probably couldn't tell you.

Noelle's eyes, though, I always compared them to a frozen lake with sapphire-colored fractures. How I could stare endlessly into her eyes, although that wasn't an option tonight with the way they were continuously rolling to the back of her head.

"Noelle was having a spell. I have better things to worry about than the wait staff's feelings." I practically beat myself up because it was I who triggered that spell with my insensitive comment. Truthfully, she looked like shit. Not aesthetically, of course, Noelle is always beautiful. But physically, she looked like shit.

"That didn't spare you from hurting mine." Noelle sighs, her gaze occupied by the Phoenix landscape passing by. I need to get Noelle to look at me, look into my eyes and really see how much I am trying.

"Noelle," I press, wincing as the irritation I feel for myself seeps through my clenched teeth. Noelle will never believe my efforts are genuine now.

"Cameron, this is why brands don't want to work with you," Samantha huffs.

"It's mutual." I hope that comment will be enough to signal to Samantha that I am also irritated at her. We can't possibly get back to my mansion fast enough. Almost every room has a lock on it. I can't wait to guide Noelle into a room, any room, shut the door in Samantha's face and finally show Noelle the respect she truly deserves.

A part of me hopes Noelle will somehow truly see me, like she always has in the past, and recognize my eagerness to befriend her again. Which will hopefully lead to her having an eagerness to bed me. Which will hopefully cause a domino effect and convince her we really should be life partners instead.

"I'm with the brands," Noelle snarks. Looks like I've got a lot of work ahead of me if I even want to just sleep next to her at this point. She looks pissed. Beautiful, but pissed.

The limousine flutters with light, dancing over Noelle's sickly tinged skin. I poke my head out to see a verandah of glittering bulbs and signage in gold cursive scripture. *The Maloney.*

"Why are we at a hotel and not at my mansion?"

"You're on your last leg. You are so lucky that The Maloney Hotels have agreed to partner with you and Angelface for the week." Samantha grits from over her phone.

"Is this our honeymoon?" Noelle's eyes widened, her words coming out in a thin wheeze. "It's supposed to be at Darlington Snow Paradise."

I shimmy over to rest my palm atop her hand, searching for any more severe symptoms.

Noelle snatches her hand away, wiping my touch on her silk dress.

"Cameron has yet to propose, but I like where your head's at, Angelface." Samantha shoots Noelle a wink. "This is the focus I need from you, Cameron."

"So we have separate rooms, right?" Noelle beams, rather optimistic, considering Samantha's ignorant character suggests she should be more pessimistic.

Samantha presses her phone to her ear, disregarding Noelle's concern.

"I can't hear you. I'm too busy trying to save this one's fickle reputation. He's got me doing god's work, honestly." Samantha slips out of the car.

Believe me, Samantha, you think your job is hard. The woman I am in love with hates me beyond repair.

"Samantha, wait!" Noelle strains, scooting towards the limousine door. Wow, she hates me so much she can't even spend a single second alone with me in a limousine. She should thank her lucky stars we're not at my house then. It's not like I was going to keep Noelle hostage in my room, but if Samantha was hovering, I certainly wouldn't have let her out.

"Let's go check in, I guess." My hand finds the small of Noelle's sweaty back. A small moan leaves Noelle's lips, and it's not one of agony either.

Oh, so you do enjoy my touch, Princess. You're just being petty.

"That woman is more akin to the devil than a god." Noelle swats my touch away. Not because she's not enjoying it, but because she is obviously embarrassed by her sweaty state.

"She's a little too good at her job," I smirk flirtatiously, hoping my advance shows her I'm not deterred by a little sweat. I'd fuck her in this limousine if she flashed me with those wanting eyes. I would rip this very expensive designer dress from her figure and count my losses on how much I paid for it. *Samantha really went digging skeletons out of my closet for this stunt.* I recognized this emerald number from an *Upon-A-Star* banquet where I saw one of the other players' wife sporting it and knew immediately I had to acquire it for my archive, in case Noelle were to ever re-enter my life. I'm thinking that may have been where the media plucked my playboy persona from, probably misinterpreting the interaction as me trying to steal a fellow player's wife, when really I was only trying to dress my own imaginary wife. Since the circumstances are no longer imaginary, I can clear my name, I guess. Exposing my clandestine shopping habits and having my baggage aired out is so worth it if it means I get to be intimate with Noelle.

When I break from my vision, I realize Noelle has slipped through my fingers like silk, but she hasn't strayed too far as I catch her gawking at the gilded building.

"Wow, this place makes the lodge look like crap." Noelle sparkles far more effulgently than this gaudy place. She turns to me with a pout. "Janny, this place makes the lodge look like crap." She repeats, her awe replaced with defeat.

"Don't worry, I won't let this partnership overshadow home." I reassure Noelle as I hurry her into the air-conditioned lobby. The brush of the cool air paints Noelle's complexion back to its healthy, freckled ivory.

"Home?" Her bottom lip quivers, finally looking my way. And now I'm gawking, completely enamored by her beauty. Her own irritation has seemed to have settled and all it took was air conditioning. If I have to plead my case in a walk-in freezer, I'll do it if it means she'll really hear me out.

How could I have been so insensitive? Noelle just had a spell, and all I can think about now is how to make her forgive me. It wasn't about me at that moment, it should've been about Noelle's health.

Noelle looks marginally better than before, but it's clear this is already taking a toll on her. I have to get through to her. It's important we are cordial in all this mess, or else she'll really do damage to her health. But I can see now is not the time for that conversation. My priority is getting this woman to bed to sleep, and only sleep.

"Good evening." The receptionist greets chipperly. This man can try all he wants, but he will never outrank Noelle's incredible hospitality.

"Reservation for Snow."

"Yes, Mr. Snow, we've been expecting you."

"Isn't that the case with every guest?" Noelle snickers.

Noelle, you troublemaker, this is why I fell for you. At least my Princess is in good enough health to jab.

"Well, yes, we had the room modified to your specifications."

"Oh, goodie!" Samantha's voice pierces through shrilly. "I think you'll be happy with the changes I've made."

"I'm not about to walk in on a spread of TickleMeKink merchandise...again. Actually, can we make that happen?" I humor, hoping to keep the spirit light.

Noelle stomps on my foot, and I let out a cry of pain. Totally deserved, definitely wasn't the joke of the hour.

"Apartment suite, just swipe your card in the elevator." The receptionist instructs. I pinch the two swipe cards. I am surprised to find these cards are heavier than any ordinary key card, they might actually be made of gold.

"Apartment? That means there might be two beds." Noelle snatches the key card from me, bolting to the elevator and repeatedly assaulting the call button with vigor. I'm just glad she's showing signs of recovery, even if she's repulsed at the idea of sharing a bed with me.

"Level 30, boss level. Come on, Janny." She swipes her card with an animated *woosh*.

I comb my fingers through the ends of her hair, hoping to cool her excitable energy. Knowing it will end up with her collapsed on the floor.

Noelle scrunches her face into a pinch and crosses her fingers, muttering quietly under her breath. "Two beds, please, let there be two beds."

Noelle tries to steady her breathing the entire flight. She has excited her heart in her spurt of adrenaline.

"Hello, two—dammit!" Noelle huffs. She throws the key card to the plush carpet in a fit. "There's only one bed."

"And it's a California king. Sam, you did it again." There goes Samantha, stroking her ego once again. But I have to admit that the bed looks so inviting, I can already see Noelle and I cuddling in the marshmallow-like duvet.

"Disappointing," Noelle deflates. *I conquer, Nono. This is perfect for the two of us.* I even feel a smile threatening at my lips.

Good job, Sam, for once you're not a pain in my ass.

"Come on, Nono, it's not the first time we've shared a bed." I wrap my arms around Noelle from behind, waddling her into the apartment. She better get used to this because the sight of that bed is bringing out the cuddler in me. And I know Noelle loved a cuddle. She must still, since she shows no sign of fight as I nuzzle into her.

"I suppose not, but don't expect to have sex tonight," Noelle says sternly with a grimace.

Guess that designer dress is staying intact after all. No biggie, my Princess needs her rest.

"Okay, Nono. But no doubt Samantha is going to want candid shots of us cuddling."

Noelle leans back into my snuggle. I nuzzle my nose into the crook of her neck. She smells of feverish sweat, but I'm not deterred. If anything, it makes me more aroused.

But she's already declared no advances of sex tonight.

"You guys have sex?" Samantha gasps. I didn't pick Mrs. Try-TheVibratingCockRing over here to be such a prude.

"Yes, we've had sex a couple of times." Noelle pipes up.

"Really? I thought you were just friends who flirted," Samantha ponders.

"We are just friends." Noelle snipes, pushing away from me as if she's just awoken from her worst nightmare.

Friends is a start, but I still hate when she uses that label for us. We've never been just friends. We have far too much chemistry. Even to this day, I can sense it in Noelle. She's trying to convince herself that's not the case. But it'll all come undone eventually, but this time it won't take six years, it probably won't even take the entire week. Because it's there, it's prevalent. Our chemistry is powerful during sex, but it's all there even when we're not having sex.

"You guys have zero sexual chemistry, so color me shocked." Samantha cackles.

All traces of amusement disappear from Noelle's face at that comment. Which is all the confirmation I need to know that a little longing still lives in her. And that fact makes her sick to her stomach.

Oh, here we go, a self-induced spell. All it takes is one stressful hyper-fixation, and the next thing she's passed out on the floor.

"Noelle, don't work yourself up over that." My eyes roll, which I regret because it was more directed towards Samantha's ridiculous statement.

Of course, Noelle and I have sexual chemistry. We've had sex, simple. Not only that, we've been fighting off having sex again. I see that same primitive urge mirroring in her eyes. She wants me just as much as I want her.

Well, just not right now, as I've shot off at the mouth and said something insensitively stupid...again. Her lips part with a scoff before wandering off to give herself a self-guided tour of the apartment.

On that note, I'm going to allow Noelle time to cool down before my mere presence hospitalizes her.

I have a date with this stubborn stain, which is ironic because Noelle caused it, and I can't help but feel like a stain in her life right now.

Noelle's disgruntled mumbling trickles into the marble bathroom as she moves about the apartment noisily. I will gladly wear the hefty bill of her destruction if it allows her to blow off a little steam with this stressful predicament thrust upon her.

I would blow off steam a little differently. Nothing quite centers me than when I can release my pent-up sexual frustrations. Which sounds rather vicious, but I would be nothing but mindful and gentle with Noelle if she consented to me fucking her.

No sexual chemistry. Who is Samantha kidding? It's all my brain can think about now.

My hand dismisses the wet cloth as it only makes the stain spread broadly and my nipples hard at the coldness. I release the buttons from their designated holes, untucking the luxurious fabric blend from my trousers.

I'd love nothing more than a repeat of what we did in the lodge. But if I know Noelle like I think I do, she's possibly passed out from a long day of hard work.

Today was as long and as hard as my fucking cock right now. *Down, boy.* I scrub my hands over my face as an attempt to purify my thoughts. I will happily settle for a timid cuddle with Noelle. Hardly a compromise, I adore snuggling with my Princess.

I brace myself to see a scene of demolition, only to find the room looks to be in immaculate order. Except the rumpled-up duvet that is sending all the wrong signals to my erection. My eyes roll when I see Noelle in nothing but a robe, on her knees, sinking into the mattress as she maneuvers her body along with her avatar on the screen.

Nintendo Switch and Mario Kart. Samantha must've organized that. Thank you again, Sam, for not being a cockblock and keeping my Princess happy.

Noelle's eyes do a double take, the remote dropping along with her jaw. I often forget about my sex appeal and the effect it has on women, but I rather like it being acknowledged by Noelle.

I approach the bed, finessing my fingers through my gelled-back hair, separating the gluey particles. Her eyes focus on my abs and I swear I see them flicker just a little lower.

That's it, Nono, take it all in. This is all yours for the rest of your life, my wife.

Fuck, I'm getting myself horny.

"Room for one more play—" I expected my knee to be met with the cloudy mattress of the California king bed. Instead, I'm tumbling down, swallowed by what feels like marshmallows. I swim my way through the white mass, coming face to face with Noelle's sunny expression.

"Ha! Gotcha! I split the bed in two."

I crawl from the duvet and burrow us together underneath. We called these avalanches as kids, Noelle would always surprise me when I was least expecting it, entangling me and her in a sheet. Even when we were on laundry duty, she would always catch me off guard.

I pull myself back from her, her panting coming hard and fast.

"You better fix your face, Janny."

"What look am I giving?" My voice sits thickly in my throat. It's almost like my body is trying to stop me from talking. Truthfully, I don't want to talk, I want to kiss and kiss and kiss.

"That look. *The* look."

"The look? Pretty sure my face doesn't show any expression." I tease, shuffling my weight on top of her. Her back bows to me in her efforts to squirm, but she doesn't appear to be trying to get away.

"We're not having sex tonight, January. I'm too tired," she whines breathily.

"That's okay, Nono." I resign from my hover above her, allowing her air supply to be clean of my hot, eager breath. "No sex."

Noelle wrestles the robe from her shoulders. My fingers tangle with the cord's knot to assist her in getting it loose. She swats away my help with her hand, striking me with a scolding glare.

"No sex."

"I was just helping you get comfortable."

She holds her disapproving stare. She's clearly not buying that my intentions were among the purest.

I resign back onto the pillow with a sigh. "Fine."

She hums pleasantly at her victory, shimmying the robe from her figure. My eyes widen when I see a distressed t-shirt on Noelle's body, one I thought the lodge's industrial washing machine had devoured.

"Nono," I start unassumingly, "Is that my Guns N' Roses shirt?"

Her face blanches as she registers her apparel.

"You gave this to me, so it's *my* Guns N' Roses shirt."

Oh, that's right. The day started with us searching the laundry room high and low for this shirt. Noelle even crawled into the mammoth dryer where she miraculously plucked out this very shirt. I declared she should keep it as a prize, as well as a token of my appreciation for her helpful nature.

"I remember, yes. Nice to know you held on to it." I rub my hand up the side of her rib. The softness of the cotton brings a million more memories that featured this shirt to the surface.

"No sex." She pries my hand from her side.

"That wasn't me coming onto you. I just wanted a reminder of how soft this shirt is."

"You can have it back, actually." She peels the shirt from her body, exposing her perky tits. Her nipples stiffen in an instant at my attention. "It has no place amongst my wardrobe."

"Right." I can't tear my eyes from her stunning naked body. I shake my enchantment by threading my head through the shirt myself.

Bad call, January.

The fabric is infused with her cinnamon scent. I'm immediately getting hard.

"Goodnight, January." She tugs a large amount of the duvet from my side of the bed, exposing my fully erect penis in my sweats. It's okay, because I am feeling rather feverish anyway as I swim in Noelle's scent. I lay my head on the pillow again, trying to fight off her potent aroma. My blood feels like it's pumping hotter and faster than usual. I find my fist bundling the shirt and pressing it to my nose. I inhale deeply.

The memories burst into full color in my mind; Noelle and I cuddling on the couch. Dancing in my room. Playfully brawling one another after a match of Mario Kart.

The wonderful innocent memories become immediately distorted in my brain. I want to make naughtier memories with this shirt. I want to fuck her in nothing but this shirt, feast on her pussy in just this shirt.

I watch her wrestling the shirt off on replay, her gorgeous tits with their raspberry colored nipples, her striking collarbones that sink alluringly deep, her freckles blossom from the divot.

She's so fucking beautiful. Even after all these years, she is still the most beautiful woman I know. I want to appreciate her beauty with much more than just observation. I desire for her to sense my gratitude as I eagerly penetrate her with fervent, rhythmic movements. I yearn to have her freckled skin sticky with sweat adhering to mine. I crave to hear her sweet, airy moans trickle into my ears, relaying her appreciation back. I desire to press my nose into the soft skin of her neck and inhale.

I breathe in the shirt again.

"Mm, fuck." I buck at the waist, jerking up from the mattress.

"What the heck are you doing?" Noelle whines as she comes to a seat.

I spring to a stand, feeling the warm wetness dripping down my legs.

"Is that...?" Noelle tilts her head as she stares at my crotch. I look down to find a stain match larger than the one Noelle caused by *accidentally* catapulting meatballs.

"Excuse me." I waddle awkwardly to the bathroom again, snipping the door behind me and releasing my cock from my sweltering sweats.

I came.

I came hard, alright.

All from Noelle's smell. I am so fucked. She hates me and here I am, ejaculating at her mere scent.

TWELVE

In The Club

Noelle

January rejoins me in the bedroom with his cheeks now flushed red, and his hair damp with sweat.

"Care to explain how fame has turned you into a bed wetter?" I try not to focus on the outline of his cock as he struts out in just his boxer briefs.

"What?"

I right my head from its fascinated tilt, snapping my jaw shut from its awestruck slack. I flick my gaze up to find January wearing an amused arch-browed expression.

"You pissed yourself." I point to his crotch, biting back my devious smile.

"Noelle, you know damn well that was cum and not piss."

"You came? Were you touching yourself whilst lying next to me?" I scoff, bundling the duvet to cover myself, exaggerating my feelings of being violated with hisses and disapproving clicks of my tongue.

"I wasn't touching myself, Noelle. I didn't provoke this reaction, it just happened." January suddenly peels the shirt from his back, and I am wondering how I provoked this reaction from him so I can continue to do so in the future.

My teeth grind down hard as my eyes rake over his heavenly-crafted body, and now I am bundling the duvet for a whole new reason, to hide my arousal.

"Here, take this back." He dismisses the shirt back to me. I snatch it beneath the covers and pull it over my head to hide my hard nipples. I can't have January knowing he provoked their vitality. "Your smell set me off, I think."

"My smell?" I lift the shirt to my nose. All I can smell is traces of vetiver. Fuck, he still uses the same cologne. The same cologne I would subtly get a whiff of every time we cuddled. Perhaps I should apologize for my overreaction to him touching himself, because I have the sudden urge to do so myself.

"Yes, I guess it's enough to send me over the edge." January clears his throat to brush over his confession. It does the opposite effect of deterring me. In fact, I want to weaponise that little piece of information.

"My smell." I repeat. Now with a confident, flirtatious air. "I really must do it for you, Janny."

"That's not new information, Nono." He sucks at his teeth as he ponders that fact with reluctance.

"Well," I prowl forward onto the bed, January inviting himself closer, falling immediately under my magnetic enchantment, "If that's you reacting to my smell, I can only imagine what reaction I could pull from you with my voice." I turn my timbre airy.

"Careful, Princess, your actions will have consequences." January crawls onto the bed again. My thighs squeeze together at his gentle scolding. I'm thinking January's dreamy, deep voice might overpower my advances and cause me to fold like a wet paper towel.

"Or perhaps even my touch," I stammer out as January tucks himself within the sheets again and yanks me close to his side of the bed with ease. I anchor myself by curling my hand around his sturdy shoulder.

I'm forgetting what the whole point of this seduction was. I know I'm supposed to weaponise January's weakness, but I didn't think I would find myself vulnerable.

I'm only milliseconds from surrendering completely and having January fuck me incredibly one more time.

"Janny," I breathe out on a swoon. I inhale again, ready to express my consent.

"Nono, please don't do this. I can see you are extremely tired. You do not have it in you to have sex right now." January cuts me off before I get the chance.

Despite my whole body being revitalized with horniness, my fatigue has a far stronger hold on me than my arousal.

"I'm exhausted. Today was a lot already." I fight the shiver at the bottom of my spine, triggered by January's feathery caress of his fingertips on my thigh. I am so languid after today's exertion that I don't even have the energy to lie there and take it.

"I know. Do you see why you couldn't come with me all those years ago?"

"January, you must learn the art of shutting the fuck up." I swipe my arm away from its crossed position on his chest, pushing with all my strength into his ribcage to detach from his embrace.

"Noelle, I'm just explaining it to you." I feel January's broad chest press into my back, my ass instinctively pushes back into his pelvis. I can feel the definition of his bulge. It almost hypnotizes me into forgiveness, but I catch myself and reign in my lust-driven adoration.

"I get it! I'm not suitable for you." Why must he drive that fact home? It hurts every time he brings it up. Which only reiterates that I'm doing this whole stunt for my self benefit. But can we really pull it off when we're always at odds? I'd have a much better time tolerating him as a fake boyfriend if he didn't constantly bring up my POTS. It must weigh on him as much as it does me.

"I never said that. I think we make a perfect pair. You're not suited to this fast-paced environment. You haven't even scratched the surface with how demanding my life is."

"Well, it's a burden I'm going to have to carry." I can only imagine those words echoing in January's mind and he's going to have to carry the burden of my unpredictable health throughout this whole stunt. "I think your lifestyle is the least of our worries. Me trying not to hate your guts will be the true hindrance."

"You hate me?" January pulls away from his hold on me. "I mean, that's what I've been telling myself in my head, but hearing it from you is something else."

I roll over to spectate his vulnerability. His cerulean eyes are fixed on the ceiling, but I know his thoughts are elsewhere.

"Yes, I hate you." Even saying it to myself feels like a punch to the gut. I don't hate January, but I certainly don't like him either. I don't know what we've got going for ourselves and how we could use it to the benefit of this fake relationship. Well, except one aspect that never went away over our ten-year separation.

"At least we have sexual chemistry. I'm sure that will come in handy with the stunt." I spin optimistically. It's an innate habit of mine that I practiced even as a little girl, finding the good in every situation. January's crestfallen expression brings out that quality in me so naturally.

I can recall the first day we met and how miserable he looked to be now living on an isolated ski lodge. I pulled out every trick in my hospitality arsenal, doing anything I could to make January's time there worthwhile.

Time will tell if he returns the favor. So far, he's been accommodating me with backhanded jabs at my health.

"You think we have sexual chemistry?" his eyes flick to me. Every other muscle stays still with hesitation, which seems to activate some sort of fight-or-flight response in me.

"Well, do you?" I fidget with the hem of the shirt that started this whole messy conversation.

"Duh. We've had sex and I'm pretty sure if you weren't so tired right now, we'd be having more sex." He transfers his palms from his steady breathing belly to behind his head, shooting me a sleazy smirk.

"Thank you, January, for reiterating that I'm the problem."

"Noelle, you're misinterpreting my words again."

"You're saying stupid shit again. I guess we can write off sexual chemistry, since it is so easily faltered by my fatigue. Clearly wasn't our strongest attribute to this stunt anyway, your publicist doesn't even buy that we have sex."

"Fuck Samantha, she doesn't know what the fuck she's talking about." January's nostrils flare at his declaration. He looks most kissable when he's irritated. I avert my eyes and draw hearts on the duvet. Something I used to do to distract my teenage-crushing heart from falling for my best friend. Only the illustrations were drawn into the snow instead. It wasn't a very effective coping mechanism because I fell for this asshole, anyway.

"Now, I hope that's not true. I hope she knows what she's doing with this stunt. I need this to work."

It really is my fault, all the setbacks with this stunt stem from me. I punch at the duvet to skew up my loving drawings.

January grabs my balled fist and presses it softly to his lips. I watch with starry eyes.

"Let's call the stunt off. I will help Darlington Snow Paradise by donating some money." January reasons. "I don't want you spiraling and beating yourself up over all of this."

"That has to be the most insensitive thing you've said so far." I snatch my hand back, rubbing at my knuckles where he pressed his tender kiss.

"Beats you having to tolerate me any longer. I'll draw up a check and we can continue to live our life as perfect strangers."

I gasp. I can not believe the gull on this guy.

"You continue to outdo yourself, January." I thrash the duvet completely off the both of us, coming to a stand. "I am not entirely shocked. You have always been completely shallow as a person. Money solves all your problems, but your arrogance started well and truly before that. When you felt you had the right to take my virginity and fucking leave—" I hiss as a sharp pain in my head interrupts my spiel.

"It's not like I was going around collecting virginities. You forget I was a virgin myself." I try to track January's voice as he moves around the room. His stabilizing palm behind my back makes me flinch. "For the record, money has solved none of my problems, at least not the biggest one of all."

"And what could that possibly be, January?" I lean my body back into his, craning my head onto his shoulder. His palms run around to my stomach. I melt into his touch.

"Having you back in my life, but that's rather simplifying it. Money hasn't been able to bring you back into my life. It hasn't made you reach out to me for ten years. It hasn't made you fall in love with me. Money is not all it's cracked up to be."

"But it'll magically solve all my problems. What makes me the exception?"

"Well, from what you are telling me, saying you hate me and all, it sounds like money could really get me out of your hair for a little while." January calmly purrs into my ear.

"Is that what you want? To be out of my hair?" My breath catches in my throat.

January presses his nose into my raging pulse. "Rather the opposite, Princess. I'm trying to get entangled with you all over again."

"Oh, January." I swoon, turning way too quickly to face him. The passionate kiss I plant on his lips mixed with my dizzy spell feels like an amusement park ride. January scoops me up and guides us back to the bed. My body surrenders completely to its need for sleep once it hits the mattress. Lethargy makes my muscles feel like cement. "Oh man, I really am tired."

"Let's get some sleep, Princess. Who knows what they have in store for us tomorrow?" January finesses the sheet over us completely. I palm at the roof of the cotton cocoon, allowing for a pocket of air.

"So we're going forth with this stunt?" I ask meekly. Even in the dark, January's abnormally colored eyes glow and I still fall victim to their spellbinding quality.

"Are we?" He pauses.

"Do you think we're convincing enough?"

"Nono, I think we have a lot going for us. We just have to be us, and I think people will be convinced."

Just be us? But I supposedly hate him, and he wants to be *entangled* with me, what even is *us*. This has become far more confusing than when it was black and white pure hatred. I am also terrible at convincing myself that I do hate January. There I went again, tripping so easily into his arms every time. It's like my adult Noelle brain powers down and teenage Noelle takes the wheel. I've really got to get a hold on that if I plan to be strictly self-serving in this endeavor, but the unconvincing part continues to plague my thoughts. It could jeopardize the whole thing. I guess that means I am still acting in my self-interest if I'm only concerned with the surface level aspect of the stunt, and have no desire to rekindle anything with January. *You hear me, teenage brain?*

"I just can't believe Samantha can't believe that we have unbelievable sex." I regret it immediately after saying it, scrunching my face in disgust. I should've been more careful with my word choice because that insinuates that January and I obviously have sexual chemistry to an obnoxious degree.

"It's really bothering you, huh?" January's smirk has my stomach in knots.

"No, it doesn't. It's just so obvious we've been intimate." I truly believe that to the average person, we look like a pair of people who have *touched genitals*. Even as disturbing as that fact is for the average person to conclude. What more do I have to do to get that point across? Do I have to acknowledge that teenage girl longing that still lives inside of me? I'm considering that as my last resort.

"I mean, you have your hands all over me. Maybe I need to be a little more handsy with you." I contemplate because January has not been shy about acting coupley.

"Now that sounds even more bothersome to you." January's mouth brackets with frown lines. His cerulean eyes, sheltered by his thick raven brows, somehow makes his humorless expression look handsome. My fingertips run along his hairline, his features soften instantly. It feels so natural to touch him. So why is it so unbelievable that we're more intimate than this? Are the touches perhaps too subtle? But that would make them read more authentically. A love that's not strictly for show.

"I like handsy Noelle." January's eyes sink close. He releases a deep hum of pleasure.

"I feel like I've always been touchy-feely with you. I was always touching you as a teen." This is by all means not me acting on my teenage desires. I'm simply using the information I know.

"Don't second guess yourself now." Even as January forces my lingering touch to remain, he does so carefully. *Just like he always does.*

Much like how Darlington Snow Paradise accommodates my lifestyle, January has always accommodated me as a person, which was always something that Sean lacked. His demanding job with long hours would have me awake late into the night just so I could see him...what I now realize is those long hours were probably just him spending time with his family. Whilst I was an after-hours afterthought. But that's not his family's fault. They should be the priority. I just wish I could be someone's priority.

"I am second guessing myself because I need this to look so convincing for the sake of the lodge. A lot is riding on the believability."

"Maybe it's just not for them to believe. I know we never had the chance to fully explore the potential of our relationship, but I don't think we would have been publicly passionate lovers. It was only a love we understood and only a love we understand."

I hum, January is not hearing me out. This has to be more of a spectacle. He's clearly enchanted by something about me if his whimsical words are anything to go by. He spreads my legs further and maneuvers his way into a cuddle. *Lo-and-behold, our genitals are touching. What more could you people want?* I fight off the urge to keep my guard up completely. I just need to let my walls down enough to appear like I'm in love on the surface.

"Nono."

My fingers thread further into his hair as I try to anchor myself on this line I'm teetering on. I gently tug at January's locks, his gaze meeting mine with a smitten smirk. God, he is adorable when he's not sulking. Even when he is sulking.

"Goodnight, Janny."

"Sweet dreams, Nono." He nuzzles his head between my breasts. My racing heartbeat is no doubt a dead giveaway of how much I enjoy having him nestled there, to my dismay.

"Look at you two!" Samantha's sudden vocal fry penetrates the peaceful atmosphere. January flinches away. My knotted fingers in his hair yank hard at his scalp, causing him to cry out in pain.

My head snaps to the elevator. I can only just make out Samantha's face behind a burst of light.

"Samantha, do you mind?" January growls as he delicately pries my hand from his hair, being meticulous as not to not hurt me by inflicting him more pain.

"This is great stuff." With another burst of light, I can only make out another figure behind the beam. "Oh, the bags are fine just there, thanks." Perfect! Maybe this bellhop can spread the news around town about this very convincing predicament he found Hot Shot Pro Hockey Player Cameron Snow in and hopefully that will lead to questions about who I am, which will lead to a domino effect of Darlington Snow Paradise being mentioned. Such a long-winded process just to give the lodge the recognition it deserves.

I'm just glad our bags are finally here, which means I can be reunited with the true love of my life. My laptop.

But first, I have to be a little opportunistic and put on a show for the camera. Perhaps Samantha can throw whichever news outlet she'll be selling these pictures to a bone and simply mention Darlington Snow Paradise upon the transaction. Then we can bypass all that *who is that girl?* bullshit.

"You really think so, Samantha?" I cup January's cheeks, giving Samantha another photo op, and the clever woman takes the hint. I make her job easier and hopefully she will return the favor.

"Don't you two look cuddly? You look as if you're ready for bed," Samantha coos.

"Yes, so why are you here?" January presses through his pearlescent teeth. I want to hook my fingers into his cheeks and tug his lips into one of his rare hypnotic smiles.

"Surely, you two aren't *actually* ready for bed. The night is young."

"It's 10 pm?" I flip January's phone over, as it lay between our entanglement. I can confirm the time is 10 pm and January did not choose the *cheeky* Jacuzzi picture for his phone wallpaper, but one of me and him from the day he got scouted. I remember being so excited for him, possibly even more excited *than* him. He seemed so devastated by the news, now that I recall. I didn't understand at that moment. All his hard work at the lodge had finally paid off, and yet he wasn't ecstatic. He clung to me for the rest of that day, which wasn't unusual for us as a pair. We were inseparable.

"10 is young!" Samantha defends, knocking me out of my daydream.

"In age, yes, time, no," January retorts.

"You kids are such old farts. I need you up and out. Seymour and Aaron are waiting for you at *The Speakeasy*."

"I'm sure they can have fun without us." January cocoons me completely. An orgasmic nostalgia sloshes in my core. I'm now realizing how much I love January's clinginess.

"Well, since you are notoriously cranky, I not only have to validate this relationship, I also have to validate these friendships."

"Noelle has to come?" January's voice reverberates against my neck. The hickey he left there a few days ago is still sensitive. I softly nudge him away, mostly because it's painful having his skin to be pressed to my bruises. The urgency to seize another moment to really sell the authenticity jolts me awake.

"Yes, I have to come. We must portray our love to the masses."

"Angelface gets it." Samantha gives me an approving nod.

I sit up and my head reels with dizziness.

"Noelle, do you even feel up to it?" January's fingers run up and down my spine, which is doing no good for my growing headache. I turn and give him a curt, squinty-eyed nod to acknowledge his question.

"Nothing a little concealer can't hide." Samantha clicks smartly.

"I don't care what she looks like, I care how she feels," January's volume borders on a bark. "She looks tired as fuck."

"I'm sure that was supposed to sound sweet, but you made it sound backhanded." My eyes narrow for a completely different reason, unrelated to fatigue and completely related to judgment.

"Don't you bicker now. Get dressed, nightclub attire. Chop, chop." Samantha tears the sheets off of us.

"I hate her," January grumbles as he wheels and hikes my suitcase onto the bed for me.

Putting on makeup and this tight dress took up way more energy than I thought it would. I'm nodding off, my head lulling onto January's shoulders. The pleasant soft jazz music playing in the elevator is not helping with fighting off my fatigue.

"You're far too tired for this nonsense." January's voice is just the lullaby my ears crave.

"I'm sure the adrenaline will kick in once you two get to the club and start grinding up on one another." I credit this to my extreme lethargy, but it almost sounds like Samantha's voice, her keyboard clacking, and the jazzy swing of music are in harmony.

"Adrenaline is something Noelle very much likes to avoid." January's fingers caress at the nape of my neck. I can feel his craving to loop a finger around my auburn locks, but I have opted for a stylish claw clip to keep my hair from contacting my skin. A boiling environment like a nightclub will no doubt make it a big sweaty, soggy heap by the end of the night.

"Fine, no grinding up on each other, but look cozy in a very indiscreet booth." The elevator ping announces our arrival. I am ushered blindly by January to a crowd of people. My vision becomes clear again and I catch on that we are now lining up to enter the nightclub.

We pass the velvet rope cordoning us off from Jojo, blessing our ears at an unfortunately assaulting volume.

"Do you think this song is an omen?" I joke drowsily to January.

"I can barely make out the song behind the reverberation."

"Leave by Jojo."

"Oh, most definitely a sign."

"Cameron!" January is greeted by a booming southern drawl I have never heard before.

"These fuckers," January huffs under his breath. "Please stay close, so I don't have to mingle too much with these meatheads."

"'Play nice' is your new motto, isn't it?" I tease with the little energy I have.

"Come join us. You've brought a friend." I am shocked to find the bombastic deep southern accent belongs to the notorious playboy of the team, Aaron Nightingale. Who is as handsome as he is tall. Photos and game replays do not do him justice. His limbs always spread to their longest capacity to take up all the space of the goal. Aaron may not get to score, being stuck in front of the goal the entire game, but I've heard different stories off the rink. This man scores every woman he's ever wanted, and there's no trouble understanding why. His dark skin makes his extremely white smile glow under the strobing lights, and his raven hair is short and well-kept. It bears mentioning again his gigantic stature, that even has me at 5'10—*6'2 in heels*—feeling dainty.

"I'm Aaron, this is Seymour," my eyes tear from Aaron's godly structured face to a younger set of features. Seymour Floss, as far as I am aware, is the rookie of the team. His skin is just as pale as mine and that is about where our similarities end, for if I am frail, Seymour is strong and full of brute. Even if he may fall a little shorter than me in heels, based on his reputation on the ice for knocking rivaling players' teeth out, I certainly don't want to cross him. He hasn't been coined The Tooth Fairy for nothing. His aloofness reminds me a bit of someone I grew up with, but his demeanor is far less charming and more unsettling. His shaggy dark brunette hair curtains a harsh, judgemental glare on me that feels personal.

What did I ever do to him?

I turn to January for answers. I can't help but deconstruct his handsomeness, too. His razor-sharp jawline is accentuated by him gnawing at his cheek, making it known how much he doesn't want to be here. His lips are full and kissable, even in a snarl. I want them on mine. Lord knows my skin can't handle his vicious love bites, leaving my skin tender days after, even as orgasmic as they are in the moment. If I'm committed to taking out my revenge on January, perhaps *hurting* him in the same ways he hurts me is the way to go.

My lips part, readying to beckon my lover and my victim to me. Only words don't escape me at first. I'm jilted by more promiscuous urges as I am verbally restrained, like my mind is punishing me with the unobtainable just at the thought of inflicting pain on January.

Visions of us panting hard and fast form quickly in my mind. Our bodies are slick with sweat, but neither of us is ashamed at that moment because the passion is so intoxicating. As he ebbs and flows from my core, making the chasm between my legs a sweltering desert.

I've always dreamed of fucking January like that, wildly and with vigor. But, alas, my health gets in the way.

Worst cockblock ever.

If by some Freaky Friday miracle, I got the chance to have either Candy or Janelle's body, kindled with stamina, I would spend the whole day fucking January Cameron Snow. And I'd fuck him so amazingly he wouldn't be able to wipe that hypnotizing smile off his face ever again.

A girl can dream.

My vision turns to darkness, a flood of ruckus hits my eardrums, and my body aches as it comes alive with vitality.

"Oh, I was dreaming." I peel my head from January's lap, as I take in the strobing lights of the club, walking my hands up to a stand. January lurches forward with a groan, making me realize my palm made a perch on his crotch. "Oops, sorry."

"It's okay, Nono."

I can't wrangle the swoon before it leaves my lips, which makes January quirk a questionable brow at me.

"You okay, Princess?" January's tender gaze leaves me breathless. I dive for his lips, halting when my heartbeat thumps in an irregular rhythm. Only to come to my senses, it's not my heartbeat but the bass of the song playing. Promiscuous by Nelly Furtado ft. Timbaland.

"Janny! Our song!" I pinch at my spinning head as I pull January up from the booth seat, his hand securing around my figure, bringing the swaying to a stop. "Let's go dance."

"Noelle, you don't look well."

"I'm fine, January," I snarl, breaking away from him and finessing myself through the crowd and onto the dance floor. Within seconds, I am swarmed by men wanting to dance with my wheezing ass. I look over my shoulder with regret. January is right there.

I throw my numb arms around his neck to support my buckling knees. I press up against him as he quietly sings the Timbaland parts to me and I wheeze the Nelly Furtado parts back.

The nightclub scene fades from my peripherals. I'm transported back to times of innocence and my desperation to change that, as January and I take the stage at Cocomo's karaoke nights. Where he's really not hearing me when I sing, *you already know that I'm all yours. What are you waiting for?* Like, for Christ's sake, could he not tell I was completely head over heels for him? I fucking wanted him more than I need air.

I'm thrust back into the present, where the situation is in reverse. January can't keep off of me, that is certainly something I could use in my favor.

I peel my heavy lids open, my vision blurry at first, clearing to January's face close to mine. Our foreheads pressed together, his eyes also closed, his brows in a deep furrow. Possibly also wrapped in a memory of us and the history of this song.

I hope he's not being too critical of his past performances, especially the ones with the pubescent voice cracks.

"Janny," I wheeze, barely audible. I can't even hear myself, so I doubt January can. "Janny, kiss me."

He appears to be shackled by this memory he's revisiting. Hopefully, this Princess can rescue her Prince. I tilt my lips, pressing mine featherlight to his, feeling his furrow melt away with each second.

I part from the kiss in need of some air. It's already so suffocating in the club.

"Let's get out of here." January makes the call I've been dying for him to make this whole outing. Only it's missing something.

Sexual chemistry.

Thirteen

Practice Makes Perfect

Noelle

I woke up feeling like Regina George when she got hit by the bus. Fatigue still strikes my body like a sledgehammer, coming down hard on my skull. It's painful just to look at the bright light on my phone screen. The harsh arena lights of the rink certainly don't sweeten the deal. I lull my head down, pinching my eyes. My vision finally crisps to the view of the influx of comments on photos posted on Aaron's story that were most definitely not taken by Aaron. The text reading, @TheCameronSnow + @DarlingNoelle. Even in my dysfunctional state, I can pinpoint what is missing from his post.

"There's no indication that we're dating." I turn to Samantha in a tizzy. "Why are there no love hearts or something saying we're an item?"

The comments confirm my dramatics.

> *@ShirtlessCameronSnow: THEY'RE OBVY JUST HUGGING GUYS! THAT WOULD BE A LAME ASS KISS. I WOULD SUE!*

@SnowThirstEdits: I love that they are just good friends; that means more Cameron for me.

@AlphaMode: Told you guys you were crazy. They are obviously just friends. You losers actually thought they were shagging. That Noelle bird could get it.

@VanessaSnow: See, guys, friends, just friends.

"No, this can't be happening." My finger continues to scroll frantically, more comments peppered with the word *friends.* That word will haunt me for the rest of my living days. "We're not convincing enough."

I look up to see January's worried eyes locked on me. I must be showing my panic in my features. I can see my chest ebbing and flowing frantically in my peripherals.

His features display nothing but concern for me, with his thick brows down-turned and his sharp jawline clenched tensely. To the casual observer, he would just come across as an asshole. Which is true, but as of right now, he is an attentive asshole.

His blades dig into the ice, his stick no longer in playing motion.

Shit, he's making his way over.

I don't want to have this conversation right now, the one about how to the casual observer we look like *just friends.* When in actuality there might be some underlying infatuation that I am trying to keep at bay whilst executing my revenge. I'm doing such a subtle job at pretending to be in love with January. So far I am the only one convinced I love him. That is a major issue.

January is almost to the threshold where the ice turns suddenly to carpet.

"Crumpets!"

My head snaps to the distraction. I should've heard those 10-inch high stompers clicking from miles away.

Janelle, my savior.

"Nelly!" I stand too quickly from my seat and I feel like I'm also floating 10 inches from the ground, twirling like a ballerina.

"Noelle!"

I stare at inconspicuous stains on the carpet as my vision sharpens once again, revealing that it was only one mysterious stain after all, and I'm certain it's blood. No doubt the damage by January's new compadre, Seymour Floss.

I snap my gaze at my friends once again.

"Candy, Janelle, am I glad to see you," I wheeze. My eyes quickly flicker to January. He resigns from the safety guard, keeping his eyes on me as he returns to his destined position on the ice. The position he has trained for his whole life, a role that is worth much more than I am.

"Noelle, you off with the fairies again?" Janelle snaps her pink acrylics in my vision. I startle back into reality. I think I'm developing a phobia of acrylic nails as my eyes wearily wander over to Samantha.

I focus back on my support network. I can't decide whether it's a win for me, knowing January has no genuine friends. There is a sliver of victory in there for me. It's clear that I'm irreplaceable.

"Sorry, girls. What are you doing here?" I turn back to my friends.

"We were flown out to Phoenix to sign some NDAs. I thought you were pranking when you said you were coming to Phoenix. Does that mean the whole marriage thing with Cameron Snow is real? Is that legal?" Janelle is asking far too many questions of someone who is still recovering from an almost episode.

"It's real…only it doesn't read that way." My eyes scan the ice, searching for the bold 10 on that famous forest green jersey. I sink into the breath that holds my lungs hostage. "And it really needs to look real."

"Wait, sit down and explain everything." Janelle tugs me spiritedly back to the bleachers. I have never felt such orgasmic relief from simply sitting down once again.

"Spill." I'm blinded by a wink of a jewel. Janelle's hands are always rhinestoned to the heavens.

A sense of grounding comes over me when I feel Candy join my other side. I'm cocooned by the most incredible women who provide unwavering support and safety. Even with my health trying to right itself still, I feel stable enough to voice my concerns to the girls.

"Well, January and I had our first public appearances together, and no one is buying that we are more than friends."

"Are you more than friends?" Candy asks, flicking her eyes from me to January. I squish down the prickle of jealousy that makes my heart speed.

"Well...it's complicated," I hush in a whisper, leaning forward to tighten the huddle, dulling the volume so Mrs. Dragon Claws behind us can't hear up. No doubt Samantha's incessant obnoxious texting—*seriously, why is your phone not on silent*—will filter out my scheme as I detail it to the girls. "I'm sort of still trying to exact my revenge."

"You cunning bitch, I knew you had it in you!" Janelle pinches my bicep, which will certainly bruise later.

"Shut up, please." I wish my heart would listen to that request too, as my pulse thrums loudly in my ear.

"It's always the quiet ones, Candy." Janelle crosses her arms over her chest, perking her already hitched-up breasts and clicking her tongue disapprovingly. "I am so proud of you." A mischievous smirk growing on her cherry lacquered lips.

"I'm surprised you two haven't seen the comments. Are we not all chronically online?" I laugh nervously.

"You know, I actually haven't taken my phone off airplane mode yet." Candy looks at her phone. I catch a quick glimpse of the photo of her graduating from San Francisco State University. She is a spitting image of her father, right down to his proud smile.

"We were advised to keep a low profile. Someone's fanbase is very skilled in *finding out someone's location*." Janelle's marina eyes narrow on me as she hums suspiciously.

I wince. I know exactly what video she is referring to. The one where I innocently demonstrated to my techy fanbase how to cross-check and pinpoint someone's exact location. My DMs were flooded the next day with *thank you* and *fuck you*, mostly due to them finding out that their partners were cheating.

Looks like I should've put my skills to work. Suppose that's where January got the idea to track down and get some background information on Sean to begin with.

I will not dwell on it. It's simply a thing of the past.

"Well, here." My brain is doing pirouettes again. I blindly hold my phone out, hoping one of the girls will grab it before it slips from my limp grip. "Every single comment states that we look *friendly*."

"Yikes, I haven't seen a comment section so brutal since...well before I boarded a plane here," Candy resigns meekly. We all get our fair share of cyberbullying, but it's undeniable that Candy gets the brunt of it. Targeting her curvaceous figure and how it contradicts her message of healthy eating. Candy Fernandez couldn't be more qualified if she tried. Janelle had put me onto her when the doctors' only recommendation to get a handle on my POTS was to correct my diet. Candy's expertise is the very reason I can live a somewhat functional life.

"No, we can fix this." And then there's Janelle, despite her promiscuous in pink look she's got going on. She's a solutionist to her core, which I can only guess stems from her education in engineering. "You just need to be intimate." Janelle tilts her head as she inspects the carousel of photos, dissecting every frame as it was a piece of machinery that just needs a gear changed out. "It's crazy how he makes ass-grabbing look so friend—"

"Do not say the f-word," I groan.

"But that's my favorite word," Janelle whines playfully, shooting me a saucy wink. "Fine...look so innocent."

"Innocent?" I'm positive every thought running through January's head is anything but innocent, especially since our reluctant reunion.

"Have you kissed?" Janelle asks.

"Janelle, we've fucked. And then I friendzoned him, just like you advised."

"You've fucked?" They both exclaim, their jaws hanging as slack as my shoulders.

"Yes, is that so hard to believe?" I straighten my posture, crossing my arms and flaring my nostrils. I'm genuinely offended by that.

"Well...a little. Can you kiss for me now?" Janelle inspects her nails as she asks the most absurd question casually. I love my best friend Janelle, but I really need her to cut the blasé approach to the matter. This has me quite stressed out.

She's probably thinking it's an easy fix and just a matter of *rewiring our connection.* What she fails to understand is I'm not a machine and there are complex human feelings involved that somehow are not reflecting externally.

If only I were a computer, I'd have no problem smoothing out this bug.

"Like demonstrate how we kiss?" I sigh, considering her question and its scientific benefits. I'm so desperate for this to work, that picking apart the mechanics of how January and I kiss is worth it. Besides, polishing up the mechanics will make it appear authentic whilst simply keeping things emotionally disconnected.

"Yes, crumpets. Cameron! Come kiss your bride-to-be."

I curl into myself once again, but not because of fatigue for once, but of pure embarrassment. I cover my face with my hands, parting my middle and ring finger, I find that January is still absorbed in his practice.

"Huh? Maybe he's like a pet, he'll come to his owner. Oh, you just gave me an idea for my next line of pleasure toys. Leashes."

I roll my eyes and release a tired sigh.

"January," I speak in my controlled drowsy drawl, my skin texturing with goosebumps as January's mint-colored eyes turn to me.

There's no way he heard me. This is simply a coincidence.

"Did you call me?" he mouths back. My heart drops to my anus as his words catch up to me in an echo with crystalline clarity. I'm backtracking our conversation, my stomach performing Olympic-level gymnastics at the thought of January hearing my revenge ploy.

"Come, come." Janelle invites January over with a flirty flourish of her acrylic nails. "Once I'm done with you two, that's just what you'll be doing tonight."

Doing what? Oh. It takes me a second to realize she's talking about cumming. I should've figured.

January's gaze bores into me, awaiting some sort of green light. I give my shoulders a miniscule shrug and it's enough to set his blades in motion.

He makes it look so easy. All the physics should be against the phenomenon that a man of January's size can not only balance but navigate oneself on two slices of sharp metal.

If my heart is so convinced I still have feelings for January, my brain will have no trouble giving it reasons why I hate January. Reason one: he can skate, I can't.

"I think you're supposed to be happy to see your husband," Janelle snickers.

I realize I am pinching my lips tensely. I soften them as January steps off the ice and clicks his blade covers into place.

I'm up from my seat, and with no thought, I ambush him with a kiss.

All laws of physics turn against this handsome fucker; standing on blades becomes impossible when you are sent weak-kneed by your bride-to-be.

It seems finding his center of gravity isn't as important as ensuring I don't fall ass over tit. His weight pushes against me, unintentionally deepening the kiss. My entire body from my thighs to my breasts presses tightly to January's front. My hands slip from their knotted position behind his neck and past the plastic shields resting on his shoulders. I huff as my attempt to touch his skin is obstructed by the cumbersome uniform.

I want to touch you, Janny.

If physics has turned against January, it appears rationality has betrayed me.

Upon that realization, that's when my fingers curl from him completely. His unwieldy height threatens to crush me as he chases for my departing kiss.

I step back from January, allowing some space for oxygen to flow freely between us and into my arrested lungs. Which also allows me space to indulge in how much I want to surrender to that kiss. How right it would've felt to do so.

But I have to stay somewhat guarded. I can't let him get away with how much he hurt me.

"Nono." He gently lifts my chin to meet his gaze.

"Janny." I swallow thickly. I don't mean to follow it with a lick of my lips, but I can't deny the quick syncopation of my heart when January's gaze quickly flickers to and from them.

"That was..." Candy's voice only just hits my senses, as I slowly transcend from my January-induced high.

"Awful! Downright awful!" Janelle rises from the bench, her platformed height gives her a few inches over me. "Allow me to show you."

"Not on me, you're not." January backs further from Janelle.

"Duh, I'm not about to be the other woman to my best friend's man."

I'm reminded of the time I was the other woman. *Ouch, that still stings.*

"Which one of you boys wants to kiss me?" Janelle calls out into the rink, giving her thick false lash extensions a tempting flutter. Groans, grunts, and splats sound from the rink. A few players clumsily tumble to the ground as others fight their way to get to Janelle first, weaponizing their equipment any way they can. Using their sticks to trip or puncture their fellow teammate.

I suppose the rules of teamwork do not apply when a babe like Janelle is present.

A player *successfully* splats into the safety guard.

"I made it, suck it, fuckers!"

I recognize the rich voice coming from under the helmet. Today's champion—or rather, the next victim to be hopelessly enchanted by Janelle—is Aaron Nightingale.

"Hey babe, aren't you lucky I moved from the goal, now you can finally score?"

"Just a kiss, Number 31." Janelle giggles girlishly.

"I can give you the rest of my phone number." Aaron winks.

Janelle hushes him with a press of her manicured fingertip to his pursed lips, her finger running along his jaw before giving him a tame peck. Aaron's eyes spring open with vitality, glossing over with a hypnotic sheen before his weight falls slack against Janelle. It looked as if he was shot with a tranquilizer dart laced with Janelle's seductive elixir. She might just send him into an overdose-induced coma, as she slips sweet and insatiable moan. She pulled her lips away from Aaron's, and at first, I was underwhelmed, but the aftermath left me rather impressed.

Janelle and Aaron definitely shag, or at least that's the impression they give. But as far as I know, this is their first time meeting.

"Thanks for being such a wonderful volunteer." Janelle tosses her long blonde locks over her shoulder, breaking from her enamored stare that has me convinced she loves that man. *That is perfect! How did you do that?*

She gives Aaron a slight nudge. His skates propel him backwards as he continues to gawk at Janelle, strutting away with sensual confidence.

"Er, anytime." Aaron corrects his tight grip on his stick before skating back to the rest of the pact, as they wait with anticipation for him to report his experience.

"See, nothing to it." Janelle shrugs, flaring her tiny skirt and perching herself back onto the bleachers.

"Okay, so how would I do that?" I interrupt Janelle's mutual perving.

"What do you mean? I just showed you." She chuckles sweetly as she breaks her stare from Aaron.

"Can I get an explanation how you made it look like you're in love?"

Janelle's amusement falls from her face, "I don't know, you sort of have to open your heart a little, give them a hopeful glimpse."

Open my heart? That is what I'm trying to avoid. I can't explicitly say that to Janelle with January present.

"Super helpful, Nelly." I roll my eyes before turning to January with a worried look, locking in on his expression that teeters on solicitous and stoic. It's incredible how the color of his eyes can leave me both threatened and safe. How one glance reminds me I'm a living, breathing person, with an *almost* functioning heart.

Samantha's contemplative hum breaks my equal parts gratitude, equal parts suffering. That sound is far more dangerous than my uncontrollable heartbeat.

We are so screwed.

Fourteen

Damage Control

January

I scrub my jersey down my face to clear my sweat riddled vision. I went harder today than I've ever gone in training; I credit it all to Noelle's presence.

As a teen I had a tendency for showing off when Noelle watched me practice, sometimes it would even reward me with a celebratory cheer. Which made running my breath so agonizingly thin until my lungs burned all worth it. Although she looks as though she's the one who has just over exerted herself on this rink instead of me. The harsh arena lights illuminate her sickly pale flesh, the dark circles under her blood-shot eyes grow darker as she sinks into despair.

I slide onto the bench she occupies, now that she's free of her influential friends, I have her all to myself. I bump my hip against hers and wrap my arm around her waist. My toes curl with giddy when she instinctively rests her head on my shoulder.

"I plan to get you to bed, Nono."

"You're really letting your teenage self take over too, huh?" She scoffs, giving my thigh a weak punch.

Too? What does she mean by too?

I have some clearing up to do first, "I meant it innocently, we barely got any sleep last night, and it shows. You look worried about something as well."

I shoot her a pout that she misses entirely; she flutters her eyes closed and her head becomes heavier on my shoulder.

"You've clearly been online today." Her voice drips with sarcasm.

"Come to think of it, I haven't checked social media for days. I have no need for it now."

"Now that I'm back in your life, your stalking endeavors have ended." She swoons dramatically.

"You said it." I squeeze her tighter to my side. I flinch when she turns to me sharply.

"You really did just go online to stalk me." Her icy eyes rake over me with judgment.

"Hey, don't make it sound creepier than it is. I prefer the term *checking up* on you."

"Like a crazy ex would do." She scoffs, retracting from our embrace.

"I mean, you are my ex-girlfriend," I state matter-of-factly.

"You consider me your ex-girlfriend?"

"I mean not anymore, we're back together—"

"January, I'm not your girlfriend and the public would agree."

Christ, Noelle, and they never will with that attitude. Noelle has to be playing around right now, she is my girlfriend, well technically only contractually before she becomes my wife. Which is a very real ceremony that is happening. This publicity might be for show, but we are actually getting married. Noelle is a smart woman, so I know those details haven't escaped her. I'm putting the emotional warfare she is implementing as my comeuppance for breaking her heart.

Little does she know she won't wear me down because my heart remains full when she is near. She's forgotten our means of flirting when we were friends was through jabbing, so if anything she's turning me on and looking absolutely adorable while doing it.

Nice try, Princess, shall we look at the scoreboard while we're at it?

"Did you get the shot?" Noelle turns her gaze behind us.

"Yep," Samantha chirps. I guess Noelle really does just see this as a spectacle for the masses.

In that case: *January: 0. Noelle: 1.*

"I need to see you two in my office immediately." Samantha's chipper expression dissipates in a flash.

I lean into Noelle and cup my gloved hand by her ear.

"Uh oh, she has the tone your dad had when we pranked him with rubber spiders in his bed. This is not good, Nono, not good."

She turns her face to me, and we are close enough to kiss.

"I still feel so guilty about that." Her cheeks rouge over, I can feel the heat radiating from her skin. "I feel guilty about this too."

"Guilty? About what?" My brows pinch together in confusion.

"Immediately means right now, you homeschooled hermits." Samantha glares from over her phone.

Noelle obediently trots behind Samantha. I have no choice but to follow if I want to ensure Noelle doesn't work herself up into an episode. And to make sure Samantha doesn't eat her up alive. Noelle has always been cunning enough to get herself out of trouble; crafting whatever excuse she can to avoid punishment, but from her defeated stride, she's about to take accountability for something.

"Take a seat, you two." Samantha gestures to the two leather chairs sitting in front of her desk. I only just realize I'm in Samantha's office. Many a-scolding has taken place here, after interviews where I was coined abrasive and stand-offish. "So."

A projector slowly unveils from the ceiling, my Instagram feed casts onto the screen. Comments are flooding in and gauging from the time in the phone screen's corner it's happening in real time. I roll my eyes at this woman's dramatics.

"As Angelface pointed out before, your public appearances are not being received as we desired."

"So, who gives a fuck?" I join Noelle in the leather chair, pulling her onto my lap.

"There's a chair—" Noelle starts.

"You will give a fuck when the place you call home goes bankrupt, leaving your *girlfriend* and her family homeless, which will no doubt lead them to go back to Ireland."

"I'm from London, actually," Noelle interjects, trying to stifle a giggle.

"Your little scare tactic will not work. Also, the stunt has had no mention of Darlington Snow Paradise." Usually, I am a little terrified of Samantha, but with Noelle here to anchor me down, I feel strong enough to confront her.

"Thank you for bringing that up, Janny." I sink into Noelle's touch as she cups my chin.

"I'm trying to solidify this honeymoon angle, but the only thing people took away from last night's outing is that The Prince of Ice has formed a court of friends. And I hate to break it to you, Angelface, but you're right there under that umbrella."

"Friends," Noelle quivers, terrified.

This is all so melodramatic, Noelle and I will fall in love again, it's just going to take time to build her trust again.

"There's hope though." Samantha exhales. "Since Cameron is displaying more sociable attributes, sponsors are coming in again."

"Oh goodie, I'm so glad your end of the deal is being held up." Noelle crashes her weight back into me hard, crossing her arm with a bratty harrumph.

"I'm superb at my job, Angelface, I found a sponsorship that will work in the stunts favor, getting it back on track to the *honeymoon* dynamic."

"Go on." Noelle leans forward on my knee, feathering her fingers whilst wearing a diabolical smile.

"Castaway Swimwear has reached out to me and wants to collaborate with both of you."

"Both of us?" Noelle's posture straightens, I want to run my finger delicately down her spine.

"Yes, the company's social media manager is an avid follower of yours, Angelface."

"That's amazing, people will see the resort through my account. Although bikinis and ski lodges don't really go hand in hand."

"I have photographic evidence that proves otherwise." I'm salivating at the thought of those jacuzzi pictures Noelle kindly blessed my camera roll with. Although I've seen Noelle completely naked on a few occasions, the vision of her only partially covered excites me. Ask any guy if the vision of the woman they love in a bikini is enough to make them cum full loads for a week. I put it down to our biology, the woman in question being exposed enough to stimulate our Neanderthal brains but leave enough to the imagination to get our caveman gears turning.

I might have to shove Noelle off my lap in a minute because I think my cock is getting a head start. I feel like I've regressed to the intellect of a sexually pent-up gorilla.

"I have a feeling you're not thinking friendly thoughts." I can barely make out Noelle's taunt. I want to swim in her dreamy accent, at least I'll be dressed for the occasion. "We'll do it!"

I'm thrusted back into the now at Noelle's enthusiasm, I can sniff out these situations like a bloodhound. I've worked with Samantha for ten years and I know all her tricks. Especially the one where she withholds important decision-altering details.

"So, what's the Catch 22?" I probe.

"Why would there be a Catch 22?" Samantha tugs at the collar of her blouse nervously.

"Samantha." I press through my teeth.

"Okay fine, so the idea was to have you wear something from their matching couple's line," Samantha reveals.

"Oh." Noelle deflates. "We're resorting to matching outfits. Well, if we must. No misinterpreting the message there, only people stupidly in love wear matching outfits."

Yeah, and best friends too, apparently. Unless...

"Wait, Nono, we used to match our outfits and steal each other's clothes all the time as friends."

I remember one time when a couple staying at the ski lodge mistook Noelle for my girlfriend because we had pinched each other's Darlington Snow Paradise hoodies. Noelle stole mine, so I returned the favor. The man leaned in with squinted eyes to read the name embroidered across my heart. *Noelle?* I then cleared up that she stole my hoodie. The guest pulled his partner closer and said; *I remember when she used to steal my hoodies, but no biggie, I got my revenge by marrying her.* I looked over at Noelle sifting the firewood and I thought to myself, *one day I'll marry Noelle.*

I just didn't think it would be under these stupid circumstances.

"Emphasis on the stupid part, Janny." She gives my head a patronizing pat.

"I have a good feeling about this, Nono, so you don't have to worry yourself sick about it."

"Great, we will shoot tomorrow at The Maloney Hotel pool." Samantha pockets her phone, only to dig it out seconds later with an incoming phone call. The projector announces the caller as *Vinnie,* his name decorated with a red heart and eggplant emoji.

A shower was much needed upon my return to the hotel; one, I was absolutely disgusting after training today and two, I had to sort out the situation in my pants brought on by Noelle sitting on my lap.

I take in my water soaked body, how the droplets perch on my muscular figure, set into motion with the tiniest of flexes. I've certainly changed in ten years, Noelle has too. Change is not a strong enough word to describe her transformation, she has evolved, as if Michael Angelo crafted her from marble himself and somehow the stone statue came to life. Now she casually roams around, unaware that she is the most heavenly looking being alive.

I consider myself pretty humble when it comes to my appearance, but based on what the media outlets portray, I definitely have something going for me in the looks department. I anticipate Noelle's swoon as I exit the bathroom, only to find her frozen in deep thought. Her ruby-hued brows arch downwards, making me think those thoughts are actually worries.

"Now, Nono, what could you possibly be worried about?"

She flinches back into motion, her fingers running over her keyboard, pretending she had been preoccupied the whole time.

"Noelle, don't deflect." I lean forward and close her laptop.

Noelle hisses, thrashing her laptop open again and pulling it away from me. "Rule number one; don't ever close an IT majors laptop unless you want to lose a limb. The one I have in mind is looking rather vulnerable under that towel, Hot Shot."

I lick my lips as she scowls at my crotch area. She scoffs, rolling her eyes, turning back to her computer and aggressively navigating her cursor.

"At least one of us is being vulnerable, you've had your guard up this whole time." I light-heartedly jab back.

She goes ahead and snaps her laptop shut for good, releasing an annoyed grunt. Gauging from her reaction she did not take the taunt with a light heart, I've appeared to have struck a nerve.

"I have to be on guard, January," she huffs.

"But you *don't* have to be," I emphasize, crawling my naked ass on the bed.

"You really are an out of touch moron." She shuffles herself off before I have time to embrace her. Composing herself, she gently lays her laptop on the desk, plugging in her charger. She exhales deeply, "I don't want to get hurt again."

I catch a glimpse of her vulnerability in the mirror's reflection.

"I know I have a long way to go earning your trust again, Noelle." I quickly rummage through the haphazard mess of my suitcase, slipping on boxer briefs. There is no way I am going to allow my wayward cock to discount the sincere statement I am about to say. With my junk safely tucked away, I cautiously approach Noelle. "But I promise you I have no intentions of hurting you."

Noelle's body tenses at my touch.

"Just like the first time," she whimpers. "That doesn't mean it didn't happen, even if it wasn't your intention. You still hurt me."

"I will continue to say sorry until it means something to you, even if that takes the rest of my life. I'll do anything for your forgiveness, Noelle, even endure your warfare, which for the record is completely one sided. I've already surrendered, I just want to make amends."

She turns from the mirror to me.

"Since when did you become the sentimental type?"

"Since I realized saving face is nowhere near as important as restoring what we had. If the world has to find out I'm secretly a big softy, I will gladly give up preserving my dignity if it means I can have your forgiveness."

"It's going to take a while to open my heart again, January. I don't think you realize how much you were my everything growing up. All the memories and fun we had were written off completely because of what you did. I didn't know who I was without you; it took me years to figure it out and build myself up again. So forgive me for trying to preserve *my* dignity."

"I completely understand. I won't rush you, and I'm sorry if I've been too forward. I want this to really work out for you. I'm taking advantage of the situation, hoping that you being forced to spend time with me will speed up the process of restoring our relationship. But my eagerness is only making you back further away from trusting me. So, I'm sorry."

"I forgive you partially, only because I'm to blame a little. My reservations about you are contributing to the implausibility of the stunt. Even Janelle says to make it look convincing, I need to open my heart a little."

Noelle's fingertips caress my palm, my lungs arrest in my chest at her touch.

"It feels like it's safe to open up a little." Noelle pulls her touch away. I chase it bringing her palm up and entangling our fingers.

"It is safe." I release my hold from her hand, easing up on my impatient advance. Noelle slips her fingers from my knuckles, feathering her touch on my palm. My eyes flutter shut, sinking into a guttural moan. My soul fills with a tender comforting only she can provide. Her hot breath hits my lips, I train the frantic energy inside of me into still composure.

My hands are itching to feel Noelle up but knowing that would completely invalidate everything she just vulnerably shared with me, I keep my yearning touch at bay. I'm listening, I want her to know through my actions that my words aren't empty. I am listening.

My good behavior rewards me with a kiss, her breathing shudders upon the connection. I caress my thumb over her pulse to tame her throbbing heartbeat, which is very much contributing to this blissful make out. Our lips part in unison and it sends my heart into an excited giddy. We are back in rhythm, just like old times. This kiss is dripping with nostalgia, I'm transported back to the rooftop of her lodge. Her cinnamon scent is all-encompassing, her moans sweet and airy. There's always this build up when we kiss, it's like I'm on a rollercoaster on an incline, my stomach twisting as I anticipate the drop. The carriage finally reaches the peak and then we finally brave the fall together.

My body lurches forward as our lips disconnect, I quickly gather my bearings.

"What happened?" I inspect Noelle first in case any medical attention may be required, the only thing wounded is her expression.

"I got scared," she meekly admits.

"Oh, Nono." I pull Noelle into a tight hug. That's enough opening up for tonight.

Fifteen

Teenage Dream

Noelle

I feel more exposed than ever and not because I'm wearing the tiniest of bikinis right now, but because my revenge plot has been foiled when I opened up to January last night. Now he is fully aware of my plans to take his emotions for a joyride, which was only making mine more confusing to understand. So now I must take my vengeance in a more practical sense. I pull the cap of the sharpie off with my teeth, carefully maneuvering my weight so as not to disturb January from his deep slumber.

I test his reaction by running my thumb over his lips; he doesn't stir, but he does pucker them.

"Kiss me," he mumbles sleepily. I wait a few moments, anticipating to be struck with his hypnotic stare. He rolls onto his back and I'm certain I'll be caught red-handed. "Princess." He clicks his tongue, resting his hands on his belly, wearing a content smile. Snores slip from him only seconds later.

"Thank you for the advantage, Janny." I lean forward and scrub the marker on his chin, fashioning him with a horrendous goatee. I'm glad January shaves his pretty face, it makes for the perfect canvas for my devious prank. With a flourish, I curl the sharpie and decorate his upper lip with the most ridiculous mustache.

You're really pulling off that mustache, Nono.

I freeze as the memory echoes in my head. Me, sat across from January at Cocomo, daringly playing footsies under the table. We'd talk about absolute nonsense, games, movies, guests. Whatever we could talk about, we talked about in great lengths. It has always been so easy to open up to January. I've always been inherently chatty, but the act of having a casual conversation with him feels way more intimate than with anyone else. Maybe it is how he actively listens. Although I would take up most of the conversational space. Whenever January got his word in, it was always to ask questions to expand on what I was already passionately rambling about.

I haven't had that kind of space to talk nonsense since. I have Janelle and Candy, but I often feel like the odd one out, but it's not their fault. They have been friends with each other much longer than I have with both of them. So, it's only natural that they will have inside jokes I don't understand or know each other like the back of their hands.

Just like how I was with January, we used to be so in tune with one another.

"Morning, Princess," January croaks.

I scream, flinching away from my destructive masterpiece, the evidence of the sharpie gets lost in the thick of the sheets. January pulls me close to his side, he hums approvingly as his fingers tangle with the knot of my bikini on the nape of my neck.

"Is this a dream or are you actually here wearing the sexiest bikini I've ever seen?"

I bite back my snickers; he looks extra ridiculous with his penned on facial hair and the stupid sleazy grin he's wearing.

"Wait until you see what you're wearing." I gnaw at my knuckles; it's way more difficult than I thought to stifle my laughter. His eyebrows animate skywards.

"Right, matchy matchy." He tosses the sheets aside. "At least we'll look stupidly in love."

"Oh, you look stupid, alright." That's it, I can't contain myself any longer. I fall backwards onto the mattress, kicking my feet about as I laugh bombastically.

"Is it really that amusing?" January combs his hair. I've clearly struck at his ego with how his gaze retreats with embarrassment.

My gut is turning sore with how hard I'm laughing.

"It's got you in absolute hysterics." My breath hitches when I feel his large muscular form press against me. My penmanship on his face is no deterrent for my arousal, I feel my pussy clench and then release on my inconvenient moan. "I love hearing you laugh, even if it is at the expense of my humility."

I really ought to be turned off right now, but I wouldn't mind kissing his handsome vandalized face. I lick my lips and he gets the hint, softly pressing his lips into mine. My eyes roll back as I run my palm over his feathering shoulder blades, this guy is built like a fucking tank.

I catch onto my indulgence, nudging him back with a soft knee into his washboard abs. *Dear god, he is hot.*

"I think we should save the kissing for the cameras." I say in a panic.

"What's on your face?" January completely bypasses my excuse, caressing his thumb over my cheek and then transferring it to his. He wipes the back of his hand across his upper lip, smearing my masterpiece. "Noelle." My stomach sloshes as he scolds me on a hiss, scrubbing vigorously at his face as he makes his way to the mirror. "Good prank, Princess."

"They don't call me the Princess of Pranks for nothin'."

"This will come off, right? Samantha is going to be fuming when she sees me like this."

"Only a face a mother could love."

"Why not a face my future wife can love?" He wiggles his brows and I'm wishing I'd penned those, too.

"Get ready, Hot Shot. Samantha is ready to plaster us all over the internet looking like a pair of clowns." I snort, tossing him the bag containing his clown uniform for this sponsorship. This bikini is truly horrific. The team over at Castaway Swimwear are trying way too hard to revive the 2000s aesthetic. Chucking everything and the kitchen sink from that era into this very minimal amount of material. I'm wearing rhinestoned lime-green hibiscuses with crochet-woven straps. Which January apparently considers the sexiest thing from the way he is drooling. I knew he lived a sheltered life at the resort, but this monstrosity is the biggest turn off I've ever laid my eyes on.

"These are kind of cool." January echoes from the bathroom.

I look from fidgeting with the low waistband of my bikini bottoms. He walks out and, just as I suspected, a huge lady boner killer.

"Please tell me you're being sarcastic."

"Obviously, Nono, we look ridiculous."

"Phew, I was thinking we both had poor taste. You with swimwear, me with men."

"So, I'm your *taste*, huh?" January toys with the crochet bow at my hip.

"Grow up, Janny." I nudge him away.

"Says the woman who drew on my face with marker while I was sleeping. That's amateur level stuff, Nono."

"I'm rusty," I whine.

"It's okay, you're still the reigning Princess of Pranks." January pulls my head into his chest. I don't fight it. I just want to stay here a little and listen to his pattering heartbeat.

"Samantha said to meet her at the pool at 7am," I meekly say into January's pectorals, I almost give into my urge to make out with his muscles.

"Let's do this, I guess," January says with a sigh, pulling me to the elevator, but not without giving me a noogie first.

"Hey." I shove him off me and run into the elevator, abusing the close button before he could slip in.

"Too slow, Nono." His voice drips with pompous, my nostrils flare as I let out a huff. I look up to find myself caged in his body, I'm not completely opposed to being his prisoner in this moment. My heart is thundering in my chest as he looks at me like I'm the hotel's complimentary breakfast.

He licks his lips, "You look really good."

I gasp, "So you can give compliments."

"Can you finally take them?" I watch the thick of saliva run down his throat, I'm surprised he has any to swallow considering he's basically drooling on me.

"You two look so..." Samantha's voice booms, I only just register the elevator doors have opened, a waft of chlorine fills the space. "Good," she finishes with a nervous gulp.

"Thank you, Samantha." I accept the fake compliment with pure pageantry, sucking my teeth smugly as I shoot January a taunting wink. He scrunches his nose in detest.

"I really should've looked into their stuff before I subjected you two to this." Samantha rakes her eyes over us, gritting her teeth.

"Really, tacky swimwear is where your ethics lie, but arranged marriage is no problem," January sulks.

"Oh, relax, Janny, we get to spend our day working in the sun." I embrace the warmth of the sun as it hugs at my skin, more like claws at my skin. "I have to use sunscreen before I burn to a crisp."

Samantha gives her acrylic nails a satisfying snap, "Oh, Cameron, put the lotion on her."

"Meticulous application is imperative, Samantha, I will look like a tomato if it is not done properly."

"Touch her *everywhere* is what I'm hearing, Cameron." Samantha motions her hands in an hourglass figure. "You have quite the ass on you, girl."

"Is that where you suggest we start?" I wheeze, I can already feel the sun biting at my flesh, it feels like it's pinching at every individual skin cell beneath my skin.

"Vinnie and I can show you." Samantha flourishes her kaftan to reveal January's team captain laying leisurely on a pool lounge chair, glossed to the heavens with tanning lotion. "Oh, you're so sexy, babe." She blows him an air kiss, Vinnie's hand flies up from his statuesque pose, catching her kiss in a fist and palming at his crotch. "Behave yourself, mister."

"God, they are worse than when they came to the lodge scouting you," I turn to January and gag.

"Because they weren't married yet, I'm pretty sure they weren't even dating." January is also wearing an expression of repulsion. "What's a bet that they fell in love at Darlington Snow Paradise?"

Lord knows, I fell in love hard at the ski lodge. It's just one of those places that has that effect on people, its secluded environment makes it swell with romantic intimacy. Makes it all the easier to focus on your partner. Darlington Snow Paradise has so much going for it already, it just needs the exposure. I'm reminded of why I am enduring this humility—*although I'm really pushing the limits of my humility today*—it's all to save *home*.

"Are you kids even watching?" Samantha scolds January and I. "Great, now Vinnie has to lather me up again."

"Gladly." Vinnie bites at his lip, I can even make out the hungry glint behind his darkly tinted sunglasses.

"No, they'll do it. Here." Samantha tosses the bottle of sunscreen to January. "Go make yourselves look coupley over on that lounge over there." She dismisses us with a flick of her acrylic nails.

I turn to January with a shrug, "I need to get that stuff on me fast."

"You can do it. I've messed up enough." January defeatedly holds the bottle for me to take.

"Gee, January, that may be true, but no need to be a downer." I pop the cap and lather myself.

"HE WAS SUPPOSED TO DO IT!" Samantha calls from across the pool.

"Can't you read, the sign says no yelling!" January retorts by ironically yelling, gesturing to the sign instructing guests; *no running, no diving, no yelling, no foul language.*

"Whatever," Samantha huffs, "you put it on him."

My nipples become sensitive to the fact I will get to touch January's heavenly-sculptured body. *Too bad the sign doesn't say no gawking.*

"Get handsy, Nono." January flashes a smile that feels like a hot summer's day. *Jesus, it's warm out.* I fan my hand over my face to cool myself. "You're getting all hot and bothered at the thought of it."

"It's just hot, Janny," I strain out, my vision sheens over.

"You're hot."

"Another compliment."

"No, I'm asking, are you too hot?" January presses his palm to my forehead. I swat his touch away as it only raises the temperature within my bloodstream.

I slop a heavy gloop of sunscreen in my palm and transfer to January's chest with a haphazard slap.

"That is quite the technique you've got there, Princess." He smiles hypnotically again.

Stop smiling, you're making my heart race.

"Yeah, get all up in there, Noelle, *feel* me—" I plant my palm hard against January's chest. With all the strength I can muster, I push this pillar of a man into the pool.

Water sprinkles my ankles, confirming the success of my attack. My vision clears and I can now indulge in the sight of a wet January. Which is anything but a humorous sight, but to keep my mind from settling on naughtier thoughts. I laugh at his soggy fate implemented by me.

My breath hitches when he smooths his hair back with his palm. I've never seen his eyes beam so brightly in direct sunlight. They are even more heart-palpitation-inducingly gorgeous when they glitter mischievously.

"Laugh now, Nono, but here's payback." January's hands grip around my wrists.

My toes grip at the slippery tiles that edge the pool, trying to fight off January's pull on me. I scream only for my lungs to fill with water suddenly; I emerge to the surface, coughing.

"You okay?" Not only is January's tender voice anchoring, but his brawny arm snaking around my waist keeps me from drowning.

"Give me a minute," I pinch out, my nostrils are clogged with water. January withdraws his hold on me slightly, his eyes scan with severe worry. I seize the opportunity, planting both my hands on the crown of his head and pushing him under water.

I thrash about to make my escape, swimming backwards to anticipate his counterattack.

He breaks to the surface, locking eyes with me, determination in his gaze. He stalks to me in a lurking swim, lowering himself so only his eyes remain above the water. I can't stop giggling girlishly, this is all so much fun. My stomach is doing somersaults as he chases me down around the pool.

I can't help but wonder if I let myself get caught by him. I stop my back-stroking arms. January collects me in a full embrace, he yields himself, fighting against the current he created. I'm gently pressed up against the wall of the pool. It's all quite stimulating, between the water jet massaging between my legs and January enfolded around me.

I wrap my legs around his waist, donning a flirtatious smirk. My heart is thundering in my chest and my pussy is throbbing between my legs. We exchange hard-hitting hot breaths, staring intensely at the others' lips.

January rubs his nose against mine before pressing a tame kiss against my lips.

"I want to preface this question with the fact that you can say no, but—"

"Yes, I want to have sex," I slip out thinly.

"Huh?"

"I'm so horny right now," I whisper into January's ear, I pull back to find him wearing the most adorable expression of awe.

"Turn more to me, I can't tell if you're kissing or not." Samantha's voice makes my horniness falter. I had completely forgotten about the sponsorship obligations. I'd been so caught up in the fun I was having with January. Which I hope will develop into more adult fun when we return to the apartment.

"Kiss for the camera." I shoot him a flirtatious wink. "Do as I say, and you might get a reward later." January's eyes animate with surprise, his palm runs along my cheek before embracing me in a kiss. I can feel myself playing up for the cameras, disconnecting me from the bliss of the kiss. I feel the climbing sensation that comes with kissing January, Samantha's incessant photo snapping fades out as I take the freefall into the kiss.

"Perfect, that'll do you two."

I go to pull away, but January hungrily pinches my lip with his teeth, pulling back into the kiss.

"Is he hurting you, Angelface, blink twice if you're in danger?"

I'm so far from being in danger, I may just be diving into complete safety. January feels like a sanctuary to me right now.

"That looks so unpleasant, it's like you're Cameron's hostage."

I push back at Samantha's comment.

"Is that really how it reads?" I pant.

"Yes, are you even enjoying yourself?" Samantha looks at me, disturbed.

I turn back to January, "yeah, I was, actually."

"Your face was all screwed up like this." Samantha demonstrates the unpleasant expression. It's hard to believe that's what my face was doing, I felt like I was melting from within.

"Who cares, you got the shot, right?" January gnaws at his cheek impatiently; his touch is even electric underwater. My libido returns in a flash, my thighs squeeze tighter around January's waist, begging him to take me back to the apartment. Honestly, just take me in this pool.

"I'm sure I have something here."

"Great." January hoists himself and me from the water, coming to a stand and walking us up the steps of the pool. Completely bypassing the towels, making us a complete hazard to the next person to use the elevator as we drip everywhere. I'm pretty sure the wetness between my thighs is not pool water.

I tug at the bow knotted around my neck; the fabric pressed against my hard nipples falls loose, freeing my breast. January engulfs his face into the cushions, moaning in a shuddering breath.

"Fuck, I get so hard for you, Noelle." His nose nuzzles into my neck, my fingers instinctively thread through his hair. My head spins as he lowers me to the mattress. I am so enchanted with lust I didn't even feel the whirlwind of the usually nauseating elevator ride.

"January, take me back."

"Huh, to the pool?"

"No," I breathe out. "To that night, take me back to that magical moment and right your wrongs."

"Couldn't have put it better myself. Allow me to take you places, Noelle."

Ugh, what a perfect thing to say. My legs spread invitingly, the crochet bows spring loose at January's hasting hands, he tilts my pelvis upwards to dispose of the wet material.

"Yes, January." Here I am, completely naked underneath January once again, but it feels like the first time. I want it to *feel* like the first time. "Take me back," I rasp. "I hope you remember what you did."

"I replayed that day over and over every night as I laid in bed. I remember everything from the way you sounded to the way you smelled, even the way you *felt.*"

I melt on a moan, surrendering my body to the pounding arousal that is begging to be released.

January peels my body from the mattress, the memory of me perched on his waist comes rushing back. My breasts tickle at his neck as we indulge in a sloppy kiss, reminiscent of our first few kisses tangled in my bed sheets back at the lodge. Completely driven by adrenaline and lust. I want to bring that energy to the here and now.

I slip my tongue into January's mouth, just like I had done that night, eager to experience all of his pent-up love for me.

"January."

"Noelle." He drives his bulge into my throbbing heat. He really does remember, that's why it's no surprise when he flips me over again in a flurry of passion. He plants his palms beside my shoulders and artfully rolls his hips into me. "Noelle." He repeats on a hiss. "I'm so hard."

He followed that sentence with *I don't know what I'm doing.* But that is definitely not the case now, he knows exactly what he is doing.

"Let's go slow."

"Yeah," I exhale.

January drops to his elbow, my core trembles as our bodies slot together.

"January," I hiccup. "I want you inside me."

He silences my yearning with a deep, sustained kiss; we break when I whine at his tender petting at my sensitive clit.

"Oh, fuck," he gutturally purrs in my ear.

"Yes!" I yelp, my body writhing against his, pleading for more friction. Preferably internal.

January slips a finger inside.

"Oh Noelle, you want me, don't you?" That's him going off script but I'm not completely mad, this still has a very living in the moment kind of vibe.

"I—" I choke. "I want you, Janny."

January pulls his fingers from inside me, pushing them back in once again. My back bows into him, our skins are mutually hot and sticky. He speeds his punctures, my nails claw at the sheets.

"Does that hurt?" he asks so tenderly.

"Feels so good, don't stop."

January nods, continuing the fingering, only this time he moves his thumb to my clit for extra simulation. My entrance flexes around his exiting fingers, my thighs threatening to squeeze together. He ignites our kiss instead of hyper fixating on every minute reaction; he knows my body like the back of his hand and can puppeteer it with just two—

"Three!" I bark at the additional pleasure.

Correction: three fingers.

"It seemed like you wanted it," January justifies with a devious grin.

"I would prefer a certain other limb if I'm completely honest." I jerk upwards when he audibly peels from my skin, running his fingers covered in my moisture through his mouth. His other hand cupping at his bulge, moaning as he tastes me.

"You taste so fucking good, Princess."

Fuck, that is so hot, my core is melting. My thighs snap together as my core convulses.

Am I orgasming?

My legs pry apart, I feel myself fill completely.

January has inserted himself amidst my orgasm, growing it tenfold with his zealous thrusts.

"Oh fuck, this never gets old." January bites down on his jaw hard, bucking forward. "Noelle!" He roars.

"No need to shout, I'm right here." My ears ring as his bark echoes throughout the apartment.

"You're right fucking here," he whimpers, his fervent thrusts slow to sensual rolls. "You're right fucking here."

"Say it one more time, just for good luck." I taunt in a giggle.

"You're." January charges his hips. "Right." I quiver at the next charge, and even though I expected the next one, it still hits me like an internal earthquake. "Fucking." I come undone completely, January joins me as I feel his length spilling within me. He collapses on top of me, enveloping me as he slips out. "Here."

Sixteen

It's All For Charity

January

"You two need to get it together!" Samantha's voice tears through my hypnosis, like she dug those razor-sharp claws into my mental projector displaying the picture of my angelic Noelle, a heavenly essence of someone well rested and in good health. Well, she looked that way before Samantha startled her and painted her skin a sickly green. "Do you know how much is riding on this sponsor?"

"What do you mean, I'm sure we were plenty convincing yesterday?" I scoot over on the bench, closing the space between Noelle and I. "Our very convincing performance continued behind closed doors." I lick my lips and give Noelle a wink, one she entirely misses as her gaze remains locked on the rink.

"Am I to believe you went back to the apartment and braided each other's hair and had pillow fights, because all you can take away from these photos is that you are old friends? Look at the caption!" Samantha wails, shoving her phone to me.

Commemorate your long-lasting childhood friendship by matching outfits from those nostalgic times.

And pictured above was a photo of Noelle pushing me into the pool, her smile looks infectious, I'm even smiling too.

"You should be happy you finally got a photo of me smiling, in fact, thank Noelle."

Noelle resembles the outfit of those *nostalgic times*, her skin a sickly key lime hue, her beads of sweat glimmer like rhinestones.

Samantha's berating fades as my concern for Noelle amplifies.

"You've made my job even harder with this whole *friendly* mess." Noelle just sits there and takes it. She appears to be far away in thought, but I know she's absorbing Samantha's unnecessary reprimanding. She cowardly trembles in her flushed skin, which is so unlike her.

She was never scared of a little scolding; she never batted an eyelid whenever Mrs. Donovan would come down on her after a successful prank. She was even brave enough to challenge the old lady with a snarky retort.

But now, Noelle looks sicklier than ever.

"Seriously, you know there's going to be a media presence today and you guys can't even pull off a convincing enough kiss," Samantha's grating vocal fry feeds into my senses again. "You're lucky no one cares about the charity match, but this has to be corrected by the charity gala, the people love spectacle and sparkle. The cameras will be on you two, dressed to the nines. I expect your relationship to look just as dazzling."

Noelle's lashes flutter as they strain to remain open, her brows pinching together tightly.

"I don't care what you do behind closed doors, whether you're just friends, or you fuck, or are sworn enemies, but it has to look more than friendly to the masses."

A small whimper leaves Noelle's lips, which I'm sure everybody but me missed.

"Do you guys even like each oth—"

"That's enough, Samantha." I cut her off curtly, holding my palm out as a visual signal. I do all of this with my eyes still trained on Noelle. "Noelle, are you okay?" I carefully press my palm between her shoulder blades, it's instinctive for her to trustfully surrender her weight.

I've got you, Nono.

"See, that's great, it just needs a little more love and tenderness, then an interaction like this would be plenty convin—"

"Samantha, make yourself useful and get her some ice water," I order bitterly, executing a glare the exact opposite of love and tenderness. My features soften from their rigidness with a familiar feathery touch at my jawline, I surrender to Noelle's *love and tenderness.*

It's all me, I'm the unconvincing one. I haven't shown softness in a decade, not since Noelle was erased from my life.

But she's here now, I can be me again.

"Cameron, cameras, kiss her," Samantha whispers, her discretion voided when her inconspicuous cupped hands megaphone the instruction. A crew of men come stumbling into the arena lugging film equipment, huge cameras that will catch Noelle and I's undeniable love for one another.

I turn my attention back to Noelle, her glassy eyes drop to my lips, parting in effect to catch what little breath she can manage in her fatigued state.

There's no way I'm kissing her like this.

"Kiss her," Samantha hisses.

"I'm not going to kiss you, Nono."

"Please...kiss me...January...kiss me." Her breathing becomes more haggard with her exerted effort.

"Sorry, Nono, you could pass out. I can't kiss you." I finesse my fingers between hers and press her knuckles softly to my lips, she watches with bated breath. "Breathe, Nono."

She wheezes upon her inhale; her gaze trailing behind my shoulder. I'm hoping she's locked eyes with a refreshing bottle of water if Samantha knows what's good for her.

"*Upon-A-Star*," Noelle slips out weakly. She swallows a dry gulp and I'm wondering why no one has given this poor woman a bottle of water. "I didn't know you were working with the *Upon-A-Star* foundation?"

I stop myself from pursuing my witch hunt on Samantha when I catch Noelle's icy blue eyes intimately; they sparkle like sun-beamed snow. It's the most magnificent sight I've seen in years.

"Yes, the *Upon-A-Star* foundation. They help terminally ill kids by fulfilling their wishes."

"I love working with the *Upon-A-Star* foundation, I've never worked with them on such a large scale before. Mostly privately with small donations, but not since Janelle has *matured* my image a little." Noelle gives a modest shrug.

Of course, I'm aware of the philanthropic work Noelle is involved in. Only Samantha is unfortunately right, nobody cares about public figures being charitable, and the masses favor scandal and infamy.

"You've always been such a giving person, Noelle."

She was always overworking herself at the lodge to ensure everyone's experience was satisfactory. Now it's my turn to be hospitable.

Noelle dives her head forward and for a moment I think she's going to kiss me, only her hot breath tickles my ear.

"January, I'm conflicted now, I don't want to make this about us, it should be about the charity. But Samantha is going to hand our asses to us if we don't start being convincing."

I pull back, Noelle's conflicting morals show with crystalline clarity in her eyes, her bottom lip quivering.

"Are you about to cry?" I hate how it rolls off my tongue so insensitively.

"No." Noelle sniffs, composing herself quickly, giving her lash line a subtle swipe.

"Sorry, Princess, that came out a lot more bitter than I liked." I really am out of practice with showing softness, I have got to pull it together. Noelle doesn't need to worry about my unrefined communication skills on top of everything else. I can tell her head is a fucking blizzard of *what ifs* and ways this could all go terribly wrong. Even though the metaphorical ice beneath is definitely cracking, and here we are doing our best to look convincing, yet we just don't.

It's getting to Noelle, and all I want to do is put that infectious smile back on her face.

Go show the world that enduring four years of braces was all worth it.

Next to come flooding through the door is a bundle of excited kids of many ages, ranging from preschool to teenagers. A soft smile grows on Noelle's lips at the sight of the joyful bunch.

"Did you want to sit with the nurses and the kids? You can finally work with them on *such a large scale*." I ask. I don't understand Samantha's plan for Noelle, but Noelle's correct, we don't need to be overly affectionate today. It was quite a selfless consideration on her part, and that is the girl I fell in love with. It's comforting to know that part of her didn't diminish when I broke her heart. Although she emphasizes that this stunt benefits her, I am willing to be exploited if it secures stability for Noelle. She's entitled to a little selfishness, she is always running herself to the point of burnout for others.

"I'd love to talk to the nurses and kids; I genuinely want to make this a great experience for them." Noelle meekly accepts. Her smile grows completely, I mirror the effulgence not able to contain my adoration.

"Okay, I'll take you there." I carefully lift Noelle from the seat and find a sea of blue puffer jackets sporting official-looking lanyards, with the bright yellow shooting star logo of *Upon-A-Star*.

"No way, you're @DarlingNoelle, I love your speed runs." A teen probably no more than 16, accompanied by an oxygen tank, perks up.

"Oh, you're a fan of mine?" Noelle perches herself beside the teenage boy, giving a small nod to the nurse in attendance with him.

"Sure am, I've even played the beta of The Battle of Blizzard."

The Battle of Blizzard made it out of Noelle's drive and into the masses. *She has so much to be proud of...I'm proud of her most, for picking herself up after I was the one to push her down the hardest and the furthest.*

I swallow my guilt. I'd much rather enjoy this connection Noelle is fostering with this sick boy, her finally getting the recognition she deserves.

"How easy is it to defeat the Yeti Master?" I indirectly poke at Noelle by asking the teen the question that I know will infuriate her.

"Just because you dropped your remote on accident that one time and somehow bypassed that level does not mean it is *easy to defeat.*" She crosses her arms with a huff, and her fiery locks slip loose from her messy bun.

"You are so cute, Nono." I bonk the faltering bundle of red.

"Janny, you're such a tosser." She tugs her hair free, and a strangled sound leaves the teen's mouth. At first, I fret, thinking I'm going to have to wave the nurse from her not-so-discreet perv on Aaron Nightingale's ass and potentially perform CPR. "Oh, sorry, I didn't mean to swear."

"You are so hot." The boy heaves dryly.

"Huh?" Noelle pinches through her teeth, the elastic perched there. I'm mesmerized by how her delicate fingers weave through that desert-colored mass. Her jawline and neck look so kissable, I can vaguely make out the faint bruises from my hickeys.

"Can you and Janelle start an OnlyFans? I'd subscribe."

And Noelle is so fucking out of here. Her fingers are still busy with smoothing out the knots of her auburn locks, I think she might have been oblivious to the inappropriate comment.

"If I were you, kid, I'd make a different wish," I grit through my teeth.

Terminally ill or not, no one is talking to my girlfriend like that.

"I'm going to the bathroom, Janny, come with me." My teeth unclench at Noelle's invitation. I toddle behind her as she releases her locks once again, strutting only a few feet ahead of me.

I'm no better than the kid as my eyes drop to her plush ass in those jeans.

"Simp." I hear the teenage boy mock quickly under his breath.

Whatever, I don't care. I am a simp for Noelle.

She slips into the ladies' bathroom, I almost blindly follow her in.

The kid is right, I'm a huge simp.

The wooden door whips open and Noelle comes out sporting a perky ponytail, with a few strands loose to frame her pretty freckled face.

She's just so effortlessly beautiful, I want to kiss—

My thoughts are interrupted when my wish becomes a reality. I didn't think I was eligible for Noelle's charity, but I sure am enjoying her philanthropy.

I press her against a set of lockers, the tinny thrash makes her jump with fright like she was caught in a compromising situation, only then does she slowly give in to her vulnerability.

I know Samantha would adore what we're doing right now; it *feels* so real and raw, I can only imagine what it *looks* like.

But I don't ponder what Samantha fucking adores. I return my undivided adoration to Noelle.

"Janny."

My heart is pounding so loudly along with hers; I can taste her buttery pulse in my throat as our tongues dance in each other's mouths.

My gloves act as an inconvenient barrier to touching Noelle's searing skin, but it doesn't stop me from journeying my hand up the jersey Samantha had given her to wear.

She's wearing my name, along with my number 10. Soon it'll be her actual name.

I love you, Noelle Snow.

"Camer—well, I guess that settles the question; you do like each other."

I stiffen at that haunting vocal fry. I'm not sure why, this is just the predicament Samantha is dying to find me in.

"The game is about to start and you're busy making out. Could you at least do it in front of the many cameras?"

"I'm being discreet today to avoid distracting from the true purpose." Noelle's wispy voice leaves me hypnotized; I cling to her as Samantha tugs at the back of my jersey. *I just want to stay here with you, Noelle.* "But we can't afford to go a day without practice." She shoots me a wink and I am putty in her hand.

We don't need practice; we have nailed kissing to a masterful degree. It feels incredible when I kiss Noelle; I don't understand why it doesn't translate in photographs. If that's the case, I should request Samantha to organize an interview where I will talk in great lengths about what kissing Noelle Winter Darlington *feels* like.

It always starts off cautionary, which is probably what the public is perceiving as unpleasant, but it never stays cautious for too long. Noelle will part her lips granting me permission to up the ante, but I always keep tabs on her wellbeing at all points during this subtle transition. Our mingling breaths will become hotter and harder, the tentativeness melting away with each exhale. Each heartbeat marks a measure of time until time itself momentarily ceases to exist. Like we have reached a high summit, we pause, take in the view, or in this case I check in on her once again. I allow Noelle to direct us through the unraveling of our passion.

Which she appears to flake on as of late, her worries about the stunt are clearly a hindrance to her letting go.

But yesterday, boy, yesterday was incredibly intimate and raw. Not just the sex, but the emotional connection we were undeniably sharing was magical. A beautiful elevation of all that we built as teenagers, coming together with the testing trials of this stunt, and flowering in a moment of unity.

I don't even register that I'm gliding on the ice until I bump into Aaron at the goal. How the hell did I end up here? I play as a forward. I shake from my trance, only for my jersey to choke on my neck.

"Bro, has Noelle mentioned anything about Janelle mentioning anything about me?" Aaron pants in my ear.

"What?" I spit irritably. I'm having great difficulty focusing on this conversation when all I can think about is yesterday. This is going to be my best game, or possibly my worst.

"You know, has Janelle mentioned anything to Noelle—"

"Get off me, Nightingale." I shake the goalie and his sweltering hot breath from my shoulder, taking my rightful position on the right of the center.

"Go Janny!" My attention snaps to a little girl with lopsided pigtails, sitting on Noelle's lap, holding up a very crafty Phoenix Badgers sign. The logo resembles more of a cat, but it doesn't bother me all that much.

The sight of Noelle waving about a makeshift green, white, and black pom-pom has me too enchanted to even care. She leans forward and whispers into the girl's ear.

"Janny, stop staring at your princess and play some hockey!" The girl's volume borderlines on shrill. Noelle winces at the preschooler.

Only when the puck passes me in a flash, do I recognize what Noelle's indirect request is.

My wish is your command, Princess.

A surge of energy strikes through my veins as it only takes me seven seconds from the puck going from Vinnie's stick to mine, and from my stick to the corner of the net in a clean, striking motion.

Fuck, that might just be my best shot to date. I'm convinced it's because my Princess is here.

The cheering from the crowd is thunderous considering the demographic consists mostly of those with bad lungs, including Noelle, who is up on her feet jumping about excitedly.

I'm immediately transported to our youth, when she would spring victoriously from the snow, every time I secured a shot in the makeshift goal we made from branches of fallen pine trees.

After exerting such intense ecstasy, she would slump back down into the snow, pinching her reeling head.

All the air in my lungs escapes in a snap, as I watch my Princess fall to the ground, disappearing behind the barricade.

My blades are quick into motion, I don't even care if it allows the rivaling team to retrieve the puck and score an identical shot to my own.

My Princess needs saving.

Seventeen

Cold As Ice

Noelle

Samantha's words continued to eat at my mind once I had come down from my spell, and my concern only continued to amplify when the weird kid hit on me. Although something as mundane as wrestling my hair into a ponytail had really worn me out, I caught sight of my pinkened cheeks.

January has only kept his teasing as friendly, just as we discussed, but even that friendly teasing has always been flirty to some extent. I advised we keep it only to our subtle flirtations because I didn't want to overshadow the true cause.

But it was *too* friendly. It needed work, so I flubbed an excuse to use the bathroom, thankfully January's dignity was so far down the toilet he followed me unabashedly.

All in the name of practicing this dynamic, the real spectacle is only a week away and if we're so friendly to where teenage boys think they can shoot their shot, we're in huge trouble.

I'll admit it's terrifying being vulnerable with January again, I don't know if I can fully trust him. But I have to overcome this restraint I keep enforcing. I'm only trying to protect my heart, I can slowly feel myself involuntarily falling for him again. I don't know whether to consider yesterday's unraveling of shenanigans as a moment of weakness or a step towards success. It felt amazing to surrender to January yesterday. Our playful dynamic was growing more and more enticing the more we taunted and jabbed, I couldn't help but fall into bed with him. My god, the sex was mind-blowing; it had all the nostalgic magic to it as well as elements of surprise that had my toes curling and my heart racing dangerously fast. I would've accepted death at that moment, finally reaching peak sexual satisfaction after ten long years of waiting. And sure, we had our little fun at the lodge, but that doesn't even compare to yesterday.

The instincts in us bubbled to the surface, the familiarity of each other's bodies settled in and we went from making waves in the pool to making waves in bed.

We were so vulnerable, so *us*. Yesterday was reminder after reminder of why I fell for my best friend.

But he seems to fight some push and pull too, although that all disappears once his hands are on me, exploring my body as much as a man at a children's charity sports game can before his publicist finds us.

But we had to practice, because how can very obvious foreplay not be convincing enough and still misconstrued as friendly?

It's been nice kissing January. His lips are surprisingly soft, perhaps because he never cracks a smile. His touch is always so attentive and gentle. I can feel the passion radiating from his palms, even through his dense gloves. His hot kiss is like a promise of satisfaction once it was safe to do so.

Any moment kissing January is always going to be one I remember.

Although I remember little of the game, it almost felt like I dreamed it. I can envision green, white, and black streamers in my peripherals, and an excitable little girl in my face, and then suddenly my vision spots.

It comes back to me in a flood.

I fainted.

How bloody embarrassing, no doubt that'll make the headlines and overshadow the Phoenix Badgers doing a good deed in working with the *Upon-A-Star* foundation.

My phone is the first thing I reach for after rolling over. I halt as my tits almost engulf January's face. I shuffle further up, fetching my phone from the nightstand before turning away from January, reestablishing the spooning position.

January's throat releases a hum that makes my core vibrate, his palm splaying on my hip, his thumb circling on my thigh.

It's all quite lovely and tender.

I recognize my face has unlocked my phone and has led me straight to the headline I feared most.

Cameron Snow's attempt at being more charitable and less cynical, Noelle Darlington, the first ever Upon-A-Star adult. Complete fail! Click here for more details.

"Oh god," I whisper in the hopes of not alarming January.

I've been demoted from beloved childhood friend to pitiful charity case. Samantha will not like this.

I flinch as I am disarmed of my phone.

"Forget those stupid wannabe gossip accounts." January muffles into my shoulder. My throat goes tight. "Noelle, I can see you're worried about something."

I turn over to face January, it's completely unfair how good he looks with bedhead, always has, and probably always will. Even with the addition of the faint icy streaks sprouting from his hairline. He'll probably lose his hair in the next ten years at this rate, and maybe that's all the revenge I need. Portraying ourselves as a convincing couple is far more important than my petty grudge. I guess this is me waving my white flag in the hopes of more heart-palpitating orgasms.

"No one believes that we're in love." I pout.

"This is all my fault, Nono." January rolls onto his back. I gawk at his buff pectorals.

I don't necessarily disagree that he is not to blame for this unusual circumstance we find ourselves in, but I don't entirely agree that it's all his fault.

"Go on." I bite back my mischievous smirk, keen to hear him beat himself up. Call me a sadist, but I think hearing him being hard on himself may be the treatment my aching heart needs right now.

He runs his hands down his face, wiping away his temporary smile.

"It's my fault, I guess all that time hiding my feelings for you as a teen is still trained into me like muscle memory. I always ensured that my intentions were friendly. If only I could switch it off and just let my heart open up completely, we might actually pull this off. But I'm nothing but a prickly tosser. Or I'm an over eager psychopath."

January's internal struggle reads completely in his features. He's trying to be patient with my forgiveness, but also resisting his old stoic ways.

On second thought, this is only making my heart tear further in two.

"It doesn't help that I haven't been soft with anyone in a decade. It hurts to smile, like that's not normal. What am I even mad at? Well, I'm mad at myself for messing things up with you. I should've stayed, I should've fought harder for you."

"January, stop." I cup my hand over his mouth, his cerulean eyes widen as he is suffocated. He pries my hand from his lips, entwining them with his fingers, pulling my weight closer to him. My head nuzzles between the eye candy I was only perving on moments ago. His muscles, although firm, make for a comfortable cushion. "You're not completely to blame, Janny. It's my fault too, I still have my reservations about that day, but I want this to work. I need this to work for the sake of my parents and my future."

"Our future." January corrects me, squeezing my hand.

Those words act as a metaphorical dressing for my wounded heart. I can almost feel the bandage restricting tightly around my heart, now thrashing and pumping against it frantically.

"You would stay with me and help me run Darlington Snow Paradise?"

"It's what I should've done all along. This Hot Shot Pro Hockey Life isn't all it's cracked up to be, well, because you're not a part of it."

My breath hitches at his honest declaration. Does this mean he's surrendering too? Is that it? This vengeful war finally ends with his remorseful statement. It doesn't feel completely settled, my heart aches with the familiar pain once again. I'm definitely not over it; it's going to take a lot for January to resolve this.

"I was prepared to be..." the metaphorical bandage frays as the pain from the past resurfaces. "I was ready to follow you around blindly. My god, how stupid could I have been, you made me feel so stupid."

Perhaps a white flag is only at half mast, I still feel strongly about that day. One nostalgic day together is not going to cure the six years of friendship he invalidated in a matter of five minutes ten years ago.

Yet here I am, opening up my heart so easily, which will undoubtedly lead to me getting hurt again.

I shuffle quickly away from January, stripping back the sheets and rising from the bed. My world is quick to spin, I close my eyes only for the back of my eyelids to act as a projector sheet. The roll of film spinning too fast with images of that dreadful memory.

"Noelle, wait, I don't want to work you up."

"I'm fine." I wheeze as my throat tightens. For fuck's sake, throat, I need you to do the very opposite of that. I need oxygen to my heart, pronto.

With strangled whimpers and unsteady knees, I thread my arms into my hoodie. Pungent with a scent so familiar and haunting.

Vetiver.

I open my eyes to find January's warm-up hoodie on my body, my havoc panting breathes the badger logo to life.

"I need some fresh air." Fuck you January, for making me feel my emotions so irrationally and frankly, immaturely. Why did he have to make me care so much about him? Why couldn't he just care about me all those years ago?

"I'll come with you," January declares, I hear the bed creak as he lifts his weight off it. I shoot January a threatening glare, or at least I think I do, I can't quite pinpoint him as the room continues to spin. "Nono, come back to bed."

Oh, so you care now?

I use the acoustics of the apartment complex to find my way to the elevator in my dizzy state, heading in the direction away from January's voice and his overwhelming presence.

"I said, I need fresh air." My knees give in as I reach for the elevator button, thankfully the carpet is plush enough to stop my kneecaps from shattering. The doors part and I crawl my way in, pressing my back against the refreshingly cool mirror. It smells of lemon, no doubt recently cleaned by an overworked housekeeper.

Crap, I need to press the ground floor.

I groan as I peel my back from the heavenly cool surface.

"I've got it." January's voice fills the space of the elevator, giving me a headache that feels like my skull is being split in two. He has the decency to join me on the floor, as mad as I am with him, his shoulder is conveniently beside me. Even his shoulder is quite comfy and surprisingly, just as muscly as his pectorals. The air conditioning is bliss in this tiny box, only the sensation is counteracted by the nauseating descending motion.

"Ground floor." The elevator announces.

I groan.

"Don't move, I'm going to carry you."

"Don't make such a farce." I slowly manage myself to a stand, January repeatedly assaults the elevator button to keep the door open as I move at a snail's pace.

The lobby is absurdly bright, you'd think we were staying in a flashy casino in Las Vegas, not a chain hotel here in blazing Arizona.

"Ugh, I need darkness." I stumble towards two art déco doors, branded in gold, thrusting my whole body into them, hoping to escape the light.

Little did I know I stumbled through the gates of heaven, the tiles are orgasmically cold beneath my bare feet.

"Noelle, I don't think we're allowed in here." Whatever happened to my partner in crime? Who would stand by me in situations just like this. Guess he's not blindly infatuated with me anymore and has no desire to let me lead him astray. Maybe he got all his sexual frustrations out and now he's done with me, just like the first time.

My blood simmers as it hits me, he's done it again, he's played me again. Here I am thinking I'm at risk of getting hurt again by being vulnerable, but the damage has already been done. All that fear of me getting hurt again wasn't irrational paranoia, it was essential. Because now I've slept with him on multiple occasions and here he is keeping me at arm's length, while I'm stupidly throwing myself at him.

I disregard January's concerns with a loud moan that echoes through the ballroom, not quite empty. It looks like someone has moved in stacks of tables and chairs ready to be set up. Perfect, more tile for me to lie on.

January grabs me at the waist as my weight falls limp, shifting his hold accordingly to my forearm as he lowers me safely to the ground. I crave for his support more than anything right now; I knew I had my reservations about him but I wasn't completely aware he still had reservations about me.

I guess he's just trying to teeter that line of respect and forgiveness. I feel stupid once again at my quick to temper reaction, he's just as confused as I am. But I'm still far too stubborn to be the first one to say sorry. That's what was missing from his declaration before, an apology. My simmering anger returns, the metaphorical wound has been reopened to where you can see bone.

"Join me, Janny." He's halfway to the ground before I get to finish my request.

"It's hot here in Phoenix, I know." January brushes away the sweat-soaked locks that adhere to my forehead.

"You were right, I wouldn't have been able to handle all of this. Doesn't help when you work me up." I try to berate with sharpness, but it all comes out in a pathetic wheeze.

"I'm sorry, I know it might be too late, and might mean too little, but I didn't mean to hurt you that day, and I don't mean to make you feel stupid. I'm just...stupid."

"A little," I jab, mostly to deflect how overwhelming it is to hear him say those words I longed for.

"A lot."

We both chuckle. I stall by averting my gaze; I don't know if I'm ready to accept his apology.

"This is so stressful seeing you like this, Nono, I hate that I'm working you up and making this experience insufferable." January scrubs his palms down his face.

"It's not just you working me up, Janny, I just feel a lot of pressure to get this right." I notice the blue and yellow ribboning that twirls into a flourished point to a banner. *Upon-A-Star.* "I really wanted to take advantage of your fame to put Darlington Snow Paradise on the map."

"Wow, taking advantage of me, Nono." He rolls his head to me, flashing me a dazzling smile in this dimly lit ballroom. "I appreciate the honesty at least."

"Well, I don't mean it with malice." Maybe a little, he sort of owes it to me. My remorse sits heavy in my sternum as January's warm gaze is unfaltering. I retreat my gaze to the ceiling of spiraling ribbons of blue and gold. "I don't want to overshadow the incredible work *Upon-A-Star* does. Despite what Samantha says, this should be the focal point...but saving the lodge is equally important to me and that can only be done with a convincing intimate relationship."

"Well, the gala isn't for a week. Let's really push the lodge's new image. In the meantime, I'll really work on being less on guard and just follow my instincts when it comes to being more romantic and less friendly."

The ping in my chest blooms into a feeling of warmth, January's efforts to right the situation makes my heart flutter.

"Instincts?" I raise a cheeky eyebrow.

"You know, like, natural urges I want to act on but never did because I didn't want to ruin our friendship," January explains.

"Urges? You're such a pervert, Janny." I give his lower stomach a flaccid slap, I curl my fist in as my instinctive urges kick in. The desire to run my hand even lower and tuck them into his joggers is flaming inside me.

"They weren't always dirty, mostly me fighting the urge to kiss you. I'm more talking about sneaking tender touches that I always flinched away from as a teen. I should give myself more credit, it was often and quite the challenge." I turn to my side, taking in January's bassy soliloquy that pairs so nicely with the hollow resonance of the ballroom.

"Why do I find that adorable?" I slip, my fingertips instinctively trace his jawline. Perhaps that's my substitute for every time I want to kiss January.

"So, what do you think?" His brows pinch into a tight furrow.

"You kissing me? Well, it needs work according—"

"No, Noelle, I meant about me just acting instinctively, I need your consent in this. I can't just grope you when I please."

"So much for not being a pervert. Keep the urges tasteful, this is a children's charity after all." I pinch January's chin, giving it a taunting waggle. His lips break into a charming smile.

There hasn't been a smile of his that I haven't wanted to turn into a make-out.

"Are you feeling better now?"

I halt my head, registering the minimal space between our lips. I was going to kiss him.

"Yes, I've come down from my episode." I retreat bashfully, scolding myself for falling so deeply under his enchantment.

"Good." He inches his hoodie I'm wearing upwards, bearing my torso. He lifts me at the shoulders to shimmy the fleece from my shoulder blades.

"January, this is the opposite of tasteful." I giggle and squirm, my back arches into his touch.

Screw it, I want to be spellbound.

"I'm just making sure you stay cool, I'm about to inject ten years of yearning into this make out, Noelle." The way he slowly lowers my back to the cool tiles has me hypnotized, my now bare flesh pressed to the freshness.

The gray sweater bunches just below my tits, January's palm splays to flatten the bundled fabric whilst subtly copping a feel.

"Janny." I slip with a moan, his tongue replaces my words.

"Bump-in will conclude at 7 pm." A stray, unfamiliar voice echoes through the ballroom.

"Shit, people," I pant into January's lips.

Without hesitation, January collects my entire body and rolls us both under a nearby table.

His quick thinking makes my heart pound excitedly and makes my arousal throb. My thighs ache to squeeze together, but January's thighs stop that from happening, which only heightens the hot sensation between my legs. The outline of his cock in the matching gray sweatpants is extremely prominent.

"Shit." January huffs.

"Fuck."

January shoots me a disapproving look.

"What? I thought we were playing the swearing game." I flutter my lashes coyly. Vocalizing the only goal I have in sight right now: *Fuck*.

"The nonsense we made up just to amuse ourselves at the lodge." January clicks his tongue disapprovingly, all while wearing a nostalgic smile.

"I know a way we can amuse ourselves now." My thumb caresses his jawline again, and I can confirm that is certainly a crutch I fall on when I want to kiss him.

"Not here, we get caught and we will be in the press, for all the bad reasons."

His reasoning puts my horniness at bay.

"As soon as we get back to the room."

"Absolutely." January's eyes somehow glow in the faint darkness, illuminating his enchanting pearly white smile.

"January?"

"Noelle." He answers in acknowledgment.

"I want to feel all of your *natural instinctive urges*." Something tells me I got a glimpse of them the other night when we went off script from our first time, I'm dying to explore that more with him.

I press my hips lightly into his bulge, and January releases an excitable grunt.

"The kitchen is here so we need to ensure there is thoroughfare..." the voice trails off into the distance.

January pulls my waist tightly against his torso, and I feel his core muscles engage as he shuffles us from under the table.

He moves so swiftly across the tiles, just like he does on the ice. His effortless grace whilst on blades has always turned me on, for once it is not an inconvenience for either of us.

We're pushing past our egos and our self-inflicted restraints, and we're both on the same page. We're about to have mutually agreeable sex.

January doesn't lower me once we burst through the doors, he continues to plummet the both of us into the elevator that had already been conveniently hailed. The stars align for us on this one, there is nothing stopping us from having more orgasmic sex.

Except the elevator itself, before it was moving far too fast, but now it couldn't possibly be moving any slower. My pussy is pleading for January's cock, I wriggle restlessly on his waist.

"Come on, come on." I crane my neck backward to see the numbers slowly count up. 26. 27. 28. 29. "Final—"

The door parts only for the apartment's interior to become a blur as January dips my body forward in a whirlwind motion. I hear a tinny scrape across the floor.

"What are you doing?"

"Ice bucket," January says simply, as if it was self-explanatory.

"It's quite early for champagne." I feel like I'm drunk off the stuff right now.

"No, Nono." January carefully perches me on the edge of the mattress. "It's for when things get a little too instinctive."

"Oh my god, yes, please." I moan, allowing my back to fall onto the mattress, shuffling my body up to the Mount Everest of pillows. The cushions are organized in a sloping concave.

Darlington Snow Paradise cannot constitute itself as a ski resort, because the slope doesn't meet the requirements, according to the Aspen Ski Committee Board. But this pile of pillows certainly does.

"I know exactly what I want to do." January's knee digs into the mattress. He sinks his weight into the plush alpine, I gravitate to him instantly, I swing my legs over into a straddle.

"Where was this confidence in your youth, Janny?"

"A *natural urge* I want to indulge in right now is to fulfill whatever fantasy of yours we never got the chance to do. Don't think too hard, Nono, I can see you have something in mind already."

God, he reads me so well. I love perching my ass on those stone-hard thighs.

"January, I want to ride you but..." some fantasies stay fantasies for a reason, not because they were never acted on but mostly because I cannot execute them.

"But what? You can ride me." January quirks a thick raven brow.

"I get tired when I ride, but I want to ride you so badly." I gnaw at my lip. There's no point in getting my hopes up, it just won't work. I've ridden Sean once, and it was the most lackluster experience of my life.

"I'll help you, Nono, we can do this together. You riding me sounds like a dream."

"You have no idea how much I've dreamed of riding your cock with intense vigor but...it'll remain a dream, if only *Upon-A-Star* adult wishes were a thing, I know what I'd wish for."

"Fuck, Noelle, are you kidding me right now." January's swagger falters at that confession of mine.

"What?" I tilt my head adorably, rubbing my hands at his beefy shoulders.

"That is so fucking sexy...you've...you've thought of me that way."

"Only since I was like 14."

"I can't believe it." His jaw hangs slack in awe.

"Did you not?"

"I definitely did, I just always suppressed them because they felt wrong to have. You're my best friend."

Something warms in me at the fact he uses it in the present tense. I yearn for nothing more than to be January's best friend, and to have him be mine. I believe setting that label in stone would probably eliminate some of the confusion about our feelings, but that is also our biggest obstacle whilst performing this stunt.

I refocus my thoughts on my promiscuity, alluring January into not so friendly circumstances.

"Well, now it's time to let those dirty thoughts of yours free."

"Did you..." January swallows thickly, I create friction with my thighs as I watch his Adam's apple bob.

"Did I...?" I breathe out.

"Did you *resolve* those daydreams?"

"You mean did I touch myself until I thought my heart was going to explode? Yes, January, yes I did...and yes I do."

"Fuck..." His eyes drop to my rubbing thighs.

"You're so stupid." I nudge him playfully.

"Hm." He whines. Fucking whines like a prepubescent boy.

"Janny, did you just whine?"

"I guess I did," January admits with a gulp. "I am so sexually attracted to you. I've always been sexually attracted to you."

"Are you kidding me? Why did we never do this sooner, you dweeb?" I pinch his cheek patronizingly.

"We could've burned through your condom collection." He swats my hand away, wrapping his fingers around my frail wrist. I can feel the vitality pumping through his veins.

"Exactly, instead of having them all expire. Do you even know why Sex Ed was introduced?" I tilt my head endearingly, fluttering my lashes to garner his attention. Not that it ever wavered from me, I have this man wrapped around my finger after all.

"It felt really sudden, I'm just glad it interrupted our book report on The Count of Monte Cristo, I was never going to finish that book."

"But you planned on finishing me instead." I wink mischievously. January looks away, overwhelmed by my obvious flirting.

"Here I was thinking I knew my best friend like the back of my hand, just to find out she's a secret minx." He huffs out pathetically.

"Call me that again, Prince."

"A minx?" His glassy eyes stay trained on the elevator doors.

Oh, Janny, this door is wide open, why don't you come inside?

"Yeah, I'll show you how minxy I can be. While I tell you why Sex Ed came to be." My eyes roll backward as I lower my swollen pussy to his bulge, he releases a long quiet hiss as our sexes make contact.

"I've had dreams just like this," he gurgles, wearing a stupid grin on his alluring lips.

"Speaking of dreams, that's how it all came about, really. My parents noticed me watching you while you practiced, more so daydreaming than spectating. So, Mum pulled me aside and straight out asked me if you and I were sexually active with one another."

"I would be so embarrassed if my mom did that to me." January snaps to attention, his cerulean eyes widening, his skin blanching.

"Well, she said it was nothing to be ashamed of, but she needed me to be honest with her so we could be properly educated about sex."

"But we didn't sleep with each other until we were eighteen, what did you tell her?" January's bottom lip sinks, his brows furrowing with confusion.

"I said, no we hadn't, but if you'd asked me one day, I would've said yes. Despite knowing nothing about sex besides what I've read in books."

"Fuck, do you know how badly I wanted to make love with you after prom, if I had known you wanted me like I wanted you? You see it in all the movies, I wanted that so badly with you."

It wasn't an official prom but more of a pitiful shindig our parents pulled together for us to live the full high school experience. But that didn't stop January from taking it seriously. Although it's not unheard of for friends to go to prom together, January followed through on tradition with a promposal that was anything but friendly. Which gives me a glimpse of hope that we might have moments like that during the stunt too. I woke one morning looking out my porch door to see a row of 22 snowmen that came up to my hips, wearing colorful Darlington Snow Paradise merchandise, all donning signs with single letters on them that read in sequence: WILL YOU GO TO PROM WITH ME?

He must've stayed up all night putting in all that effort for me, just for us to decapitate their heads with hockey pucks. Well,

January at least, my strike was always far too weak. He was rather handsy that day with me, which wasn't uncharacteristic, but the placement of his touches were more intimate than ever. He even guided me through a clean shot to behead a snowman, of course my brain was far too foggy to celebrate. So, I rewarded my impressive shot by appreciating my best friend's handsomeness.

"I wanted that too." I plant a palm to my heart, feeling its rapid rhythm. "Anyway, I think Mum immediately told Mrs. Donovan, and sure enough, Sex Ed was implemented the next day."

"You're more sadistic than minxy, Nono, creating more schoolwork for us." His palms run over my ass cheeks. How I would love to have me guide me through whilst I ride his cock with intense enthusiasm.

"You should've asked me, January, you have no idea how blindly in love with you I was," I release on a purr.

"I think I have a pretty good idea, being entirely in love with you."

My breath hitches, I'm too afraid to ask if that is also in the present tense.

"I guess you can't exactly say blindly, considering all my flaws are completely at the forefront of who I am. With my mysterious burdensome declining health."

"I've never seen you as a burden, ever. I find my hockey career more burdensome, how it inhibited me from always being close to you."

I guess that confirms he means it in the past tense, but he also referred to the lodge as *our future*. So, he sees us being in love in the future? Now, I definitely need clarity.

"Really, January? You'd give up all of this for me, you may have been lying about your feelings then, but don't lie to me now."

"I would give all of this up in a heartbeat...if we pull this stunt off, I might even retire. I just want to be with you, Noelle, and live out the fairytale ending I've always dreamed of. You are my dream, Noelle, if I could make a wish, that is what I would wish for."

"You'd be so sick of me after some time, it might be considered terminal." I chuckle even though I know it's the truth. It's clear people are tired of my inconvenient fatigue. I have to do the most mundane of things slowly and steadily.

"No, I'm patient, Noelle, you know I'm patient. You turned me from an entitled, impatient, testy, 11-year-old into a man who feels such deep love for you. You did that. You, Noelle Winter Darlington, thawed January Cameron Snow."

"You said testy." I snort.

"Come here, you." January presses his soft lips into mine, his pulse beats in time with my own. I can feel the thumping as it amplifies in this tonguey kiss. "Your dreams are going to come true, Noelle, you're going to ride your Prince."

My core melts at that declaration, his hands pinch at the ribbed elastic bottom of the hoodie, journeying it over my head. My nipples stand with attention, especially when January's focus is on them.

I reignite the kiss, threading my hand between us and fishing out January's cock.

"Oh, you're touching me. *Putain.*"

I giggle, "*Baise-moi.*"

"I will *fuck you*, Noelle, with absolute pleasure, *tu es une belle femme.* I've got to get my Princess nice and wet."

"Your Princess." My heart races at that claim, I've only ever imagined January saying it laced with lust and now my daydream has come to fruition.

I'm so enthused by the news I take all my ecstatic energy out on January's cock as I pump quickly. Which takes more of an effect on me than it does on January, my heartbeat succeeds my pumping speed.

"Noelle, *putain, putain oui,* mm, fuck, yes." January's breathy moans make me dizzier. I press my forehead against his, trying to work my fist faster.

"Wait, Nono, you're burning up."

My vision is spotting, even behind my closed eyelids.

"I'm okay," I wheeze out.

"Nono, stop touching me for a second and just catch yourself."

"We're just getting started, Janny, I can't stop now."

"Your forehead is on fire, let's just relax a bit. Take it steady." January pries my hand from his cock, pulling me close to his chest as he leans over the bed.

My back arches, pressing myself more intimately into January, my breasts couldn't possibly pancake more. I surrender to the blissful, harsh cold of the ice cube as January trails it down my spine.

"Does that feel good, Princess?"

"So good." I shiver as his hand runs up the nape of my neck and around to my collarbone above my heart.

The cube diminishes quickly; I see January's hungry look in his eyes, or rather thirsty look, as he stares at the liquid pooling in the hollow of my collarbone.

"Thirsty, Hot Shot?"

"Would it be weird if I drank the water from your pretty collarbone?"

"I want you too," I moan.

January's lips press to my collarbone, sipping the small pill of water dry from the divot, suckling on the skin, clearly aiming to bruise.

"Get a fresh cube." I pluck the remains of the ice cube. January leans forward once more, I press the ice cube to the tip of his cock, running it down his hard length.

"Oh fuck, Nono, maybe don't do that." He hisses through his teeth.

"That doesn't feel good, Prince?" I pout, hoping the sensation would work in tandem with his throbbing tip.

"I'm just agonizingly stiff right now and you never learned in Sex Ed what happens to a penis in the cold."

"No, what happens?" I furrow my brows, genuinely unaware of what is happening.

"It shrinks in the cold."

"It shrinks in the cold? Was it always shrunken at the lodge?" How I could live for 28 years and not know this about a penis is beyond me.

"Not always...not when you kept me hot."

"Was that often?"

"It became more frequent the older we got...the sexier you got."

"So, you did take notice." I click my tongue disapprovingly. "All those times I thought I was making a fool of myself and you—oh my god." I hiss when I feel ice run along my lower belly. "I like that."

"Yeah, Princess?"

"Yes, Prince." My fingers weakly wrap around January's wrist, I try to push his hand lower but he fights against my desire. "January, please, please try it."

"I think it might be a bit too cold for down there, Nono."

"Put it in your mouth and lick my clit." I don't even know where I plucked the idea from, it certainly wasn't in my daydream arsenal. "Please, Janny, I want to try it."

"I...I want to try it, too. I'm going to lay you on your back."

"I want to ride your face. Your handsome face that all the magazines claim is the prettiest face in all of sports."

"R-ride my f-face." His cheeks heat over with an adorable intense blush.

"Can I?" My stomach jostles as January shuffles further down the pillows, he gives my ass a firm squeeze. I squeak as I launch my hips up from his pelvis, the ice cube perched between his teeth as he shoots me a wicked smile. That effulgent smile is enough invitation to have me crawling with blind adoration. My knees line up with his ears, his eyes glass over. He seems distant in thought, yet equally present as he drinks in my sensuality.

I run my palms over my breast as they become sensitive and hyper-aware of January's lingering gaze.

"*Une second*." I brush my hair from my shoulder, collect two ice cubes from the bucket, and slip them over my erect nipples. I slowly lower myself, using January's hot breath as a guide, my eyes already pinched shut as I indulge in the euphoric dizziness all the contradicting temperatures are causing.

He tugs my knickers aside, splitting my folds with his tongue, the ice cube perched on the tip. I let out a shivering moan.

My hips rock slightly in search of the sensation again.

"Oh, Janny, I like that."

The ice cube dissolves quickly in the heat of my arousal, I come into complete contact with the texture of January's tongue. I press further into his stiff licks, triggering my thighs into a trembling frenzy.

He hums as he smothers his face further into my spasming pussy. The tip of his nose pulls at the hood of my swollen clit as his tongue slightly penetrates my hole. My abdomen tenses before it surrenders to the orgasm that is crawling down my spine.

"Cum for me Princess. That's my girl."

I don't know why, but the thought of being *my girl* to January ignites me with energy.

"Claim what's yours, Prince, be inside your Princess."

I shuffle off January's face with gusto; I think I may have enough energy to ride January's cock, like I've always dreamed of. I can feel the adrenaline building inside me, I inhale deeply, trying to preserve my excitement.

I'm cursing myself as soon as I slide down January's rock-solid abs, I'm fatigued by the time I feel January's tip caress my hole.

"Take your time, Princess, we've got no plans today. We have all the time in the world."

I slick the last remaining droplets from the cubes of ice I was using to stimulate my nipples down my torso.

January's copping a few remnants on his chiseled chest as well.

Fuck, my best friend is so hot.

"I'm getting you all wet, Janny." I slide my hand up his front, saliva naturally building in my mouth at the sight and the *feel* of his muscles. He's so fit. I'm embarrassed by how much I polarize that fact.

Maybe, it's time to test the limits of my fitness. I reach my hand between my legs and retrieve January's cock in my hand, lining his length up with my entrance and pushing it in slowly.

The sensation of being full gives me a second wind, I plant my palms on January's sturdy shoulders, gearing up to thrust manically.

I get three good thrusts before I tire.

"This fucking condition is ruining my life, especially my sex life," I grunt as my hips roll in a weak, flaccid motion. January is suspiciously quiet, I peek through my lashes to find his expression is one of transcendence.

As if he's a million miles away in a serene rainforest, his mouth agape as though he's anticipating a droplet of dew to land on the tip of his tongue. It's never looked more inviting, I'm almost tempted to abandon his cock and revisit his face.

His teeth clench together as I become more intentional with my slow rolls, I can't go fast but I can certainly control direction. I try all sorts of motions, and January responds with all sorts of sounds, hisses, and moans with each change of direction.

January stares distantly at my middle, I can't tell if he's faded from boredom or if this is doing it for him.

"I wanted this to be fun."

His eyes flash with return.

"What are you talking about, this is so fun." He pants, his hands moving about my body with presence.

Welcome back, Janny, welcome to my body, it's all yours.

And that's the truth, January is the only person I could surrender my body to. He knows my limitations best, and he's the only one I trust to push those limits with.

"I wanted to ride you with vigor, this is placid at best." I slow my roll, pulling up January's length at a timid pace.

"Uh fuck, I like placid. Fuck, you've got me good, Nono."

He yelps as I push back down again.

"I think I'm going to come." He throws his head back heavenwards, his Adam's apple protruding with temptation, bobbing as a whining moan gets caught in his throat.

January's a whiner.

Who would've thought with such a bassy drawl. I don't hate it, I might even like it.

How the most minuscule of movements has this 6'3 mountain of muscles whining. *Fucking whining.*

I shift my weight, so the plushest part of my stomach rests on January's hard v-line. Using all my reserved energy to pull up January's length once again.

"Ah, fuck Noelle, you feel the whole of my cock, every fucking inch with that beautifully tight pussy of yours." January's palms leave my ass cheeks hastily, clawing at the sheets. "I'm trying so hard not to punch my cock into your magical pussy. I love this other world you are transporting me to right now, I want this to last forever."

"But I am hardly doing anything." My brows pinch in confusion.

"You are rocking my entire world." January releases a string of hyperventilating huffs. "Huh, fuck, Noelle, I want this to last forever, but I don't think I'm going to."

I sink back down again. January smacks his head against the pillow, groaning in agony. His fingers pinching at my hips briefly before flying to his face, scrubbing at his flushed features.

"Don't come, don't come, don't come."

"You were right, this is fun. I feel I'm playing you like a joystick. I move it left." I do as I say, January's whole body jerks up. His hand grabbing at my hip like he's seeking refuge from the intense pleasure. "Or I could go right." I roll my hips circularly to the right, my head lulling heavenwards as the sensations hit all the right spots for me.

"Or up and down." I more so use the buoyancy of the mattress, rather than execute the movement.

I can feel January's tip caressing my internals with each minute bounce. I lick my fingers and start playing with my clit.

"Janny."

"Nono." He echoes my pleasure with a whine. "Noelle, Princess, I'm about to finish." That statement triggers me into excitement, I bounce eagerly, wanting to feel the sensations of January's cum inside me.

"Come. Come. Come." I dig my knees into the mattress, ricocheting January's pelvis into me.

Fuck, I'm coming. And so is January.

Our bodies release from their wound-up tightness, melting into the blissful aftermaths of our eruptions. My pussy feels so slick and full of January's cum, I almost don't want to get up and go to the loo and pop my birth control.

"Noelle, I need you in my life." January pulls me closer to him, hiking me up, his now soft cock slipping from my still-flexing entrance.

"For this purpose only." I can barely concentrate on this conversation, I can feel the cocktail of pleasure running down my walls, it sends a shiver down my spine.

"For everything, my happiness depends on it. You make me euphoric."

"That was—"

"For the love of god, please, Noelle, do not friendzone me again, don't say the sex was interesting because I know what I felt and it was—"

"Fun."

January's defensiveness falls to disbelief, "So fun."

"I have to go pee."

"Come back to bed afterward."

“Of course, Prince.” I place a featherlight kiss on January’s cheek, he cups my chin with gentle assertiveness, redirecting the kiss to his lips.

“Go piss, Princess.” He winks at me, flashing his hypnotic smile.

I play along with his ridiculousness, curtseying politely. Falling from the balletic form to scoop up January’s Phoenix Badgers hoodie, slipping it over my flushed skin, the wool cocoons the warmth radiating off my body.

EIGHTEEN

Too Cool For School

January

I lay in Noelle's heavenly heat, waiting for her to return from her peeing intermission.

Christ, that was something else. Tame in practicality, but my cock couldn't possibly handle anything more than what she was providing. I feel my length twitching as I mentally replay the vision of Noelle's breasts and me having a very arousing staring contest. I'm not entirely sure who won, but I believe it was me. But then again, my eyes couldn't help but stray to her pretty flushed cheeks and how her ice-blue eyes popped against the crimson color.

Ice hockey championships be damned, I'm a winner now that Noelle is back in my life.

"Don't tell me you're exhausted after that?"

I hear Noelle's wispy voice first and her tender touch on my cheeks next. I relish in her caress, blindly reaching for her to pull her impossibly close to me.

"Nono, Princess, cuddle with me." I press my lips to her feverish pulse. My eyes spring open with urgency.

"Don't look so worried, I'm okay…we barely did anything."

"Tell that to my cock, you left quite the impression for *barely anything.*" I reach my palm over my bulge as the damn thing continues to squirm.

Noelle's nimble fingers tug at the elastic of my sweatpants.

"We barely did anything." I flinch as her breath caresses the tip of my cock.

"Fuck, Nono. Leave the poor thing alone, he's been through it. Tease my lips if you must." I thread my fingers into her auburn locks, still knotty from her bedhead. She smirks mischievously before taking on the offer, cupping my sharp jawline with her trembling fingers.

I can tell the tame experience has also left her a little fatigued too, I ensure our make out is of the same caliber.

As much as I love having my tongue tied with Noelle's, I appreciate these mellow kisses most. Slow-paced and sporadic, I can take my time enjoying every single one.

"You two are still asleep?"

The grating vocal fry interrupts my enjoyment. Noelle flinches away from me, slowly returning to my side when she takes in the sight of Samantha over her shoulder.

"For fuck's sake, Samantha, how did you get in here? It's key access only!"

"I got myself a key, duh." She flashes the maroon and gold key card identical to Noelle's and my own.

"We were having sex!" I roar, a familiar hand muzzles my mouth. Many times, Noelle's soft palm has quieted me because Princess can't handle a little trash-talking when we play video games.

"Not so loud." Noelle gurgles, snuggling back into my bare chest again. My heartbeat is exposed by her ear, probably exploding her eardrum by how deafeningly loud it is.

"Sorry, Princess." I peck at her temple, surrendering to this serene moment.

"Puh-lease!" Samantha sucks the serenity from the room with her boastful volume. "I don't believe you two were having sex for a second, and that's the problem." She narrows her eyes on me with lethal accusations.

So I am the one to blame for the lack of believability.

"But I took matters into my own hands. Rise and shine, bedbugs." Samantha tugs at the duvet, the blanket pooling at the foot of the bed.

"Ah, I don't have any pants on," Noelle squeaks, pulling her knees to her chest and stretching my hoodie over her knees.

I maneuver my body to block her as she shamefully shivers.

"Oh, she's here!" Samantha announces as her phone illuminates her face. "You guys have five minutes to get ready, I will return."

Fuck, that's a threat if I've ever heard one.

Also, who is *she*?

I pull Noelle into my side as she hurries past me in a flash. Now sporting my sweatpants that are far too cumbersome for her skinny figure, except they sit artfully tight on her full ass. I scoop her into a kiss, and she surprisingly surrenders. Maybe we've finally figured this out, all we had to do was surrender to our instincts. I will no longer ignore the voices in my head whenever I want to kiss Noelle, I will simply act. With how Noelle responds, I have to believe she agrees.

The kiss is sweet and tame, but it's electric. My fingertips resting over Noelle's excited pulse on her neck, I circle my thumb. My lips pause as I allow her to retain oxygen in her blood, to get her sweet heart beating normally again.

"Awful." A foreign voice reeking of entitled judgment breaks our enchanting intimacy. I pull away from Noelle with a snarl.

I assume this is *who* Samantha was referring to before.

"Who the fuck are you?" I growl, and my palm spreads on Noelle's back protectively, pulling her tightly to my front.

"Cameron, for the love of god, stop being such an asshole," Samantha scolds with a hiss.

"Samantha, there is a stranger in our hotel room, not to mention I'm pissed off that you have a key card of your own."

"When aren't you pissed off," Samantha scoffs. "This, for the record, is Eshika Patel. She's an intimacy coach in Hollywood. She helps actors who despise one another look like they are ready to fall into bed at any moment."

An intimacy coach? Is Samantha for real at this point?

"For the record, we do not kiss *awful*. Everybody needs to stop saying that. Kiss me, Nono." I push back Noelle, my palms planted on her shoulders. Her fingertips press against her reeling head. Oh god, that was rough of me. I caress my fingers lightly over her temple as a nonverbal apology.

"That's the whole point, it's not supposed to look switched on. A kiss should catch you off guard while still keeping its natural magic. You two make it look stiff and calculative. Like you are androids."

"We don't need an intimacy coach, Sam." I get a good look at the mentor Samantha has hired to mold our relationship into a convincing one. She's wearing more gold than there is in this tacky 1920s-themed chain hotel. Eshika's bangles, stacked up to her elbow, clack loudly as she and Samantha shake hands formally. She's wearing a dress made from a floaty and flimsy fabric, as if she dyed the air the color of passion.

I completely disregard her advice as she continues to ramble on nonsensically. Thankfully, she's gesticulative enough to drown her own nonsense out, as her abundant gold bangles bang together like a chaotic choir.

"Hm, I sense an instinct to protect her, you guys have a history. But judging by her wearing her shoulders as earrings, she's not completely trusting of you."

I turn to Noelle and notice that she's lifted her shoulders stiffly to her ears. She drops them quickly, her face blanches at the analysis.

"Do not shift all the blame onto Noelle, we've discussed it actually, and we know exactly what we need to work on. We don't need you, Eshika, was it?" I genuinely don't care if I'm addressing this invasive stranger correctly.

Samantha runs her palm down her face, exhaling a loud, obnoxious groan of frustration. *Welcome to my world, Sammy, I hate this too.*

Eshika's kohl-rimmed chocolate eyes scan us with precision.

"I think we're being reprogrammed, Janny." Noelle leans into me, I subtly inhale her scent. *It doesn't get more intimate than that, does it?* I chuckle, catching her joke and sacrificing my inhale.

"What is the most intimate you two have been?" Eshika purrs, pianoing her golden fingertips on her heavily blushed cheek.

"We've fucked, if that's what you're asking. Mere seconds before you rudely arrived, actually," I spit out.

"Wait, you guys had sex today?" Samantha's eyes leave her phone for once.

"Yes. Does she not look freshly pounded?" I hiss bitterly.

"Tasteless, Janny, very tasteless." Okay, I agree with Noelle that better wording could've been chosen on my part, but I'm irate by this overreaction. So, our chemistry is a little stunted, Noelle and I can figure this out on our own.

"She always looks like that." Samantha's gaze turns to her phone once again, I swear I'm going to break those acrylics off in her sleep.

"Like what?" Noelle's bottom lip sinks into a pout.

"Y'know, run down." Samantha shrugs casually.

"I look run down?" Noelle whimpers.

"No, Angelface, I get the look you're going for. He's into it...I think." Samantha tilts her head, locking eyes with what I hope is my most murderous stare to date.

"Both of you need to leave," I order with a roar.

"Wait, Janny, maybe we could use some professional mentoring."

Noelle's balanced voice pierces through like a knife to my senses. Thrusting me to return to them and realize that I am being irrational. You've got to be joking, how Noelle can side with Samantha on this ridiculous investment after she just insulted her, is beside me.

"But we don't need the help. We talked this out. I think we fixed this." I feel an almost smile crawl to my face as the success settles in.

"It seems we figured you out, but I'm not there just yet," Noelle reasons.

What?

"She's not even close. You say you had intercourse only less than an hour ago, yet she's not emotionally fawning over you." Eshika injects her unwelcome opinion.

"Fawning over me, now you're just making shit up," I scoff.

"It's all in the eyes, it appears that you two can engage in sexual intimacy on a surface level and remain emotionally detached. It's clear there's a layer of disconnection."

"Look, Janny, it's both our faults, at least people can see that clear as day." Noelle sighs, defeatedly.

"I trust Noelle completely." I hate how my voice wavers because I do trust Noelle. Why wouldn't I? She's my best friend.

"Yes, but you're aware that she doesn't trust you."

"You're making this sound like it's all her fault, then."

"Listen, you two. I've scheduled a little romantic outing tomorrow to fix all of this." Samantha gnashes at the both of us.

"We were in the middle of fixing it when my dick was inside her!" I roar, I can feel Noelle trembling against my palm.

Samantha tilts her head, wearing a contemplative look. "I don't see it."

"Neither do I," Eshika chimes in.

"Noelle, do you want to have sex so we can show them we're doing this just fine?"

"I am feeling a little run down." Noelle's head lulls onto my shoulder.

"You two need to leave." I comb my fingers through Noelle's locks, fluttering my eyes closed. I hear a camera shutter and can only guess it's from Samantha's phone.

I don't care, all I care about is protecting Noelle in this entire process. I will fight off every dragon that dares to come near my princess.

My princess.

For once, Samantha takes on my command and leaves, escorting Eshika Patel, intimacy coach to the stars, out with her.

Thank all the ice hockey lords, now I am alone with Noelle once again.

"I need to lie down after that." Noelle's precious eyes stare up at mine, glassed with fatigue. Maybe the sex did take her out more than she's letting on. I scoop her up bridal style and lay her softly on the bed, her hand runs weakly along my neck as she sinks into the mattress. I crawl onto the bed next to her, fluttering the sheets over us again.

This is all I want in life, to be with Noelle, privately. Love on our terms.

I catch sight of my frantically buzzing phone, only giving it attention to turn it on Do Not Disturb so Noelle and I can cuddle in peace. I catch the aggressive all-caps text message.

CAMERON! DATE IDEA THAT IS IMPORTANT TO NOELLE NOW!!! STOP IGNORING ME!!!!

I growl, quickly unlocking my phone. It doesn't take much for me to pluck an answer to Samantha's urgent question.

Grand Crayon.

I don't even care that I misspelled my reply. If only *Upon-A-Star* could help me wish these fuckers away for good.

Nineteen

It's Nice To Have A Friend

Noelle

I am so glad Samantha allowed January and me to stop off at Walmart for a few snacks. I have the Nintendo Switch powered up and I'm honestly extremely excited to spend the day road tripping with January. It feels like old times. Until it dawns on me...it feels friendly.

I act in a panic and link January's hand to mine as we stand side by side in the checkout line. January's eyes drop with surprise at the intimacy, shooting me a look of confusion before finally closing in.

Yes, dummy, we're supposed to look like we are dating.

We are next to be served, January dumps his mountain of chips and lollies onto the moving belt. I'm thrust forward in a fright when his hand smacks hard against my ass, I turn with a huff.

"January!" I bite, rubbing at the sting.

"Sorry, I'm kind of shit at this relationship dynamic...sort of only been in one for ten minutes."

"Puh-lease." I dismiss all of my snacks onto the moving belt. A selection I'm sure would give my dear friend, Candy, a heart attack if she knew this was my nutritional intake for the day.

It allows my hands to return the favor. He cries loudly, earning the whole checkout area to observe the amusing sight of a 6'3 man tenderly rubbing his ass.

"You're Cameron Snow." The checkout girl gasps.

"Yeah," January answers as he continues to massage his ass. *Men are such babies, honestly.*

"Oh my god, are you that girl everyone is unsure he's dating?" Her eyes bore into me next. In fact, everybody seems to invest their eyes on me. I take so long to answer, I'm sure the milk belonging to the lady behind us in the cashier line is spoiling.

"Allow me to put an end to the mystery, Noelle is my girlfriend. My beautiful, masochistic girlfriend," January presses through his teeth, ending his derriere rubbing to fetch his wallet from his pocket.

I straighten my posture proudly at the label, mostly resonating with the masochistic part, I get a kick out of seeing January suffer.

And it is nice to be called beautiful after being told I look rundown yesterday. I'm doing my best in this agonizing heat and January's hectic schedule has me ran off my feet.

"Girlfriend. Aren't you lowkey a player?"

Wow, you have some gall to ask January a question like that, but that's the thing with today's generation. Confrontation doesn't scare the living daylights out of them.

"Noelle's the only woman I've been with. For years."

Okay, January, let's not give the media too much to talk about, before they misconstrue me as a cheater. Hurry and pay, let's get out of here before Samantha calls Candy in for damage control once she sees all this junk food we have.

I'm going to need to fly the girls out to the lodge once this is over...but it's never going to end. I need a girls' night in.

"Don't you have a mystery man? Shane or whatever."

The almost mention of Sean reminds me of that cherry on top of my emotional damage cake. *How many tiers is this fucking thing at this point?* "Oh, he's just my mistress when it's playing season, don't tell Cameron." I shoot the cashier a wink, and she is not picking up on my sarcasm. *Great, I just went and fueled the flame.* Her eyes widen as she quickly scans the rest of the items and completes our purchase. She eagerly whips her phone out, disregarding the next customer in line—*I am so sorry about your milk, ma'am, it is definitely spoiled by now*—she frantically types away on her phone. I swear she discreetly tilts her phone to take a photo of us.

Oh shit, Samantha might be the one in need of doing some damage control on our public image after all.

"Let's go, Princess." January tugs me out of the store, pulling me in front of him and shielding me from all the supermarket spectators.

"You fucking cheater!" I dislodge my seatbelt and lunge at January as he somehow beats me for the third time in Mario Kart.

"I'm not cheating, Nono, I'm just a better player than you." January cradles his palms on the back of his neck, peacocking with an arrogant smile.

"Swap the remotes," he and I say at the same time.

"I knew you were going to say that. Here, Nono, I promise I'll still beat you."

"You two act like literal children." Samantha rubs at her temple as if she were our mother, and certainly berates us like one.

"I can't help but regress to my teenage self when I'm with Noelle...I'm working on it, though." January resigns his hands into the sleeves of his hoodie, only he slips them out again to link my hands nearby. Even his small attentive smirks make me want to kiss him.

Since my fingertips are busy, I cannot rely on my crutch.

I snap a peck on his lips.

"Great stuff, please keep this dynamic for when we get to the Grand Canyon. Why seeing a bunch of red rocks was so important to you, I do not know."

"You were the one who organized this trip," I roll my eyes, shooting January a look and nod that reads *can you believe this woman*? It actually earns a small chuckle and a lopsided grin, which has my inner teenage girl screaming into a pillow.

"Actually, Cameron did. I received an extensive list this morning via text of other date ideas." Samantha smugly exposes.

"January," I coo.

"Just trying to make up for hurting you, showing one little slice of the world at a time."

"Naw, now you're considerate. Too little, too late, Hot Shot." I snap another peck after my taunt.

"We're here. Thank god, this dynamic feels fragile." Samantha rockets from the car, urging us to do the same.

"Stay in the car, I'll open your door, Princess."

"You know it's way more romantic when you don't announce it."

"Sorry, level 1 boyfriend here." January offers me his hand, flexing his arm as he lifts me from the SUV.

Boyfriend. January Cameron Snow is my boyfriend. It's so strange to say...it doesn't feel particularly wrong, but it doesn't come without its pressures.

"Well done, maybe you'll actually get to level up next time you open the door for me."

"Well, it might be difficult with the prank we have planned today."

The Glad Wrap completely slipped my mind, as many things do when I'm gazing into January's cerulean eyes. There's no way they expect January and me to spend copious amounts of alone time together and not execute a prank of some sort.

Samantha's gaze is always glued to her phone, which will make it easy for us to sneak away today. I just realized I haven't checked mine all day, I've been so preoccupied with genuinely enjoying January's company again. Maybe the walls are coming down.

Is that what I want? Or is that just what I want to convey?

My vision is painted with crimson and for a second I think I'm having my worst spell yet, that somehow blood has somehow seeped into my retinas. But I'm mistaken, my view for once is breathtaking, not completely void of dizziness as my eyes travel along the endless scarlet rocky chasms.

"Wow, I can't believe this place made it out of my screensaver."

"Looks just like the view from my place." January's robust deep voice hits intimately in my ear, his palm splays on my stomach from behind, guiding my weight backward into him. It somehow stabilizes my dizziness, having a pillar of strength to ground me.

My fingers thread through his knuckles, I'm almost convinced that we're dating.

This reminds me we are not, and I need to be careful of handing my heart over so blindly as I did in my youth. I must teeter the line of being vulnerable with January without actually falling into that very consequence.

It doesn't help that this very moment reminds me of the time January hauled me up the very top of the lodge's slope on his back. All because I was mildly curious about what the view was like at the top of the incline. The view was underwhelming, masked by a sheet of fog.

"I can't say I have a view like this back home." I giggle. "Take a picture of me, Janny."

"Of course, Nono." January's hand slips into my jeans pocket, my lips part with a gasp. If this isn't convincing enough, maybe they should hook me up to a heart monitor, that'll expose the truth.

The insufferable truth is that I still may have feelings for January.

I hope I'm hiding the panic in my eyes as I turn to face the camera, these pictures will make it to the masses. That's the whole point of this outing, is to get as many photo ops as possible. It just feels so natural hanging out with January, I almost don't care if we get any evidence of us doing so.

"Did you get the canyon in the background?" I ask, hopefully the landmark can distract from the crisis that is probably homing in my plastic smile.

"It's hard to miss, Nono." January hands me back my phone, only to retract. "Wait, let me send these to myself."

"Attempting to expand your wank bank."

"You already did that with those jacuzzi photos, thank you very much for that." January dares to wink at me. It's frustrating, where was all this outright flirting in our youth?

"You infuriate me, you know." My eyes roll.

"What? You gave them to me yourself, I am not a pervert."

"Sure, Jan."

"That's it. You drove me to do this, you left me no choice. This is becoming my phone screen. Don't stop me, I'm doing it." I watch as January swipes indecisively on what is essentially the same picture of me. "This one. Done!"

"I dare you to post it to your socials." I narrow my eyes challengingly.

"Oh, game on, Nono." He returns the stare on me, before flicking to his phone. "I'll even post it to my stories."

"You're bluffing," I jab, my finger looping around a thread of my hair, twirling it girlishly as my lashes flutter.

Ugh, what is wrong with me? Am I...am I regressing to my teenage self? Fawning and gawking over January for no reason but him just existing.

"Done!"

"Prove it." Why can't I stop? Why is flirting with January so addictive?

"I even mentioned Darlington Snow Paradise, what level of boyfriend did I just level up to?" He presents his phone; I quickly catch the caption.

Playing tourists with my one and only. Sweating like pigs out here in Arizona, can't wait to be back at @DarlingtonSnowParadise.

"Nicely done, Janny, but you have one more quest to complete before you level up." I rock back on my heels, my weight clumsily tumbles. I catch myself, but that doesn't stop January from stopping my fall.

"Defeat the Yeti Master, I can do that shit with my eyes closed." He wiggles his brows tauntingly.

"No, not defeat the Yeti Master," I press through my teeth. "Add my initials to your bio."

"Oh, duh, why didn't I think of that? You were always the smart one, Nono."

Not as of recently. Stupid brain and heart, can't you see this is all just pretend?

"Nono, let's go. We have to stay focused," January slips my phone from my palm, as I make up for my lost screen time from this morning. I was just gawking at the NWD in @TheCameronSnow's bio. "You didn't think I would do it, did you?"

"Not really, no."

"I'm being uninhibited now, Nono." That confession drowns out the agonizing squelching sound of the glad wrap rubbing against each extra layer applied around Samantha's personal driver's car.

I move my roll counterclockwise, running into January as he speeds around excitedly. I thread my roll around his back, tugging him closer to me.

"Why weren't you like this when we were younger?"

"Er, wrapped in glad wrap?" January quirks a thick raven brow.

"No, so bold and uninhibited."

"I already told you, I didn't want to lose you as a friend. Which was a good call, because when I confessed, I ended up losing you as a friend."

"That's not why we stopped being friends, January." I tug at the glad wrap aggressively, feeling it tear a little behind January's back.

"Yes, I know it was because I was a fucking asshat." He steps closer to me, tilting my chin to meet his gaze.

"I thought you were the person I knew best, but it seems like we were hiding a lot more from each other than I thought." I say all this without breaking eye contact, even though my heart aches agonizingly as I revisit those haunting emotions.

"Only to protect the longevity of our friendship."

"But you saw me as helpless, just like everybody else. I thought you were the one person who was in my corner."

"I am in your corner, Noelle."

It's staring me right in the face, I don't trust January when he says that. He's got a lot of ground to make up for.

"MY CAR! WHAT HAVE YOU DONE TO MY CAR!" Samantha's vocal fry is substituted for a shrill screech.

January bursts into hysterical laughter, breaking from our glad wrap cocoon. I take a moment to realize that we've already pranked Samantha. I am so in my head.

"Nono, look at her face." January swipes his finger along his lash line, collecting a tear. He's wearing the most sunny smile I've ever seen him wear.

It's incredible how a phenomenon like January's smile can make me feel nauseous and grounded at once.

I can't help but mirror his joy.

"I see. Hilarious."

"Unwrap this right now!" Samantha orders with military fierceness.

"Hey, this part is fun. Have at it, Nono." January's biceps flex as he tears through multiple layers of glad wrap at once. Meanwhile, in my fragile state both mentally and physically, I'm still working on my first layer.

The more layers we unravel of the wrapped car, the more my brain unravels in my head.

Can January and I pull this off? Not the glad wrap, but this whole fake relationship thing. My distrust of January is so multifaceted not even I completely understand why I'm not so willing to forgive him, he's trying so hard for me. I can sense his desperation of wanting something with me. Friendship? An actual relationship?

I guess I should ask what I want. So I'm prepared with whatever January has in mind.

January's wrap tangles with mine. The both of us ending up in a Lady and The Tramp situation, only with glad wrap and not a string of spaghetti.

His wheezing laughter comes to a sudden halt, the gentlest touch tilts my chin heavenwards.

"Hey, you okay?"

"Yeah, I'm fine."

I am so not fine.

Twenty

Run Around, Run Down

January

It only takes one look at Noelle Winter Darlington to see that she is burned out. Between the long car trip to and from the Grand Canyon yesterday, her adrenaline spiking every time she passed me in Mario Kart, and the biggest contribution to her burnout, this stupid fucking charade. No wonder she is feeling rundown.

But here she is in a Maloney complimentary robe, squinting at her computer as she tinkers with what essentially looks like numerical gibberish to me.

The fluffy lapel slips from her shoulder, revealing her flushed, freckled skin. I train my eyes on the droplet of sweat running from her temple.

"Noelle, you should just relax tonight."

Her fingers continue to click away at her pastel pink keyboard, her icy blue eyes shoot me a look of steel.

"I know you saw the comments from yesterday's outing," she spit irritably.

I have and they're getting comparatively worse. There was even one who compared us to her and her uncle taking a picture at the Grand Canyon. Mentally looking back at the photo, the posing could've been a little more romantic. I should've kissed the woman, I am madly in love with her after all.

But we've spoken about touching more, kissing her whenever I felt might not be off the table.

"Can I kiss you?"

"Ugh, it's like you don't even care about the lodge, I've always just been a quick fuck to you," she huffs, quickly collecting her laptop and shuffling off the bed.

"Wait, no, that was in poor taste and shit timing. I can see that you're stressed, but let me add some context to my question."

"I'm pretty sure I know the context, you want to kiss and hopefully lead into sex. Correct?"

"No." I won't deny I'm a little aroused by Noelle in nothing but a bathrobe, glaring at me like she's the smartest ass to grace the planet. "I was asking if I can kiss you when we are out and about to lend some legitimacy to this charade. I want this to work out so the lodge can benefit from it. So, I need your permission to kiss you whenever I please."

"That's all hunky dory." Only Noelle Winter Darlington could make hunky dory sound sexy. "But the general public says you kiss me like they kiss their grandma. Obligatory."

Which is weird because any chance to kiss Noelle that arises I seize with enthusiasm.

"Can I kiss you now, then?" I quirk a suggestive brow.

"What's the use, you just don't get the art of kissing. How do you kiss any other woman?"

Crap, how do I get out of this one? By telling the truth, I suppose. "I don't."

"You mean to tell me what you said in Walmart wasn't a lie?" Noelle's features soften as she drinks me in, seeing me in a new light. She looks so beautiful as she does so, Noelle *seeing* me is like transcending to heaven.

"No." I pocket my hands in the pouch of my hoodie for some grounding, I feel I could sprout wings and fly away.

"No wonder you're so one-track-minded." Noelle's girlish giggle is making something sprout, that's for sure.

I almost jump up on all fours like an excitable pup when she joins me on the bed once again.

"I need you to stay focused and really work on the authenticity of this connection. I'm not blaming you, I know I also have some work to do." Her hand threads into my damp locks, if I had a tail it would be going ballistic right now. "Yes, Janny, you can kiss me."

"Now?"

She presses her forehead to mine. "Whenever," she whispers, her soft, warm breath caresses my lips, triggering something primal and protective inside of me.

Like a lion tamely snoozing in a cave, only to be awoken by his lioness lover. I want to circle her seductively, her eyes trained on my every move, glittering with anticipation and desire.

I press my lips firmly to Noelle's, and my hands immediately toy with the knot of her robe. Focusing on the sensation on my lips, I snatch my hands away. I pull apart momentarily, allowing Noelle to correct her shallow breathing.

"You're. Not. A. Bad. Kisser." She starts and pauses after every word. "By any means, I certainly feel the effects of your kiss."

Feel the effects of my kiss? Like how I feel the effects of *your* kiss? I want to bare my teeth at anyone who dares flash a smile at you, who dares to enter the orbit of your celestial energy.

"See, I'm already short of breath," she pants. "I just think we need to work on being more grand with it, create a canyon of our own with our mouths."

A chuckle slips from my lips at her ridiculousness.

"I keep it tame so as not to tire you out." My thumb brushes her bottom lip instinctively, and her breath hitches. I pull my palm away from her cheek hoping to release her lungs.

"I figured as much, but the subtlety isn't reading to the masses. So it's something I'm going to have to adjust to, you've been very aware of my body, and I trust you to know when to stop."

"I trust you too." I bite back my victorious grin.

Her eyes light up like I've never seen before, the enchanting ice blue iridescent with invitation.

I welcome myself in once again. My palm splays between her shoulder blades as her muscles feather to press against me. Already I feel the taxing effect flood over her from her brief spurt of enthusiasm.

"Keep going," she pants, her breath coming hard on my teeth. I realize I'm smiling. What psychopath smiles when he kisses? I guess I do. "Janny, I said keep going."

Oh right.

Noelle is the one to attach our lips once again, her approach is thick with fervor. To my surprise, there isn't any trace of desperation. If the people witness a kiss like this and still have the gall to call it disingenuous. I honestly wouldn't even care, so long as Noelle keeps kissing me like this.

"Why is this actually..." her voice trails off.

"Good?"

"Amazing!" she corrects with a burst. "I guess I'm not very reactionary when we make out, what have I been depriving myself of?"

"The both of us. This feels so hot." My tongue presses for permission to tangle with hers.

"Very hot." Noelle's body twitches beneath me, I can feel the searing heat from her nape, her head lulling back with heaviness.

"Are you losing steam?"

"A little..." she struggles out. "Please keep going."

"I'll lay you down to ease the effort."

"That's counterproductive...oh god, I am so dizzy though," she squeezes out agonizingly.

"I'm stopping, Noelle, I can't keep kissing you when you're having a spell." I slip my hand from her back, I can feel her fiery flesh through the terry cloth fabric.

"I am not having an episode, I'm on the brink of one. There's a difference, Janny."

I inspect her facial features before trailing down her body, her cheeks rogue with an apricot-like pink that only emphasizes the sickly green of her complexion. Her eyes are glaring at me as I make my observations, my eyes avert to the sheen on her cleavage.

"I'm calling it."

"Are you fucking serious?" She pushes her palms into the mattress, her elbows shaking before she collapses onto her back once again.

"You said I have a good read on you and you trust me to make that call—"

"Well, my trust has been revoked. We were actually getting somewhere, but you just quit on me, out of the blue. I'm honestly not surprised." Noelle rolls her body to a stand, she falls like a bag of sand with a thud.

"Noelle!" I scurry to the edge of the bed.

"I'm not unconscious," she whines, pressing her back up against the mattress. I can see her temple throbbing as she squeezes her eyes shut.

I rely on my instinctive attentiveness with Noelle and run to gather a handful of ice. No matter how uncomfortable the freezing sensation is in my calloused hands, I can imagine what Noelle is experiencing right now is far worse. I tolerate the discomfort for her. I would go as far as to have the pain transferred to me if I could.

She flinches when I press the ice cube to her temple, her fingers wrap loosely around my wrists. The pinched furrow in her brows smooths out. Her eyes roll open and focus on my lips, she swallows dryly. Her eyes meet mine.

"I'm disappointed."

Those two words from Noelle's lips stab painfully at my heart.

"I'm sorry, Nono, I didn't want to trigger you into a spell. I do that enough by unintentionally riling you up."

"I can't tell what's intentional and what's not anymore. You say you're in my corner but seem to back away so quickly." Her hiss melts into a pained whine.

"Noelle, you cannot possibly use that against me. This is your health we are toying with here."

"This isn't going to work, January. No doubt you were going to make this call soon anyway, but I'm doing it first. I quit."

"What? Quit? Quit how?"

"Help me push these beds apart so I can get some fucking rest." Her words are weak, but her threat still cuts through strong. I silently oblige to split the beds, not wanting to rile her up anymore.

I can't tell if those are tears running down her face or droplets from the melted cube.

She sniffs.

That answers my question.

Devastatingly, those are tears.

Twenty-One

Hot 'n' Cold

January

"Can you wheel that thing a little quieter, can't you see my girlfriend is sleeping?" I turn to see Noelle shuffling herself to a lethargic seat. "Great, you woke her up. That'll be all, you can leave now." I usher the hotel staff, who delivered the room service I ordered in possibly the noisiest manner known to man, back into the elevator.

"No tip, sir?" The guy has some nerve.

"After that service, no way."

"I'm so sorry about him, he has this disease where he's an asshole to everybody. Not even his *girlfriend* is safe." Noelle brushes past me, blocking my scowling glare at the pushy staff member. Instead, I'm met with an unsightly knot of auburn. "Thank you so much for delivering the food."

"Apologies for waking you, ma'am." I roll my eyes at this absolute kiss ass, who in comparison makes me look like even more of a jerk.

"It's okay you didn't, his tyrannical rampage did. Thanks again." Noelle's lethal glare at me contrasts her sweet clarification.

The elevator doors finally close.

"You know when you say girlfriend like *girlfriend,* all aloof and shit. It doesn't add authenticity to this." I gesture to the both of us. "Now he's probably filling in the blanks, what if he thinks you're a prostitute?"

"That has to be the worst apology you've ever given me, January." Noelle rolls her eyes, lifting the silver dome to release a waft of steam, ribboning up to the ceiling. *Fried eggs.*

"Those fucking idiots, I ordered scrambled!" I roar, prying the dome from Noelle's nimble grip and smashing it back onto the plate in a fit.

"Fucking idiot, you still haven't said sorry." Noelle crosses her arms, flaring her nostrils.

"What's the use now, they fucked up your egg preference."

"You really are fucking stupid, January." She knocks the dome off-kilter with a fierce smack, storming off to her suitcase, and hurling it onto the unmade bed with a burst of adrenaline.

Fuck! There I go again, being an insensitive prat.

"Wait Noelle," I call, swiveling indecisively from the eggs and back toward the bed.

Fuck it, I'd rather eat cold eggs than receive Noelle's cold shoulder.

"Is it your life's mission to disturb my peace or something?" Noelle hisses, threateningly flipping the lid off her suitcase with all the strength she can muster. I plant my palm timidly on hers, peeling her hand from the zipper. It's enough to counteract her intention. She stumbles back with wide eyes, shocked by how much she underestimates my firm assertiveness, whilst remaining gentle with her. I can tell she's reconsidering the trust she revoked yesterday, I know her best.

A scowl paints on her angelic contemplative features, I guess she's decided she's not reinstating that trust then, despite it being in her best interest.

"I'm leaving, January. I'm leaving *you* this time." She manically cheers.

I don't know what to say, how to stop her from leaving. A few choice words come to mind, but I know she'll dismiss them instantly.

You can't leave me, Noelle, because...I love you.

She sighs, tightening her robe before refolding her clothes haphazardly into the suitcase.

"Noelle, I am so sorry." I start stupidly, she huffs with a dragon-like flare of her nostrils. "I'm not going to rile you up." I crawl onto the bed, dismissing my humility. Hoping my expression comes across as desperate and pleading, not sulky and stubborn. "I'm sincerely trying to make everything up to you. Especially for what I did to you ten years ago, ten days ago, and even ten minutes ago, as well as last night."

Noelle sinks defeatedly, all the fight and anger dissipating from her body. Though I know her surrendering is involuntary.

"I want to take you out on a date. An actual date that cannot be misconstrued as friendly or formal. I owe you a night of actual romance, something I failed to deliver on all of those occasions I let you down. I want to do this to make it up to you, but mostly because I like you, Noelle." Her raspberry-colored lips part with surprise, I welcome that smile that threatens at the corners of my mouth. "Noelle, you look so beautiful when you're shocked." Her lips press together again as she swallows thickly, and my smile drops with a lick of my lips. "Honestly, Noelle, I don't even care if people see us on this date, I only hope they do for the benefit of the lodge. But I just want to take you out, because I do, I like you. And I hope this is a stepping stone in rekindling that undeniable love we had for each other." I feel giddy saying all this to Noelle again, the nostalgic nerves running through my veins like electricity. And I love every second of it. "So, what do you say?"

I'm expecting her eyes to glitter with euphoria like the first time we confessed our feelings, any second now.

Her face pinches into a grimace.

Oh god.

Her lips part to speak.

"Cameron!"

SAMANTHA NOT FUCKING NOW!

"You were going to say something, Nono." I encourage Noelle to continue with a panicked huff.

"Cameron! Why aren't you ready?" Samantha scolds.

"For what, exactly?" I ask in a gravelly grumble.

"Press conference, gala, hello. I thought Seymour, being the youngest, would be like wrangling a toddler. Get dressed, would you? Angelface has to hurry also, you may be *in love* and time is an illusion when you're *in love*, but not in this case." Her irritating claws are painted an obnoxious red today, which my vision colors with as she makes air quotes.

"Press conference, no." I scrub my palms over my face. This is not fucking happening.

"Press conference, yes, actually."

"No, I plan to take Noelle out on a date today." My voice breaks with a whine, like some pathetic prepubescent teen. I'm basically displaying the same desperation I had as a teen when it came to Noelle liking me back.

"We scheduled a date yesterday, and it did your publicity no favors." Samantha reminds through her teeth, obviously still unhappy with the results.

"This isn't for publicity, I'm doing this because I like her." I clarify.

"You like her?" Samantha raises a brow, flicking her gaze to Noelle. Her eyes avert with a snarl pulling at the corner of her lips. She looks as though she doesn't even want to be friends with me, let alone date me.

"Yes, and I've done the worst job of showing that." I plead more so to Noelle than Samantha. This makes Noelle resign from the conversation altogether. She snatches at some sort of pink fabric conveniently in her vicinity, slipping into the bathroom before I can get a defensive word in edge wise.

"Fuck." I curl my fingers into fists.

"Worse than the worst." Samantha drives in on the fact.

"Thank you, Sam. So, I will be absent from the press conference because I'll be dating Noelle Darlington."

"You won't be." My skin textures with goosebumps at Noelle's airy British accent, I barely recognize the gut-punching declaration.

"I won't be?" I turn to see Noelle's hairline soaked with dampness, small splotches of wetness around her breast and torso soaking the baby pink wrap dress she opted for today. *She looks hot.* No, she looks worked up and flustered, sweating like a pig even. Yet, my brain bypasses that with how adorably summery she looks. "You certainly look dressed for the occasion, Nono, looking pretty in pink."

This dress is turning me into a lovesick teenage boy, it makes me want to steal my neighbor's unruly daisies and gift them to her.

"No, January, because I meant what I said last night. I quit."

Focus, January, she's unwell. She tugs at her phone charger viciously, throwing it into her suitcase. I plant my palm in the center of her suitcase, inhibiting her from doing it up. She meets me with a challenging, sweat-riddled stare.

I can't believe I'm breaking her heart again. Why do I keep doing this?

I part my lips, ready to speak.

"You quit?" Samantha snorts. "You can't quit, you signed a contract."

Noelle's red face flashes white instantaneously, her bottom lip quivers, and I'm positive she's about to burst into tears.

No, not again, don't cry, Nono.

"She can quit if she wants...is that what you really want?" I ask, hoping she'll seriously reconsider, although there's no reason she should. I'm just a stupid prickly tosser, this is all my fault.

"Nope!" If only those words came from Noelle's lips instead of Samantha's.

"I told you not to sign that soul-selling contract." I regret that being the first sentiment out of my mouth, I should apologize profusely.

Say sorry, you stupid prickly tosser. Say sorry and tell her you love her. Do something to make this all better. Don't quit on her.

"Yes, I get it, January!" Noelle's excessive volume snaps me to attention. "I told you so, I told you so, I told you so. Whatever, I'm doing this, I guess. I don't have a choice. This is the green light to make this super convincing, even with how much I hate you right now."

She hates me.

Again.

"Hey, it's your bestie, Noelle." My blood boils as Aaron wraps a chummy arm around Noelle's shoulder, I'm meticulous in its removal, ensuring I am gentle with Noelle and firm with Aaron. "Wow, Cameron, relax. I'm not stealing your best friend; I wouldn't mind stealing hers, though. Any chance Janelle is free Saturday if she's feeling philanthropic and wants to join me for the gala? A little afterparty for two afterward, if you catch my drift."

Noelle simply shoots Aaron an ice-cold glare, continuing to fan herself with the press pass Samantha had organized for her.

I plant my palms on Aaron's shoulders and guide him up to the table lined with chairs for all of us. I am insufferably placed between my hand-selected *besties,* quick-to-temper Seymour Floss, and quick-to-bed Aaron Nightingale.

"Sheesh, she looks PO'd, brother. What did you do to her?" Aaron leans over to me, discreetly asking through the corner of his mouth.

We scuffle our chairs in, my eyes dart straight to Noelle. Yep, still wearing the same face of disappointment, from the hotel to the conference hall.

"Something I'm desperately trying to stop; letting her down." I say with zero discretion, I have nothing to hide with Noelle. Not that she's sparing me even so much as a thought right now.

"Trouble in the sheets, I can give you tips for going down on a woman." Aaron's voice booms over the speaker. "Oops, testing testing. Just seeing if you are all paying attention." He covers his blunder by sleazily charming the crowd.

My eyes momentarily break from Noelle to Samantha, dragging her palm down her face. At least I'm not the disappointing client for once. I see Samantha lean into Noelle; her face somehow looks more sickly after whatever Samantha tells her in clandestine. I guess somehow, by Aaron's stupidity, I'm still the most disappointing client. I think the worst, and maybe she's trying to set Noelle and Aaron up.

Not fucking happening.

Noelle locks eyes with me after avoiding my gaze for the past 30 minutes. I unfortunately have a good read on Noelle and I know what Samantha has just told her is not good. It's conflicting to receive such an unsettling warning from the prettiest face ever to exist. Her damp hair now forms soft loose curls that frame her scowling, delicate features.

"Princess," I slip stupidly from my mouth.

Noelle shakes her head disapprovingly. Samantha contradicts Noelle with an enthusiastic nod.

Thankfully, the media has no interest in asking me questions; I have quite the reputation for *answering back*. Which is what you're supposed to do when someone asks you a question, but according to Samantha, my answers are always disrespectful and gruff.

Opposed to the bloke to my right? Every answer is a sexual innuendo, then I've got Dr. FistyCuffs to my left snorting at everything like a high school boy.

I disregard those meatheads, fading out the meaningless questions of the report. Probably directed at our captain, Vinnie, who is about the only person who will give a flawless answer they are looking to put on their tacky clickbait website.

My vision sharpens on Noelle, but darkness engulfs her vision as her eyes continue to flutter shut. I discreetly flag down Samantha, but she's all heart eyes for her media-trained pet husband. Getting a hold of her is hopeless when she's in this state.

I scan the room for a chair Noelle could make her way to, preferably one against the wall, so she has support along the way. But all the chairs are in uniform rows and columns in the center of the room.

The flattering v-neckline of her dress gives me a clear view of her heaving cleavage, I watch as her skin flushes pink in real-time.

I can't just sit here and watch, I've got to fucking do something.

"And that's how you score—" my abrupt chair scrape cuts Aaron's deep southern drawl off.

"Cameron, bud, what are you doing?" Vinnie catches my bicep as I stalk past, my underestimated strength coming in handy as I pry my arm from him. I jump off the stage with a heavy thump.

"What the hell are you doing, get back up there," Samantha berates.

"Gladly."

"Janny, what are—" Noelle's body falls limp immediately at my touch.

So much for trust revoked, Nono.

I hike her onto my back; I feel her cheek, heavy on the top of my hair. Her breasts press against my shoulder blades, she grips her hands together tightly.

"I've got you, Nono." My large hands on her soft thighs are proud of that statement.

"Janny, I don't feel well." Her breath feathers my earlobe.

I carefully hoist myself back onto the stage. Slipping Noelle down slowly, purposely doing it behind Aaron's ridiculous 6'7 frame in case this pretty pink dress of hers betrays her and rides up.

"Take a seat, Nono."

She falls hard into the chair.

Twenty-Two

The Damsel Is Distressed

Noelle

The cameras flash frantically, and quiet whimpers I'm sure only dogs could hear slip from my lips.

"No cameras!" January barks by my ear. The flashing stops, and my pinched features melt away into disbelief.

"Janny." My fingertips blindly reach for January, caressing his cheek gratefully.

I'm thankful for January's quick thinking, no one looks out for me like him. *I guess he is in my corner.* So, I should do my best to make this entire operation as smooth as possible since I don't have a choice. I'm stuck here, but I could do what he does and sulk about it, or I can take advantage of all of this exposure. I'm sitting in front of dozens of cameras right now, I'd be an idiot not to strike while the iron is hot.

"Question for Cameron!"

"Cameron! Over here!"

"Question for Mr. Snow."

"Your question better be, is she okay and nothing else?" January grumbles into the microphone. Half of the opportunistic crowd reclaims their seats they sprung up from.

"Cameron, is she okay?" A reporter calls out.

"I'm okay," I wheeze out.

"British?"

"Airmail girlfriend?"

"Up and coming model, how did she meet Cameron Snow?"

"LA Fashion Week? Sport Spartan had a collection of streetwear?"

I thought my imagination was vivid, but the amount of false stories these reporters hush amongst themselves is impressive.

"Who are you?" A reporter asks me directly, piercing through the conspiratory whispers.

I tilt my head back, searching to see if January is still in proximity; he stands menacingly over me like a surly—*and kind of sexy*—bodyguard.

Which makes me say this next statement proudly.

"I'm January's girlfriend, Noelle Darlington."

"The rumors are true. Girlfriend, not friends." I overheard a reporter discuss.

Yes, exactly, not friends. Print that in bold! Turn me into a GIF! Spread the word!

I feel January's firm body curl over me, I instinctively want to crane my neck back so he can leave bruising kisses on my neck. It clicks where the instinct comes from; I opened up so naturally to January's love when we fucked back at the lodge. The vision of him hurled over my body as he had the fiercest orgasm that was ten years in the making. The feeling was undeniable then and I can only imagine it reads that way right now.

"For now." January's voice booms over the speakers. I meet his intimate cerulean gaze. I'm thrust back to the memory of our first kiss. *Should we or shouldn't we?* Replaying in my mind. Much like now, he gave me the decision, allowing me to evaluate the situation, and be the one to make the final decision to cross the threshold of friendship.

"January," I slip with a moan, his tempting lips cracking into a smile.

"Cameron Snow is smiling!" a reporter shouts out in disbelief.

"Cameron Snow is in love!" Another shouts.

I break into a beaming smile myself.

"January Snow is kissing me," I announce between the two of us, before closing in on the alluring kiss that hovers between our electric chemistry.

The cameras flash in a frenzy again, thankfully disregarding January's command from before.

There is no way anyone can dismiss what the press is capturing right now as fake, reserved, or friendly. This kiss is identical to the passionate one we first shared at 18. My heart is pounding with the same eagerness it had back when I felt our lives together were about to begin.

Nono and Janny against the world (or Phoenix was a good start).

Here we are now, our tongues tangled together once again, and that feels like a possibility again.

We break apart, our hot haggard breath cocktailing together. I can't keep the smile off my face.

"That was..." January starts with a huff.

"Fun." I finish his sentence.

"So fun," he says through a chuckle.

"Cameron! How did you meet?" The reporters begin their chaotic questioning again.

"Snow! Snow! Over here! How long have you been together?"

"That's the conclusion of the conference." Samantha's grating Valley girl vocal fry is actually welcome this time.

"You okay to walk?" January's breath tickles my ear, sending a shiver up my spine, only to ricochet back down to my pelvis with a tremor.

"I can walk with you by my side," I wispily reply.

"Of course, Nono, we're attached at the hip."

January presses his forehead to mine, I inhale his homely vetiver scent.

"With how much sex we're having, it's barely just an expression of speech anymore, but a fact." I tease on my exhale.

"Fuck." January replies with a salacious hum, his teeth nipping at his bottom lip.

"Sure." I wink, biting my cheek mischievously.

January pulls my limp weight up with ease, wrapping his arm around my waist, I can feel his muscles feather as he does all the heavy lifting. I am still slightly dizzy, but with January's help, I don't think I'll make the headlines for face-planting off the stage. Not this time.

January punctuates his supportive guidance with a peck to my temple.

"You kids were great up there." Samantha is all pearly white teeth upon her greeting, hanging off her husband excitedly as he takes his place beside her.

I feel great about all of this too; I think I'll celebrate with my best friend...and boyfriend.

"Samantha." January starts sternly, I watch him with anticipation. "Do not come to the apartment for the rest of the day, understood?"

Samantha flicks a knowing gaze between January and I, "Reading you loud and clear, Cameron."

She's buying it! She believes we have sex.

Twenty-Three

Olaf, Olaf, Olaf

January

"Look, January."

I'm looking alright, how this pretty pink dress has adhered to Noelle's ass cheeks and her sloping hips, emphasizing her tiny waist. Sure, she's also got a massive sweat stain on her back, but I kind of have the desire to grow it tenfold. I want to make her sweat.

"When Snow said 'For now'," Noelle pries one hand from her phone to do air quotes, before continuing to recite the article that was quickly birthed from the press conference, "the audience was confused at first by the subtext behind those measly two words. Crowds suspecting that Noelle Darlington, 28. I don't know why my age was necessary. Was merely a temporary fling for Phoenix Badger's number ten. But if you were lucky enough to witness the chemistry they had in person, it is undeniable that the pair are on the path to be wed. And if what I saw was true, my guess is a proposal will happen soon. Really soon." Noelle concludes, her breathing thin as her excitement grows. "January, people are believing we're in love-"

I cup Noelle's cheeks and bring her into a passionate kiss; she hums sweetly as her arms link around my neck.

We are so not faking anymore. I love you, Noelle, say you love me too. This can't be pretend.

I go to slip from the kiss, Noelle charging her lips against mine again. I rub my hand along her back, hoping it will soothe her eagerness. She grips my wrist fiercely and moves my hand to her ass; she purrs ferally at the contact. We part with a wet pop.

"Let's celebrate." She wrestles the knot of her dress free, her auburn locks obstructing her vision. I gently pry her hands from the bow, polarizing her commanding puppeteering. The belt is now in a stubborn half-bow tangle.

"Just rip it, I don't care," Noelle pants, her heaving cleavage is right in my line of sight, but I stay focused on the challenging puzzle that is this garment's fastening. I'm losing my patience so quickly, that I may just take on Noelle's request to, "Rip it, Janny!" Scratch that, her demand.

I have had quite an influence on her.

"I'm trying not to ruin this dress, you look so pretty in it."

"Ugh." Noelle grunts, flicking the skirt up as she throws her head back, I notice her arm working in stroking motions.

"Are you...touching yourself?" I swallow dryly, I hear a faint snap under my strangling grip, and the blush-colored material unravels from Noelle's body. It's like Christmas day and Noelle is the gift I've always wanted.

"January," she moans as she speeds her stroking, I slowly peel the soft cotton from her shoulder, before removing it from the other, the dress falls to her working arm. "I can't stop."

"Should I rip it?" I cusp the limp material in my hand.

"Fuck, yes, rip it!"

I curl my fingers, pulling the fabric to its absolute limit of stretch. Noelle groans orgasmically as the dress sounds a slow-paced tear.

"Mm, fuck, you are so strong, January."

I whip the fabric from her arm, my fingertips travel down her forearm, and my thumb glides past her pulse. Gently, I pull her hand, which is frantically stroking, from her bud, bringing it up to my lips and sliding my tongue over her knuckles. I wrap my lips around her fingers, tasting the sweetness of her juices, my eyelids flutter at the orgasmic taste.

"January," she says breathlessly, my eyes refocus on her. She looks dazed and enchanted, but mostly extremely fuckable.

"Noelle," I croak primitively, her knees faltering as I prowl forward. Lucky for her, I anticipated that reaction and plant my palms on her derriere, lifting her to the mattress.

I back away, observing the angel lying on the duvet.

The love of my life and the girl of my dreams.

I'm tempted to whip out my cock and pump it into its firmest state and push it straight into that already soaking pussy of hers. But we've already flown too close to the sun last time we didn't use a condom.

Although, luckily, Noelle had birth control.

But it got me thinking about our future together. I'm yet to discuss it with Noelle, but I would adore having a family with her. I believe together we'd make incredible parents. Our kids would have an incredible childhood growing up at the lodge, something I can vouch for.

"Here." Noelle presents a holographic square wrapper.

We'll invite Aunty Janelle and Aunty Candy around for Christmas. I guess Uncle Aaron and Uncle Seymour are welcome, too. How could I possibly forget the kids' godparents, Samantha and Vinnie?

"Earth to Janny." Noelle giggles, rolling the condom on my firm cock herself.

"Look at you putting those Sex Ed classes to use."

Her hand doesn't leave my cock, her grip tightens as a wicked smile grows on her face.

She kneads her nimble fingers into my length; I feel my balls become firmer. My eyelids sink closed, her fondling is relaxing and arousing, complete and utter bliss.

This whole stunt has been so stressful for both me and her, it feels good to be gentle and calm in this moment.

The heat and moisture consuming my ballsack disturbs my peace.

Oh fuck, my ballsack is in Noelle's mouth. Pinch me now.

"Noelle, Princess, Baby, Honey, Sweetie."

Noelle inhales with a gag, spitting my balls out. Her coughing fit turns into a chorus of laughter.

"I'm sorry, that was so funny. Princess, Baby, Honey, Sweetie."

"You didn't let me finish...Minx."

"I'll show you minx, Hot Shot." Noelle rises to her knees on the mattress, her touch abandoning my cock and acquainted with the band of my sweatshirt. The one that now smells like a concoction of cinnamon and vetiver. She discards the garment haphazardly. My hand reaches for her cheek, but I miss it as she launches her head forward. Her tongue presses just above my belly button and hotly glides up the center of my abs, passing my pectorals before punctuating with a mischievous peck on my lips.

If I sat teenage January down right now and explain what his seemingly sweet and innocent best friend is doing to him in the future, he'd probably stand up and call me a big fat liar.

Noelle aligns her breath with my cock, even wrapped in the geode holographic condom the heat pierces through. Which is why Janelle makes a superior product.

My mouth salivates at the thought of being inside Noelle's steaming hot pussy, I barely noticed my sweatpants are suddenly bunched at my ankles.

"You going to keep those on while we fuck or...?" my eyes refocus on Noelle's ice-blue naughty stare. I flick my ankles free from the flannelette shackles, welcoming myself onto the mattress with my best friend/love of my life/girl of my dreams.

All I can think of is how lucky I am.

"January, before we start, don't stop until I say Olaf."

"Our safe word." I can't help but smile at myself. "Those Sex Ed classes have been quite practical."

Mrs. Donovan did a wonderful job in equipping us with the best experience for getting down and dirty. We must invite her to the wedding.

I plant my palms beside her shoulders, her ice-colored eyes widening with enchantment, "Ready?"

"Ready," she breathes out with a small nod.

I push myself into her entrance.

Fuck, nothing will ever compare to this. I let out a pathetic whine, my eyes rolling back, my mouth gaping with a gurgle. I hope Noelle can read that these are all signs of appreciation.

"Janny, yes, fast and rough."

"You sure?" I know I am more than capable, all I did during the years Noelle was absent from my life was eat, sleep, and workout. So, to say my stamina is impeccable is an understatement.

"Please, January, don't pity me." Her hands thread into my locks, already damp from the sweat of the pure adrenaline I get whenever Noelle is naked in my presence. She clenches her fist in my tresses, pulling my face close to hers. "Now fuck me, Hot Shot."

I reach my hand between us and pet her clit as I roll my hips fluidly into her.

Oh, she's wet. So fucking wet. Impeccably wet.

I speed a little, my thrusts vocalized by the excessive moisture. Noelle inhales sharply, her eyes locking with mine.

I scan her for any sign of discomfort.

"Like that." Her body melts into my rapid thrusts. "That feels good, Janny, don't stop."

I can feel a pathetic whine building in my throat, I try manipulating it so it comes out as a grunt. Only my efforts to roughen up my moans also reflect in my hips.

"Janny, fuck, oh, fuck, Olaf, Olaf, Olaf."

Shit. I pause my hips in an instant.

"Are we done?" My whine slips out with the concern.

Noelle's palm presses to her heart, she applies pressure as she inhales deeply.

"I'm going to pull out, Nono."

"No, January, wait." Her eyes avert from me. I sense her embarrassment radiating off her skin, her eyes glittering with tears.

"Noelle, you are not a burden to me, I'm having fun with you, don't feel guilty." I am certain I have just counteracted every deprecating thought in her head.

"Screw you for being able to read me so well." She breaks into a smile. The pad of my thumb catches the stray tear that runs down her temple.

"You want to keep going?" I ask attentively.

"Just a smidge slower." Noelle gesticulates with a pinch of her fingers.

"Does it hurt?"

"No, it feels incredible," Noelle releases her tight grip from my hair, massaging my scalp with tender gratitude. "My heart just feels like it's about to burst out of my chest."

"We could maybe try it in moderation. Should we make up a new code word for *stop but don't pull out*."

"Sven." Noelle decides instantaneously.

"Keeping it in the Frozen family, I see."

"Most quotable movie ever."

"I'll try not to whine like a little bitch, I was concentrating on grunting instead of whining and I think all my frustrations channeled into my hips." I wriggle slightly. Noelle hums with appreciation, continuing the circular motion.

"I like it when you whine, it's pathetic."

"Ha, ha, Nono."

"Finish me!" Noelle declares in a deep, bassy tone, imitating the announcers in fighting video games.

"You're the master, Yeti." I jab.

"Hey!" Noelle's detestation melts into a moan as my hips find a pleasurable rhythm once again. "January, fuck, this is perfect, my heart feels full but not like it's going to burst."

"Thank fuck, because this feels fucking fantastic."

I can feel her arousal grip tightly around my cock.

"You want me, Noelle, you want me so bad. Minxy girl."

"I do, Hot Shot, I want you," she declares airily.

"Oh fuck," I slip in a whine. "God, that is not attractive."

Noelle outdoes me with an equally horrific wheeze.

"Looks like we are mutually pathetic losers and with that discovery I am about to finish." I steady my elbows and realign my posture to articulate every moderate punch of my pelvis.

"Me too." Noelle's back bows into me, her entrance flexing at the base of my length, I can feel her copious amounts of cum dripping onto my balls.

"Oh fuck, that's hot." I feel my ejaculation sprouting from my tip with light-speed. "Noelle, Princess, Baby, Honey...oh yes."

Noelle giggles, wriggling me from her entrance. Her fingertips press to my cheeks, featherlight, bringing me into a tame make out.

I love you, Noelle Snow.

Twenty-Four

Take It Easy

Noelle

Oh my god, I can't believe it.

"January, wake up, wake up." I jostle January, his soft snoring coming to a halt.

"Huh? What's wrong?" He stirs in the sheets and groans when he realizes his arms aren't possessively wrapped around my waist. He quickly corrects that, his eyes landing on my laptop screen. "Wait, is that the booking calendar for Darlington Snow Paradise?"

"Yeah-ha!" I gnaw at my bottom lip excitedly.

"And that's six confirmed, fully paid bookings for next month."

"Yeah-ha!" My pitch heightens with excitement.

"Is this because of us?"

"Yeah-ha! Yeah-ha! Yeah-ha!"

"Oh shit, go Nono!" January sits up, offering his palm, and I smack mine against him with a celebratory high five. Only to catch myself as the tingle settles from the forceful exchange. That is far too friendly, a couple would celebrate with a kiss.

I push my laptop to the side, pressing myself against January's bare chest, hurling my thigh over his and smothering my lips to his agape mouth.

"Oh, Noelle." His palms splay the entirety of my bum, he moans richly into my throat.

"It's working, Janny. Marrying you might actually be worth it!" I pant, pressing my rear into his massaging fingers. The seductive glint in his smile falters.

"How should we celebrate, Nono?" His hands adjust to my hips, it feels far too friendly, despite me perched on his semi-firm cock. I feel a sense of panic to maintain this high we are achieving with our convincing chemistry.

"I don't know, I wouldn't mind going on that date of yours."

A lot of things make my heart speed up to an unhealthy rate, mostly negative things, standing for too long, stressful situations, and agonizing heat. But there is one trigger that I welcome wholeheartedly—*pardon the pun*—when January's face lights up euphorically.

"You feeling up for it, Nono?" Concern twitches at his brows.

"I mean, you don't mind if it's not for show? What if we just hang out here for the day and rent some shitty movies that no doubt make up the entire catalog on this hotel TV? Get some rubbish food and just...be."

"Like how we used to."

"Yes." The maintenance doesn't always have to be in front of the cameras. The solid product comes from the practice behind the scenes...or so I tell myself, so I can keep enjoying January's companionship. Even though I really ought to keep things strictly professional with this stunt.

But a part of me wants this so badly. I want to live out my teenage girl fantasy and be January Snow's girlfriend, for real.

Is it safe to do so, though? The people believe we are in love, and I believe we were all those years ago. But if we were to fall in love now...is it enough for January not to break my heart again?

"Let's do it, Nono." I guess my mind has been made up for me. I'm doing this. We are doing this.

I have to avert my eyes to stop my heart from whirling with giddy. He's wearing the same boyish smile he wore whenever we hung out as friends, the same smile that made me think of him as more than friends.

If only January wasn't devastatingly pretty, I could just keep my heart at bay, but if he's going to actually put in effort to be sensitive and romantic. I don't know if I stand a chance.

It was so easy falling for him the first time and now he's ten times more handsome with his premature grays and sharp jawline.

Not to mention he's got the shoulders of a refrigerator, and is so tall and well-proportioned.

Sure, he's a little grumpy, but it's kind of adorable. He's not angry at anything in particular, he's just got the personality of Eeyore from Winnie the Pooh.

And I kind of love him for it.

I kind of love January.

Oh fuck.

Katy Perry's *Never Really Over* plays in this Walmart, soundtracking my internal crisis. I roll my eyes at how fitting it is to my dilemma rattling around in my brain. Who would've thought a catchy pop song would have such a visceral effect on me?

I do what I do in any dire situation. I consult the girls for some advice. In this case, I think I'm in love with a man who will inevitably hurt me again.

@DarlingNoelle: girls??? Candy??? Nelly???

Please, girls, someone be online.

@TickleMeKink: you called.

@WhatIsCandyEating: you called.

@WhatIsCandyEating: JINX!

@TickleMeKink: talk to me, crumpets, I can sense your crisis all the way from Vegas.

@DarlingNoelle: I really need to get you girls out to the lodge as soon as I get back.

@DarlingNoelle: but this is an SOS. I need help, advice, a bitch slap. SOMETHING?!?!?!

"Noelle?" January calls for my attention tenderly.

I quickly pocket my phone away, my face burns as if I was just caught doing something nefarious.

"You okay?" For fuck's sake, January, don't look at me like that or I will probably be the one to get down on one knee.

"I'm good, just messaging the girls."

"Remind me to meet them one day under less ridiculous circumstances."

"Our wedding?"

I remember envisioning a symbolic wedding with January, an idea that blossomed in my youth when I started viewing him as a lifelong partner. Darlington Snow Paradise, at the start of the snowfall, with the snow at its most pristine white, has always been my dream location for our wedding. I'd have a gown to match, although I'm no longer *complete,* thanks to January all those years ago, I'd still wear snow white. It would be small and intimate, being each other's only friends, our guest list probably wouldn't exceed our parents. But I never wanted a big wedding, I just wanted one with January.

"You still want to get married?"

"I said so this morning that it'll be totally worth all this trouble." And not to mention my soon-to-be husband is destined to be a future DILF who knows me like the back of his hand.

"I just wasn't sure if you liked me like that, I actually thought you hated me."

"I hated you at that moment, but..."

"Things are looking up for the lodge you like me again?" January raises a concerned brow.

"I tolerate you at best." Masking my crisis with a joke, because I know I am falling for January and it's certainly not to do with the mutual benefits of this arrangement. I'm simply just falling for him.

"Tolerance, the grounds of a fruitful marriage." January sells theatrically, I'm sent into a horrendous snorting fit.

It wasn't even that funny. *Oh fuck, I'm soooo gone.*

I clear my throat, "Excuse me, I've left my friends on read."

"By all means, don't keep them waiting. My ears are burning, though." January rolls his cerulean eyes, my own eyes track the circular motion, anticipating the conniving smile to crack on his face.

Just like old times.

"I won't be long." I look over my shoulder once more to see January has actually moved to inspect the variety of chips. "Get the—"

"Got them!" He holds up the cheese-flavored Doritos I was about to order. God, this man is killing me with how well he knows me.

I unlock my phone to an influx of screaming messages.

@DarlingNoelle: sorry guys, I couldn't talk he was hot on my tail

@TickleMeKink: ooooh anal, is this your first time, crumpets?

@DarlingNoelle: very funny, Nelly.

@TickleMeKink: it's been radio silent in this chat, I'm still waiting to know how big.

@DarlingNoelle: not as big as the dilemma I'm in.

@WhatIsCandyEating: I'm back! What did I miss?

@TickleMeKink: lock into therapist mode, Candy Cane, this one sounds like a doozy.

@DarlingNoelle: I think I like January again…

Both names shoot up from the keyboard, notifying me they are typing. I try to steady my breathing, it's out there now. It's no longer just a thought in my head. Now it's a materialized idea and hopefully, my girls will help me process it.

@WhatIsCandyEating: this is amazing, Noelle, does he like you back?

Always the optimist my dear Candy, guess when you eat clean, your mind is also clean. I look over at January, only he's missing. How the hell do you lose a supermodel in a supermarket?

@DarlingNoelle: sent a voice memo.

"As a matter of fact, I do like her very much."

I could vomit my heart as January's finger releases from the voice recording button. The message automatically sends through.

"So much for not riling me up, my heart is pounding." I elbow him away with the very little strength I can muster.

@TickleMeKink: OMFG HES WITH YOU RIGHT NOW!!! CAMERON HIIIII!!! BE GOOD TO MY GIRL NOELLE MWAH MWAH!!!

@DarlingNoelle: sent a voice memo.

"And you be good to my boy, Aaron Nightingale."

"Okay, enough fun for today." I go to lock my phone, January's tilts the phone his way, and I can only just make out the wording of the lengthy message.

@TickleMeKink: Man won't stop dming me to catch up, he doesn't know me like that. Do me a favor and put him back to factory setting, I think he's broken.

"Ha, that Janelle is funny. Aaron is a dickwart." January snarls.

"Only a certified dickwart could make that observation." I jab.

"Don't push me, Noelle, or I'll send a voice memo to your gal pals declaring my love for you. How's that for a jumpscare?"

"It would certainly make my heart pound." Why does my heart feel like it's launched in my throat? Are we joking? Are we pretending? Is this real? It's like a question tornado in my head right now.

"Let's go check out some ice cream for dinner." January pries my flaccid hand from my pounding chest and links our fingers together.

Our pulses mix, beating with the same syncopation.

Only to break them apart when a blissful coldness caresses my skin in the frozen aisle.

Freezer aisle today, wedding aisle tomorrow.

My mind dangerously concocts visions of the metaphorical day...it won't stay metaphorical forever. According to a contract snuggled away in Samantha's office, I will marry January Cameron Snow.

January links my hand with his own across my stomach as he hugs me from behind. He plants his chin on top of my head.

"I'm having so much fun with you, Noelle. It feels simple, just like how it was when we were kids." The hum he sounds after his sentence reverberates in my skull, momentarily soothing the chaos swirling inside.

"I'm having fun too." I slip into a moment of vulnerability.

I never really got the chance to consult with my girls, thanks to Mister Mic Hog over here. Guess that's payback for me hijacking his press conference yesterday.

Something in my gut is telling me not to let my guard down just yet.

Ugh, I really needed that chat with my girls.

"Decisions, decisions, Nono. We can get a couple if you want, we have our own personal ice cooler." January gestures to the colorful canisters behind the frosty panel of glass.

"That you demanded for." I pinch at the skin on the back of his veiny hand, my juvenile punishment interrupted as I trace my fingers over his protruding veins. To think his fingers have been inside me and I haven't even witnessed them at work, far too enveloped in the pleasure to open my eyes and spectate.

"Can't have my princess melt to death."

"You spoil me," I smirk to myself, pursing my lips when I catch my infatuated reflection.

"You appreciate everything I do for you."

"I do." I breathe out. "Mint Choc Chip." I finally decide.

"I think it's about time we did our rematch of Blizzard, Nono." January heaves the five bags he insisted he carry up to the room. I may not have ever seen his hand muscles at work whilst inside me, but boy, I'm coping quite the arm candy show now.

"Are you referring to the rematch I declared all those years ago?"

"That's the one, Princess, I'm willing to do so now. I'm giving you the chance."

"How noble of you, Prince." My teeth nip at my bottom lip. I think I am this close to giving January another chance at my heart.

"I'm giving you the chance to finally lose to me for good."

On second thought.

"Tosser." I arm myself with a pillow, throwing it at the giant. Of course, he skillfully dodges it. "Fine. Rematch. I'm about to bring you to tears, Hot Shot."

"Oh, it's on, Nono." His eyes narrow with a challenging stare.

"I have a HDMI cord on me, get ready to—"

"Eat yellow snow." January finishes for me.

I growl falsely through my teeth. I can't say that my predictability to January is bothersome, I just wish I had somewhat of the same certainty with him. Even in his stoic state as a teen, where to the average outsider he was an unreadable enigma, I still read him just fine, until all I knew was challenged by that miserable day. Ten years we've been apart, yet things feel like they haven't changed, but not everything feels quite the same.

The HDMI cord strangled around my knuckles is turning them white, I release myself from the shackles of my memories. I have to trust that January isn't like that anymore, we've had huge developments in our friendship, and even our romantic relationship seems to be thoroughly explored...well the sex part, that's for sure.

"You remember when we drove two hours out of town for a new HDMI cord?" It feels like my lips are moving involuntarily as I nervously recite the memory.

"Because Snowflake chewed through the other one, I remember."

I look up from the cord at the wrong moment as I see January strip off his Metallica shirt. That made him look like every bad boy (that I was adamant I could fix) I read in books. For his, you guessed it, Phoenix Badger's hoodie.

My Janny is such a homebody.

"Snowflake." I coo subconsciously, jolting back to the conversation at hand. Snowflake was the precious, wild, snow bunny January and I harbored in my bedroom, keeping the pet secret from our parents. That was until he had to explain why we needed a new HDMI cable. They did not buy that they magically fray over time. It didn't help that Snowflake revealed himself, as we were explaining why it is essential to my inevitable career as the world's best video game developer.

"He threw us under the bus, after all the snowmen that sacrificed their carrot noses for him." January clicks his tongue disapprovingly. I can't help but giggle girlishly, January is just so *dreamy* sometimes.

I am in big, big trouble; I need to stop this now.

"You know that's when I started falling for you," I state coyly, digging my foot into the floor bashfully. "Even after my parents tore through us for harboring a pet snow bunny, you still stuck by me in all of my schemes and pranks. I certainly thought you were attractive before then, but you stayed by my side, even when I was clearly trouble. That made my teenage girl's heart go crazy. What girl doesn't dream of having a pretty boy as her unconditional partner in crime?"

I don't know why my mouth thinks reciting all this information is necessary...possibly because this is the moment I pinpoint as *I'm falling for January 2.0.*

"I've always been with you, even if it gets me into trouble. I wouldn't have it any other way."

"We were kind of little shits growing up." I snob off January's advancement for a hug by leaning behind the TV in search of the correlating port. January sighs dramatically, holding the TV so I don't get crushed to death.

"I don't think we outgrew that phase, Samantha would probably still consider us to be little shits," January adds to my dismissive comment, my attempt at making things friendly. I'm giving myself whiplash, jumping the fence that divides friendship and infatuation every five minutes, I do not have the mental stamina for this.

"I really missed you, January. Why did you never visit?" Great, I guess, I've landed myself on neither and am being stabbed by the metaphorical cast-iron fences' sharp spikes. Now, I'm bleeding out as the memory that created the fence in the first place resurfaces.

"You have no idea how much I missed you too, I thought you didn't want to see me again." January reasons. I feign tinkering with the cord, to avoid this very vulnerable conversation, even though I was the one to prompt it.

"I was just angry in that moment when I said that, I didn't think you'd stay away for so long, I thought you'd come back after the season. I forgave you long before then. But then you never did, and the next season came and passed, and the next, and the next, and the next. I thought we were closer than that." I say as I aggressively take my frustrations out on the plug, the cord may just fray from my pressurized twisting.

"We were, we are. Noelle, you have no idea how much time I've wasted." January carefully pulls me from behind the TV I am shielding my vulnerability with, he pauses contemplatively like he's trying to find the right words to say.

"Stop thinking about what I want to hear and just say what you mean." I whine desperately, "I'm sick of guessing, of figuring you out, because no matter what, I'm always wrong about you."

"I'm falling in love with you, Noelle!" January bursts out. "That scares me a little because it feels way deeper than last time and I know you are nowhere close to where I am with my love for you. And this isn't me trying to pry an answer out of you now, but yes, Noelle, I'm falling deeply and more in love with you."

"Oh."

January chuckles, "Just *oh*?"

"Yeah." I have no words.

"I have more to say."

"Go ahead."

"I don't want to dogpile it all on you."

"My god, is there a lot more?"

"Yeah-ha."

"Oh."

January's lips purse with uncertainty, "It can wait."

"Tell me, Janny, it's helping me recognize some things within me." I guess I finally have the answers to those questions eating at my brain. What do *I* want?

"Wait, are you...actually, no. I will not pry an answer out of you, but hopefully, my words can turn what you're fighting internally into something more manageable."

I let out a whimper at January's considerations. No one in my life will even compare to January in that way. No one has ever been so thoughtful and attentive.

I give January a nod to continue.

"As a kid, I always saw you being in my future, hopefully as my wife, but there was a part of me that knew it wasn't entirely possible. But since we've started doing this admittedly stupid stunt, some of it fabricated yet parts of it feel undeniably real, either way, the vision has become clearer. A future with you seems so within reach, I think my heart is convinced it's happening right now. That you are my girlfriend and I am your boyfriend, I genuinely plan to propose, then get married. My heart has even thought beyond that."

"Beyond that?" My bottom lip quivers.

"Well, I've always dreamed of having a family with you, Noelle, don't you think we'd make great parents? I know I wouldn't model my parenting after my parents. And you probably have some things you wouldn't use from your parents, but I think their shortcomings with us are great knowledge for when it's our turn. If you want kids. Is this too much for you to hear right now?"

"January, I put a disturbing amount of detail into our metaphorical future as a young girl. You are barely scratching the surface of what my sick mind concocted."

"I'd love to hear about it all one day, Nono."

"Shall we play *Blizzard* while I process that avalanche of information," I suggest. I don't have all that much to consider, except what my wedding dress is going to look like and how to tell January I'm also falling in love with him.

It's safe to surrender to my feelings, a pillow of snow awaits below to cushion my fall.

Twenty-Five

Snowfall

January

It felt so good finally getting how I feel off my chest, I won't feel like such a prat when I gift her the things I have been accumulating in my wardrobe at my mansion. I can't even call that place my home, because Noelle is my home and sanctuary wrapped up in one.

I open the velvet jewelry box for the six thousandth time; the diamonds wink at me more and more brightly with each greeting, I cannot wait to see how superb they will look on Noelle's pretty collarbones.

It's an absolute injustice that they are separating us to get ready for the gala. Samantha justifying how unreliable we've been since we've fallen in love with one another. She's not entirely disgruntled by that fact, but I am entirely disgruntled that I have to be separated from my best friend/the love of my life/the girl of my dreams. Especially after airing out my feelings only last night, it feels cruel.

"If it makes you feel any better, Vinnie and I can't get ready in the same room."

"Do not bring up vibrating cock rings at this point and time, Samantha, I beg of you."

"No, Vinnie mostly ends up bickering with me, because he won't admit he looks far better looking than me in his suit, very frustrating. So, we get ready separately and find out what the other is wearing when we arrive at the event."

"I can't wait to be married." I slip, imagining Noelle and myself bickering over silly little things like that.

"You're going to live an extremely happy life, Cameron." Samantha smiles warmly at me.

"I'm already living it, I'm sure." Usually, I try to shake my publicist's presence, but I am honestly so incredibly grateful that she is here to keep my jitters at bay. I am proposing tonight and although Noelle contractually has to say yes, it doesn't ease my nerves one bit.

I just hope Noelle isn't fighting any sort of nervousness alone.

"Who is with Noelle right now? She's not alone, is she?" My hands ball into fists on the makeup chair arms.

"No no, I invited Candy Fernandez to the gala too, the board disapproved Janelle's invitation because of her mature image."

"I'm sure Aaron's stoked about that." I roll my eyes.

"He indeed threw quite the tantrum. He is down bad for her, I don't know who I feel more bad for; Aaron because he doesn't stand a chance with Janelle, or Janelle because she has to put up with an ego like Aaron's. I'm calling it, I feel bad for me most."

"The PR gods give their toughest clients to their most capable agents."

"You flatter me, Cameron. Angelface has softened you up quite nicely." Samantha nods approvingly at me. "Come on, let's put an end to this separation anxiety."

"Really?" I fly from my seat, the fragile structure collapsing underneath. I couldn't care less, I'm about to see my Princess again.

"Let's go, kid." I barrel out the door of the makeup boarding room set up just for my hair to be styled. I catch my reflection; it looks no different from when I rolled out of bed this morning. My suffering wasn't even worth it but I'm positive Noelle is going to be a vision tonight.

"Samantha, what are you doing to me?" Seymour obstructs the room I know Noelle is inside, I can feel it in some weird soulmatey way. I hear Aaron's bassy voice and then a string of girlish laughter, my jaw clenches.

"Move it, Floss."

"No way, Snow. Sam has some questions of mine to answer."

"What are you talking about, Seymour?" Samantha's eyes roll with a twitch.

"Why is she here?"

"Noelle is my soon-to-be wife, punk," I snarl, planting my palm on the door.

"Not her, the other one..." Seymour turns sheepishly on himself.

"Candy?" Samantha quirks a brow.

"Yes, that one, why is she here?" Seymour dismisses with a nonchalant air. I'm not stupid, I can see when a man is infatuated.

"I hear she's your date, Floss, looks like Nightingale is going empty-handed for once. That man needed to be brought down a peg or two."

"Gross, she better not be my date." Seymour gags. "Also, don't mention that to Aaron, he'll reply with how he'll let Janelle peg him twice...that is not how I wanted to find out what that was. So embarrassing and in front of what's her face?"

"Your date, Candy Fernandez. Watch out, Seymour, or Samantha, will set you two up. The snowflake ring is mine, buddy, so back off." I taunt, the kid has got to learn to relax and not be the victim of everything.

"Do not do that or I will quit hockey for good." Seymour threatens.

"Actually..." Samantha taps her sparkly tipped nail to her chin contemplatively.

"No, Sam, I'm begging you."

I quickly slip into the room as Seymour claws at Samantha, desperately pleading for her to change her mind.

My hypothesis was correct, Noelle is a vision tonight, but even with the predictability, I'm still not entirely prepared for how beautiful she looks right now. A powder blue silk contoured to her body, Swarovski crystals accenting all the right places, slipping in unison with her natural womanly curves. My eyes trail up to the feature I muse about the most. Her collarbones. A mesh-like cape draping from her right shoulder, snowflake accouterments cascade down to her bust, decreasing in size, depicting a snowfall.

My Ice Princess to my Prince of Ice.

"Don't you clean up well." She greets me with a hypnotic smile, emphasized by an all too arousing shade of red.

"As do you, Princess."

"What, this old thing? I heard it was hiding in the back of my soon to be fiancée's wardrobe."

"All rumors." I taunt, presenting the maroon velvet box. Only when her hand caresses it, I notice her hands are wearing pristine white gloves. She is truly the image of sophistication, but she's always been perfect in my eyes, when she's clumsy, when she's bored, when she's angry, when she's dizzy.

"Janny," she breathes out airily, I snap with urgent attention. She clutches her gloved hand to her heart, patting to regulate its rhythm. Perhaps this was overstepping a little. "You haven't bought anything this fancy for me in years...it's just like old times. You used to buy me the most lavish of diamonds to make up for all the physical fun I missed out on."

"I wouldn't say you're missing out on physical fun anymore." I flash a dazzling smile, she releases a sound that almost shapes into a sneeze. She made this sound a lot when we were teens, and my dumb ass is only realizing that it's her version of fawning.

Suck it, Eshika Patel, intimacy coach to the stars, we didn't need you, anyway.

"Can I wear it tonight?" Noelle asks so meekly.

"Of course, Princess, want me to put it on you?" I beat her to her next question.

"Yes, please." She turns her back to me, sweeping her auburn locks to the side, revealing her kissable nape, constellated with freckles. I snake the string of diamond droplets between my fingers, lacing the necklace around her neck, ensuring my knuckles briefly caress her collarbones. I try to suppress the shuddering breath that collects hotly on the roof of my mouth.

"You look absolutely beautiful, Noelle," I whisper in her ear, pecking her lobe softly. A shiver travels down her spine and ricochets back up, stopping at the metal clasp resting at the top of her vertebrae. "So beautiful." I repeat.

"You two look adorable, do you want a picture together?" Candy offers as she tugs down the golden sequin fabric wrapped around her thighs. Seymour makes a disgruntled sound that delays my acceptance of Candy's offer.

Boy has got it as bad as me. I'm seeing all the signs I had as a kid.

Candy is polite enough to shoot him a friendly smile, not bringing too much attention to his quiet tantrum he is throwing in the corner.

"Say lactose free cheese!" Candy giggles infectiously, I immediately turn to Seymour, as he releases an irritable puff from the corner of his mouth.

Yep, that boy is gone.

"Smile, Hot Shot." Noelle elbows my rib.

"That's not a challenge with you here, Princess."

"You guys are so cute, when will it be my turn?" Candy swoons dramatically. I catch the end of Seymour's eye roll, his eyes averting with contemplation.

"You see what I'm seeing," I whisper to Noelle in confidence.

"Seymour totally has a thing for Candy."

"Yeah-ha."

"Funny, you could pick up on Seymour's crush, but not my blind adoration for you."

"My denial blocked me from seeing the truth, but I'm so glad I'm being honest with myself and my feelings. Look where it got me." I give Noelle's waist a pinch.

"Well, let me be abundantly clear, January Cameron Snow, I like you a lot."

It's not the love declaration I hoped for, but my heart still palpitates at the distinct labeling. She *likes* me and that is a start to what will blossom into an eternal love. I may just be the one to rip off the band-aid and make it abundantly clear to Noelle Winter Darlington that I *love* her.

"Ready to dazzle and sparkle, Princess?" I offer my arm chivalrously.

"You bet, Prince." She plants a peck on my cheek.

Twenty-Six

The Ice Princess

Noelle

"Cameron, Noelle, this is Shirley Harris, Director of Philanthropy, and Julia Reed, Administration Assistant for *Upon-A-Star.*" Samantha introduces us to two silver-haired women donning black gowns.

"So lovely to meet you both." I graciously accept their offering of handshakes. "You do incredible work."

"So do you I've heard. This is the first I'm seeing Cameron Snow at one of these events, he usually has someone attend on his behalf and buy out the whole auction catalog." Shirley's eyes scan down January's figure.

"Yes, it's true, Noelle Darlington thawed The Prince of Ice. You'll be seeing a lot more of me, Noelle adores your organization's mission, almost as much as I adore her. She hopes to work more with *Upon-A-Star*, now that she's completed her hazing by being seen in public with me."

"January," I hiss, rolling my eyes endearingly. "Don't make me tell these lovely women what happened to said auction catalog. He spoils me." I crane my neck to showcase the diamonds.

"I would word it differently," January scoffs.

"How would you word it, Hot Shot?" I narrow my eyes playfully.

"I don't spoil you, I show how much I love you through material means. And you really appreciate the gifts."

My heart leaps into my throat.

I love you. January just said he loves me.

"Well, you two are very lucky to have found each other." Julie gushes with a hand to her heart.

"Our friendship is worth more than any diamond."

Friends! January, you are giving me serious whiplash right now.

"To call your partner your best friend is truly the best gift in life." Samantha swoons.

"Is it, though, when your partner is Vinnie?" January jabs, Samantha scoffs with offense.

"Well then, if you'll excuse me, I have to go find my husband/best friend. I'll leave you two to mingle, don't burn any bridges, Cameron." Samantha turns to me. "Keep him in check, Angelface."

"So." I turn back to Shirley and Julia, as they redirect the conversation with that simple word. "What do you do for a living, Noelle?"

"I'm a Data Administrator at Darlington Snow Paradise," I say meekly. It feels embarrassing to mention the decrepit lodge I call home, especially when I'm surrounded by luxury of the highest grade right now. "But really, that's just a fancy way of me saying I take care of the bookings."

"You're being modest, Nono." January jumps in. "This woman provides top tier hospitality. The lodge is already such a spectacular location, but Noelle is the one that makes it magical."

"Thank you, Janny."

"And."

Oh God, there's more? How could there be more, I don't do all that much at the lodge?

"Noelle is also a game developer."

"Oh, well, it's not my profession, I dabble more than anything."

"No, she's the real deal." January enthusiastically announces, his lips breaking into a hypnotic smile. I pray I don't stumble over my next words as my heart palpitates.

"Until I'm on Nintendo's payroll, I'm technically not the real deal."

"Your game is as valid as anything. It's called The Battle of Blizzard, it's like Zelda in the snow." January excitably explains his lackluster description.

"That was such an enthralling description, Janny." I roll my eyes.

"I'm just trying to give you a podium, Princess, so you can big note yourself."

"You are so embarrassing." I snort. "How would you like it if I said January has the best and most consistent shot in all the NHL? The man has laser focus, nothing can falter his concentration."

"Except you." January jabs.

"I guess I'll be the start of your demise." I snort.

"You two have something very special." Shirley coos.

"If you'll excuse us, I'd like to get a hurry on this demise."

"It was lovely meeting you both."

"We'll be in touch in the future." Julie gives me a wink. I can't restrain the gasp of disbelief that leaves my mouth. Is this really happening? Am I about to work with an incredible organization that provides chronically ill children with the childlike wonder they deserve? I could never really be hands on with the charity in the past, that's when I took the development of The Battle of Blizzard seriously. I always hoped that the profit made from the game would go towards *Upon-A-Star*, equipping the foundation with financial support to bring magical adventure and endless wonder to children hindered by their ailment. Knowing exactly how that feels, being confined to my bedroom most days. Any physical activity we offered at the lodge was far too taxing on my heart as a young girl. Here's to hoping I get to work with them close enough to make the project come to fruition.

"Until then, wishing you two the best in your relationship."

Relationship. It's really working, people believe we are in a relationship...

I mean, are we?

I can confidently say that January and I have definitely rekindled our friendship, but has the love that we secretly harbored been revived too? With the incredible sexual connection, we've been able to fully explore—hopefully continue to explore—in combination with January's emotional suitability and his abrupt love confession. It certainly reads as a *real* relationship to me, it certainly looks like we're in love.

I feel like I'm in love. I know it would crush me if January were to leave me, he's my companion, he's the most understanding person. If he were to leave me, it would leave a massive hole in my life...just like it did the first time.

"Noelle." January exhales. I register that we've been pulled away from the crowd into a secluded corner, decorated with a fern that tickles at my bare back. But the tingling sensation that takes place in my fingertips as January holds them intently garners all of my attention. "Noelle, I just want to clarify a few things with you."

"Okay." Is all I can pathetically sputter out. What is wrong with you, Noelle? This is January Snow, your friend since we were eleven years old, you can talk about absolutely anything with him. Just not the one thing you desperately want to ask him most.

Do you love me?

"I know I've made it clear about my feelings for you; I'm falling deeply in love with you. Well, there have been some changes to that."

Oh god, I'm about to vomit my heart any second now, this could go one of two ways and I'm not prepared for either.

"Noelle, you have been there for me my whole life, even when we had no contact for so long. A lot of what you said and did for me as a teen really shaped me into the person I am today, I carried little pieces of you throughout my whole life even in your absence. Now, having you back in my life, those fractured pieces are molding back together, and I realize I am my best self when I am with you, Noelle, you bring out the absolute best in me."

Oh my god, is he proposing?

"You make me beam from within, you melt my frosty exterior from the inside, Noelle. No one but you has that effect on me, I love the way you make me feel, I want to be this happy forever."

He is definitely proposing. Why am I trembling like a chihuahua?

"I just hope that I have the same effect on you, Noelle. I know I'm a total asswipe sometimes, okay, most times. But I'm working on it for you. I want to be the best version of myself and I want to be the best version of the person you need most in life."

"You are, January," I squeeze in weakly.

"I am? What a relief. Stunt aside, I'm being completely transparent with you, Noelle Winter Darlington, I want to be with you for the rest of my life. I love you, Noelle."

There it is.

January Cameron Snow loves me.

I couldn't be more ecstatic at the news until the truth finally buries me under like an avalanche. A truth January has been blunt about from the very beginning.

January Cameron Snow loves me and I can't keep up.

My hands clench into fists as I feel the symptoms of an episode edging on. Whimpers slip from my tight throat, my head feels like it's full of hot cement, pushing at my taut skin as if it wants to push through my pores. It feels like I'm sweating thick molten, my tears are of the same fiery texture.

"Noelle?" I faintly make out January's concern. "You don't look good."

"I don't—" I can barely finish my sentence, it feels like coal is being poured down my throat, the sharp edges scratching at my esophagus.

My knees buckle and I feel January's spontaneous support under my elbows.

"I knew I shouldn't have said I loved you yet, because you don't."

"I don't?" I peer up through my sweat drenched lashes. Where did January get an assumption that I don't love him?

Do I love January?

Even in my feverish state, at my absolute worst, I know I love January Cameron Snow, I don't understand how he could love me. My health won't allow me to keep up with his lifestyle and I don't think my love will be enough for him to stay.

I part my lips, readying to say the three word sentiment, only for my jaw to fall slack. I want those words to slip out of my mouth, but more than anything, I need water to run down my searing throat.

"Water! Can somebody get my girlfriend water? For fuck's sake." January huffs under his breath.

I feel my body gently guided to the ground, the skirting of the wall digging into my back, but it's not nearly as painful as the hellish wallpaper. Who lines the walls with 300-degree flames?

"Stay here, Nono, I'll be back with some water."

I hear January's panicked footsteps fade out. The wallpaper seeps completely black, everything goes silent.

Twenty-Seven

Avalanche

January

I had completely forgotten how much of an ass I made of myself finally professing my love for Noelle, finding out that she doesn't reciprocate the feelings.

What am I supposed to do with myself, now that the love is unrequited? Suppose it's always been unrequited, it's just now been confirmed.

Of course, Noelle doesn't love me. A woman so incredible as her, who deserves so much more than this. I've done nothing but pull her into my bullshit. Bullshit she is far too bright, far too kind, far too loving for. And I've repaid her by running her into the absolute ground. My heart felt as if it was going to explode, I have never seen a spell of such vicious nature. I was almost certain Noelle was about to die.

I nearly killed my best friend by telling her I love her. I'm no prince, I'm a fucking monster.

"#ThePrinceOfIce and his #IcePrincess," Samantha snickers from the winged back chair in the apartment's corner. My eyes have not left Noelle, as I stand at the foot of the bed looking over her like I am a lion protecting my wounded mate. Only I was the one to maul her. "You should see these comments, Cameron. Everyone is so convinced and more importantly obsessed with your relationship they're amid workshopping a ship name. What started as #Camelle is now #Janelle but that is confusing Noelle's *Darlings*—"

"Shut the fuck up, Samantha." I roar as if I am the apex predator. She pulls her phone close to her chest, her eyes wide with fright. I pinch the bridge of my nose at my overreaction. Noelle gets me this way, she pulls out instincts in me I love and instincts that I despise. My overprotective instinct being one of the negative traits Noelle brings out of me. "Sam, I'm just feeling very..."

I can't even pinpoint my feelings. Only one sticks out pungently, it's crazy to say, but I'm feeling *love* right now. I know I may not look like your stereotypical picture of a man in love, I'm not giddy, or plucking petals from roses. I'm feeling true, deep love, the kind you feel when you've failed the subject of your desires. The guilt and shame you have to process. The paranoia of whether the love of your life will even forgive you. The anticipation of how the dynamic will now change. The dread that comes with knowing that the other lover will now be apprehensive to trust. The hard side of love.

"#Joelle," I say, deflated. This is as close as I'll get to an apology, because truly Samantha is a huge part to blame for Noelle's current state.

"Huh?" Samantha unfurls from her diminished demeanor.

"That'll be our ship name, #Joelle."

"Oh...okay." Samantha hesitantly unlocks her phone; the click is deafening in the thick tension that lies between us.

I turn my gaze back to Noelle, my blood pumps with urgency as I've noticed she's stirred.

"Janny?" She weakly calls.

I hurry to the bedside, crawling onto the mattress but still maintaining my distance.

"I'm here."

Noelle's eyes remain closed, her hand blindly reaching out for my touch. I guess not all is lost.

I link my hand with hers as it flutters with anxiety.

"It's okay, I'm here, Nono." I reassure her, caressing my thumb over her knuckles. Her skin is red and flushed, almost like she's covered in a rash. Even just her palm feels like it's 100 degrees. "Nono, I think you should go back to the lodge."

Her eyes flick open into narrow slits.

"Go home?" She weakly strains. The sight of her beyond the point of burnout is painful to watch. That heavy sense of love washes over me again. I want nothing more than to embrace her and carry her back to Colorado myself, lay with her in the snow until she looks like my beautiful Princess again.

"Yes, Nono. I think you should go back to Darlington Snow Paradise, where you can go at your own pace."

She turns her head away from me, a whimpering cry slips from her lips and then comes the tears. My heart breaks in two.

Her diaphragm collapses with a large exhale, her features read with conclusion. She rolls her gaze to me once again.

"I want to go home, January."

"Then you're going home, Noelle." I swipe my knuckle gently across her cheek, collecting her hot tears.

Twenty-Eight

Love Is An Open Door

January

Samantha has fortunately agreed to Noelle returning home to Darlington Snow Paradise, unfortunately she has forced me to fulfill contractual obligations. The stunt has fucking worked alright and we're all feeling the aftermath. Noelle reaping the promised benefits of the arrangement of this stunt, generating revenue for the lodge. And I am suffering the consequences, cleaning up my asshole reputation, securing myself more brand deals.

That is why I'm stuck in this chair being prodded with a makeup brush, readying for my pretty face to be planted in front of the camera, so I can play mannequin for Sport Spartan and their overpriced gym wear.

Thankfully after this shoot, I'm getting straight into my Rolls Royce and heading to the airport where my private jet awaits. chartered for Aspen, Colorado, and I will finally reunite with the love of my life/best friend/girl of my dreams.

Noelle has been reporting to me throughout this obligatory hell that her health has improved since she has been back home. She is so thankful that I made that call…but I can sense there is something she is not telling me.

I thought we didn't hide our feelings anymore, Nono?

"Alright we got the shot."

I'm thrust back into my reality, I hadn't even been actively modeling, but they've got the shot, so I couldn't give a fuck. I don't even bother to change out of the apparel they provided me for the photoshoot; they were no doubt going to give it to me for free. I grab my duffle bag and shoot for the door.

"Cameron!" That fucking Valley girl vocal fry.

"Yes, Samantha."

"Don't you want to thank your sponsors—"

"Oh, right, thank you for working with me again. Apologies for my sudden departure, but I have to propose to my best friend." My farewell is pageantry perfection.

I don't even bother to wait for the elevator.

I fly straight down the stairs.

Into my Rolls Royce.

Drive onto the tarmac.

On my jet.

Off my jet.

And only when I hear the crunch of snow beneath my feet do I exhale with serenity.

I'm home.

I take in the lodge, the snowy mist creates a halo-like glow around the main lobby. I know my angel awaits me inside; I don't waste a second longer. I drop my duffle at the door, greeted by the tender crackle of the fireplace. The lobby embraces me in a hug with its warm temperature, which probably means Noelle has a tiny fan working overtime beneath her desk.

I approach the desk, her fiery locks peeping out from the top.

"I have a booking for the Noelle suite, party of two."

"Janny!" Noelle hoofs her chair back, the intense force crashing into the large painting of the Colorado landscape behind the reception.

I don't know what copped a harder brunt, the painting or me, as Noelle hikes herself onto my torso, wrapping her legs around my hips.

Our lips knot together in a panting, passionate kiss.

I missed you so much, Nono.

"January, I missed you."

"Yes, me too." I pull her impossibly tight to my chest.

"I'll see if Mum can cover the reception, I *need* to spend some time with you." Noelle tries to catch her breath once again as she explains.

"I need you too, Noelle."

"Mum." She couldn't possibly sound more British. She hikes herself from her koala-like hold on me.

"Yes, Noelle—Oh, January is back! I'll cover, you two catch up."

"Thank you, Mum." She plants a grateful peck on her mom's cheek.

"I'll catch up with you and David a little later on, now I just need some time with Princess." I nuzzle my nose into the crook of Noelle's neck as she rejoins my side.

"Take your time, sweethearts," Johanna graciously encourages us.

Perfect! Noelle all to myself.

The ring box bangs against my thigh and is the weight of a brick in my tracksuit pocket.

"January, I'm so glad you're home. The lodge has been crazy busy, but It's been a good kind of busy." Noelle recounts as we trek across the small plane of snow to her lodge's porch.

The door skidded open with ease, no sign of security at all.

"Nono, I've told you about this door."

"Yes, I know, but only you know it's unlocked." She plants a sassy peck on my lips that silences my next retort. "I kept it unlocked in case you flew into Colorado in the middle of the night and wanted to cuddle."

"Samantha kept a watchful eye on me, otherwise I would've snuck out like a rebellious teenager every night."

"Just like old times." Her eyes glitter youthfully.

"I really missed you." We both slip in unison.

"The past week without you has been very difficult." Noelle sinks into her mattress, for once, in a non-sensual manner.

"Ditto." I join her by her side. "But I'm here now."

"For now..." Noelle sinks further into the mattress.

"I'm here for a while, actually." My reassurance doesn't influence Noelle.

"Until you leave again." Her shoulders curl in defeat.

"But not forever. I'll be coming back."

"January, I love you."

I almost keel over with how visceral an effect those words have on my body. It dawns on me that this is the first time Noelle has said those words back to me.

The taste of bile builds in my mouth as I recall the sour note we left on; I thought she didn't love me.

"Noelle, I love you too—"

"But..."

But? How can there be a but? We love each other, full stop, there is no run-on sentence, no objection, we are mutually in love.

"I can't marry you, January."

That ring box may as well be a cement block tied to my waist, and it's pulling me deeply into the ocean. It's like Noelle has pushed me into the oceanic abyss and no matter how much I try to thrash against the water, the weight keeps pulling me down further and faster with each inch of a struggle.

"You can't marry me? But you love me? I don't understand."

"January, I can't marry you because this could never work." The tears flow, but my palm is already on her cheek to catch every single one.

"It took some time to get our footing again. I think we had it all along. It was always there for us privately, it was the public who struggled to see it. But it's not for them to see, it's for us to *feel*. And I feel intense, true love for you."

"January," she hiccups. "I know we love each other, and I love you just as intensely, but with my health and your career, I don't know if our love is enough to persevere."

"That is what love is all about, Nono. Defying the odds. I know that sounds corny, but I want to be corny with you. I want to spend the rest of my life with you. My parents gave me a path in life, but you, Noelle Winter Darlington, you've given me purpose." With my free hand, I pull out the tiny velvet box, using my thumb to flip the top off, so my touch can remain on her warming crimson cheeks, still flowing with tears.

"Only the love of my life would propose to me with Justin Bieber lyrics," she sniffs a chuckle.

"I love you, Noelle, will you marry me?"

Her hesitation is creating a stone inside my belly, she holds her terrified gaze on me. I can read the contemplation behind her eyes. She's trying to find the courage to tell me something, I'm silently pleading for her not to say it.

"I love you too, January, but I can't marry you. No, I won't."

My hand presenting the ring falls limp, the snowflake diamond cascading onto her duvet with the same print. It's comically ironic that this was where our love first blossomed under these sheets, and this is where it will seize.

"I'm sorry, I won't do that to you. I hope you don't feel used, I really appreciate all you've done for me, not just during the stunt but my whole life. You've shaped me into the person I am."

"So that's it? But, Noelle, we love each other. I don't think I could love another person, I never have."

"Neither have I," she chokes out.

"Then be with me," I'm on my knees this time, maybe that's all she needs, is a little bit of tradition to persuade her to say yes. How could I be so idiotic not to get on one knee to begin with, I really am a prat with romance? But I want to spend my whole life trying and successfully romancing Noelle, she just needs to say yes.

"No."

A ping from my phone rips me from my daydream, I keep replaying my whole life and where I went wrong to have Noelle reject my proposal. Now we're playing pretend again, only this time we are not fighting off firing breathing dragons as princes and princesses. No, were pretending to be happy and completely dancing around the awkwardness of the situation. I think I am doing a far better job than Noelle with hiding how numb I feel inside right now, my stoic muscle memory has kicked in once again.

Another vicious ping snaps me from my analytical gaze on Noelle. I flick my eyes discreetly to see a text from Samantha.

Engagement ring photo, stat, kiddo!

Crap, how do I tell Samantha there is no photo, because there is no engagement? My gaze flutters on Noelle again, she's looking at my phone, her hands wringing nervously in her lap. I guess we are fighting fire-breathing dragons, after all.

"Excuse me, I need to make a phone call." I excuse myself from the lobby, no longer filled with an embracing ambience but now a lethal chokehold.

"It's Samantha, isn't it?" Noelle asks meekly. I nod in confirmation. "We should tell her together."

"She will not take it well." I warn Noelle.

"I know." She swallows thickly.

"But I'm on your side, Noelle, no matter what, I'm always in your corner, even if it gets me into trouble."

A small whimper slips from her lips.

"One last *battle* for old time's sake." I shoot Noelle an encouraging smile, I feel my palm being gently unfurled from its clenched fist, Noelle's featherlight touch caressing my palm before weaving our fingers together.

"I'm sorry again." She sincerely apologizes. I give a curt nod in acknowledgement.

I inhale deeply as the phone rings on.

"Cameron! Facetime me! I want to see the ring on her finger," Samantha greets enthusiastically, Vinnie pops into the frame with a toothbrush in his mouth.

"Show us the ring, kid." Vinnie muffles, Samantha pinching his chin, they exchange a foamy kiss. "You're going to be just as cringy as us, you two."

"Sam..." I start. Samantha's smile wipes from her face.

"I want good news only, Cameron Snow."

"Noelle and I aren't getting married."

"Why not? You do love each other, no? Or are you two better actors than I thought?"

"I love January," Noelle chimes in.

"And I love Noelle."

"And that's the problem and why I can't marry him, I would ruin his life with how unpredictable my health is. I can't keep up with his lifestyle, which will lead me to being unwell, often interrupting his work. I'd be making your job so much more difficult, I hate to say it, but I am his priority. He will probably become an unreliable client if he hears my health is in decline, I don't think he's above skating off the rink mid-game to fly to Colorado."

"I plan on doing that whether or not we are married, Nono."

"Ugh, you can't, you won't." Noelle swats my devotion away.

"Except you will." Samantha's vocal fry pierces through. "You think you have a choice, it's all there in your contract. You will get married."

"But January's career will be ruin—" Noelle stops herself as Samantha disappears from the screen, showcasing the phone screen of Noelle and I in a celebratory embrace when the dragon first signs me to Phoenix Badgers. "She hung up. January, I'm so sorry," Noelle blubbers, I pull her protectively to my chest.

"No, Nono, I'm sorry." The lump in my throat turns into shallow hiccups. I realize for the first time in my life I'm crying, and I'm sure it's for absolutely everything I've suppressed for the 28 years I've been alive.

Twenty-Nine

Snowy Matrimony

Noelle

"Aaron, get away from me before I pass out from how strong your cologne is, also you're slobbering." Janelle plucks Aaron's pocket square from his suit jacket, dabbing the same baby pink fabric as her bridesmaid dress to the corners of his mouth.

"Janelle, allow me to explain the benefits of a wedding hook up." Aaron huffs like a dehydrated dog.

"Don't make me stuff this thing into your mouth." Janelle threatens the pocket square, now crumpled into a ball, ready to be inserted into Aaron's mouth.

"Go on then, why the hesitation? Because you want to hear my argument. Wait no longer, Babydoll. The benefit of a wedding hook up is that you will most likely never see the person again and you get an orgasm at the end of the day."

"Is that a promise?" Janelle threads her fingers around Aaron's tie.

"Yes, to both never seeing me again and especially the orgasm. Hook ups are really the only reason to have weddings, honestly."

"Oh, I don't think that's true, weddings are occasions to celebrate two people in love, don't you think?" Candy chimes, turning to Seymour for support.

"I'm not in love," Seymour gags.

"Oh." Candy retracts with surprise. "No, um, but Noelle and Cameron are...Noelle?"

I return from the foggy enchantment I was under. It was like I am watching my world through a sheen glass window, like I'm a spectator of my own life. Is this the epitome of an out-of-body experience?

"Am I getting married?" I shudder.

"Yes, because you love Cameron." Candy reminds me. Pretty sure most people who are in love don't need reminders they are.

"Right." I exhale. "No, right, I know, this is all just a dream come true." I press out in a fluster.

This is possibly my worst nightmare, this marriage is going to be a disaster.

I love January but I can't marry him, I can't keep up with him. But I don't want to hold him back, and that's what he was trying to tell me all along. I am nothing but a burden to him, I'm dead weight that he'll carry for the rest of his life if he says *I do*.

Why has he changed his mind on the fact that I could never be with him, why does he think love will conquer all? This is not a fairytale, our love will not cure me of my dreadful episodes.

I clench onto my bouquet as I immediately recognize the instrumental of Nothing Like Us by Justin Bieber. Christ, January is so perfect for me, he even organized my favorite song to be my entrance song. He completes me, if I'm the music, he's the lyrics. But I am anything but perfect for January. I do nothing but distract and reorganize his priorities, all because he has this innate instinct with my health. Something that will not work well with his career now on an incline again.

"Go, Noelle." Samantha hisses for me to tread the carpet, lined with flickering candles, I can feel her fluttering out my veil behind me. The ivory satin of my mermaid cut wedding dress is like a prison with a built in sauna. I'm having flashbacks to the vicious episodes I was a victim to at the start of this stunt in that emerald satin dress. My erratic short breathing dispenses tiny clouds from my mouth, I feel I'm wearing my body's entire water contents on my flesh.

The delicate piano melody absorbs my senses, transporting me back to January and I dancing around his cabin. A daydream I visited often whilst sitting on my crummy apartment couch with Sean chewing loudly in my ear.

I nearly married that man, a man I never really loved...I used Sean as much as he used me. I needed to escape the fact that I knew January was never coming back to me.

But now, here I am, walking down the aisle of his and I's wedding, about to be permanently bound to one another in the name of law. My eyes look up and even through my snowflake detailed veil I can make out January's concern in his haunting cerulean eyes.

"Smile." Samantha instructs as she presses through her own plastic grin, finessing my veil before I step up to the altar. My features pinch tightly with worry.

January dusts the snowflakes from my vision, even in his own worried state he makes the most handsomest groom. He's my groom. Teenage Noelle would be screaming into her pillow right now, meanwhile I'm screaming internally as I am about to ruin this man's life forever.

The pastor's mouth drops to speak, January holds his palm up, stunting his words.

"Noelle, I love you, but what's wrong?" He whispers in my ear.

"Nothing...I love you too."

"Shall we begin?" The pastor interjects bitterly.

"Yes. Let's get married." I squeeze out. Shit shit shit shit shit.

"We are gathered here today..."

Oh fuck, it's happening. Heart, I need you to compose yourself; I know you're feeling a lot of things right now. Mostly guilt.

Oh God, I'm so sorry January for what I'm about to do to you.

I gasp as a droplet slips from my lashes down my cheek and dissolves as it hits the snow in a flash.

"I do."

My head snaps to January's proclamation.

"In sickness and in health."

"I do," January says with his whole chest.

My heart feels like it's going to leap out of mine.

No, January, you're making a terrible mistake.

"To have and to cherish, for as long as you both shall live."

"Absolutely, I do." January's worry dissipates into a hypnotic smile, making mine wisp away with the light snowfall.

Snowfall...just like how I'd always dreamed our wedding to be like.

I say my vows in some sort of trance, each promise bringing back a blissful memory of our youth, experienced right here at this lodge.

"I now pronounce you husband and wife, you may kiss the bride."

January cradles my face in his palm, my shoulders tense up to my ears.

"Are you feeling okay? I won't kiss you if you're not." January whispers into my lips, making my head spin delightfully.

"Kiss me."

I'm a fool, I had all the power to prevent this mess. Instead, my stupid heart took the wheel instead of my head and sealed my doomed fate with a kiss.

January pulls back from my stiff lips.

"Sorry," I lilt quietly. "Kiss me, please." I encourage once again, hoping my internal crisis doesn't slip through to the kiss.

January's bottom lip feathers mine, "Are you sure?"

"I'm sure." I want to surrender completely, I want January to kiss me like he did that night in the dark ballroom, with passion and longing. I want to be with January Cameron Snow because I love him. But what I want isn't necessarily something I can have.

"I love you," I croak through my tears. "I'm married to my best friend."

"Yes, you are, Princess. And I'm married to mine."

The beginning of a castle crumbling to pieces.

THIRTY

This Is Why We Can't Have Nice Things

Noelle

"All that work for nothing!" Samantha roars, her nostrils flaring.

"The stunt worked, who cares what people say?" January chimes in with bitterness, still trying to cozy up to me. I only inch further away, I don't know how he can long for my touch when I've ruined his life indefinitely.

"Well, if you want those bookings to continue to flood in, yes, you do care what people have to say," Samantha hisses.

"Looks like you needed my help after all." Eshika soundtracks her entrance with her metallic bangles clanging about. "I haven't seen a more miserable bride since the Russian model, Svetlana Romanov."

"Svetlana Romanov?" Samantha chimes in brightly, as if the name strikes her with familiarity.

"Yes." Eshika confirms.

"My husband blew off a date with her for a date with me, can you believe that?" Samantha gives her flat ironed hair a cocky toss over her shoulder.

"I don't see it," January pokes dryly, turning to me with hopeful anticipation glittering in his cerulean eyes. Samantha evokes into her dragon form once again with a huff.

"Very funny, Cameron. But it's true, I organized the date and then canceled the date. Looks like she found another fish in the sea."

"Something you should do, January," I meekly chime in.

"What?" his head snaps hastily back to me. "Noelle, we're married."

"And we should divorce at the soonest notice, preferably before the season starts." I anxiously bunch the ribbed cuffs of my snowsuit over my trembling fingers.

"You want to divorce?" January unburies them, holding them with a firm sense of grounding.

"How many times do I have to bring up the contract," Samantha groans. "You guys are stuck for life. You can't divorce."

"I'm not going anywhere, not this time." January discreetly inching closer to me. I'm pressed up to the couch arm, I'm sure January is pleased he has me cornered. His hot breath caresses my lips softly, I can't restrain my lips from leaning into his and connecting in a kiss.

"I don't think it will take much to restore at all, the passion is as clear as day now. It's now a matter of displaying it to the public and the image is restored. The newly wed couple *are* happy." Eshika dissects our make out.

"Okay, keep kissing you two." Samantha's camera flash bleeds through my closed eyelids.

"No," Eshika starts, "it's going to take a lot more than a photo of them kissing."

"What do you propose then, renewal of their vows?" Samantha lowers her phone hesitantly, I'm thankful to not have a device shoved in my face like I'm a zoo animal imprisoned, on display for people's viewing pleasure. Since when did the world become so voyeuristic? Enjoying seeing two people make out and prod into their sex life.

But if I have to subject myself to a few more staged make outs, I will if it means January doesn't have to renew his vows.

Oh God, please no. It was bad enough hearing him stupidly devote himself to me once...even through sickness and health.

"I propose a sex tape." Eshika reveals with a metallic flourish.

"A sex tape? There is no way we are forcing Noelle to objectify herself in the name of saving this stunt, we love each other and that is the only people it concerns when it comes to our love." January protests.

"It doesn't have to be an actual sex tape, you forget my line of work, Cameron. I choreograph intimate scenes in film and stage for a living. There will be no display of genitals if you truly wish not to show them to the world. Although we all know the question on everyone's tongue."

"How big?" I slip with a deflated sigh.

"That's nobody's business," January huffs.

"Do you really think that me being a sulky bride will affect bookings?"

"Absolutely, without a doubt. You only got those bookings in the first place because you two looked so loved up." Samantha answers honestly. No beating around the bush.

I knew this...and I also know hype can be fickle, so it's best to use it while we have it.

"Okay, let's make a sex tape." I agree.

The noise that leaves January's mouth is an awkward mix of arousal and detestation.

"Noelle?"

"Yes, January, we have to, for *our future.*" I know mentioning what is most at stake here would persuade him into a hard yes. His eyes glitter dimly with hopefulness again, I can tell the visions of *our future* are playing behind those glassy eyes.

"Fine. For our future." January gently tangles our fingers together. "She will not be naked, will she?"

"She will be, but there will be no nudity shown." Eshika reassures.

"Whose filming this?" January's grip on me tightens possessively.

"I have a crew on call, and don't worry, they film full frontal shots on the daily, they are completely desensitized to seeing naked bodies," Eshika explains.

"That may be so, doesn't mean Noelle is comfortable showing her body around others."

"I mean, I'm not ashamed of what I look like—"

"That's not what we're talking about here, Nono. This is going to be leaked and you know the internet as well as I do, this video will go viral. Who is sharing this video? You will certainly not be using Noelle's account."

"We'll make a decoy account today."

"What about @NovemberRain." I suggest. "It's practically useless now, why not get suspended with a bang, quite literally." I chuckle, only for my amusement to slip away when it comes flooding back in what the production of the tape is for. To save our marriage...or the public image of it, at least.

"@NovemberRain it is then, you two will film tomorrow at noon," Samantha orders. "Eshika, call that crew of yours, were filming a sex tape."

Thirty-One

Lights, Cameron, Action

January

Well, this is fucking shit.

I'm thinking Noelle isn't the best at making logical decisions, but I'll keep that to myself. Frankly I've attacked her character enough by diminishing her to her unpredictable health. But Noelle is so much more than her health, and she's certainly far more than a pawn in this ploy.

It has officially turned from ridiculous to absurd! A fucking sex tape! Real or fake, is an absolute ridiculous ploy to resort to.

Now, Noelle and I are standing in our robes in her cabin, whilst extravagant light setups roast us slowly like marshmallows.

"This is so fucking shit." I shuffle on the spot, my eyes averting from the man tinkering away at a bulky camera.

"I'm sorry, January," Noelle sniffs. My gaze snaps to her hastily. Her flesh spots with beads of sweat, her skin coated with an angelic sheen. I try not to get caught up in how beautiful she looks even when she is suffering from an episode. I want to hold her closely, but I know that will only make her entire body feel like a hellfire.

"No, Nono, I'm sorry that I got you into this mess and I'll be seeking new representation after all of this fuckery, even if I have to leave the badgers. I'll join the Colorado Cowboys if I have to. I absolutely should. I've always wanted to play for them." Actually they suck, I've always made that opinion. No matter who they scout, they never seem to nail the on rink chemistry, the Phoenix Badgers may not be a team full of camaraderie but we somehow are a well-oiled machine, the swapping out of players and using each other strengths to our advances is a mechanism that never gets choked up. The Cowboys, however, turn the ice rink into an absolute circus, their tactics are sloppy, and although the Badgers have their fair share of egos, these guys can't seem to squash their narcissism aside to score a single goal. In conclusion, they are dogshit. But its worth being a part of a sucky team and even staining my golden goal statistics if it means I can stay here in Colorado with Noelle.

"January, you used to shit on the Colorado Cowboys all the time." Noelle quirks a ruby-toned brow.

"Yeah, well, they won't be once I join their team." I'll fit right in with my cockiness.

"You'd give up playing for the best team in the NHL for the team who have ranked last for the last 17 years." She crosses her arms, her robe falling loosely around her breasts, exposing her flushed decolletage.

"Absolutely," I strain through a dry throat. Being in love with Noelle is full of contradicting simultaneous feelings, like how her beautiful body can leave me both aroused and concerned as it sways nauseously.

"You think you're such a great liar, January, but I see right through you. Your team will be a complete burden to your playing, and it's bad enough your wife is." A droplet runs down Noelle's cheek that I am positive is not sweat.

"Stop saying that, Noelle, you are not a burden, and if you are, then I want to be burdened my whole life." I pull Noelle into my arms, finessing the robe from her shoulders to prevent her from overheating whilst in my comforting embrace.

"That's it, kids, start warming up those lovin' arms." My blood sears at the sound of Samantha's voice.

"Do we really have to do this in front of you all?" I hiss, planting my chin on Noelle's crown, and squeezing her with protective tightness. "This is way too staged for a casually leaked sex tape."

"Hm, you're absolutely right." Eshika chimes gesticulatively, her bangles tolling in agreement. "Everybody out! They're going to do this their way."

I think I'm warming up to Eshika Patel, intimacy coach to the stars.

"I agree. It should be recorded on my phone." I thread my fingers once more through Noelle's soft locks, prying us apart. Tearing my phone from its case and snapping it into place on Noelle's streaming tripod. I swipe the picture of us at eighteen, a time when we were innocent, opening the camera. My jaw drops when I catch the sight of the technicolor lights dancing along Noelle's collarbones, that mini nightclub on her desk is making her skin look like Aurora Borealis.

Noelle is returning the favor of showing me the wonders of the world, and she's doing it right here in the comfort of her cabin.

"Everybody out now, I want to make love to my wife." I pull Noelle in once again, my thigh finesses between the slit of her gown, rubbing my knee into her crotch.

I hear a clammer of footsteps.

"Don't forget to press record!" Samantha yelps out.

The door snips, I flick my eyes over with a quick glance. "Good, they're gone." I retract my knee.

"More than good." Noelle's fingertips thread into my hair, I catch onto her seductive stare.

"You really want to do this? You really want to film an actual sex tape?" I know what I want to do, make love to Noelle so continuously until my phone runs out of storage, and it's got a lot. I stopped taking photos of things once Noelle and I went our separate ways, nothing was worth capturing as a memory.

"Well..." Noelle rings a long tuff of raven hair around her finger. "What if we made two?"

"Two, do you really have it in you to fuck twice—"

"Sh!" She releases her hand quickly, moving her featherlight fingerprint to my lips. "What if you film a fake one, for them, and then we film a real one, for *us*?" Noelle's finger traces along my jawline. Can you believe I am wrapped around that nimble little thing?

"Something to look back upon every anniversary." This is technically our honeymoon, I suppose, the final stage of the PR stunt agreement. Once that fake tape is filmed, it's over. Everything promised to Noelle with this arrangement will be fulfilled once that sex tape goes live to the world. Then we are free from the shackles of pretending, the contract is null and we get to start our life anew. Now that is a memory I want to capture on film, something I can look back on time and time again. When my hair has gone completely gray, and Noelle has aged like fine wine.

"Mhm...something for me to touch myself to while you're away, not that my imagination has failed me in the past."

The words *while I'm away* have my stomach in knots. I've got to figure out a way where I can remain in Noelle's vicinity, even with us legally bound in marriage and her always being a quick FaceTime call away, it's not enough. I've spent the last decade loving her parasocially, I want to do this wholeheartedly and completely physically present. I want to watch this sex tape of ours together on that batted up leather sofa, not as a viewing party on Zoom.

"So I've been told." I inhale crisply. "Yeah, okay, let's fake one for those fuckers and then make real sweet true love just for each other."

"Oh, Janny, take me." Noelle leaps her entire weight into me.

"Maybe we should do the fake one first? So we can really focus on one another for ourselves." Make the fake one, then while making the real one, it will be like crossing a magical threshold. We will go to places we've never been before but have longed to go. Noelle will expand my imagination just like how she always has, where we are going there will be no point of return. We are crossing through a fantastical portal to our future, one that will be fruitful in love and friendship.

"Good point. We should figure out how we're going to be discreet about it." Noelle's logic grounds me once again. I've got to keep my fanciful dreams at bay just a little longer, even though I am eager to cross the line with my wife.

"We could do missionary, my body can cover all the explicit bits." I present my large stature, my chest covers Noelle's torso generously and then some. If only there was a way to prevent the spectator from seeing her long, alluring legs.

"And what about your *explicit bits?*" She reaches around and gives my ass a nail-digging squeeze.

I yelp, jumping forward and pressing completely against her. The urge to take her there and then flames hotly. "If I have to show my ass to the world, so you don't have to, so be it." I exhale to regulate my thick, panting breath.

"You do have quite the ass, January." Noelle softens her groping. That's just so like her to turn something that needs to be taken seriously into a moment of mischief, where I blindly follow through with her ploys, which then molds into my mind as a memory.

"I modeled my personality after it." I wink, Noelle snorting adorably as I scoop her up and lay her on the mattress. *Oh, I fucking want her, I fucking need her.*

"Let's fake fuck." I scoop Noelle into my arms. Let's make this five-minute sex tape a swift process whilst still upholding an aspect of authenticity, so I can make hot and passionate love with the woman of my dreams.

"Don't forget to hit record." Noelle pushes past me to press record, I move with her as she presses against my chest. The ding sound signals me to put on quite the show.

I know for a fact I'm blocking the view of the camera already, only to ensure Noelle positions her naked body in a way that won't leave her exposed. But I'm the lucky guy who gets to see it all, uncensored. Noelle tilts her head past my hip.

"Nothing for you to see there, Princess." My robe's knot falls loose with a single tug.

"Oh my, just like in those old pornos." Noelle giggles, her eyes drop to my cock, her jaw clenches and her teeth grind. "Oh, fuck."

I fall forward onto the mattress, planting my palms beside her shoulders. I know my enormous frame is big enough to shield her spindly figure.

I lick my lips as I ogle at her striking collarbones and how they contrast with the soft curves of her breasts.

"Nono." I breathe out thickly, my arousal is building thickly in my throat, along with the urge to taste her.

"Janny." Her foot caresses up my thigh, locking around my hips, her other limb joining shortly. I didn't really account for those who might have foot fetishes, but they are certainly copping an exclusive view of my wife's feet right now. Hopefully, the sight of my ass is enough to deflect their boners. "January."

"Fuck Noelle, you look beautiful right now." This tape may be fake, but I am not good at hiding my true feelings anymore, I think I broke that habit back in Phoenix. "I want to taste you." *I need to taste you.*

"Taste me," Noelle moans, her eyes turning white as her ice blues roll.

"Nono." I discreetly call for her attention, her lashes flutter before her eyes meet mine. "How am I going to eat you out and not expose you?" I mouth to her.

"By using those gigantic hands of yours, Hot Shot." Noelle guides my left palm to her tit, my dick twitches immediately at the contact. A saccharine moan slips from her lips as her back bows into my touch.

"Hm, fuck, okay." I plant my other palm on her other breast and lower myself to my knees. "I'm going to eat you out, Princess."

Noelle's thighs tremble as I feel my hot breath ricochet on my cheek, in fact, that may just be the heat radiating from her pussy. Seems like she can't help but have all her feelings on display, too.

"January, yes, please, for real."

For real? My eyes train on her, I lick the air. Her pelvis jerks up, her pussy making contact with my chin, leaving a wet residue.

Fuck, I want to take my palm, wipe her juices away, and lick it clean.

"So wet, Princess."

"January, please," Noelle pleads. I hook Noelle's leg over my shoulder and come to a stand. Her trembling limb falls to the crevice of my elbow as I lean forward and whisper in her ear.

"We're just pretending for this one, right, Nono?" I croak.

"Yes," she whispers, and my cock twitches eagerly. I swear that thing has a mind of its own, how could it possibly be excited at the prospect of *not* eating Noelle out? Unless I am only just realizing I have a tease kink.

"So I'm not going to actually eat you out." I search for confirmation, my cock grows firmer as I narrow in on Noelle's pretty features.

"Not yet, at least." Noelle runs a soothing palm down my face, I'm not sure if it's an attempt to arouse me more or to calm my horniness. It's certainly achieving the former.

"Okay, got it." *You hear that penis, not yet at least.*

"January." Noelle cups my face in a kiss. "I love you."

"I love you too, Noelle." I peck her lips once more before trailing kisses down her body, my palms move to her breasts once again. I can feel her stiff nipples on my palms, which sends my dick into the ultimate twitching fit. I always thought of myself more as an ass guy than a tit guy. Truth is, I'm just a Noelle guy. I peck Noelle's inner thigh, her pelvis bucks up again, ricocheting her pleasure through her legs. I nip at the same spot with my teeth, her reaction is just as visceral and completely convincing for the camera's sake. I try my tongue on the same spot.

"Oh, Janny, fuck."

Her entrance flexes with invitation, so she's definitely not faking her arousal. I can't exactly say I'm faking my arousal either, as my cock comes to a full stand. I kiss tenderly at the spot I've been suckling, holding my lips where her panties would sit.

"Oh, January, I love you."

"I love you too, Nono." I grumble wetly into her heat. My mouth is both dry and swimming with saliva. Her knees jerk into a bend, she shudders a moan.

My palms massage at her tits as I caress her bruising flesh with my tongue. The overstimulation has all of Noelle's flesh tinting pink, her core flexing and releasing with each stroke of my hot tongue.

"January, yes."

Noelle's pussy is soaking by this point, the temptation to move my tongue over by a few inches and just feast is undeniably strong.

"Noelle," I groan gutturally. It almost sounded like the prowl of a lion.

"January." Noelle's moan contrasts mine with an airy lightness. Her delicateness makes my primitive instincts front in my brain, I want to protect her and possess her and most importantly please her.

I move my lips just above where her folds meet, a sharp gasp leaves her lips. The bony mound of her pelvis jerks into my chin, no doubt leaving a bruise there.

I'm sure her moisture will cure it. I dip my chin between her folds, sweetly kissing the mound, creating a bruise of my own making.

"Stubble, hm, fuck, January."

I nearly stupidly remove my hand to touch my cheek, inspecting the sharpness of my stubble. Noelle and I must still be completely in tune as she gently dismisses my hand from her breasts, replacing it with her own.

"Touch me," she lilts.

I quickly scrub my light stubble, Noelle hastens her hips into the texture.

"Hm, fuck, Janny."

My jaw clenches, trying to restrain my tongue from unfurling from my mouth and parting her folds, devouring her tempting juices.

I position my arm in what is hopefully a convincing enough position to look like I'm fingering Noelle without actually fingering her.

I peer over my shoulder to see if we're still in frame, my chin glitters with moisture.

Oh fuck, this looks so real.

"January," Noelle purrs, she licks her raspberry hued lips, threading her fingers through my tresses. She guides my gaze back to hers with a mischievous flick of her finger under my chin.

"Noelle." I turn my head profile once more, inserting two fingers into my mouth, dragging them out.

Noelle releases a shudder, I press my fingers to her panty line, tracing the faint imprint from the elastic of her panties. Fuck, I'm dying to see the back and what illustrations her panties have painted there. I really am an ass guy, after all.

Noelle flinches, the flesh is obviously sensitive from my previous smooching. She rocks with my strokes, squeezing at her tits as agonizing whimpers slip from her mouth. I maintain the rapid fingering motion as I rise to her face once more.

"You okay?" I whisper into her lips.

"No."

"We can stop if it's too much."

"It's too much and not enough." Noelle bucks her pelvis, my fingers slipping between her folds momentarily. "January, please fuck me."

"You mean *insert*?" I wink, showing that I, in fact, won't be inserting.

"I mean." Noelle leans further into my ear. "Fake fuck me already, so we can actually fuck."

"Okay, you got it, Princess." I declare, with a peck on her lips.

I remove my finger from her panty line, licking the remnants of what juices I catch.

Grabbing at my cock feels like torture right now, its twitches are like pleas to push into Noelle's wanting pussy.

Not yet, buddy, soon.

I groan as I pretend to push into Noelle, collapsing forward and catching her lips in a kiss. I roll my hips, which causes Noelle's folds to split. My cock may not be inside her, but it is still feeling the throbbing sensations of her heat.

"Oh, fuck Noelle, you make me weak." I pull my hips back, my tip caresses her clit. "So fucking weak."

I hold my hips in place, feeling her bud flutter beneath my tip. She rocks gently into my length.

"January, I—" her words cut short and her thrusts quick, only to suspend into long pulls running along my length.

"You feel amazing, Nono." My words vibrate pleasantly in my throat. I feel hyper aware of my internal reactions, possibly because I crave to be inside Noelle so badly. I can feel my hot blood coursing through my veins and circulating hotly at my pelvis,

"Yeah-ha," Noelle trembles, her chest rising and falling frantically. "Fuck me, hard and fast."

I take on the command and rub my cock on her heat with vigor and speed, rolling my hips in to apply pressure.

"Oh fuck, January, that feels so good." Her fingertips run along my back, her nails locking into my flesh, triggering me to thrust faster. "Oh, Janny! Yes!"

I'm grunting like a neanderthal, I can't even materialize words for how good this feels. So, I stick with uncouth grunts.

"I love you, Prince."

"I love—" I pause, my balls are aching as they become firmer. The image of my blood pumping through my cock forms vividly in my mind. "I love you, Princess." I finally manage out. "I love you so fucking much."

We may be faking sex right now, but I really love Noelle to an unmeasurable degree. She was crazy enough to film a fake sex tape to save our asses. What part of that doesn't scream *love of my life* material?

"Noelle," I pant, leaning forward. "Noelle, fake orgasm right now, so I can make actual love with you."

"Yes!" she yelps. Her body tenses suddenly before melting into a tremor.

"Atta girl." I brush the auburn strands that stick to her forehead, my eyelids rest lazily as I take in all her colors. A trickling wetness down my cock tears me from the spectacle.

"I just finished." Her raspberry lips break into a seductive smile.

I can't help but mirror her charming grin, I peck her forehead. She matter-of-factly did finish.

"*Je t'aime,* Nono." I peel from her sweltering skin, ensuring I don't expose her as I go to stop the recording. I release a hard exhale when the ping sounds, signaling the video has stopped.

"Wow," I huff, planting my hands on my hips. "That was a lot harder than I thought it would be."

"How so?" Noelle lilts from the bed, now tangled in her snowflake sheets.

"There were multiple moments I wanted to make that real then." I shake my head, wearing my biggest grin to date, I even slip out a laugh of disbelief. *We just filmed a fucking sex tape.*

"Well." Noelle's fingertips run along my stubble. "Technically, it was all real, because this is real."

"It is real, isn't it?" I grin, bringing her into a dreamy kiss.

"That has to be the best edging I've ever experienced." Noelle's hands explore my back muscles with her featherlight fingertips.

"I guess you're right, it wasn't really all that fake at all. We're just broadcasting our foreplay to the world." I can't keep my hands off of Noelle, some part of me has to be touching her at all times. She's a necessity to me now, she's water, she's oxygen, she's essential. *She's my wife.* I aim to be the most incredible husband that she finds me to be just as essential.

"Do you need a little intermission before we go full primal?" I flash a charming smile.

"Just five minutes to catch my bearings, some of us weren't completely faking," Noelle pants out thinly, my smile drops from my face, worry washing over it instead.

"No, you actually finished, but I barely did anything." Besides some sloppy clitoral stimulation, I'm surprised how minimal contact brought on such an intense reaction from Noelle.

"Sometimes it's not what you do, but who you are that gets me going." Noelle manages through an airy lilt.

"That makes complete sense to me, like that time you rode me. Oh fuck, I still have dreams about it." Honestly, I could—*and have*—finished to just the thought of Noelle, not even her naked, just Noelle's existence is enough for my penis to erupt with cum.

"I guess we know what we're doing for the real thing, huh?" Oh fuck, my cock may just erupt now. She's going to ride me. I'm going to feel those silky, smooth thighs rubbing against mine, I'm going to see her core muscles flex as her arousal grows. I'm going to witness those gorgeous tits of hers bounce freely.

"Noelle," I croak dryly, as I drool over my wife. I clear my throat, trying to align Noelle's health as my priority. Let's get her into good shape so we can make our mutually shared dream of riding the fuck out of me come true. First, I must ensure she is hydrated. "Did you want some water, Princess?"

"That would be lovely, Peasant, I mean Prince." She grins mischievously, finessing her long legs together. *That's it, Nono, get those pretty thighs warmed up for some real activity.*

"By all means, call me husband, I think it's a good middle ground." I wink back.

"January Cameron Snow, my beloved husband, fetch me a glass of water," she plummily demands, waving her hand with a pompous flourish.

"Right away, Noelle Winter Darlington, my beloved wife."

Thirty-Two

Promiscuous

Noelle

"They are all outside, looking at the floor as if it's the most interesting thing in the world." January clicks the door shut with a bump of his hip, armed with two glasses of water. The overflowing liquid spills over the edge and runs down January's well-defined forearms, threading majestically through the muscular contours. *That has to be the hottest thing I've ever seen.*

"They're just waiting around?" I croak out dryly. January's eyes widen with urgency, he hands me my sweating glass of water.

"Yep. Get this, I told them we weren't done. Not even close, they'll be waiting for a loooong time. I have no intention of rushing."

"Really?" I don't know what has me in more disbelief, that January told the entire film crew we're not done—I can only imagine the stun on their faces, no faking in here, fellas—or the fact that January wants to go on for a *loooong time.* I just hope I can keep up, because although he has no intentions of rushing, I have every intention of fucking him wildly as I can.

"That's what Samantha said, and I said nope, just taking an intermission. Then she said I look wrecked, so we must actually be making love." I watch as January takes a pull from his glass, the droplets running down his neck makes me want to rub my pussy on his bobbing Adam's apple. As January bathes in his sloppy drinking, realization floods over me. Samantha believes we make love. Now all she has to do is spread it like I'm spreading my legs.

"Ha, take that Samantha! We make love and we've got the tape to prove it." I peer seductively over my glass, teasing January with a brief glimpse of my swollen pussy. January's brows jump in surprise, a smirk growing on his lips. He dismisses his glass onto my side table, crawling atop of me, gently parting my knees. I giggle, feeling the refreshing water slip from the glass and onto my breasts. A primal growl leaves January's lips, his palm splays over my tit once again, his breath breaking with a shudder.

"Except we weren't actually making love in that, just pretending, just like the stunt." January massages at the tissue of my breast, biting so hard on his bottom lip. I anticipate him to draw blood.

"I wasn't pretending." My back bows into his touch, my moist fingertips leave the glass and thread through his hair, January simpers pathetically, quickly composing himself with a clearing of his throat.

"I know, I could feel your not-pretend hatred for me." January retracts his hands from my body, now I'm whimpering and pleading for his touch.

"I never hated you, Janny. I was just disappointed," I state with reassurance, signaling through lazed flirtatious eyes he is welcome to touch my body.

"I know and I will never let you down again, I will spend the rest of my life making it up to you." He tenderly rubs at my side near my ribcage, I can tell he's dying to touch my breasts again. But to right his wrongs, he's restraining himself, like his adolescent training has kicked in.

"You can start with a kiss." I occupy my lips around the edge of the glass, yielding him from kissing me. I mischievously peer over the edge, watching his brain tick away on how to defeat this obstacle. *Where's your Yeti Master now, Janny?*

"I will do much more than kiss you, Noelle." His hands finally make contact with my aching breasts again, he displays a devilishly handsome smile of his own.

"I never said where you'd be kissing me, January. You've got a lifetime's worth of groveling to do." Although most is forgiven, I have to admit I like teasing January, and I believe the dynamic is mutual.

"Lucky me." January licks his lips.

I reach to place my glass of water on the side table, knowing my ass is obscuring his complete sight.

"I'm ready to begin my ass kissing, Nono." From what I can gather, January has pressed his cheek to my derierre, his bassy voice vibrating through my pelvis.

"Close, Janny, so close. Certainly in the vicinity though—" I gasp when he slips between my legs and wraps his large hands around my thighs, pulling my weight down to his face.

He hums when my heat makes contact with his mouth, this time no ice cube to separate the searing sensation. The spike in temperature makes me instantly dizzy.

"January, I need to lie down, but please don't stop."

I maneuver my weight off of January and onto my shaky arms. The mattress springs from its sunken position, January coming to a stand, making the mattress available for me to flop down on.

"Are we recording this one, too?" January says with a hiss as he nods to the camera, my eyes flick down to find his hand tending to his balls.

I roll my head to catch myself on the phone screen, January's cerulean eyes remain lustfully on me.

"I'd like to make a real one for us," I say meekly.

"You're not going to pick apart and analyze its authenticity afterwards, are you, Nono?" He quirks a thick raven brow.

Crap, he's caught me red-handed, that was my exact intent. There is no way how I truly feel doesn't completely read on my body, and especially when we are experiencing peak intimacy whilst having sex. I don't think there will be all the much difference between the fake one…which proves we've never been faking.

"Because you should know, Nono." January presses record. "Everything I feel for you is real." He stalks his muscular frame back to the bed, enveloping me in his arms. I reach for the sheet and shelter us from the camera's view.

"And what I feel for you is also real, and it's for your eyes only, Hot Shot." I want to live in the moment with January. Although this sex tape will serve as something to jog our memories when we are senile, there is a part of me that doesn't want to put on a show. I just want to be completely present for once.

"I love you, Nono."

"I love you too, Janny."

January and I's lips catch in a perfect union, his soft, unchapped lips make mine tingle. January's entire body pressed against me makes me tingle. His rock solid middle pressed to my soft stomach, his firm thighs entangled against my wet, trembling thighs. His dark demeanor coming together and merging with my sunny outlook. How we polarize one another, yet that strengthens our bond. It makes our love defiant.

He's ice and I'm fire, yet he's the one melting my core.

"Nono, I need to taste you," he desperately declares through a hot, wet breath.

"Yes, Janny." My fingers thread into his raven locks, I feel the sheet haphazardly fall past his shoulder as he travels lower, leaving us exposed to the chilling Colorado air. But the room feels more like a sauna in the Sahara Desert, a complete inferno akin to hell.

But the feeling is heaven.

My diaphragm flinches as January's hot tongue splits my folds again. January's arms scoop under my thighs, the sheet completely abandoning us, leaving us exposed. The feeling of his hot breath cocktailing with the heat of my pussy is spellbinding. I'm grateful that it's all being caught on tape, because I certainly want to revisit this, even if it is only as a third party spectator. Thankfully, this tape is for our eyes only. Our love is for us, we don't have to prove a damn thing. I don't care what people say; I don't care if the hype dies out. I just need January to stay.

"January." My lungs feel like they could tear into two, but it would be an absolute pleasure.

January grumbles on an exhale, "Say my name, Princess. How I've missed my name, how I've missed you."

"I've missed you too, January. I've missed this, us, everything, so much."

My back bows when January nuzzles deeper into my pussy, his tongue working at my entrance whilst his nose toys with my clit.

"Holy Justin Bieber, no one does that better than you." I inhale sharply, my legs threaten to squeeze together. January's aquiline nose emerges from my pussy, his lips pinching at my clitoral hood, his tongue flicking at my sensitive bud. "Oh, January."

My hole flexes desperately for stimulation. If anyone is good at reading my subtle body movements, it is January. Within seconds, my pussy is occupied by January's finger, skillfully stimulating me with hook-like caresses, puncturing inwards and outwards.

"More, please," I beg. My brain is foggy right now, the sensation is bliss, but I crave more, I want more of January. I want him faster, I want him rougher, I want more of his body parts inside of me. January inserts a second finger, speeding the rhythm and articulation. His suckling on my clit also intensifies, triggering my thighs into an intense tremor. "Hm, fuck."

"My name." I only just make out January's voice amongst my moisture.

"January. Yes, January Snow. I will marry you." I am incomprehensible right now, I can't even remember the date, I don't even remember my name. All I can think of right now is *January Cameron Snow.* "January." I come undone, I feel I might evaporate, completely consumed by heat. My thighs become slick with wetness and may be the only thing keeping me cool right now.

January rises from his crouched position by my sex, observing as I continue to twitch, thrash, and steam. It is physical bliss to have the cold air caress my body, but it is emotional agony to not have January pressed against me.

He cleans his fingers of my finish as he looks on, my eyes trail lower at his free-standing erect penis.

Having his fevered body pressed against mine may be too much to handle right now, but perhaps just my lips pressed to his cock will suffice.

It takes all I've got to push myself from the mattress, but it's all worth it when the tip of January's cock caresses the roof of my mouth. His eyes roll back with a moan, I engulf his length, releasing a muffled moan of my own.

"Noelle."

Oh right, that's my name. I completely forgot, I would've gladly been referred to as January's Princess for the rest of my life.

His cum free hand plants on the top of my crown, I want to tilt my head up and see what expression is being paired with those pathetic whimpers. January's firm grip only allows me the pleasure of viewing the bulging veins of his twitching abdomen, I'm not complaining.

"Fuck, Princess."

I finesse my tongue over his slit.

"FUCK, PRINCESS!"

January's knob twitches, hitting the roof of my mouth repeatedly. I feel cum spread on my tongue, but I don't stop. I use the moisture as lubrication to devour more of his length.

"Noelle, I will cum again if you keep this up."

I suppress the gag that is building in my throat; I dismiss his empty threat and take it as a challenge. I want to work his cock like some sort of oral joystick, control him and defeat his *Yeti Master* until it's nothing but constant snowfall.

"January," I moan, knowing the hot breath in the back of my throat is probably agonizing bliss paired with the vibration of my voice. "Ugh, January, so big."

I tighten the suction on my cheeks, his length anchors in my mouth. I bob my head quickly, my fingers blindly reaching for his ballsack, kneading a single one in each hand.

"Oh, fuck this! I need to fuck the shit out of you, Noelle, right now."

January's palm gently presses against my searing forehead, but I'm persistent with puncturing my mouth with his cock.

"Please, Noelle, I'm gonna make a fucking mess in your mouth."

I hum at the delicious prospects.

January's hips buck forward suddenly, I gag at the fierce punch of his tip against my uvula.

He pulls out quickly when my hold loosens out of surprise. His cock painting my breast with his cum, I embrace the rainfall like a proud pornstar. I mean, I am halfway there with this all being recorded. I cannot wait to watch that blowjob on replay, over and over and over. January's stream of cum seems endless. Until it suddenly just...stops. With heavy breaths, we expect more to come.

"I suggest we get a condom on my dick right now and I pound that hot pussy of yours."

I look up to see January's chest heaving, his cheeks are adorably rosy.

"Sure thing, Hot Shot."

January simpers, more cum flows. I roll my eyes with a giggle and reach into my draw for a holographic condom. I tear the packet with my teeth, pinch the tip of the rubber, ready to roll it onto January's cock, that he is now pumping at frantically.

"It just won't stop," he scolds his penis.

"He's got 10 years of suppressed sexual frustration, Janny, don't be so hard on the little guy. It's going to take a lot of sex to cure him of this continuous stream of cum." I tease, giving January's disheveled locks a tussle.

"I'm trying to will it to a stop." January squeezes out, I watch his abdomen flex attractively, exposing veins that remained hidden during my blowjob.

"Fucking hell, January," I pant, my blood runs cold and flashes hot at how much of a stud my best friend and husband is.

"I know, I'm getting pissed off, too." His handsome face contorts into his usual irritated expression, only making him even more handsome.

"January, fuck it." I toss the condom aside. "Please, just fuck me like this."

"Noelle, I'm in the middle of ejaculating." January stares at me like I'm crazy. It's not the first time we've had unprotected sex, I took precautions then...I haven't decided whether I'll do the same now. That is a post insemination discussion, I think. As for now, I need January's cum inside me.

"I don't care, fill me up, Hot Shot." *January, listen to me for once and fucking fill me to the brim.*

"Oh." January's expression softens. He plants his palms into the mattress, digging his knees into the cum covered duvet. I shimmy back up to my pillows, spreading my legs widely. My core anticipating being filled with January's length and his ever-flowing load. I feel his finish drip down my entire heat, from my clit to my entrance, flexing eagerly as he lines himself up with my hole.

"We're doing this again," January says with a tremble.

"Doing what?" I can barely concentrate, I've already surrendered my body to the sensation of being full before it's even happened.

"Unprotected sex. This is dangerous, Noelle." January pierces with sternness.

"I don't feel like I'm in danger." I flutter my lashes open, hoping the serene peace I feel translates on my face.

"Neither do I." January's jaw clenches as my hole claims his tip. "I'm in, I'm going all the way."

"Yes." My whole body submits to January, I feel utter completeness. Completely safe, completely loved, completely *his.* I have no fear that he will let me go ever again, he wants me and he wants me for forever.

My hips follow his movements as he pulls from my center. Usually, the part of my brain that is linked with my anxious attachment style would kick in, worrying that my lover will abandon me. It was especially prominent when January and I started to have sex again. But that part of my brain no longer activates, I simply just love the feeling of being filled by January. I don't want his cock to leave my body for even a second.

"Nono," January hisses, his fingers wrapping around my hip, holding it in place as he pulls out slightly. A simper slips from his lips.

On second thought, I love hearing January whimper and simper pathetically, so perhaps partial removal is okay.

An airy moan slips from me when he pushes in again, he grips his other hand to my hip. Slowly and articulately repeating his tender pull from my core and re-entering. "January."

"YES!" His voice peaks shrilly.

"Don't hold back. I mean it." I lock eyes with him, he's wearing his signature concerned face. "I said what I said, January, fuck me like you've never fucked me before."

"But I—"

"Zip! Do it, Janny, I'll be fine. In fact, I'll be satisfied." I squirm, feeling my canal squeeze his length, begging for friction.

January doesn't deny my body of its needs any longer, he rolls his cock into my pelvis at a steady pace. My reaction is visceral, my upper body jerks upwards, pressing against January's briefly before crashing down again.

January catches me before I complete my fall, cradling the back of my neck as he continues to blissfully roll into my pussy. He collects my lips into a kiss, I'm the one to slip my tongue in. This all feels so undeniably passionate. And that's all that matters, is how it feels. I wouldn't even mind if the phone suddenly reached full storage minutes ago and stopped recording, I feel completely present right now with January.

"Your pussy feels so good, Noelle, I love you, Princess." January devotes with a whiny glottal.

"Your cock feels fucking fantastic, Janny, I love you too, Prince," I slur through my orgasmic dizziness.

January speeds suddenly, lowering both him and me to the mattress before letting me absolutely have it.

And oh my fucking god, I need January to fuck me like this for the rest of my life. The friction is so intense; it feels like we're starting a fire in my belly. Not even January's copious amounts of cum could extinguish, it's a wildfire between my legs right now.

"January, I'm going to—"

"Come for me, Princess. Come for me."

My breath comes thin and snappy, my diaphragm expanding to store breath but failing miserably at my lackluster attempts to collect oxygen. I let the winded sensation take over my body, surrendering to thunderous moans building in my throat and the earthquake that is living in my veins.

"That's my girl, Nono." January rolls slowly, my autonomy is lost as I feel my body go numb. It's like I'm on a rollercoaster that is thrashing my body around wildly. And I am ready to line up and ride again and again and again.

Next time, I'll most definitely be riding January with extreme vigor. I have a feeling this sexy session is going to take me three to five business days to recover, but I'm hoping it's like a hangover where you cure it by drinking more liquor. In this case, take more of January's incredible cock.

"How are you feeling?"

I open my mouth but no words come out, my throat is obscenely dry. January is quick to reach for my glass of water and press it to my lips. I take a long, well-needed draw.

"Thank you," I say crisply.

"It's the least I could do." January shrugs, his palm still planted at the bottom of the glass in my shaky, weak grip.

"For fucking my brains out, thank you, Janny. I want you to fuck me like that every time, please and thank you." I muster with what little breath and energy I have, which doesn't showcase my full extent of enthusiasm.

"Maybe, just on special occasions." January swipes sweaty auburn locks from my eyes.

"January," I press through my teeth.

"Okay, yes, fine. Every time, my wife." January submits to my request with a beaming smile.

My wife. I can't help but mirror his grin at that.

"My husband."

Thirty-Three

Afterglow

Noelle

I can't tear my eyes from my phone as I watch January and I *make love*. Even though the act we are undertaking has a more unloving nature.

"I look pissed." January's thumbs massage into my shoulder blade, I didn't even realize I was, as Eshika would say, wearing my shoulder as earrings.

"And I look ill," I say on a collapsed breath.

"For the record, Nono, I wasn't pissed. I was in fact very aroused. You certainly didn't look ill as I looked down on you so angrily. My god, I really do need to fix my face. That is unsettling." January tilts the phone towards him, his teeth grinding loudly in my ear.

"I think you look handsome." I peck January's tense jawline, his pinched expression melts instantly.

"And you look beautiful as always, Princess." He delicately tucks a lock of hair behind my ear, pulling my chin towards him and planting a soft kiss on my lips.

"Thank you, Prince." I smile softly, only for it to break into a frown. "This is not the fairytale ending Justin Bieber promised me in his song."

"This sex tape thing wasn't ideal," his admiring smirk tilts into a handsome grimace.

"Thankfully, the public are seeing this one. Our fake one is much less vomit inducing." I click on the link in @November-Rain's link tree, immediately my stomach is nauseated. "Well, not completely, I still feel sick that this is out there, but it's what had to be done."

January's discontent hum sends a shiver down my spine.

"Why don't we stay offline today, I'll treat you like the Princess you are." His thumb glides over mine, threading his fingers through my knuckles and locking the screen with his thumb over mine. My home screen now displays the image I recently changed it to; January and I making snow angels. A time of innocence, although looking at this picture, it's all right there in our eyes. How this very obvious but subtle undertone of infatuation never read during the publicity stunt will always rack my brain, even when I was hurting most I was still undeniably infatuated with him, despite how much I was in denial.

I wipe it all from my mind; I don't need to worry about pretending or being convincing, because all of this is real to those it matters most. January and I.

"Really, Janny?" I feel my eyes sparkling as I stare into January's dreamy ones.

"I'm thinking of taking a trip into town, going to the bookstore and then drinking ourselves sick with one of everything at Coco-mo."

"Coco drunk karaoke?" My demeanor perks up.

"A must." January spins the office chair suddenly, I yelp as I try to find something solid to root myself from my reeling head. I feel January's warm palms grab a hold of my cheeks, my vision defines with clarity and my mind is quiet again.

"I love you, January." I snap a peck on January's lips, which breaks into a beaming smile.

"As much as the circumstances are not ideal, I couldn't be happier that we finally figured *us* out."

Suppose there is a silver lining in all of this. I couldn't be happier myself, everything I dreamed up as a young girl has come true. I guess I got the fairytale ending I wanted after all, just got there by unconventional means.

"Let's take your dad's SUV and fill the backseat up with books, video games, and movies."

"And where will we put them, Janny?" My eyes flick to the brimming bookshelves peeking through the timber archway that leads to the reading room.

"We'll get a new bookcase while we're at it, we'll put it in your room."

"Oh, I forgot to tell you," I begin my scheming charade by mindlessly clacking at the keyboard. "There was a mixup with your booking here at Darlington Snow Paradise, so we've had to place you in the Noelle suite permanently."

"What an upgrade." January presses his forehead to mine.

"It is a shared space, with only one bed, I'm afraid." My breath thins out, my heart speeds at January's proximity. I don't know why I'm having such a visceral reaction to January right now, we've been far more intimate than this only just yesterday. Perhaps the prospect of sharing a space with him permanently is making all of this teenage fantasy puzzle click into place.

"Who am I rooming with?" January purrs gutturally.

"Me."

"A premium upgrade, if you ask me."

I melt with a swoon when January finally kisses me.

"So, technically, we'll be putting a bookcase in our room," I huff through the kiss.

"Our room. Does that mean my Slash posters can integrate with your Justin Bieber ones?"

"I suppose so." I roll my eyes endearingly. "I want my old CD player back, even though CDs are obsolete now. So much has changed."

"For the better, I think." January pulls me from the cooling gel of my chair cushion. "I can't wait to see how we evolve together."

That all sounds so wonderful, it's all reminiscent of old times but with something new. A life I thought would never get a chance to live, a life spent with the love of my life, here at the place I most call home. But truthfully, January has always been my home, our love is home. Now we get to take that vessel of lover and continue right where we left off and fill it with memories.

I ponder on our drive into the village the other large ski resort's skirt, Darlington Snow Paradise, is merely a blip amongst its dominating neighbors. What's next for him and I? Will we ever actually get the chance to have kids? It's comforting to know January also wants kids, but when do we enter that stage of our life? Will my health be a hindrance? I can already see us growing old and gray together, our hair turning as white as the snow surrounding us, but the middle parts of our life together are still foggy for me. What happens with January's hockey career? Is this it? The stunt is over and he gets to tie his decade long career up in a nice little bow. All that effort was not only to bring security to my future, but it was also an attempt to bring longevity to his career.

My wedding ring glints in the peeking Aspen sun, the moment feels like a sign from the universe that this will work in our favor. Our soulmate bond is far too strong to sever.

"I have a confession," January starts out of the blue. I look up to find the city center is in view, it sparkles in unison with my wedding ring.

"Me too, you first." I fidget with the ring as I hold my gaze on January. It's the ultimate comfort to be looking at him and know that this physical object ties us together for eternity.

"Okay, well, that ring...that ring was always yours. I pre-ordered it from the Gala's catalog knowing that you would adore it, and from the way you're always staring, I am correct." A devilish cocky smirk grows on his face. I hum contemplatively as I take in the dazzling snowflake ring again.

"Okay, my turn." I can't fight the conniving grin on my face. "I already knew that, January."

"Oh shit, you did?" January gulps cartoonishly.

"Yes, Prince." I snicker.

"Then I guess you know about your secret wardrobe at my mansion." January runs his hands nervously through his raven locks, now I'm being humbled by his handsomeness. "I should get all of that moved here."

"You spoil me," I swoon.

"Just trying to level the playing field with how much you better my life and me as a person. It got me thinking about what kind of person I want to be in the future." January jumps out of the car before I can even ask.

I'm shocked to find him opening the door for me.

"What level boyfriend am I up to?"

"Husband level." I wrap my arms tightly around his abdomen. He slips his mittened hand into mine and we journey into the bustling street lined with shops.

I can feel people's stares on us but it's no match for my husband's vicious guard dog glare, his thick raven brows furrowed deeply, his mouth quivering into a snarl. It appears all the online buzz has made its way offline, whispers and mutters of both admiration and disgust slip from onlookers.

"Say that to my face!" January bursts suddenly, I bring him down from his aggressive energy by caressing his bicep, catching the fearful expression of a group of teenage girls.

"Janny." I snap my finger to garner my beloved guard dog's attention. His head whips to me with the speed of light, now wearing the frightened expression of the now snickering teenagers once wore. "Don't worry about people, get lost in me and me only."

January's puffed out chest collapses, "Just defending you, Princess."

"Come on, let's go to Frosty's."

Frosty's is a child's dream and where January and I spent most of what little money we earned doing jobs around the lodge—well, most of my money—January always rationed his to buy me lavish gifts on special occasions. Looks like the tradition lived on even in my absence.

We enter Frosty's quaint shop front entrance; the magic nostalgia greets us. Walls lined from floor to ceiling with video and board games, books and movies of all genres. Small packages full of adventures that I can live from the comfort of my bed. Which sounds sad, but my inhibitions never got me down because I always had great company.

I loop my arm through January's, leaning my head on his shoulder as he browses the back of a video game.

"It's no *Blizzard*. I don't think you realize how much The Battle of Blizzard has ruined gaming for me, it's all I ever want to play." January slots the gaming cartridge back onto the shelf with an unsatisfied hum.

"If only Justin Bieber could *ruin* music for you, so you can fangirl with me." I snuggle extra close to him, hoping my touch will also persuade him to become a Belieber.

"Hey, I like some of his songs." His hand rests gently on top of mine and if he asked me to like rock and roll music at this very moment. I would honestly take it the extra mile and become a hardcore groupie.

"Yeah right." I break our touch apart, partially to keep my superior taste in music.

"To prove it, I will sing Baby at karaoke word for word without even looking at the screen." January narrows his on me, leaning done and pressing his forehead to mine. My breath escapes me. Can hockey players have groupies? Because I am January Cameron Snow's biggest fan.

I catch myself before I lose all my autonomy over January's love spell.

"You're on, make a bet?" I drive my forehead further into his. My heart flutters still, it's incredible how we've kept our playful friendship in our love. I wish everybody could feel the way I feel with January. My husband and my best friend.

"You wouldn't be my wife if there wasn't some moral corruption behind your ideas." January collects my hand in a vigorous handshake, he pulls me into his chest, shooting those sexy challenging eyes on me. "You're on, wife."

"You have no idea how much my inner teenager screams whenever you call me your wife."

"Happy screams, right?" He quirks a brow.

"Yes, high pitch fangirl screams to be exact." I have officially entered fangirl territory, I'm forgetting what Justin Beiber looks like, every crevice of my brain is occupied by January Cameron Snow.

"No way, teenage January does the same thing whenever I call you my wife. I'm convinced I've been hit in the head with a puck and I'm just in a wonderful coma."

"Tough! I'm actually your wife, forever!" I say with a spooky, dramatic flair.

"I got so lucky."

"Last one to the register is a rotten egg and has to pay." I'm sprinting before I even finish my sentence, I look over my shoulder to find January making his way to the register at a leisurely pace. Even committing to the bit by pulling his debit card out in slow motion.

"You can ring these up while my husband takes his sweet ass time. You've proven your point, Janny."

"Hey, you're from the—"

January stumbles into a run, joining me at the counter. "Nope, what is this sex tape everyone is talking about? I would love to meet our doppelgangers one day, don't you think, Princess?"

"Janny, she didn't even mention the sex tape." I pinch the bridge of my nose.

"What? I was just going to say you're the kids that live in the lodge down the street. Guess you're not kids anymore."

"He has the gray hairs to prove it," I quip quickly.

"I used to come work with my mom on the weekends and you guys would always come in as teenagers, I thought you were both the coolest. We only ever spoke once, I wasn't allowed to serve customers being only nine, but you told me about a video game you were designing."

"Tia! I remember you!" My eyes flick to her name to see if I'm correct.

"You do? It was so long ago." She shuffles nervously on the spot like she's experiencing her own restless fangirl moment.

"This one never forgets a face," January pipes up, giving my rib a jab with elbow.

"What's this about a sex tape? I thought you were a hockey player and you're still designing video games?" Tia's perception of me is clearly altering her mind as we speak. She probably sees me as less of a hero now. I guess this sex tape will haunt me for the rest of my life, no matter what career path I endeavor. That should give me merit to pursue game development wholeheartedly, since my reputation is already stained, the only storyline there is to follow is a comeback.

"Yes! Yes she is. You're famous, honey! And not because of your orgasms." January pulls me into a rough hug, poking at my cheek.

"No, that would be Janelle." I loop my fingers through the bag. "Thank you so much for these, Tia. You're always welcome at Darlington Snow Paradise."

I tug January out of the store, clearly his stupidity has caught up with him because he is as pale as a ghost.

"Nice one, Janny." I roll my eyes, stirring through the contents of the bag, fishing out sticks containing pure sugar. January and I would devour these by the dozen until it had our hearts buzzing.

I bite the end off with my teeth, handing one to January. He misjudges his reach and the sugary powder dissolves into the snow. "I worry that you might slip over the microphone at karaoke, pull it together, would you?"

I tear at another, maneuvering his hands to grip onto the sweet tightly.

"Wow, I'm getting war flashbacks to the stunt. It has been one hell of a fortnight, huh?" January tips the sugar stick into his mouth, emptying the contains in one swig. He shivers, the color returning to his face. "Sour apple."

I devour my sugar stick, overcome with saccharin overload. "Cotton candy." I bite down on the crystal grains. I always had this fantasy as a teen where January and I would get two opposing flavors of sugar sticks and we'd make wonderful new concoctions in our mouths by French kissing. "Are you okay?" I ask, January still in deep thought.

"Yeah, I'm okay, just thinking about everything you've been subjected to. It doesn't sit right with me."

How January can remain so mellow and composed, whilst my heart feels like it's buzzing just from one sugar stick.

"It's not all that bad." I shrug, it's all I really can do. I fear if I animate anymore, I might have an episode. "You don't look well, Janny."

"I'm well if you're well."

"You're probably not in the mood for karaoke now. I had a sure win with this bet, too." I kick the snow in defeat, immediately clutching at my heart afterwards. Okay, I can no longer tolerate sugar sticks at 28.

"Oh, and you still do." I catch the mischievous twinkle in January's eyes, he looks to the mountains nonchalantly, but I see straight through him. He always looked to the mountains when he found me *overwhelmingly beautiful*. Which proves we have never been just friends. He always called me beautiful, crying out loud. "Janny?"

His smirk is a dead giveaway that he's up to something.

"You can't pull the wool over my eyes, January, I am a prank mastermind—"

"Oh, but I can." I'm cast into sudden darkness, my nose being tickled by fluff. I toss my snowsuit hood off my head, I see January poking his tongue out in the distance.

He nudges into an elderly woman in his cocky backward trek.

"Act your age, would you," the elderly lady huffs.

"Sorry ma'am, my wife just turns me back into my giddy teenage self."

"You look familiar." The lady removes her spectacles and squints at January.

"Watch any good sex tapes lately?" I taunt. Payback time.

She gasps, "Why, I never!"

"Gotta go. Come on, Nono." January presses through his teeth, I blindly make my way to the Cocomo entrance, my vision impaired by my uncontrollable laughing fit.

My giggling settles when January snuggles into my neck, I'm embraced by his vetiver scent.

"Order one of everything, Princess, I'll go put my name in for karaoke." He pecks my cheek, already at the tablet, to request his song. The costume box is the next target in his line of sight, he's sporting the same angry expression he has when he fucks me. Which I gathered is his face of determination, going to endless measures to impress me.

"Noelle! What can I get you?"

I turn around to the familiar voice, Violet has been a spectator of January and I's adolescent love, it's too bad she never got to come to the wedding. It was more photoshoot than a wedding. I'll definitely have to discuss with January if we could marry under less contractual circumstances.

"I heard the news." Violet breaks me from my reverie of January.

"Oh, did you?"

"You kept it really small, huh?" Violet sighs.

"Yes." I can't exactly explain that it was all a stunt, she'll think my love for January is all just for show. We've only just made people believe the truth again with a convincing fake sex tape. Oh, the irony.

God, I hope Violet hasn't seen me shagging my best friend, fake or not, this woman has known me since I was four.

"Regardless, you two look happier than ever. He's been gone for so long."

"But he's back now." I remind myself. January is actually here.

"And I'm here to stay." January's voice rings warm and true.

"January, my goodness, you've grown into such a handsome man."

"With a heart of gold because of this beautiful, cheeky woman." January cups my face.

"Oh, it's so nice to see you two finally work out those feelings you always danced around. I remember when I found January looking up *how to tell when a girl likes you* on the internet cafe computers."

"To be fair, I looked up *how to tell if a guy likes you* on the reception's desktop at least once a week. If not that, some variation, *how to tell if your best friend is in love with you, how to tell your best friend you're in love with him without saying I love you—*"

My ramble cuts short as I feel lips upon mine, ones I couldn't mistake for anyone else's except my husbands.

"Welcome to the stage!" Bob, the MC and Violet's husband, announces. "January? He's back? J-Dawg, come grab the mic."

Someone needs to tell dear Bob that adding dawg after the first letter of your name died out well before January or I were even born.

I snicker as I watch January gallop onto the stage, he couldn't be further from his celebrity person Cameron Snow.

No, he is completely himself right now. My Janny.

January stays true to his word and will serenade me with his rendition of Baby by the man I'm having a mental affair with.

That's right, I'm cheating on my mental husband with my real one. I think I'll just mentally divorce Justin Bieber altogether.

I can't believe this is my life forever. What is next for us? I honestly don't even mind the millions of possibilities, so long as those millions of possibilities are with January.

"*I know you love me.*" I wince as January starts far too high, his voice croaking and it's giving me flashbacks to his puberty days.

"*I know you care.*" It sounds even worse in his bassy drawl.

"*Just shout whenever and I'll be there.*"

"I'm willing to forfeit my bet, just please stop singing." I'm this close to plugging my ears with these marshmallows.

"No wait, I got this. Just let me do a chorus."

"Get on with it, then." I roll my wrist in a gesture that shows for him to continue.

"*We should have a baby, baby, baby, oh.*"

"Ha! Those aren't the lyrics! I win!" I jump from my seat. Crap, I didn't even bet anything. *Wait! What did January say?*

January is right in front of me by the time I register his words.

"A baby?"

"Yeah, we should try for a baby, or at least look into seeing if it's safe for you to carry a baby. If not, we can look into alternatives, but I think we should start a family."

"January." I cup my heart as it fills with a warm fuzz. "A family?" My lashes become heavy with tears.

"Oh god, I've accidentally offended you again, haven't I?"

"No, January."

"It's just, you gave me such a wonderful childhood, I'd like to repay the favor with our own child. Imagine how happy that child is going to be having parents like us?"

January as a parent, he's certainly attentive enough to care for a small being. I recall one winter he offered skating lessons for young children and since I skate just about as good as the little ones; I joined in on the class. January was so patient and gentle with the kids as they fell on their bottoms and burst into tears. And he was especially patient with me, I even got special treatment hugs, although I think they might have been fall preventative hugs. It is always a joy to be in my best friend's embrace.

"I'd love to start a family with you. I'll speak with a doctor as soon as possible."

January and I are officially leveling up in life.

Thirty-Four

Baby, Baby, Baby, Oh

January

I hurry to the reception desk, taking advantage of the rare interval where Noelle isn't checking in guests. This place is swamped with couples. With each couple's dynamics I observe, from the bickering to the blatant ignorance of each other, favoring their mobile phones over their significant other, it makes me appreciate the friendship that is the foundation of Noelle and I's love.

"Nono, have you eaten today?"

Her ice-blue eyes look up from the computer, "I have." Contemplation melts her features into realization. "I have not."

"You're in luck, I made you hot cocoa and told everyone swarming the snickerdoodle tray that this was a bad batch. Now it's yours entirely." I finesse the tinfoil from the plate, laid there to keep the cookies toasty warm for icy fingers. It was all Noelle's idea to preserve the treats' heat in tinfoil, the guests often comment on how the cookies taste and warmth added to their experience. It was always the little things Noelle thought of that made this place a winter wonderland.

"Janny, those are for the guests." Noelle clicks disapprovingly.

"Yeah, I know, but what kind of husband would I be if I didn't reward my wife's incredible hospitality?" I flash a smile I know will have Noelle putty in my hand.

"Alright, give me the cookies." She reaches up for the platter with grabbing hands, like how a toddler would, and I'm reminded of our appointment today.

We're seeing a doctor to see if it is safe for Noelle to carry a child. *Our child*. Which is unbelievable to think. I'm going to be raising a family with my best friend.

"Breaking news: this actually is a bad batch, too much cinnamon, they taste spicy." Noelle smacks her tongue to get rid of the taste.

"No such thing as too much cinnamon." Especially after being deprived of Noelle's cinnamon scent for a decade, I could snort that stuff from the jar.

"By all means, burn your taste buds." I collect the tray once again and nibble at each bite size snickerdoodle on the platter. I fight the tears prickling in my eyes as the spicy flavor overtakes my senses, my tongue goes numb, my ears burn, my flesh turns hot. I hum, content. "Delicious, Princess."

Noelle rewards my ridiculousness with the prettiest eye roll. It feels incredible to acknowledge thoughts like that now and not be swallowed alive by shame.

"Oh my god! It's her!" A shrill girlish squeal fills the entire lobby, the platter nearly goes splat on the floor as I flinch at the high pitch. "It's him!" I pull the platter away possessively as an energetic blonde bounces in front of me. "Oh my god, you are yummier in person."

I bite down on a cookie viciously, chewing unattractively, the crumbs falling haphazardly. I don't know what burns hotter, my irritation at this lady's obvious flirting in front of my wife or this flaming cookie.

"It's them," a man drawls unenthusiastically.

"Checking in, guys?" Noelle chimes and I'm suddenly turned into a starry-eyed fangirl. *More like checking you out, meow, my wife is hot.*

"Yes!" The blonde finally stops breathing heavily on my cookies and turns to Noelle. "Oh, you are so gorgeous in person."

"Yes, she is." I agree with a chomp of my cookie. An attempt to keep my salacious hunger to rail her on this desk.

"You two are so adorable on Instagram, we are such big fans of your love." The blonde returns to her partner's side, looping her arm through his as he continues to mindlessly scroll on his phone. Which I always found fascinating when men are always on their phones around their other half. The only reason I ever looked at my phone was to *check in* on Noelle. Now that she's in my life again, I barely have time to doom scroll, and I couldn't be happier.

"Jessica and I are *huge* fans," the man drawls flatly. I catch the tail end of a flaccid slap from the blonde on the man's forearm, he pockets the device with a sigh.

"Josh, please. Don't mind him, he's just got jet lag. I just know this place is going to rekindle our love. What do you guys do for fun around here?"

"Well, there's not much to do here except enjoy your partner's company," I explain, shooting Noelle a warm smile. Her beauty slowly takes my senses over, my mouth becomes both wet and dry, my nose is working overtime to catch the scent of cinnamon soaked into her skin. My eyes cannot decide what to appreciate first. My ears, however, are unaffected, my visual exploration is stunted when I hear a reluctant groan slip from Josh.

"Silly question, but enjoy your partner's company by doing what?" Jessica chimes in hesitantly.

"Make sex tapes." Noelle beams mischievously.

"Nono, you cheeky devil." I become hyperaware of my ears as they heat with embarrassment.

Jessica gasps, "I wasn't going to say anything, but since you brought it up, can we get the room you guys did it in?"

"I'm afraid not—" I start.

"Sure, you can." Noelle stands, my words are inhibited with a cookie shoved into my mouth. "Let's get you checked in."

I stand stupidly, crumbs falling from my tasty muzzle. Noelle's mischievous giggle springs me back to life. I devour the cookie, finishing it with a big gulp. I round the reception and lean close by Noelle's ear.

"Princess, that is false advertising."

"January, I think you forgot we got fake married to get this place booming again, let me milk it." Her breath tickles my ear, I'd much rather it tickle my tongue with the help of hers. Would it be entirely inappropriate to kiss my *fake* wife in front of these people?

Noelle does the honors of closing in on the kiss whilst I swim in my doubt.

"Which reminds me, we need to have a real wedding," I whisper sweetly in her lips.

"I'd love to do that, Janny." Noelle speaks at a normal volume, which reminds me I have nothing to hide and nothing to prove. Our love is our love.

"You two are so cute," Jessica squeaks, ruining the romantic mood.

"Alright, you're all checked in and I am going on a break." Noelle pushes back the desk check. I'm so enamored by my wife now being temporarily free from her work obligations, it takes me a moment to realize she ran over my toe. "Enjoy your stay at Darlington Snow Paradise!" Her sweet British accent is a cure for all pain.

"Thank you, thank you, thank you. Honey, I'm so excited. Let's make a sex tape."

The man bursts to life at that proposition, his honey blonde lover tugging him to the suites.

"I give that a week." Noelle and I say in unison.

"I am so grateful I married my best friend." I nuzzle into Noelle's neck.

I can detect Noelle's tension in her body as I drive down the slick road and I know that her rigidness is not from the occasional slip of the tires.

She's pondering the worst-case scenario, it's obvious to see. Her ruby-hued brows pinch together tightly, her precious eyes glass over as spiraling thoughts completely preoccupy her mind. I hate to think I was the one who made her this way, overthinking situations and nervously expecting the worst to come. All because I never clearly communicated how much she means to me. I won't make that mistake twice. I need her to know she will always mean everything to me, regardless of what the doctor has to say.

"Nono, no matter what happens in this appointment today, I love you and we will always be a family. There's so many ways we can expand our family, but we're enough already, you've always been more than enough for me. You were and are everything I've ever needed."

Noelle turns her tear-constellated eyes to me.

"I love you too, January, I just hope that it's safe for me to carry. I'd like to experience that phase of my life with you."

It warms my heart that she wants this just as badly. To think there was a time I was going to die alone, because there was no way I was going to get over Noelle. So much has changed in a few weeks reuniting, finally forging the future we both mutually dreamed of.

"We have so much ahead of us now that I'm staying at the resort." I want to seal it with a kiss, nothing can unravel the beautiful bow that ties our loving connection together.

"So, you've spoken to Samantha about not returning this season?" Noelle's eyes illuminate, the teary distant fog has cleared, revealing their true effulgent qualities. Her words dawn on me a second later.

"It's on my to do list." Now I'm the one who's tense.

"January," Noelle scolds me with her airy London accent. I love how she says my name, angry, happy, and especially when she's horny. What a time to be named after a month. "January." She asserts with more threat, my stomach twists with fright and curiosity.

"I'm going to discuss it with her after this appointment, you're my priority from now on, Nono. How it should've been all along." I tangle her fingers with mine, giving her an anchoring squeeze of her palm.

"You already cause that woman enough strife, please make sure you talk to her after the appointment." Noelle's hand is weak in my hold, it only makes me want to cling on tighter.

I can't let her slip away; I won't let her slip away. I will call Samantha first thing after this appointment and tell her with cemented conviction that I will not, I repeat, will not be returning to the Badgers this season, or next, or ever. I'm done with that going down that path, I'm doubling back to my comfy sanctuary that is Noelle Winter Darlington. I will not bow down to my publicist and her unethical practices any longer, I am utterly shocked to find Noelle is standing by her. It's true I've caused her strife, but Samantha wore Noelle down until she was paper thin.

"Wow, you're siding with Samantha now, after she ran you into the ground."

"I consented to the stunt, thank you very much." She tilts her nose heavenwards. God, this woman's profile is angelic, and her stances are incredibly stubborn. All the more reason to love her.

"It doesn't retract how unethical it is," I scoff, gripping tightly to the steering wheel. Perhaps Noelle is still playing her little mind games on me, knowing Samantha gets under my skin. Her supporting Samantha is certainly encouraging me to cut ties as soon as possible. I will act with the speed of light, swiping my metaphorical machete through the professional tie that holds me to my publicist.

"Are you regretting being forcefully married to me?" Noelle's tone shows she is only jabbing, knowing very well that I've been dying to marry her since the day I left. My grip on the steering wheel relaxes.

"Absolutely not, but I meant it when I said we should get married properly for friends and family, right? No press allowed." I guess friends will include Noelle's chronically online friends, but I will confiscate their phones before the service. This wedding will be private.

"I would marry you a million times over, January," she swoons, sinking her chin into her palm and admiring me. If I didn't have to keep my eyes on the road right now, I'd kiss her.

The small clinic comes into my view. This is it, this is the start of Noelle and I's future being set in stone.

"This is it," Noelle exhales. What a relief it is to be on the same page again, we are finally back in tune with one another. So much so, we were thinking the same thoughts.

"Yep." I stifle the emotional cocktail that is swirling in my stomach, excitement, nervousness, love. Lots and lots of love.

"I hope it's plausible." Noelle's playfulness from before dissipates with the cloud that accompanied her words.

"Only one way of knowing." I inhale, my shoulders sitting tautly against my ears.

"Right." She unfastens her seatbelt, I release my breath quickly and hurry around the car to open the door with utmost chivalry.

"You're really driving this husband material thing home."

"Just following my instincts, Nono."

"You're ridiculous." She pinches my cheek as she slips her long legs from the car and plants her feet on the ground.

Being such a small clinic, the process of notifying the reception was swift. Accommodated with only five waiting room chairs and a knock off Van Gogh painting. We sit with our hands entwined, Noelle jittering in her seat.

"It'll be fine, I'm staying regardless." Better wear down the coward inside of me, ten years I've put up with Samantha's crap. That wouldn't have been the case if I knew how much Noelle wanted me back at the lodge, so not another second to waste. I'm back here now and I'm here to stay. With Noelle beside me, I know I will have the courage to confront Samantha.

"Even if we can't have a baby?" Noelle squeezes out.

"Yes, Nono, I already said so." I pull our hands apart so I can embrace her completely at the waist, I'm this close to pulling her onto my lap. Just like old times.

"Pretty sure you still need to get Samantha's word." She raises a fiery brow, her smirk letting me know that she's onto me and my clandestine plans to get her close as possible.

"Pretty sure Sam works for me, so it's a matter of giving her my word," I state obstinately. Noelle hums, impressed, scooting herself closer to me and flashing her charismatic smile.

"Well well well, aren't you quite the Hot Shot Pro Hockey Player," she lilts, looping a long lock of my hair around her finger. She could puppeteer me with that strand alone. She's had me on strings since the day I met her, there's not a thing I wouldn't do at Noelle's beckoning call. Which makes her come across as manipulative, but believe me, I consent to everything because I see beyond Noelle's mischievous surface.

"Not anymore, now I'm Noelle Snow's Hot Shot Pro Husband." I swipe the auburn lock obstructing her vision, revealing her enchanted eyes. I see her tender heart that is full of love.

"I love you," she swoons.

"Noelle Snow?" A woman in a white coat, holding a clipboard, calls from the corridor.

"That's us!" Noelle jumps up, swaying as her knees buckle.

"Easy, Princess." I guide Noelle to the room with gentle pats between her shoulder blades. I slowly lower her to a seat on the bed.

"I am Dr. Weaver. For once I am seeing someone who hasn't injured themselves snowboarding, skiing or ice skating. So thank you for keeping my day fresh. How can I help you two?"

My eyes haven't left Noelle as the doctor does her spiel, Noelle is sobering quickly. Her skin looks vibrant and healthy again. Her eyes lock on me with worry.

"Do you want me to tell her?" I ask gently, Noelle meekly nods, averting her eyes guiltily.

"Well, we want to start a family, but we're worried that Noelle's postural orthostatic tachycardia syndrome—yes, babe, I know what POTS stands for." I chuckle as Noelle's worrisome eyes animate with surprise. "We worry it might not be safe for her to carry, and may provide complications during childbirth."

"Well, there's been no known evidence of POTS being any major hindrance during pregnancy, how severe are your symptoms, Noelle?"

"Life-inhibiting. Well, in a controlled environment they aren't as frequent, so I wouldn't say life-inhibiting, only in moments of duress or fast-paced environments." My blood boils, I actually look forward to an unfriendly phone call with Samantha after this appointment. As much as I want to postpone it and curl up to Noelle next to the fireplace, she is the reason I must follow through. Then I can enjoy Noelle without interruption, I moment's pain for a lifetime's pleasure.

"I am very accommodating to make sure she barely has to lift a finger." I quickly add.

"And you will be present during the pregnancy?" Dr. Weaver asks.

"Absolutely, I'm retiring, so I'll be around her 24/7." If I speak it into the universe, maybe it will manifest with ease.

"Help me." Noelle whispers loudly through cupped hands, her angelic features expressing fear.

"Princess, come on now. Just this once, we have to be serious." Then we can be the absolute dirtbags we were as teens.

"Okay, you're right." She tilts her head on my shoulder, I don't fight the soft smile that tugs at the corners of my mouth.

"Well, if your husband is qualified to take care of you?" I register Dr. Weaver's presence again.

"Believe me, he knows my body better than I do." Noelle snorts.

"Well, then I think it's safe for you two to try for a baby if you're completely up for the task."

"I feel like I've been training for this my whole adolescence."

"Oh sure, all those early morning puck drills will certainly assist you through my pregnancy." Noelle's eyes roll, her sarcasm drips like honey and I'm about to lick it up with my sharp retaliating tongue.

"Our pregnancy, Nono. We're a team in this."

And just like that, she's melting at my promises, this time they are not empty.

"Looks like we're retiring Janelle's holographic cock cozies too." Noelle pinches my chin, shooting me a saucy stare. I'm instantly thrust back to the times we had unprotected sex. Man, it would've been convenient for her to have fallen pregnant then, I suppose we were still on the rocks a bit, so it's for the best that she didn't. I would hate to think we'd have to raise a kid out of obligation, or if she aborted it instead, which I would've backed her decision whole heartedly. Thankfully, I do not have to ponder those what ifs. It was just a matter of coming to terms that we are made for each other. Suppose things happen in due time, but with my seed planted in Noelle would've been substantial support for my argument against Samantha. But my intense love for Noelle is all the evidence I need to plead my case.

"Beginning my true calling, being your husband and the father to our child." I punctuate with a kiss to Noelle's lips.

THIRTY-FIVE

Epilogue

January

Noelle had finished reading the pregnancy test packaging long before we even got out of the car, now she's just staring blankly, consumed by her own spiraling thoughts.

I pull her closer by the waist as we tread up to the inviting entrance of Darlington Snow Paradise. Beyond these doors our future awaits, no matter what the outcome, I will always be there for Noelle.

"There you are, kid."

My gaze finally tears from Noelle. Lo-and-behold, my pocket-sized publicist has made an appearance.

"What are you doing here, the stunt is done," I sneer. No need for niceties anymore, I'm no longer a Hot Shot Pro Hockey Player.

"Uh-duh, now you can reap the rewards with a sponsor-rich season."

"I'm not playing this season."

"According to a 17-million-dollar contract, you certainly are. Now hurry, we've got to get you to Phoenix for training photo ops. I need fresh pictures for your sponsors, you look miserable in your old ones."

"And I'll continue to be miserable if you take me away from my wife."

"It's for the season, you'll be back—wait, what's that?" I follow Samantha's line of sight, gawking at the box Noelle is toying with stressfully.

"We're pregnant," I announce recklessly. "I'm not leaving her while she's pregnant, I promise the doctor I would be there. And more importantly, I promised Noelle."

I lace my hand with hers.

"I mean, we don't know if I'm actually pregnant, but we didn't use protection for the sex tape." Noelle clarifies.

God, I hope my sperm is working overtime to find an egg, and with gusto. I know it would be completely out of line for me to ask Noelle to pee on this pregnancy test right now, but it would give me the utmost satisfaction to shove a positive urine-riddled test in Samantha's face.

"Either way, I'm staying here so we can continue trying." I say defiantly.

"You're coming with me to Phoenix—"

"No! I'm not, Samantha!" I roar. A few guests tremble at my outburst, clutching tightly to their luggage, but I don't stand down from my threatening stance. My blood races turbulently through my veins, and my vision blurs with a red haze.

"Janny, breathe." Noelle's voice is like an anchor in a rough sea.

"I can't breathe. I can't live without you any longer, Noelle." I pull her impossibly tight. My heart steadies itself with Noelle's familiar shape pressed to mine. I nuzzle my nose protectively in the crook of her neck.

"Look kid, one more season is all I ask. And then you can go off and play mommy and daddy."

"No—"

"January, look at me." I release my hold on Noelle. "We can postpone our plans for half a year. 17 million is quite the set up for a family."

"But you're priceless to me, Noelle, to start a family with you today cannot even be commodified."

"But your pretty face can." She giggles lightheartedly.

"Noelle." My heart is breaking that she's not taking the matter seriously.

"Looks like it's two to one, Cameron. This is your farewell season, go out with a bang—"

"If I'm doing this, I want every moment I'm not needed for a work obligation spent with Noelle. Video chats between sponsor duties, training and games. Bye week I'm spending here in its entirety. Multiple days off between games, I fly home here or you arrange for her to stay in Phoenix. Where she will not be planted in a hotel room but will share a bed with me in my mansion."

"Anything else, Hot Shot?" Noelle snickers.

"One more thing."

"What's that?" Samantha looks up from her phone with a smug expression. She thinks she's won. She's about to be humbled, big time.

"Noelle falls pregnant, the contract is void." My statement holds so much strength, I feel like I'm bolted to the ground. My shoulders rolling back as my confidence grows, a warmth spreads through me with Noelle's idolizing stare.

"You're quite the negotiator, Cameron." Samantha taps the side of her phone contemplatively.

"Those are my rules, you don't like them, I don't play."

A quiet swoon leaves Noelle's lips, I feel like a storybook hero. Finally, the hero I was always supposed to be for my Princess.

"Okay, fine," Samantha resigns, turning her glare onto Noelle. "What are the odds you'll fall pregnant in the next five months?"

Noelle

It's been an entire week since January had left to return to the hockey season. And still that familiar feeling of abandonment haunts me as I close up the reception for the night. The walk from the lobby to our lodge is bitterly cold. Usually, I would take advantage of the crisp cool that lingers in the air, but I would much rather January's clingy touch making me feverish to a dangerous degree.

I fall onto my bed, wishing I had the body of the man I love most to curl up to, but this is for the best. It was, after all, a part of the contract to better January's career. Now it's his turn to be advantageous and set us both up for an incredible life together.

I cast a look at my wedding ring, its effulgence glitters through my teary eyes. *Five months, Noelle, You just have to be strong for five more months.*

I miss his presence, his gentle touch. Bye week couldn't possibly come soon enough. Maybe his voice will be enough to anchor me.

I snap my phone from its charging cord; it vibrates in my hand.

It appears my husband had the same idea as me. I swipe away the call screen, intimately meeting with January's dreamy cerulean eyes.

"Hi Princess," January shivers.

"Prince, I was just about to call you." I shuffle myself up to the mountain of pillows on our bed. "How are things?"

"They've got me working like a dog, I've never needed you more than ever. I really fucking miss you." He pulls the phone close to his lips, puckering a kiss into the camera. I wish I could feel the warmth of his lips on my skin.

"I really miss you, too." Now I'm holding the screen closely, so close, my eyes are crossing. I want him. I need him. I need him here right now. I need to hold him close before I burst into tears.

"How are things at home?" His bassy voice breaks me from my crisis.

"Things are good, bookings are still steady, which is nice. I'm just glad I can keep busy while you're away, it distracts me from how much I miss you. It doesn't really work, though; I can't help but think of you. Think about us, and the future we potentially could have." My palm runs along our snowflake printed duvet. "Just the other day when I was doing the laundry, I couldn't help but brainstorm baby names. Your absence has made me incredibly clucky."

"Let's hear them, Nono."

"Hear what?"

"The baby names."

"Oh, well, they're pretty absurd. I went a little crazy amid the loneliness."

"Oh, Nono, I'm going to get to you as soon as possible." A cloud of smoke leaves January's mouth.

"Where are you? You look cold? Are you at the rink?" I cannot decipher January's whereabouts when the camera is basically pointed up his nostrils.

"Yeah, yeah, I'm at the rink. I'm just skating before I'm plucked from the ice and sent to another photoshoot against my will. Now more important matters; baby names."

"Oh, well, you know how we both conveniently have winter related names, I was thinking we could make it a thing as the Snow family."

"That's so freaking adorable, so what do you have so far?"

"Well, I was thinking, for a girl, Avalanche, Ava for short." I can picture the little munchkin now. She'll probably be as spunky as her mother, but have the looks of her father. I hope our children possess all of January's good looks.

"Oh." January's brows pinch together.

"Told you I go loopy when I'm lonely." No doubt poor little Ava will be born with this same confused scowl on January's face when she realizes what her full name is.

"Okay, and how about for a boy? Bobsled." January chuckles heartily, triggering a flutter in my chest. That smile, I really hope our children have that charming smile. And here's to hoping that don't get any of my genetics and end up needing braces.

"Close! I was genuinely thinking Sled. Isn't that the stage name of that guy in that band you like?" Little Sled will no doubt follow in the steps of his father and be an avid lover of rock bands. Not without an appreciation for Justin Bieber's discography, influenced by mwah.

"You're thinking of Slash, but I do like Sled. It's kind of rock and roll."

"Are you jabbing?" I narrow my eyes square into the camera lens, hoping to look menacing on his phone screen.

"No, Nono, I like it." He scrunches his nose, which means he does like it and he finds me adorable. I can feel myself glow from within.

If only I had that pregnant glow about me. *One day, Noelle, patience.*

"Our poor kids are going to have to be homeschooled with names like Avalanche and Sled."

"Ava Winter Snow and Sled Cameron Snow. I like it."

"I love you, January." I slip out, feeling the sentiment tingling on the tip of my tongue. Tears slip from my lashes and down my cheeks.

"Oh, Princess, don't be upset. I love you too."

"I know, I'm being an absolute baby, I'm going to be seeing you in a matter of weeks." I sniff, wiping my tears.

"Actually—" The sound drops out.

"Hello? January? Hello, are you there?" I hold the phone up to my ear. Nothing. "He's gone."

Can I really go on with just these sporadic phone calls? Probably not if the reception is going to be so spotty. I just need him here with me. Or I could fly to Phoenix? It'll do a number on my health but I'm sure January will be please for some low-activity dates. Even if that date may just be him lying next to me while I recover from the plane trip over. Will it even be worth it if we can't completely enjoy each other's company because of my deteriorating health?

"Oh, Janny, I wish you were here." I whine, falling onto my mattress in defeat.

"I'm here." My head snaps to my screeching porch door, my ears are blessed with January's homely timbre.

"Janny!" I spring up from our bed, pulling his weight toward me. We tumble like an avalanche back onto the mattress. "You're here."

"Only for a couple of days—"

"No, let's not worry about that. You're actually here." My hands explore his solid frame, gripping and groping at muscles I've missed dearly.

"I see your hands are making up for lost time." He flashes that hypnotic smile, and I feel my pulse speed up in my chest...and my pants.

"It's about to be my mouth, too." I pinch his chin, willing him into stillness so I can kiss the fuck out of my husband.

"Kiss me, my beautiful wife."

I collect our lips in a fervent kiss. The kindle that was slowly diminishing with each passing lonely day, bursts alight with passion. January lifts my surrendering body with ease, shuffling the both of us further onto the mattress.

"I only just got here but—"

"Shut up, January, and impregnate me!"

To Be Continued...

Acknowledgements

Here we are folks! Another notch in my belt. My first ever attempt at writing in first person, how did I do? Actually, I don't want to know. Admittedly this was a challenge for me, I often find it easy to write in third person but as a personal goal, I'm trying to mold myself into an all rounder as an author. I hope my attempt was sufficient enough. I have a few people to thank that made this all a possibility.

Firstly, thank you to my incredible cover illustrator, Jace (@curatedjays on insta). Seriously such an incredibly talented artist and amazing friend, it was an absolute joy working with you and I can not wait to work with you for the rest of the Phoenix Badgers series.

A big thanks to my character art artist, Aida (@algart on insta) and Reisha (@Riesha_chan_art on insta), you both captured my vision so beautifully.

A special thanks and shout out to Maggie at Hopeful Romantic Books, for carving out the time to really flesh out the cohesiveness of this plot.

And of course, my beautiful betas, you truly helped shape this book into what it is. Justine, Siham, Elizabth, Katie, Chloe and Maggie. Thank you all so much for your support throughout.

I also want to thank BookishBubblyPR, you're help has been imperative in this process, thank you so much for your networking and overall assistance.

Special thanks to my bookish friends, Lou, Liv, Bindi, Simone, Aleish, Kate, Rebecca. You guys pull me through this demanding hobby day in and day out, your constant reassurance is what got me to the end. Thank you, thank you, thank you.

I'd like to thank my personal friends, Liam and Sabrina, who although aren't readers, support me through this endeavour.

About the author

Brittany Carson is an Australian Author who believes she was born in the wrong era, albeit witnessing the greatness that is Taylor Swift, which proves that she was born in the right one. You can find her constantly daydreaming about the past and future, but never the present, unless she is with her darling guinea pig, Percy, then she is always present when with "the light of my life". She aspires to write more novels, especially tooth-rotting, sweet romantic comedies and she hopes to inspire other writers to write their stories too.

Printed in Great Britain
by Amazon

60350289R00211